Now What?

BARBARA J. HAMBLEN

Order this book online at www.trafford.com
or email orders@trafford.com

Most Trafford titles are also available at major online book retailers.

Printed in the United States of America.

ISBN: 978-1-4669-6420-4 (sc)
ISBN: 978-1-4669-6422-8 (hc)
ISBN: 978-1-4669-6421-1 (e)

Library of Congress Control Number: 2012919393

Trafford rev. 10/11/2012

Trafford
PUBLISHING®   www.trafford.com

North America & international
toll-free: 1 888 232 4444 (USA & Canada)
phone: 250 383 6864 ♦ fax: 812 355 4082

This book is dedicated to
my wonderful daughter, Kathleen,
with all my love and without whose
help and encouragement
it would never have seen the light of day.

Chapter 1

Johnny, cocky as any banty rooster, strutted up to the huge front door of the magnificent Southern-style mansion. In a semi-circle behind him, nine people plus a big rusty-red dog made up a fair-sized, silent group on the large veranda.

Johnny kept his finger on the intricate bell button till the heavy door suddenly burst open and, huge though the doorway was, it seemed to be filled by a tremendous pile of definitely female flesh topped by mounds of variegated blonde hair.

"Johnny! My leetle Johnny!"

Johnny, who was about one quarter of her size, grinned from ear to ear and said, "Hi, Big Mamma. How's tricks?"

She scooped him up in a big, mushy hug. "You are the trickiest trick that's been here for a long, long while, leetle Johnny." She put him back down on his feet and looked over the crowd gathered on her front porch. In spite of her generously large and smiling mouth, most members of the group were more than aware of the diamond hard stare she raked over each and every one of them. Her gaze stopped momentarily on the three young men—costumes or uniforms?—could be either—and totaled up their probable worth, tax included. "Is this a delegation from the city fathers, or are they customers?" she asked.

"We need help, Big Mamma Alice, and I knew you'd be the one to come to—for a price." Johnny poked her in the vicinity of her ribs.

Alice laughed, patted Johnny's head, and said, "I can't refuse a smart little cockerel like you anything, leetle Johnny." She pinched his cheek. "Come in. Come in and tell Mamma Alice what you need. If I haven't got it—I'll get it." She caught sight of Rusty. "A dog? A huge red dog? That might be a leetle . . . we have cats." Her laughter boomed out over the formal garden.

She swept them through the deeply carved double doors into a large, marbled, beautifully appointed reception hall where, from the far end, a wide, graceful staircase rose up.

About three steps from the bottom sat two Siamese cats. Rusty saw them the same second they saw him—instant cat-and-dog thing. With three leaps and a slide, Rusty was on the bottom step and the cats were near the top of the case. As Rusty gained the top of the flight, the two howling cats were through an open door with Rusty in hot pursuit.

Within seconds, screams from at least two females shattered the elegant calm.

One of the men in the group bounded up the stairs muttering curses on Rusty's head. Rusty's vibrating barks turned to howls, and the cats' screeches had reached a record-high pitch.

It became impossible to carry on a conversation where they were. Alice bellowed, "Into the salon. Shut the door. It sounds like a bloody cat house." Suddenly realizing what she had said, she roared with fresh laughter. "Get that, leetle Johnny? Sounds like a cat house."

Johnny laughed hysterically—partly at Alice's joke and partly as a result of the last few nerve-racking hours—laughter that could just as easily have turned into deep sobs and tears.

The group didn't get the joke and so looked politely at the two.

Through his tears, Johnny saw the puzzled looks on the others' faces, which set him off again.

"Jeez, don't you get it? That's what this place is—a cathouse."

And it was—for miles around, it was the most elegant, the most select, and the most expensive house of ill repute.

There were varying expressions on the faces of the nine. One of the women looked shocked while another curled her lip in disgust. The men were stoic.

Big Alice didn't miss anything. She boomed out, "Yes, a whorehouse." She looked up and down, with a calculating stare, at the one with the disgusted look. "Interested?" Saw her expression. "Too bad. I've room for a tall, cool, elegant lady type." Her piercing blue-gray eyes glittered. "Too bad."

"Now, my Johnny boy, what do all these people need, and how much will they pay?"

"The police are after them, and they need secret transportation back to town."

Alice had seen and heard a lot in her lusty life, but the idea of such a weird mixture of people, all being in the same bind, sent her plucked eyebrows hairwards. "All of them—together—and a dog? Come on, leetle Johnny, what for?"

"A great misunderstanding on the part of your police." Another one of the men had stepped in to speed up negotiations and to prevent Johnny from blurting out any part of the truth.

"If possible, madam, we also would appreciate some water for us and Rusty and maybe the use of the facilities?"

"That's easy." Alice rang a tinkling bell, and immediately six young lovelies, all of different sizes and colors, came giggling in from two directions.

"Listening at the doors again, were you?" boomed Alice. "Marion, close the curtains. It's more than possible that we might get some official visitors."

At that moment, Rusty and the two cats walked cheerfully into the salon together, evidently on peaceful terms, and another young woman came in behind them. "They," indicating the animals, "have decided to like each other instead of tearing each other apart."

The young man that had chased Rusty upstairs came in behind them. As he rejoined his group, he did his best to smother his laughter.

"Oh, and Alice," the young woman added, "I could see a string of flashing red lights coming up on the highway. I'm pretty sure I could hear sirens."

"They probably eez coming here—probably about theez new group here. We need to make some arrangements, and that may not be too easy—eet depends on a few things."

One of the men pulled out a wad of money.

"Well, that settles one of them," Alice said.

The sirens were getting louder.

"Okay, leetle Johnny, queekly—take them to zee bolt-hole." She noticed the concerned looks on some of the faces. "Don't worry—it's a secret suite that should be safe from a casual search. I'll do my best wiz zee cops. I'll send food and water. Hurry. Go!" She called the girls together and issued her orders. They drew the drapes in the dining room and generally made things look like any other early evening. She ordered food to be put on the table and had the girls sit down ready to have supper.

Alice stood at the huge window that looked out over the front gates. The red lights glowed, and the color bounced off the treetops. The sound of the sirens got nerve jangling louder.

"Quick, Marion, let's get ready to do a—a—."

"Diversionary act upon our dear Fritzy?" Marion suggested.

"Yes, and I bet good old Captain Fritz Wheeler must be leading zee pack. Ordering all zee red lights and sirens is the closest he'll ever get to being a wheeler-dealer."

"He's a little short in the brains department," Marion said.

"Yes, maybe, but he eez a good gringo." Alice sneaked a peek out the window. "He and his partner are getting out of the car." She scanned the room for any telltale signs of strangers and hurried slowly to the big front door just as the chimes sounded.

"Come in, come in, my mucho macho Fritzy," she bellowed out. "What games are you playing now with all zee flashing of zee red lights?"

"Hello, big Mamma Alice." He grinned with pleasure when Alice all but scooped him up in a large bear hug, gave him a huge kiss on his forehead, and plopped him back down on the floor.

"And who eez this cute fellow that came in wiz you?"

"That's Officer Joe Vallisio, my driver."

"Well, you grow them zo cute in Vegas." Alice chucked Joe under the chin. She turned toward Fritzy. "So, my handsome Fritzy, what ezz ziz all about? All ziz blinka blinka red lights and howling sirens enough to wake a polar bear in . . . in . . . ?"

"The Arctic," Marion supplied.

"My sweet Marion, you are zo, zo—smart." She beamed at Marion. "You must take after your mother."

"Probably." She shrugged and half-smiled.

Fritzy looked from Alice to Marion and back, as usual, wondering. "Well, it's a long story." He looked at Alice and sent a little signal about how he just might like a bite to eat and something a little interesting in a glass.

Alice caught the signals. "Fritzy, my dear sweet Fritzy. Come in and sit down with the girls and me and have some supper. You, too, Joey. But, Fritzy, tell Joe to tell the other cars to go back to zee—zee—," she snapped her fingers, trying to find the word.

"Headquarters," Marion supplied.

"Yes, zat place. And then come back here, queek, and have supper with the girls. I can hear their sweet little hearts fluttering now, you handsome boy, you." Alice's laugh boomed out again.

"Come wiz me, sweet Fritzy," and she almost carried him to the dining room and sat him at the table between two adoring, luscious young things. "Hurry back, Joey, there's a good place for you, too."

Alice went to the head of the table and took her rightful place. She tinkled the little bell and told Janice, the young woman that came in, to start serving supper. "And bring the usual drink for our dear friend, Fritzy."

The chimes sounded again.

"Marion, go and let in zee heartthrob."

Marion went out into the reception hall and then led a nervous and blushing Joe into the large and elegant dining room. Marion sat Joey between two lovelies who immediately made an almost overwhelming fuss over the young officer. It was evident that he had never been here before, but he hoped it wouldn't be his last time.

"Now, my macho Fritzy, tell us what's going on. Eeet must be terribly exciting for all zat noise and blinka blinkas. Janice, a refill for our Fritzy."

"Well." Fritzy enjoyed the limelight and wanted it to last. "There have been some weird going ons in the desert in the last few days, so we were scouting around near the vicinity." Fritzy paused for a mouthful, chewed, and swallowed it. "My, that's so tasty. What is it?"

"We will find out later, Fritzy. Get on wiz zee story." Alice didn't want to sound too impatient.

"Where was I? Oh, yes—in the desert near the trouble spot. Well, we were cutting through the Saguaro tract to get to the Cacomistle plains when we saw a smashed-up and abandoned red car, and nobody was anywhere near it, so we stopped to have a look and take down the particulars." Fritzy held up his glass to Janice for a refill.

Janice looked at Alice, who nodded "yes" but signaled to make it weak.

"Thank you, dear, you make a great drink."

"And?" Alice tried for patience.

"We suddenly saw a big car coming at us at around a hundred miles an hour. It just missed our cars, and when it passed by . . ." Fritzy cut off another large mouthful, looked at it, smelled it, chewed it slowly, loved it, and swallowed it.

Everyone but Fritzy saw Alice ready to erupt like an oversized volcano. Through clenched teeth she said, "And?"

"There was no one in it. Wasn't that strange? No driver, no passengers. No one. Then, about a mile away and heading north, we saw a big moving dust pillar, and we could make out that it was another car. We didn't know if anyone was in it or not." Fritzy made an extended pause and said, "That was great. Um-m, is there any desert—by any chance?"

"AND?" Fritzy, even sunk in his fuzzy feelings, caught on that Alice was getting just a little impatient for the end of the story.

"Then I called for backup and tried to figure out what our next move should be. Then we got orders to report back to command headquarters. But I remembered that you were close to the vicinity where all this queer stuff is going on, and since you usually know what's going on, I thought we should come in here to see if you had any information on anything. Besides . . . anyway, thanks for the wonderful meal, as usual, and . . . and . . ."

"You are more than welcome, Fritzy. And eet is time that you should go now, and you need to write out your reports and go home to your worried wife."

Joey, after his wonderful meal and exotic dinner companions, got up from the table and came to get Fritzy. "Okay, Chief, I guess we'd better get on the road again."

"You're right, Joey, m' boy. Have to report to headquarters." He seemed to be feeling his drinks just a little. "For only two years and three months more, then, I can report to the golf course." He heaved himself out of his chair with a helping hand from Joey.

Big Alice and Marion and a few of the girls got them to the door and waved them an animated good-bye.

Alice turned back into the foyer, and Marion thankfully shut the door and locked it.

"Now, Marion, bring up zee guests and let's see eef we can find out what zees is all about."

In a few minutes, Alice heard the group coming from the back of the house. She waited for them in the dining room, which had quickly been cleared and relaid with tea, coffee, and bits and pieces to go with the drinks.

"Come in. Come in. Leetle Johnny, you sit here beside me. I thought we should sit at zee big table and talk like zee big—big—," she turned toward Marion.

"Company boardroom conference," Marion supplied.

"Good idea," one of the men said.

"Tell Mama Alice what goes on and what eez needed."

Johnny, sitting close to Alice, said, "I thought Happy Harry might . . ."

Everyone at the table looked from Johnny to Alice.

"Yes. My clever leetle Johnny—that's who I had in mind. With his fleet of cars and hearses, he should be able to arrange something for tonight."

"Hearses?" Old Bill spoke for the first time. "He's an undertaker?"

"You could say that," Alice said. She looked closely at him with pleasure—liked what she saw.

"I s'pose he's part of the local Mafia," Bill added.

"You might even say zat, too. Why? Squeamish?" Alice laughed.

"Nope. Just wonderin'." Bill sat back in his chair. "Probably the best idea for this here situation."

Questions and opinions began to flow and fly in all directions, all at once, and with increasing volume. Rusty added some short, shrill barks as his two cents worth. After a few minutes of this unproductive and confusing table talk, Alice boomed in. "Enough! Enough! Who are you?" She pounded on the table with a heavy spoon. "What eez theez all about? Why do you . . .? Who are you . . .?" Her voice became louder and louder on a rising scale, heavy with frustration.

Then one of the two eldest men spoke in a quiet, sonorous tone. Everyone at the table was still; they recognized the quiet voice of authority. "First, dear Alice, my name is Mosets, and we can't thank you enough for sheltering us in our time of real need." He paused for a moment. "It is a complicated and an almost unbelievable chain of unseen events in which all of us have played a part. After giving it some thought, I have decided, if all of you are willing, on my solution."

He had their complete attention.

"I am, in effect, going to pick a bouquet of flowers—one from the memory of each of us and of all the events in the last four days. This will be as if each flower saw its own part of the memory. Then, my bouquet, in its entirety, will be placed in your memory, dear Alice, and then you will know all there is to know right up to this moment."

Alice, for about the only time in her life, was speechless. Her mind was full with a variety of thoughts and emotions. Then she asked, "How? How can you do zeez thing? Is it dangerous to me? Will theez bouquets thing hurt me?"

"No, I assure you, dear Alice, it won't hurt. It is no more dangerous than reading a book or watching the TV." His low, calm, stately voice soothed the fears away.

"This young lady on my left is trained in thought transference. So may I continue? Will you welcome Tarla into your thoughts? It is totally up to you, dear Alice. When she has finished, you will know all there is to know. Will you trust me?"

"Yes, Mosets, I feel zee trust for you. Zee transfer thing. Will it take a lot of time?"

"No, dear Alice, maybe five minutes. Very well. Everyone, relax, and Alice, lean your head back and be calm. I will gather my bouquet and give it to you."

Mosets entered the group's minds one at a time—he gave each memory to Tarla, and she put them in their proper order and slowly and softly placed them in the mind of Alice. Tarla made sure that Alice was calm and receptive, and then she left as gently as a falling flower petal leaving the whole story in Alice's mind.

Chapter 2

"Finally. Finally, we're on our way." Sarn rubbed his hands together and yelled, "Vacation, here we come." With a showman-like flourish, he locked in the last control switch. With arms flung out wide, legs stretched to the limit of his console, he gave a mighty stretch. Then, laughing, he turned his chair around, leaped up, grabbed his sister, Tarla, as she stood up from her navigation console, and spun her in circles.

"Sarn," she gasped, "put me down. Put me down!" They were both laughing. "Put me down before we break something. Like me, for instance."

"Settle down, Sarn, before we land before we planned." Jorl, captain of the ship, and Tarla's husband, had just finished his end of the takeoff procedure. He turned toward them, laughed, and said, "Put her down, Sarn." He stretched his shoulders and rubbed his fingers through his wavy, auburn hair. "Seems like forever since I could just sit still."

Sarn, with a grin from ear to ear, his mop of curly red hair flying and green eyes dancing, let Tarla down. She wobbled a bit. Her long blonde hair had come loose from its pins and had been flying around in arcs of bright gold.

Sarn turned around and said to Khair, Jorl's brother, "How about you, Khair? Even you must be a little excited."

Khair had just entered the command cabin. He balanced a tray with a bottle of bubbly and four glasses on it. In his usual low and calm voice, said, "Yes, I am. It's been a long time since we four have all been together and even," he smiled and quietly gave each one a glass, "going on a vacation." He opened the bottle and poured drinks. "Here's to a great one."

"I'll drink to that." Sarn still had the grin.

They clinked glasses and said cheers and love all around.

"I wonder if the women on Salda are still as gorgeous as ever," Sarn said.

"What women?" Tarla asked. She tried to remember whom he meant.

"Any women," Sarn answered.

"Oh, Sarn," she shook her head but couldn't help smiling at him. Since the day he was born, when she was only six years old, she felt a big sister's protective tie to him that had never gone away.

"Don't worry, Tarla dear, we'll be good. Me and the cousins have a lot of catching up to do." In the middle of a laugh, Sarn suddenly stood stock-still. He appeared to be looking and listening inward.

"What is it, Sarn? What's wrong?" Tarla knew her brother had extra keen senses for anything to do with mechanical things. They'd been saved a few times by his knack for feeling situations that others couldn't.

In a puzzled tone of voice he said, "I felt a shiver in the deck plates." Sarn continued to concentrate. Everyone stood still and tried to feel what Sarn had experienced.

"There . . . did you feel that faint bump?" Sarn quickly passed his glass to Tarla and headed for the engine room.

Jorl and Khair put down their glasses and followed Sarn. Jorl called over his shoulder to Tarla, "Check out the signal path to the mother ship. We just might need it."

They came back within a few minutes, and each one scanned their areas of the control room.

"Nothing's wrong down there," Jorl said. "And nothing up here shows any sign of trouble."

"Blazing suns, there better not be. That would be a total pain in the . . ."

"Sarn," Tarla warned.

They continued on with their drinks and conversations. In the middle of a word, Sarn caught sight of a small red light that had flickered on for just a split second.

"What was that?" Sarn jumped to his console and concentrated on watching the area around where the red light had flashed. For a few seconds, the three watched Sarn.

"Khair, Tarla, go to your command consoles." Jorl sat at his console and assumed his official rank of captain.

All four of them were highly trained officers in the Planetary Federation and Space Exploration, so the response was immediate. It was instant, disciplined order. Each sat at their station and quickly and efficiently scanned their controls.

"Reports, please. Navigation—Tarla?"

"Signal path laid to mother ship. All controls registering proper course to planned destination. No interference, sir. We will be entering time warp in thirty-five seconds. All controls responding correctly."

"Engineering—Sarn?"

"All controls show pulse wave working at 100 percent. No peripheral failure of any modules, sir."

"Life support systems and communications—Khair?"

"All controls show perfect working order, sir."

"We have entered time warp, sir," Tarla reported.

Suddenly, out of the corner of his eye, Jorl barely caught sight of a system warning light on his command console as it flickered on for the space of an eye blink. The red light flashed again.

"That's . . ." he turned to Sarn. "Anything on your console, Lieutenant?"

"No, sir." Suddenly, a small, baleful light quivered into life on Sarn's console. "Sir, flashing red light on module 63x." In quick succession, three of the nearest warning lights lit up. Like a contagious fever, the rest of the panel flashed red danger signals. Jorl's console joined the red light brigade.

With gut-tingling suddenness, the small space racer filled with the urgent jangling of the alarm system.

"Khair, kill the alarm." He turned to Tarla, "Propulsion system is shutting down. Add that info and the time to your general emergency signal." Jorl, an experienced captain, for the benefit of his crew and his ship, in any emergency, operated with iron self-control.

Tarla turned back to her console. Her eyes gave away the instinctive fear she felt; however, the discipline of intensive training enabled her to carry out her duties quickly and efficiently.

"Emergency drill," Jorl ordered. "Everyone into their space gear. Tarla, note probable course and destination. Khair, send out an extreme emergency signal and include Tarla's navigation info. Sarn, activate manual retro brakes."

A series of "Aye, Captains" answered. The crew bent to their tasks.

Tarla tried every "trick of the trade" that she knew to plot their position in space.

Khair, meanwhile, sent a coded repeating arc signal into space that gave their last known coordinates. "Any idea of the map designation, Tarla?"

Tarla looked up, biting her full, soft lips in consternation, and said, "The attitude we've travelled in subspace for the last five minutes could have put us anywhere in the universe. I have a partial fix . . . maybe."

"Good," Khair said. "Can you give me any of the coordinates, Tarla?" As usual, Khair was the model of cool and calm.

The wild slipping and yawing of the vehicle added to the tension.

"I've locked onto Desig. 4, Space 3, Sector 14," she replied and tried to brace herself.

"Got it," Khair said. First Lieutenant Khair Sandu, Jorl's brother, put emergency gear beside the three people and said, "Suit up, everybody." He quickly got into his own gear. "Something is familiar about Sector 14. But what is it?" His mind continued to think. He snapped his fingers. "That's it. Tarla. Isn't Sector 14 totally outside our known borders?"

"What? Give me a second to locate it. Yes. There it is, totally . . . it blacked out." Thoughts raced across her face. "Oh, blast," she said under her breath when her console screen started showing a fantastic mobile color display. Suddenly, Tarla's viewing screen totally blacked out. "Now, we're flying blind, Jorl. I didn't have time to get any further description of the destination."

"Well, that's an interesting addition to the brew. But we'll know soon enough. Unscheduled landing in four minutes, forty-five seconds."

The one-piece survival suits were almost paper-thin, lightweight, and impervious to fire and cold. They fit snugly over their uniforms from the bottom of their boots and snapped into the neck of their helmets.

Sarn reported, "We have a jammed guiding mechanism—propulsion system totally shut down—sequence and secondary control systems have also started progressive shutdowns." As the other three watched him, he continued to search for some kind of a solution. "The pile is heating up. Now into the red. Ten degrees from runaway . . . eight . . . seven . . . six . . ."

The pace of the countdown slowed somewhat.

"Any hope of bringing it under control, Sarn?" Jorl asked, knowing the answer would probably be negative.

"Three . . . two . . . one . . . no, sir! It's now totally fused." Jr. Lt. Sarn Dreela, engineering officer, realized the imminent danger, but he still muttered under his breath. "Blazing suns, what kind of a piece of . . . garbage did they stick us with? Wait till we get back—fur will fly. Blazing comet tails it's . . ." Sarn continued to mumble and grumble.

Khair, placid even in the face of who knows what, was yanking out the rest of the survival gear from the storage locker. "Put this on, Sarn," he said as he thrust a helmet at him. "And, eh, maybe you shouldn't turn the mic on." Khair's lips twitched in a fleeting smile. "Here are the rest of your Mamas." He handed each of them the clear bubble space helmets with breathing devices and communicators already installed. They rapidly completed their individual duties and locked themselves into their survival helmets.

"I think I hate these things," Sarn said.

"Let me check your helmet lockdowns," Khair said. He went to each of them to make sure all was done correctly. "Activate the padding and lockdowns on your seats."

"And, blazing suns, brace for a crash landing."

Jorl reached for Tarla's hand and gave half salutes to the two men. "My wife, Tarla—my brother, Khair, my brother-in-law, Sarn—I love you, and we will survive this, eh, detour."

A pulsing silence filled the small control room that spoke more than words ever could.

"Activating survival cushion." Khair pushed the emergency slide control up.

Quickly, the control room filled with a spongy substance. It was resilient, tough, and fireproof. It closed around the four of them like separate cocoons. Their only communications from now until after the crash would be by the radios in their helmets.

The shock-absorbing cushion did its job so well that it was difficult to tell the exact moment of impact.

Khair counted the elapsed time. "It's now three minutes and twenty-six seconds since countdown began. The cushion should begin disintegrating in . . . ninety-seven seconds."

"If there's no fire and no radiation and a few choice things like that," Sarn grumbled.

"Sarn, don't be a black beyond," Tarla whispered. "So far we're safe."

After a short pause, Jorl announced, with heartfelt relief, "Landfall complete."

The "all-clear" chimed to life. It signaled—no fire—no radiation—no danger.

"The cushion is disintegrating," Sarn shouted. He pulled off his helmet, relieved to be free of it. "Blazing suns, we made it!" He leaped out of his chair and started to do a little dance. "Wow," he said. "A little tilt to the deck." He laughed as he nearly lost his balance.

"Lucky again," Khair sighed with relief. As space exploration officers, they hadn't always been quite so fortunate.

Within two minutes, they were completely free of the cushion and could now assess the damage. They stripped off their suits, relieved and happy to be alive and unhurt. They took the time for a few thankful hugs.

"The navigational console is dead," Tarla reported. "I've tried everything I could to reset, or bypass, the problem."

"Same thing with the bridge." Once more, Jorl tried every control switch on the whole console. "There's no response at all."

Sarn was flipping switches and twisting dials. "Not even a blip out of this one." His green eyes were snapping with annoyance. "I hate it when equipment doesn't work. His mop of red hair was as wild as ever.

"Oh-h, great suns. Here's another problem." Tarla was still seated at her console.

"What now, Tarla?" Jorl, concerned, stood behind her chair.

"All the trackers are blown. The signal recognition units for friendly or hostile ships are useless. And to top it all off, the celestial maps and their information are lost. We can't even follow the Federation's main directives."

"Then we'll just have to be more alert and not worry about Federation rules. I won't be surprised if we're beyond the Federation's jurisdiction anyway." He gave her a quick hug.

The four of them went on a detailed inspection tour of the interior of their damaged space racer.

"Look at that," Jorl pointed. "I'd guess that almost forty percent of our hull is crushed inward."

Sarn had looked closely at the extent of the damage. "The engine well has to be crumpled into at least two thirds of its normal space. See? You can see where the crushed hull has rammed into the pulse wave area." He pointed to the propulsion unit. "It's sad to see."

The whole engine room presented a disconsolate picture of a cold, useless jumble, totally beyond repair.

"Well, not much to save in here." Khair shrugged his shoulders. "Might as well take a look outside."

Sarn sighed. "Great way to start a vacation."

Khair smiled. "Just look upon it as a little detour."

"Or, better yet, look upon it as a newly discovered vacation land." Jorl laughed at the expression on Sarn's face.

Sarn, lips curled in a sneer of sorts, said emphatically, "Humph!"

Khair hooked up a small auxiliary power pack and took as many readings as possible. "Well, according to everything I can determine from this unit, it will not only be safe to breathe the air outside the ship, but also the available readings here compare favorably to the chemical and biological content of the atmosphere around our own home planet. It's safe for us to leave the ship."

"Now that is pure, sheer good luck," Jorl said.

"Oh, isn't that wonderful. It could have been . . ." Tarla smiled and relaxed a little.

"Things don't seem quite so difficult now," Khair said.

"Well, I guess that depends on how you look at it. We don't know where in the universe we are, and our means of escape is busted. But you're right. We're all alive and well, and we'll think of something," Sarn said. His high spirits resumed, and he gave Tarla a hug and started to look around.

The portholes were covered with an opaque substance, and the gangway was jammed shut. Sarn said, "I need something to . . . hey, this will do. A few smart whacks with the spanner should make the hydraulic lock let go. That should free the mechanism that activates the ramp."

It did.

As the ramp started to open, a curtain of sand drifted down and a cloud of heat boiled in.

"Blazing comet tails," Sarn yelled. He was directly under the drift before he could jump out of the way. He spat out a mouthful of sand and sneezed violently.

Tarla, on her way past Sarn, grinned at him and said, "Heavens bless you," and continued on down the ramp. Jorl and Khair followed.

Jorl stopped in front of Sarn. "Oh, you missed that little tiny bit of sand right there on the tip of your ear," and flicked it off. Sarn jumped. Jorl kept on going with the grin still on his face.

"I'll get you for that." Sarn followed them down to see what was what.

After one quick look outside, Tarla was a little discouraged and dismayed. "Nothing but sand and rocks in all directions. We're in the middle of a desert." Because of another episode earlier in her career, she didn't care much for deserts.

"Well, that sure beats the middle of the ocean." Sarn grinned, still trying to beat off the rest of the sand.

"Or," Khair said with a slight shudder, "the middle of a deep swamp with heat, bugs, and who knows what hungry inhabitants."

All of them went further out of the ship for a closer look at the surroundings.

"Well then, this seems to be your lucky crash." Jorl playfully poked Khair, who was the least emotional of all of them, in the ribs.

"And I sure hope it's my last," Sarn sighed deeply. "Somehow, crash landings will never really agree with me."

"I don't think that they ever really agree with anybody," Jorl said.

"I can't imagine why I ever joined this outfit anyway. Must have caught a germ or something."

Jorl laughed. "Go on, we did everything but lock you up. You wouldn't let us get away without you."

. "Now, let's get down to the serious business of survival." Khair, with his rather long and sculpted face, black hair, and soft brown eyes, always preferred the positive side of any situation. "First off, we have a fair supply of food and water and enough weapons, all of which will give us time to decide our next move."

After further inspection, Sarn's clever mind, clicking over like a high-speed computer, arrived at the only possible conclusion that he could see. "We should be able to salvage most of the equipment, and we'll build the rest . . . Hm-m-m." His expression reflected his deep and concentrated thoughts as he paced around the sand and rocks.

"Build the rest of what, Sarn?" Jorl asked, looking around for what Sarn saw.

"A new space racer, of course." Doubt cast no shadow on Sarn's well-defined, freckled face. When he turned around to reenter the wrecked ship, his carrot-red hair blew in the breeze, curlier than ever.

"Hold on a minute. Do you even know what you're saying? Having a small attack of space fever, maybe? We can't just—just build a new—just like that." Jorl snapped his fingers, and his face registered total puzzled amazement. After a short, thoughtful pause, he said, "Still, when you stop to think a minute, why not? We are all highly trained technicians, and Sarn is the best improviser in the whole fleet. Why not? We can at least think about it." Excitement flared in his eyes.

"Well, for one thing, even on this planet—whatever it is, I bet you'll need some kind of money . . . if this planet will even have anything that we might need . . . maybe it isn't even inhabited." Tarla's mind was roaming all over the probable problems. "We're surrounded by an empty desert!"

"Tarla, if it's inhabited, we'll find a native and ask questions. That's easy," Sarn told her.

Tarla was still turning over the thoughts in her mind. "Our first and most important law is that no member of our Federation shall allow any native on any planet to be aware of our identity unless expressly ordered by the Federation."

"And, Tarla, you told me not be a black beyond," Sarn said.

"Yes, you're right," Tarla said with a smile. "Now, Sarn, how about you try to recover the star maps, and then maybe we can find out approximately where we are." She smiled at Sarn as he gave her a hug.

"I'll get on it right away, and then we'll get to work." Doubt wasn't one of Sarn's faults. He totally believed in solutions.

Khair held up his hands to Tarla and Sarn. "For right now, we must hide the ship, then we'll have a 'how' discussion. Okay?"

"Right, she's just about buried herself in the sand anyway," Jorl agreed. "From the position of this planet's sun, I would say it's early morning. We should have plenty of hours of daylight left. Let's get to work."

Jorl, one of the six captains under Admiral Emslin of Federation Space Command, had orders to complete two relatively simple assignments, one on R'Alta, the third of the five out-planets of the Ambre Mees Arm, and the other on Costa in the same arm. Because Zarlleella, their home planet, was in the spiral that was next to the Ambre Mees Arm, they wouldn't be far off their planned path to their vacation planet, Salda. That was the original plan.

"Well, everybody, we did the two jobs that we were sent to do," Jorl said. "So now it's our vacation time, a little different to what we had planned, but who knows what'll develop—I choose to think of it as a new vacation spot."

Tarla and Khair both smiled and entered into the spirit of the game.

Sarn gave him a slightly sour look. Then his expression cleared. He threw himself into the project. "I'll rig the electron gun and blast that sandbank down over her." His petty annoyance was forgotten, and he began to enjoy the novelty of the situation.

Khair, examining the position of the ship, added, "We can also burn a hole into the side of that stone ledge and make a permanent ramp into the ship—prevent a native stumbling around the crash site and finding her."

"Let's get at it." Jorl started back to the entrance ramp.

They reentered the racer to get the necessary equipment and spent the best part of the day hard at work hiding the ship. Between the heat and the unaccustomed labor, a fair amount of harsh words in a few different languages flew with the sand and rocks.

"Finally. We're done" Jorl said and stretched his arms and back. "You couldn't tell that there's a space vehicle hidden here. Well done, everybody. Now, how about we see if we can activate the auxiliary system? Then get cleaned up and see if the food processor still works and order ourselves a nice meal."

"Blazing suns, yes. After all that dirty work in the blistering heat, I have doubts if I'll ever feel cool and clean again. I'm starved."

They reentered the ship and Khair inspected the auxiliary system.

"It's undamaged. At least we can be thankful that the auxiliary system for housekeeping is independent and is still showing one hundred percent active," Khair said.

After showers and a good meal, they decided to make an early start in the morning to begin exploring.

Sarn had been paying only slight attention to the conversations during their late-in-the-day supper.

He got up from the table and said, "I want to see something." He excused himself and took a quick trip to the engine room. He came back to the table muttering numbers under his breath.

"Sarn, would you like a little more to eat?" Tarla asked. "Sarn?"

"What?" Sarn's mind had only half surfaced. "Oh, no thanks." His eyes were still looking inward. He suddenly got up from the table again and headed for Tarla's navigation console. Once there, he turned and twisted some of the controls. He got up again and headed to the engine room to return once more and plunk himself down at the navigation console again.

Jorl and Khair watched him and then looked at each other. "Interesting," Jorl remarked.

"Very," Khair agreed.

"Tarla! Come here!" Sarn called with excitement. "Look!"

"What? Did you . . .?" Tarla rushed to look over Sarn's shoulder. "Sarn, you did it. That's the introduction to the program." She gave him an excited hug. "Here, let me at it." She almost bumped Sarn to the deck as she began searching for the partial coordinates she had managed to save.

Khair and Jorl also stood behind her as she manipulated the dials.

"Here's the information we need. It's the celestial map of an unknown solar system. See? It's tucked right on the edge of the known universes." She read out loud the probable statistics of the solar system. "It says that the system has a large sun and eight planets. What a relief!" Tarla clapped her hands with heartfelt thanks. "At least we have a good chance of finding our way home from here. There wasn't any info about life on the planets."

"We just have to wait and see," Khair said.

At the breakfast table the next morning, the conversation ranged from having landed on an uninhabited planet and, if peopled, what level of development and what living form the inhabitants had. With nothing to base anything on, they realized that they had to take their chances and try to find out firsthand.

"What about our uniforms?" Tarla asked. "That's all we have as we sent all of our vacation clothes on ahead."

"Well, it's a cinch we can't go naked, so we'll have to go as we are," Sarn said. "Maybe just remove the insignias. What do you think, Jorl?"

"I agree."

Khair nodded. "I agree as well."

"There, problem solved."

Their uniforms consisted of reasonably close fitting pants, silver-gray tunics, and knee-high, soft leather black boots.

"I guess they're ordinary enough to be unnoticed in a crowd," agreed Tarla. "Oh, and I'll take the language converter with me. Maybe there'll be a knowledge center we can use to learn the language." Tarla tucked the small unit into her carry case. "Of course, we don't even know if there is any kind of a civilization, and if there is, what level they have reached in technology. Oh well, I'll take it anyway." Then she realized what she had assumed. "I mean, if there are any inhabitants that we can communicate with." Tarla's mind suddenly hit her with a new thought. "Depends on the crowd. What if they aren't built like us? More arms or legs—maybe none—not even built out of the same stuff as we are. We would probably stand out in that crowd."

"Yes, that is an important point." Khair smiled at Tarla. "We will just have to wait and see."

In a short while, they had gathered up the things that they thought they might need for the next few days, which also included a couple of small weapons for each of them.

The four of them took the few steps in the short passageway they had created and were grouped around the mouth of the cave entrance. They each took one last look at their ship, then pushed a slab of rock over the cave mouth, and looked at what they had done.

"Rather like a period at the end of a sentence," Khair said in a quiet, thoughtful tone.

Each of them was silent as they stood there in the hot sun . . . half-formed thoughts swirling around in their heads . . . and their hearts.

Jorl stood back and critically surveyed the crash site. "Looks just as natural as it was before we hit it. Now, we should scout around and see what we can find."

"I certainly hope it gets cooler. Because, right now, it's almost too much to stand." Tarla lifted her long hair from the back of her neck.

"It should—as soon as the sun goes down. At least, that's how it usually is in the desert," Khair said. "The gravity is about the same here as it is at home—maybe even a little lighter. We should be able to make good time."

"And cover a lot of ground," Jorl said. "The sooner we make contact with the inhabitants, if any, the better."

Sarn had been listening to the remarks about 'making good time' with a slight, slack-jawed expression. "Do you mean walk? On our own feet? Across that stinking desert? In this heat?"

"You mean you brought your mini jet?" Jorl said

"Oh, blazing suns." Sarn heaved a long sigh.

Tarla laughed at him. "Never mind, Sarn dear, because, hopefully, Jorl will soon find a native vehicle—then we'll ride."

Khair laughed. "If he can figure out how it works, and then maybe you'll prefer to walk."

All of them, including Jorl, laughed at the memories of some of Jorl's battles with anything that couldn't head for open space.

"Jorl . . ." Tarla suddenly felt the whip of an ugly thought. Her deep purple-blue eyes reflected her only half-hidden concern.

Jorl noticed her pallor. "Tarla, what's the matter? What is it?" He put his arms around her.

"I'm all right, Jorl. Maybe it's only a reaction—or the heat. It's only—what if—what kind—maybe they are . . . Jorl, maybe this planet isn't . . . what if the natives aren't human? I mean, what if they aren't like us. What if they're savage plants, or hostile wildlife, or hostile energy forms? What if we can't communicate? What if . . . ?" Tarla wasn't used to not having this critical information available to her.

Jorl put his arms around her and said softly, "Easy, my love. Easy. We've been in places like that before and survived. We're highly trained officers of the Federation. And we have to find out—we'll never get home just sitting here. Anyway, it can't be too much worse than some of the places we've found ourselves in . . . and remember, we've always managed to get out." He hugged her close. "Look, if we're on a planet with inhabitants, it will probably be okay—if we aren't—we'll just have to try harder to make it okay. Okay?" He hugged her again. "Okay? Now, let's get at it."

"Okay," Tarla said with a small smile.

Then, hands on hips, he turned and scanned the miles of the hot emptiness surrounding them. "Time for action, people. Get your ESP working, Tarla. Tell us which direction to take."

Tarla concentrated—watching and listening inward. "It's only a faint mumble of sound, but it's coming from there." She pointed in the direction of the sun.

"Then that's the way we'll go," Jorl said. They started off over the seemingly endless desert.

They had been walking at a distance-eating pace for about an hour when Tarla slowed and put her head to one side, apparently listening. "A human thought pattern is coming closer. At least, I think it is—human, I mean."

"Which direction, Tarla?" Jorl scanned the desert all around them.

"That way." She pointed to their left.

Jorl studied the land in that direction. "I see a dust cloud rising. Maybe it's a vehicle. Could be a road over there. If we hurry, we should be able to intersect its course."

They stepped up their pace and soon came to a track that bore some resemblance to a road.

Coming toward them, at a great rate of speed, was a peculiar vehicle; open to the sky and bounding along with, apparently, a complete disregard for comfort.

"The driver is humanoid," Khair said. He permitted only a faint trace of relief to show.

"He sees us. He's going to stop," Tarla reported.

"Good," Jorl said. "On guard." He held up his arm as the vehicle came closer.

The driver turned out to be an old man—toughened by wind, weather, and hard living.

"This clears up another problem," Khair said. "He must be an inhabitant."

Tarla breathed a deep sigh of relief and said, "Life forms like ourselves."

The old man stopped beside them in a cloud of dust, looked them up and down, then spat over his shoulder. "Wal, now, what have we here? More damn-fool lost rock-hounds?"

Tarla didn't know the language, but with her trained and well-developed talent to mind read, she could extract the vocal sounds suggested by the thoughts of the old man. She activated the language conversion unit and put the earpiece in her ear. "How clever of you to guess, sir." She gave the man one of her beautiful smiles, which almost melted the old man's heart. Tarla blushed at his thoughts as the old man let his watery blue eyes behold her from neat foot to the top of her blonde head. "Do you think you could give us a . . . lift to the next town, sir?"

"Yup." He spit. "That'd be Vegas, about forty miles away. I'm on my way there myself. Get in. You sit in front with me, and them other three can ride in the backseat. Put your stuff behind the backseat."

Tarla translated for her men, and they climbed into the backseat of the uncomfortable looking machine. Tarla sat in the front.

When they took off with a gravel-spinning jerk, Sarn yelled, "What the blazing suns is . . .?" His chin bumped lightly off the back of the front seat. "I'll bounce one off him," Sarn yelled. Khair and Jorl forced him to sit back down.

They tried to endure the bumps and bounces with good grace. Except for Sarn—he didn't really believe in suffering of any kind, especially in good grace, or in silence.

The old man, indicating the three in the backseat with a jerk of his head, said to Tarla, "Yer friends furriners?"

Tarla, knowing that suspicion often breeds violence, felt a wriggle of the need for caution. She caught the thought of South Asia and quickly replied, "We're from South Asia. We came to your wonderful country to study this interesting desert for our university. I help them with the language problems—and, and things—you know . . ."

"Yup. A nursemaid. I wish I had a maid like you. Yup, I sure do. Even an old desert rat like me might settle down if he had something like you lookin' after him."

"Really, sir, I don't know . . . as I . . ."

The old man laughed. "Oh, don't worry about me, lady. I'm too old and tired to chase women. Relax."

They hit a particularly hard bump. It made Sarn swear in pain. "Blazing suns, tell the old coot it's just as easy to go around some of those rocks and holes." He started to get up off the seat.

Khair and Jorl both grabbed Sarn and sat him down with a bump.

"Bit rough, ain't it." The old man grinned. "Bounces bodies around like peas in a pod. Good machine, though. These here jeeps can go anywhere, hardly need a road."

"Jeep?" Tarla repeated. She tightened her grip even more.

"Yup." He turned and beamed a wide smile at the men in the back and repeated, "Good machine—stand up to anything."

Jorl, Khair, and Sarn were holding on for dear life. Jorl and Khair had the added chore of keeping a firm grip on Sarn who was ready to throw caution to the interstellar winds and pound some respect for the human frame into the old man.

At last they entered a wide highway paved, thankfully, and picked up speed.

"Should be in Vegas in twenty minutes," the old man informed Tarla.

"Your kindness is, is . . ."

"My pleasure, m'lady. I was comin' this way anyway."

They entered the outskirts of a city. Finally, they drove up a wide, busy street full of mobile machines and crowds of people.

"Where can I drop you folks?"

"The next corner will be fine, sir."

The old man pulled to a stop, and the four jumped out. Tarla beamed at him as she thanked him. The three men smiled and nodded—Sarn with a tightly clenched jaw and fists.

"Lady, a piece of advice from an old man—don't go back into the desert without takin' a proper guide. People die out there." The old man spit, put the jeep in gear, muttered, "Crazy furriners," and took off with a bark of rubber—possibly his unspoken opinion of crazy furriners.

The four smiled and waved until he was out of sight—swallowed up in the heavy traffic.

"Well, here we are on a corner, in a strange city, and in a strange world," Jorl said. He tried to take in the whole scene at once.

"I don't mind strange cities. It's the alien worlds that throw me," Sarn grumbled. "And my bones will never be the same—the miserable old . . ." He gently rubbed his rear end and groaned pitifully.

The other three, expressions a little solemn, watched Sarn.

"Poor old Sarn. Always getting picked on. Suffering so much," Jorl teased. He patted Sarn on his rear end.

Suddenly, the tensions of the last few hours left them. Their youth, health, and natural high spirits asserted themselves. They began to laugh. Suddenly, all their problems, all their concerns, seemed to take on a more manageable quality, to seem not quite so insurmountable.

The crowds flowing past them looked at the four, tall, handsome people seemingly in the middle of some huge joke—half wishing they might be invited to join in.

In a few minutes, they simmered down and, feeling relaxed and more able to cope with the unknown, moved on. They started off arm in arm down the sidewalk with no other thoughts in their minds but to figure out the lay of this new land.

"We need to find a quiet place where we can sit and talk," Jorl said.

"And, more importantly, give Tarla a chance to zero in on some helpful thoughts and information," Khair said.

"Good plan," Sarn totally agreed with them. "Come on, let's go."

Chapter 3

The brilliant desert sunset began to fade. Instant darkness closed in. Within five minutes, the seemingly endless street blazed even more brilliantly. The scintillating lights of every imaginable shape, size, and color appeared to be signs advertising places of amusement. The street illumination and vehicle lights were tame in comparison.

"It's wonderful," Tarla said. "Breathtaking." She turned a complete circle, entranced with the shifting splashes of color. "Let's go that way. This part of the street seems to be darker than a way up that end. I think I can see . . . water fountains? Shooting water high up into the air. Look! Hundreds of colored lights up there. Hear the music?"

Jorl laughed at Tarla's excitement and took her hand and started up the crowded street. "Come on, everybody. Stay together."

"Looks like an exciting place to visit," Khair said. "Seems as though we picked a good place for an unscheduled stopover."

"Blazing suns, they act like they're all high on a nerve bomb," Sarn said.

The density of the crowds and vehicles doubled and redoubled.

"Well," Tarla tried to look every way at once—taking account of the clothes, the excitement that seemed to tingle all through the scene, the lights, the music—"We don't have to worry about how we're dressed. Look at them. Every sort and kind of clothing you can imagine."

"That's luck. We won't be noticed," Khair said.

"And feel the excitement. Hey. Maybe we're in one of the native sin cities—you know, like Corsta is in the home system."

"You just might be right, Sarn," Jorl said. He, also, couldn't seem to see enough. "It's almost overwhelming."

"Wonder what they call the local booze—wouldn't mind a blast of something." Sarn rubbed his hands together and licked his lips.

"All the thoughts I'm getting—and it's like a huge tidal wave—are about getting money and having fun," Tarla told them.

"Great. Here are four more of us. But no booze. Not for a while, anyway. We have to stay on our guard. At least until we know more," Jorl said. They walked slowly down the street enjoying the scene—the smiles, the lights, the laughter, and the just plain fun of it all. They looked in the window of one place they saw, and it seemed to be a public food station. People were sitting at tables that had what appeared to be food on plates in front of them.

"It doesn't look like a—a—very nice place," Tarla said. "It looks a little bit dark and seedy." She was still entranced by the sights further up the street.

"They're eating, and I'm starving," Sarn said.

"By the setup it looks public," Jorl said. "Maybe it will be a good place to practice being like the inhabitants."

"Wonder what all those machines are—looks like some kind of a game." Sarn's curiosity of mechanical things was fully alerted. "Let's go in!"

Khair shrugged and said, "Might as well."

Jorl turned from the window and asked, "Can you tune in on anything, Tarla?"

"Too much. It's flooding my brain." She held her head and closed her eyes for a moment.

"They seem to be so . . . so . . . avid . . ." she raised her head and laughed. "Oh, I know why . . . those are gambling machines. That's why there' so much noise and excitement and . . ."

Sarn, eyes gleaming, interrupted her. "Let's go. Come on." He pushed open the door and left no time for further discussion.

The sounds of machines, people, and music blasted out at them.

"Well," Jorl shrugged, "What's to lose?"

"At the very least, our hearing, maybe?" Khair shrugged and followed.

Tarla came up to Sarn who was standing in front of one of the machines pushing buttons. "You're supposed to put money in first, Sarn," Tarla whispered to him. "That makes the machine start."

"That's logical," Sarn agreed. "Khair, Tarla, help me figure out how they work." He looked up and grinned, "If that machine we rode in is any indication, it can't be too complicated." His eyes continued to dart all over the machine looking for details and information. "They look sort of familiar. Seems to be some resemblance to units I've played with. Can you find out anything more about them, Tarla?"

"See all those tapes running around? Well, when it stops, if they show the right pictures, you win."

"It's mechanical then," Khair said. "What we need is a magnetic control. Sarn, did you . . .?"

"Oh, yes. I never leave home without one." He patted his case, pleased with himself. "Hey, Jorl," he whispered, "shield me while I get the sender out and make a small adjustment."

"Wait a minute. It's too dangerous out here." Jorl looked quickly around the crowded room. "There must be a bathroom. This seems to be a public place, and some of the rules apply in any civilization. Tarla, have a scan around."

She did. "It's the second door down at the end of that row of machines."

"Khair, you wait with Tarla. I'll go with Sarn," Jorl said quietly.

The two of them headed for the washrooms. On their way down the narrow aisle, two girls were coming toward them. One stopped in front of Jorl. She put one hand on a rounded hip and the other behind her neck—the classic pose—and said, "Hello, handsome. Where've you been all my life? Huh, baby?"

"Yeah, baby," the other one said and, while cracking gum at a machine gun rate, she shot her hip in the grand old burlesque "bump and grind" style.

Jorl didn't understand the words, but the look is the same on any planet. His tanned face crinkled in a wide grin as he put an arm around each of them and dropped a light kiss on their foreheads. He shook his head and pointed to Tarla.

"Oh, taken already, eh?" the first girl sighed. "Well, that's bloody life for ya."

The other one sighed, "A hunk like that. Why be surprised?" and the two continued on their rotating way.

"Come on, lover boy, we've got a lot of work to do." Sarn lightly punched Jorl on his arm, grinned, and opened the door.

They had the room to themselves long enough to replace Sarn's watch with the altered magnetic sender. It looked like a fancy chronometer but, by manipulating the stem, the user could now control simple moving parts, either mechanical or digital, with seventy-five percent efficiency.

"On a strange planet one day and already planning crimes," Jorl said.

"Tch, tch," Sarn clucked and shook his head.

"Sarn, you've got a streak of larceny in your soul a mile wide." Jorl couldn't help but smile at him.

"Yeah," Sarn agreed. He put up his wrist to admire the sender.

They went back to where Tarla and Khair waited.

"All set?" Khair asked quietly.

"All set," answered Jorl. Meantime, Tarla had spent her time watching people at the red machine with an ATM sign over it. She whispered to Jorl and Sarn to look at the red machine and whispered, "That's the money. Now, watch that short, pudgy man over there."

The little guy went to a machine, put in a small card, punched some buttons and got some bigger paper from it. They continued to watch as the little man looked at two machines and then put one of his papers into the third one. Immediately, the machine seemed to come to life and made loud, musical type noises while flashing colors and pictures. The little man then started to push buttons. For a few minutes, they quietly watched both the little man's machine and the other two machines close to it.

The little man looked at it for a moment and then punched two buttons. All the tapes started turning and then stopped. The little man punched another button, and the tapes started rotating again. All this time, the four had been intently watching the action.

Sarn's eyes were flashing as much as the machines. Even his red hair seemed to be crackling with excitement. "That's a simplified mono version of our multiple and three D gambling machines. Wow," he whispered to the other three.

Suddenly, the little man's machine went crazy, and so did the little man.

They watched all the excitement happening when a young guy came up to the little man and counted out quite a few pieces of paper money.

The man on the machine next to the little man's appeared to be unhappy. His face had one large scowl written on it as he slammed down on a button. His machine made a loud noise and spit out a small piece of white paper. The disgruntled man took it over to a desklike counter with screening all over the front of it. The girl behind the counter exchanged his small white paper for a few other pieces of paper. They looked the same as the ones that had come out of the red ATM. Presumably, it was some of his planet's money.

"Gentlemen," Sarn said. The excitement made his green eyes gleam. "Remember that time in cadet school when we needed a 1.07 electron transductor? And that lump of a kid had a full box of them and wouldn't give us one unless we either paid through the nose or became his servants for a month?"

"Indeed I do. Remember, Jorl?" Khair laughed with Jorl at the memory.

"And do you remember how lucky we were to manage to save our hides from being nailed to the wall by the dean of the academy?" Jorl asked.

"Oh, yes, I do," Sarn said. "But let's do it anyway."

"Good idea, Sarn, but remember the council and be smooth—and fast." Jorl cautioned. He turned to Tarla and spoke softly into her ear, "You stand watch."

The three men, apparently in deep conversation, worked their way closer to the little man who was counting his money with glee. Suddenly, Sarn seemed to trip over something, couldn't catch his balance, fell on his back, and his feet flew out from under him, right smack into the stranger's ankles, who obeyed the law of physics and lost his balance, flung up his arms, let go of his money and tried to save himself from a fall. Paper flew everywhere. Sarn helped the man catch his balance, held his arm and attention, and smiled and apologized in a loud, never-ending, concerned voice. The loud use of his language added to the confusion.

Khair and Jorl picked up the money quickly, and making loud and foreign noises and gestures, brushed off the little man's clothes, giving him his money in wide, rapid gestures, and backed away, still smiling and nodding and talking until they reached Tarla who had hardly dared to breathe.

"I don't see how that performance could fool anybody. Did it work, Khair?" Tarla asked in a soft voice.

"Yes, I snagged a few pieces,"

"So did I," Jorl said.

"Let's go. Come on." Sarn headed for the machines.

They took a few minutes to understand the machine's operation and what pictures were needed to win the most money. Then Sarn put three money papers in the slot and Khair pushed the button. The pictures blurred around. By delicately manipulating the stem of his meter, Sarn sent a blast of energy that made parts composed of the molecular weight of all the pictures needed for the big win to attract each other. This time it didn't.

"Where's the sign called a jackpot? Where's all the winning noise." Sarn looked all over the machine, annoyed that nothing was happening.

"Wait a minute, Sarn," Tarla spoke quietly as she read the words on the machine. "It has to be three pictures, or else some kind of an arrangement of them," Tarla whispered.

"Humph," Sarn snorted. He made a small adjustment while Khair put in another three papers and pushed the button.

Nothing.

Sarn mumbled and grumbled under his breath, lost in deep concentration. "Okay, now try."

They watched intently.

"Five sevens—with flames on them," Tarla whispered. "You did it."

Suddenly, bells rang, lights flashed, music blared, and the word jackpot lit up the screen.

They looked around for the same young man that had arrived when the little man had won.

"Oh, Sarn," Tarla said, giving him a hug and a kiss on each cheek.

"Yeah," Sarn grinned from ear to ear.

The same young man came over and counted out a tidy pile of bills into Jorl's hand.

"Great! Now we can eat!" Sarn said, rubbing his hands together and patting his stomach. "Hear that noise? That's hunger calling. Let's get one of those stalls in that other room. And I deserve a drink of the local poison."

Soon, they were settled into one of the cramped booths. Sarn, his eyes searching everywhere, said, "Wonder where they keep the auto food dispensers?"

"I've been watching," Tarla said softly. "I think they do it all by hand." She hoped to forestall a small explosion by Sarn.

"You mean the food is handled by strangers?" Sarn was disgusted. Even more so when a swinging door opened, and they caught sight of the muddled kitchen and a sloppy, big-bellied man with a dirty cloth draped around his middle, throwing food on plates.

A tired, bored waitress sauntered over and made a careless swipe at the crumbs left by the last occupants. She came back—order book at the ready. "What'll it be?" she asked, totally disinterested. She looked blankly at the four of them as they carried on a conversation in their own lilting, liquid accents. Mostly, it was an argument with Sarn, who didn't relish the thoughts of food handled by such a motley bunch.

Hurriedly, Tarla scanned the rather empty mind of the waitress and pulled out the uppermost impression that seemed to be of food. "Four hamburgers, four chips, and four beers, please," she ordered.

"What brand of beer, and tap or bottle, ma'am?" She stood, poised, her eyes on the order pad, and a pencil at the ready.

"Oh, ah, any kind of tap, please," she answered after another hurried peek into the waitress's mind.

The waitress slouched away, and they heard her shout out the order.

"What in blazing stars did you ask for? Never mind, don't tell me. No matter what you ordered, it's still going to be boiled virus with microbes on the side and uric acid to drink."

"Sarn, that's an awful thing to say," Tarla hissed in a whisper.

"Anyway," Jorl said, "it won't hurt a tough gut like yours, Sarn."

"How do you know? We haven't eaten yet."

In a short while, their waitress showed up with a tray full of food. She plunked plates of food and glasses filled with an amber-colored, bubbly liquid in front of each of them.

They looked at the questionable food and then at one another.

"Now what? What'll we eat it with—hands—feet maybe?" Sarn poked at the hamburger.

"It smells good, so eat it," Tarla ordered.

"Are you speaking as a senior officer, or as a sister?" Sarn asked. He eyed the food thing with a wary eye.

Tarla was saved from replying by the waitress who slouched over again and plunked down some knives, forks, and a bottle.

"Well, that's some improvement," Sarn said.

"Those people over there are holding them in their hands to eat them." Tarla said quietly.

Sarn looked up and watched for a minute. "Okay, Might as well. What's this bottle of red stuff?" He opened the top and smelled it. "Well, it smells good." Hunger was driving him, so he pulled the thing called a hamburger apart and squirted some red stuff on it and put it back together. With his eyes clenched shut, he took a big bite. His eyes opened wide. He was pleasantly surprised. "Hey, it's not bad. Try it, Jorl."

Jorl didn't quite trust it that Sarn wasn't trying to pull a fast one. He looked at Sarn intently and saw nothing but wide-eyed innocence in Sarn's expression. Usually, that could be taken as a bad sign. Still doubtful, he put in the red stuff, put the burger back together and took a careful bite. "Hey, you weren't joking. It's pretty good."

Meantime, Khair had reached for the pale yellow liquid. "The glass is icy cold, and I'm as dry as that desert out there." He lifted the glass and downed half of it without a pause. "Phew. It's good—slightly bitter but good." He licked his lips, then tackled a hamburger.

"Put the red stuff on it. Makes it even better," Sarn said. Then he took another big bite.

"Great. Now you try the beer." Khair took another long swallow that emptied his glass. "I'd like some more of that, Tarla. Will you order another one for me?"

Sarn watched him. "To the black hole with it." He picked up his glass and took a big swallow. "Blazing stars and speeding comets. Not bad. Not bad at all." He finished the glass in short order. "Hey," he looked at the waitress and then at Tarla, "How do I get her to come back?"

"Call 'waitress'—nicely, Sarn." She lightly tapped him on his arm. "Behave, Sarn."

"Waitress!" he bellowed.

The girl came over and said, "Yes. What can I get you?" Her tone of voice left no doubt that she couldn't really care less—just do her job and leave it at that.

Sarn held up four fingers and the empty glass. "What's the word, Tarla?"

"Beer," she replied softly.

"Beer," Sarn bellowed again.

"Sarn, I doubt if she's deaf—and remember, it's slightly alcoholic."

"Great, just what I need. You want some more, Khair? Jorl?"

"You just ordered it," Jorl replied.

"They're for me." Sarn held up eight fingers again.

"Sarn, one more each is enough," Tarla whispered sternly.

"Eight?" asked the waitress.

Sarn gave in quite gracefully and held up four fingers. "Tarla, we want more—what are they called?" He pointed to the hamburgers.

"Hamburgers," she replied.

"Hamburgers," Sarn shouted. He held up eight fingers again.

"You're learning the language at a great rate," Khair said and smiled.

"It's the important matter of comfortable survival with Sarn," Jorl said and laughed.

The waitress came back with four more pints and eight more hamburgers. They thoroughly enjoyed the food, which tasted much better with the beer, and soon there was neither a crumb nor a drop left on the table.

"I don't know about you, but I feel much better for that." Jorl patted his stomach.

The waitress brought a piece of paper, laid it on the table, and stood waiting. Jorl picked it up and recognized the symbols as mathematical. "Must be the bill."

"Will there be anything else?" the waitress asked a little impatiently.

Tarla answered, "No, thank you." Then she caught the thought of money for the paper and more besides. "I think we're supposed to pay her now and also leave her a . . . a tip," she told Jorl. "The tip is a sort of a present."

"What for?" Sarn asked.

"Because she brought our food, I guess," Tarla replied.

"Well, isn't that why she's here?" Jorl asked.

"Yes. But it seems to be the custom, and she's wondering how much we'll leave for her. Also, her back aches, and her feet hurt," Tarla reported.

"Well, blazing stars, give her some bills. Maybe she'll even squeeze out a smile." Sarn took some of the paper money out of his pocket, heaped it on the table, and pointed from them to her. The girl's mouth and eyes opened in amazement. She couldn't believe it.

"Wow! Thanks a lot. Wow." She scooped the bills off the table and into her apron pocket and ran for the kitchen.

"See? What did I tell you? All it takes is money, anywhere," Sarn said. He was a little flushed, bright-eyed, and feeling happily fuzzy. "Come on, Jorl, Khair, I need the washroom. Too much intake with no output." He led the way to the men's room. The other two followed.

Tarla waited for them. When they came back to the booth, they picked up their packs and headed for the front door and the street. They stepped out into the cool night air, cheerfully pleased with themselves.

"Things seem to be going nicely," Jorl remarked. "Let's try one of the other places . . . where all those bright lights are. There has to be something a little better than that one."

"Oh, yes! One of those with the big flashing lights." Sarn began to feel the excitement of the city along with the beer. "I think that one was a dive."

"Well, dive or not, we have a stake and full bellies," Khair reminded them.

They happily ambled their way up the broad and fun-filled street.

"We soon must think about a place to sleep," Khair said.

"And a vehicle," Jorl added.

"But for now, just let's gamble and drink." Sarn rubbed his hands together. "Great vacation so far. Might as well enjoy it."

"Since there's nothing we can do about our problem right now—why not?"

Ahead of them, a man stepped out into the street, waved his arm, and shouted, "Hey, taxi."

A vehicle pulled over to the curb. Two couples got in, and away they went.

Without saying a word, Sarn stepped out into the street, waved his arm and shouted at the nearest moving vehicle. Not being a taxi, it didn't pay any attention. He yelled at the next one. A head stuck out the car window and yelled something back. It sounded like, "Whatareyarsomekindanut er something?"

"What in blazing suns goes on?" Sarn was highly annoyed. "What did the space rat say, Tarla?"

"I think it was something rude," Tarla replied.

Khair, pointing to a sign on the roof of a vehicle, said, "I think the public conveyances are marked like that."

Sarn stood on the curb, his green eyes examining every vehicle that passed. "Hah! That's one." He waved his arms and shouted, "Hey, waitress!"

"It's 'taxi,' Sarn," Tarla corrected.

"What's the difference? Look, it worked." Sarn chortled when the car pulled smartly to the curb, and a man leaned over and said, "Where to, pal?"

Sarn turned to Tarla. "What did he say?"

"He wants to know where we want him to take us."

"Let's get in." Sarn hopped into the front seat with the driver, and the other three got in the back.

"Where'll it be, folks?"

Tarla hurriedly sorted through the cabby's thoughts and said, "To the nearest good hotel, please."

The taxi driver pulled away from the curb. Sarn and Jorl watched his every move.

"That would be the Dunes," replied the cabbie. "Hope you got a reservation." He darted in front of another car that had slowed. "Strangers in town?"

"Yes. And we're really excited to be here," Tarla replied in her sweetest tones.

Khair watched the street as they merged into the traffic. All of them were a little anxious at the apparently uncontrolled rushing about of noisy vehicles and of the hundreds of people. They drove up one street and down another and finally arrived at a large, glittering building set in floodlit, extensive, well-appointed grounds.

The taxi pulled up to the impressive main entrance. A huge doorman marched over at a stately pace and opened the car doors with a flourish that matched his resplendent uniform.

Sarn reached back to nudge Khair. "Do we salute or just bow low?"

Tarla smiled, "No, just tip."

The taxi driver said, "That'll be $15.75, folks."

"A bit steep," muttered Jorl. He'd figured out the monetary system. He started to pull out a bill.

"Yes, and he's thinking tip," Tarla whispered to Jorl. "And so is he." She indicated the doorman. They walked across to the main doors that the general of something held open.

Jorl shrugged and paid. They entered the main doors. Before they had a minute to organize themselves, a briskly determined bellhop met them and practically snatched their cases right out of their hands.

"That's his job," Tarla hissed at Sarn, determined to forestall any argument.

"Hey-y," Jorl whistled softly. "Now this is more like it." They wended their way to the desk. The vast, elegant lobby was crowded with sparkling, well-dressed men and women.

"Yeah," Sarn agreed. He happily scanned the female crop. "Just look at all of them, Khair."

"I agree. But take a look at the ceiling. It's amazing."

The three men tore their eyes away from their sightseeing to go with Tarla as she walked over to where a desk clerk was watching her with pleasure written all over his face. "Yes, madam? How may I help you?"

Tarla quickly took a peak inside the clerk's mind. "Accommodations for four, please," Tarla said softly.

"Do you have reservations, madam?"

"No, I'm sorry. So much confusion, so much hurry, hurry," she fluttered her hands like little exhausted birds.

"Oh . . . I'm afraid . . . for four? I don't think . . ."

"But maybe you can help me?" She smiled brilliantly and tossed her beautiful mane of golden hair and looked at him pleadingly with her dark purple eyes opened wide.

He melted. "The hotel is full, but . . . well, yes, I believe I have a vacant suite."

"Oh, thank you. You've saved my life."

He blushed with pleasure and confusion, and it took a few moments longer than usual to complete the necessary arrangements before he could hand the bellhop the key.

"I hope you'll enjoy your stay with us, and if there's anything, anything at all that I can do, or the hotel can do, to make your stay more pleasant, please don't hesitate to ask."

"You are a kind man." Tarla could grasp only about half the words the desk clerk had said, so to make up for it, she smiled meltingly at him for the evident trouble that he had taken.

"Ease off, Tarla, before he's on his hands and knees begging for a pat on the head or licking your boots," Jorl whispered, grinning.

They followed the bellhop into an elevator and waited to see the result. When they stopped, the floor indicator said 4. The bellhop led them out of the elevator and down the hall to a door and used a key to open it into a series of rooms that now seemed to belong to them—a large, well-furnished living space, two big bedrooms, and a huge bathroom. It also had a balcony that overlooked one of the swimming pools.

The bellhop was busy doing the usual things—trying every door, cupboard, and window.

"Tip, I suppose," Jorl said to Tarla.

After a quick peek into the man's head, she said, "Yes."

"That's the name of the game on this planet," Sarn said."

"They're not auto-servos, Sarn. They're real people."

In a slippery sort of a voice, the bellhop announced, "The dining rooms, bars, casinos, and room service are open. Will there be anything else?" The bellhop gave them their elevator key and left his hand obviously extended. He smiled knowingly, "And I mean anything else."

"Not now, thank you," Tarla said.

Jorl gave the hand a bill.

At last they were alone—finally able to breathe in freedom. They sprawled into the nearest big chairs to enjoy the first comfort since they had crashed.

"Well, I guess we could say that we've accomplished a fair amount since we, ah-h, dropped in, or down," Jorl said. He grunted as he pulled off his boots and wiggled his toes. "Wouldn't you agree?"

"Blazing stars, yes," Sarn agreed.

"But there's a long way to go before we can get home again," Khair sighed.

"Well, right this minute, I'm for a long, hot bath." Tarla had inspected the bathroom and figured out the arrangements. "Imagine, time for a long soak in hot, soapy water—nowhere to go and nothing that I have to do. Glorious."

Soon they could hear her splashing and singing while in what they presumed was hot and soapy water.

"We'll toss for the next turn," Jorl said, sprawled comfortably in the big chair.

"Fair enough, if you promise not to cheat," Khair agreed.

"Cheat? Khair, I don't cheat." Jorl's grin spoiled his try for injured innocence.

"Not when we're looking, anyway," Sarn said, lazily scanning the room. He spied some form of an instrument on the table beside him and sat up, curious. "What's this, I wonder?" He reached for it. The top part lifted off the base, "Looks like some kind of an antiquated communicating device." He examined the two ends. His eyebrows rose when he heard a voice coming over it—gabbling out a string of unintelligible sounds. "Someone is in contact with us," he said, amazed.

"What're they saying?" Khair came over to listen.

"Blahfjfladlghjdls; amnfkgnma," answered Sarn.

Khair laughed. "Stupid question."

"Here, listen, Khair."

Khair, at six feet six inches, was as tall as his brother, Jorl, and just as strongly built. Both of them had the well-defined muscles of a trained athlete, but Khair had straight black hair and brown eyes, where Jorl had softly waved auburn hair and greenish eyes. Like Jorl, he had a pleasant look with an easy smile. The most serious of the group, he was more inclined to look a little harder before he leaped. He came over to listen but it made no sense to him, either.

"Yes, definitely squawks," he said and passed the unit back to Sarn.

"We'll just have to wait for . . ." Suddenly, a wide and wicked smile split Sarn's face from ear to ear, and he shouted into it, "Beer! Eight!" Another rattle of squawks came out of it. Khair and Sarn both shrugged. "Beer! Eight!" Sarn yelled into it again and put the device back on its stand.

"Damn fine idea, Sarn. Unless you're talking to traffic control, or Enforcementors, or something else in the law line," Jorl laughed.

"We'll soon know," Sarn replied and rubbed his hands gleefully.

Tarla eventually came out of the bathroom followed by a cloud of steam. She was swathed in towels and held her wet clothes in her hand. "That was pure heaven. I'm thankful that the uniforms dry quickly because, as you know, I didn't have time to pack and bring my traveling trunk." She ran into the bedroom—wet, clean, and happy.

Jorl won the next round, and mumblings of disgruntlement followed him to the bathroom.

"Even when I watch, you manage to do it," Sarn said, vexed.

"What do you mean? I wouldn't cheat you, Sarn. I'd never do such a thing."

"Oh? And I should believe you?" Sarn was sure that, somehow, Jorl managed to cheat.

Jorl threw back his head and laughed. He shut the bathroom door just in time to not be hit by a hard thrown cushion.

Khair and Sarn were suddenly electrified by a loud knock on their door. Khair catwalked over to it, and Sarn took a position on the other side of the doorjamb, prepared for anything. Khair opened the door. There stood the same bellboy holding a tray full of the beer they had ordered with one hand and the other hand obviously held out.

Sarn whooped and grabbed the tray, and Khair gave the startled bellboy some bills. Khair smiled and shut the door. He and Sarn went happily to work on the cold, foamy drink. Khair took one into Jorl.

Sarn knocked on Tarla's bedroom door, "Hey, Tarla, want a beer?"

"Sure do." She stuck an arm out, and Sarn put a beer in her hand.

Within an hour, they felt like new people, inside and out.

"Now what?" Khair asked.

"I think we should have a few hours' sleep, and tomorrow we'll worry about what comes next." Tarla yawned. It was catching.

"Good idea," Jorl said. They suddenly realized just how tired they were.

They found their beds and crashed, sound asleep within minutes.

Chapter 4

From halfway up the cloudless, brilliantly blue sky, the sun sent dazzling shafts of light streaming earthward. One busy little splinter of sunshine sneaked in a window and played in Sarn's eye till he woke up.

Disoriented for a moment, Sarn looked over and saw Khair in the next bed. In one big tidal wave of thoughts, he suddenly remembered everything. He stayed lazily where he was, comfortably stretching and yawning, until a cacophony of female squeals and giggles got the best of him.

"Do I hear what I think I do?" He jumped out of bed and ran to the balcony for a look. "Yes, blazing comet tails, I do."

And there they played—dozens of females, all shapes and sizes, in various states of undress, cavorting in a huge pool of sparkling water. He breathed a sigh and stared, entranced. He rubbed his hands together and grinned wolfishly.

"They're gorgeous. Hey, Khair, lazy slob, wake up." Sarn fired a pillow at him, which brought the sleeping Khair instantly to his feet, poised for anything.

"One of these days, I'll bash you for doing that to me." He rubbed his eyes and yawned.

"Come here and have a look. Just look. This time, you'll thank me."

Khair weaved himself slowly over to the balcony and blinked in the strong light. Then he, also, grinned from ear to ear. "We're still asleep, Sarn. The last time we got ourselves stranded, they were short, warty, and bilious green. This is far too much luck." Khair watched the scene below with pure pleasure.

"Feast your eyes, Khair. Just look at them."

"Um-m, yes."

"What's out there that's so interesting?" Tarla asked. She was standing in the doorway. Then she heard the distinctive sounds. "Of course. Girls, I bet." She and Jorl joined them on the balcony.

The three men watched the curvy confusion with pure enjoyment.

"That's enough," Tarla said with a laugh. "Get dressed and let's find some food." She turned to leave. Jorl followed her and grabbed her by the waist. "And you're still the pick of all the galaxies." He dropped a light kiss on her soft lips.

She hugged Jorl close. "And so are you."

"I think I must try that someday," Sarn said.

"What?" Khair asked. "Try what?"

"Being married."

"Hah. Pin yourself down to one? You?"

"What do you mean—'hah'. Sometimes, I think I'd like to be married. Look at Tarla and Jorl. And, if I remember correctly, you were married and loved it." Sarn was suddenly contrite. "I'm sorry, Khair. I shouldn't have said that. I know you're not quite over the shock of Mara's death yet. But it was a long time ago, and—" Sarn gave Khair a sympathetic hug.

"That's okay, Sarn. Yes, it was a long time ago, and I am mostly over it. But sometimes, I wish—oh, a lot of things."

"Come on, let's go and find some breakfast and enjoy this great day. Come on."

Soon, the four of them were assembled in the living room.

"Well, crew, are we ready to face this new world?" Jorl asked.

"Today," Tarla said, "our first order of business is to find out where we are."

"Correction," Sarn said. "The first order of today is to find some food."

"I agree to that," Tarla said.

"Then maybe a little look at the, eh, pool?"

"Don't push it, Sarn." Tarla couldn't help laughing. "You're still a spoiled brat, you know."

"Oh, yeah. But you love me anyway. Come on, let's get started. I'm hungry."

They found the dining room without any trouble and had a cheerful and satisfying breakfast without committing any glaring errors. Even Sarn, pleased with the better quality food, didn't grumble. "I really liked that egg thing."

Afterward, they crossed the spacious lobby and went out into the late morning sunshine. With a fine sense of direction, Sarn guided them toward the swimming pool he had seen from their balcony. The four handsome strangers created quite a stir. They made a striking picture when they seemed to glide, as lightly as a breath of air, over the brilliant green lawns.

"Gee, who are they? They're gorgeous. Do you think they're movie stars?" breathed one voluptuous lovely.

Her more reserved friend, sitting at the same table, sighed lightly.

Tarla and Jorl looked at each other, then at Sarn and Khair, smiled, and slowly moved over to an umbrella-covered table. This left Khair and Sarn free to enjoy themselves.

"Gee," the shorter girl said. "Oh, gee." She looked up at Sarn with her big pansy eyes and full, smiling lips. Sunlight enhanced the gold highlights in the soft blonde hair that crowned her pretty face. "Oh, gee."

"Yes, indeed," agreed the willowy, coolly beautiful brunette. She watched Khair from her slightly downcast eyes.

Chemicals mixed.

Instant ignition.

An immediate understanding flared between each pair.

Khair and Sarn spoke a few words in their own language to the girls.

"I don't understand a word you said, but it sounded lovely. Just lovely." The shorter of the two girls clasped her hands together and held them to her chest.

Carol said to Khair, pointing to herself, "My name is Carol." She pointed to Eloise and said, "Eloise."

"Gee—wh-what's your name?" Eloise made an involuntary shiver, maybe because Sarn put his arm around her and gently nibbled her ear. Sarn spoke a few words to her. "Gee. Maybe you don't know how to speak English, but you sure do know your body English." She giggled. "Look—goose bumps."

Carol and Khair, both more reserved, still made progress.

"What—are—your—names?" Carol enunciated clearly. She pointed to Sarn and Khair.

Sarn suddenly caught on. He pointed to himself, "Sarn." He pointed to Khair, "Khair."

"Sarn? Sarn. Oh-h-h, that's nice. It sounds so foreign. I love foreign things—eh, people." She blazed him a smile that hit him square in his libido.

With charade-like gestures to go with the words, they managed to understand one another and even ordered drinks from a hovering waiter.

Jorl and Tarla smiled at the picture the two couples made under the shade of a huge umbrella. Then Jorl and Tarla walked over to them.

"Sorry to break in on you," Tarla said, "but we really do have things that must be done."

"That's what we have been working on." Sarn patted Eloise's arm and grinned wickedly. He introduced the girls to Jorl and Tarla. Tarla spoke in her slightly accented English.

"Gee, your sister speaks pretty good English," Eloise said.

"Thank you, Eloise, but I'm afraid that we must take Sarn and Khair away for a while."

"Not for too long, I hope," Carol said quietly, a husky edge to her voice. She looked at Khair as she spoke.

"Soon again," Khair looked deeply into her eyes.

"Gee, no-o, not for too long." Eloise sighed. Her pansy eyes looked right into Sarn's snapping green ones.

Tarla was nearly bowled over by the physical waves leaping from the thoughts of all four of them.

"Tell the little star shines that we'll see them later today, Tarla." Sarn never took his eyes away from Eloise.

Tarla obliged and, making polite noises, she and Jorl shepherded Khair and Sarn away from their apparent conquests.

Chapter 5

"Gee," Eloise sighed, "oh, gee. Isn't he gorgeous?" She watched Sarn and the other three walk away.

"Simmer down, Eloise."

"But didn't you feel it? The—the electricity?" Eloise was all but quivering with excitement.

Carol thought for a moment. "I know what you mean, and yes, I did, but don't get carried away. We don't know anything about them."

"Oh, Carol, I have this funny feeling. I think he's for me, no matter what."

"Earth calling Eloise. Come back. We've got errands to do." Carol gathered up her things.

Eloise, her head full of thoughts of Sarn, absentmindedly gathered up her own bits and pieces.

"Come on, Eloise. We're going to run out of time."

"I'm coming. But Carol—isn't he wonderful?"

"Oh, I'm sure he is. Come on now, let's go." Carol rattled her car keys a little impatiently.

"I wonder if we really will see them again? Don't you want to see Khair again, Carol? Wait for me. I'm coming. Carol?"

Carol was a few feet ahead of her, and as she waited for Eloise to catch up, she turned and said, "Yes, I would like to see Khair again. But—we shall see what we shall see."

"Aren't you even a little bit excited? Just a little bit?"

"You're bouncing around enough for both of us, but, yes, I'm—intrigued. Now, come on. We have to get to the drycleaners, the bank, and the grocery store. Want to or not."

"I know we have to, but . . ."

Getting out of Carol's big blue Oldsmobile sedan in the shopping center's parking lot, Eloise said, "Oh, what a dull drag—doing dumb errands on a day like this. We should be doing something spectacular."

"Well, eating is good. We need some money, and you need your dress," Carol said. "And don't forget, we're going to the Financial Association's ball tonight. Paul and Dennis are coming for us at seven o'clock. So come on." Carol looked at her watch. "It's already two o'clock."

Once they were back at their apartment, they decided to take a few minutes to relax and have a cup of tea.

Eloise still gave off waves of excitement. "Aren't Tarla and—was it Jorl? Aren't they lovely people, Carol? As a matter of fact, all four of them are just plain gorgeous."

"Yes, I agree, they are. And Tarla is absolutely beautiful," Carol said softly.

"So are you, Carol, just as beautiful," Eloise spoke with absolute conviction.

"Not like she is, and besides, you're biased." Carol gave Eloise a tender look. "Beauty doesn't last no matter what you do to keep it. I'll grow old and ugly. Then nobody will want me for anything."

"Oh, Carol, you're always so hard on yourself. You're the envy of all the women who know you. You'll still be beautiful no matter how old you get." Eloise giggled and said, "Now, for once, I get to say it's you who has to stop being silly."

Carol had to laugh. "However, envying me is silly. Most of these women have husbands and children—someone to love them for what they are. They know where they belong." She gave a deep sigh.

"Oh, my dearest Carol, believe me, your time will come, and you'll have all of everything you ever wanted."

Carol couldn't help but smile at Eloise's earnestness. "That would be very nice. Now, enough silly talk. We have to get ready."

"Carol, I—I—" Carol saw concern written all over Eloise's face.

"Okay, Eloise, what's on your mind?"

"Well, I've been worried about something for quite some time. It's about Paul. He's a very nice guy, and I really like him. It's only that, well, he seems so—flat—somehow. Especially just after meeting Sarn today." Eloise, for reasons she didn't understand, had gently discouraged Paul, who was still pressing for an official engagement. "I think I know why I don't want to marry him—why I was holding off. I just met Sarn once, and I never, ever felt like that, not even once, with Paul."

"But Paul is a nice man," Carol said. "And he's solid and stable and has a good dental practice. He'd make a good husband."

"That's it. There's got to be more to marriage than that. I like him a lot, but he's not . . . I don't feel . . . and he's not much fun."

Carol laughed. "You've been around too many first graders for far too long. They're always and continually on the loud move."

"Maybe." Eloise had to laugh at what Carol said. "But I love being a teacher. And that's one of the main things that really bothers me about Paul. He tends to think a wife's place is in the home, and . . . and . . . well, I don't want to give up teaching."

"I totally agree with you. That kind of thinking is right out of the dark ages. You're absolutely suited to being the teacher of the little whirlwinds." Carol smiled at Eloise with affection. "I'd spend one day in that classroom, escape, go home to bed—for hours—with a good supply of aspirins and cold compresses. I don't know how you stand it."

"I know, but I love it and I get a big kick out of all the kids. And, anyway, I sure wouldn't want your job. Nothing but big piles of papers and numbers—by the truckload. Yuck."

"Remember, Eloise, you love what you do, and you don't have to give it up for anybody."

Carol, a chartered accountant with a most prestigious firm in Nevada, was well suited to the profession. She was calm, clever, and kept her cool in any situation. Dennis, the partner with whom she usually worked, was a well-respected member of the firm.

"Dennis is a nice man, too," Carol said. "I always know what to expect and how he thinks in any business related topic. I will say that we make a good team. I mean, I admire his talent—he is a brilliant accountant." Carol looked thoughtful. "Still, I have to agree with you. With him, it's mostly business. Nothing more than that—at least as far as I'm concerned."

"There, see? I told you."

Carol laughed. "You sound just like one of your first graders. But I do—see." A sad expression slid across her lovely face, a sudden memory of her life in the orphanage.

"Oh, gee, Carol, I'm sorry. Don't be sad." Eloise knew the whole story of Carol's life—the death of her parents at an early age, nowhere to go, no one to belong to, and placed in an orphanage.

Carol spoke in a soft voice. "I'll never forget that terrible feeling of aloneness. I was only five years old. I couldn't understand what had happened. Where were my Mummy and Daddy? Why did they leave me at that place? I was all alone. When I got older, I knew it wasn't their fault. The orphanage told me a drunk driver killed them both in a car accident. At the time, all I knew was that I was lost.

I think maybe that is why I rather like the thought of someone like Dennis. Not that I would ever marry Dennis. I don't feel anything even remotely romantic for him. But he does represent safety and stability and to not be alone. It could be a little tempting. So, all things considered, maybe Dennis would be . . ."

"Oh, Carol, maybe Khair is the answer—not to just settle for Dennis."

"Now, Eloise, don't start." Carol's eyes welled up in tears.

"Oh, my dear Carol." Eloise quickly sat beside her on the chesterfield. "Have a hug and a tissue. Please don't cry."

Carol, quickly wiping away a stray tear, smiled and said, "That's enough self-pity for one day." She gave Eloise a hug. "I'm just being silly. I suppose Dennis is still the best answer . . ."

"No, Carol. No! That would be just—settling. Maybe . . . maybe Khair will be the answer." Eloise's thoughts were on the bright, shiny future that might include Sarn and Khair.

"Don't start on that again, Eloise. You've read too many romance novels and have put too much meaning into a poolside meeting. We'll probably never see them again."

"Will you agree to at least wait and see? I know that Dennis is, well, it's supposed to be a secret, but . . ."

"But what, Eloise, what are you talking about? Come on Elly, what are you hiding? Tell me." Carol took Eloise's hands and insisted on an answer.

"Well, I saw, I mean, he showed me . . . I promised not to . . ." Eloise squirmed mentally and physically.

"What?"

"I can't."

"Yes, you can. What?"

"Well, Dennis . . ."

"Eloise."

"He showed me the engagement ring he's going to give you tonight."

Carol looked shocked. "He what?"

"He . . ."

"I heard you." Carol's expressions ran the whole gamut from incredulous to indignation and back. "Why would he even think such a thing? There's been nothing in our relationship to suggest marriage. We have a friendly business relationship. We went out to dinner a few times and we went to a couple of plays, but that doesn't mean I would marry him." Then Carol laughed, "I mean, he's a very laid-back person with not even a hint of, um-m, desire, let alone connubial bliss. And he carries the meaning of "laid-back" to a ridiculous level, and I really don't even know that much about him—as a person, I mean, not just as an accountant." She got up and paced around the living room.

Happily, Eloise thought to herself, *there would be no settling for Carol now.*

"You're right. Settling won't do for either of us," Carol said. "When you think about it, we've shared a lot of life together, right from when I first met you in grade four and your dad adopted me the next year on my tenth birthday when I was in grade five. You, your dad, and me—we three made a happy home, didn't we? I still miss him so much. Andy was a good man and a wonderful father." Carol had a faraway look in her eyes. "He took me in and treated me as another daughter, and gave me a home. I even had my own room. I felt cared for and loved."

"I was only nine when my mum died, but I knew how terribly sad and lonely Dad was, and I know how happy we made him. Do you still remember what he used to call us, Carol?"

"Yes, of course I do," Carol spoke quietly. "He always called you his 'little bundle of sunshine.'"

"Yes. And he called you his 'starry summer's night.'"

"I wish Andy was here now."

"So do I," Eloise said. "It's a year already, and I still can't believe it. But if there really is a heaven, then he's up there now, and he'd be telling us to 'buck up and enjoy life,'" Eloise said with a big smile. "So we will." She jumped up and said, "Our decisions have been made. No settling!"

"Decisions feel great. No marriage to Dennis, and even if nothing comes from the pool thing, it doesn't matter. I'm not going to worry about it." Carol stood up and did a cat stretch.

Eloise's face lit up with happiness. "Me, too, for both of us. Maybe even with Sarn and Khair."

"Eloise, please don't pin your hopes on something so unreal. You're just laying yourself open to such disappointment."

"But, oh, gee, I just know." Eloise poured some more tea and held up her cup to Carol, "Let's drink a toast. Here's to happy meetings and a new chapter in our lives."

"Okay. I'll drink to that." Carol smiled at Eloise and her boundless enthusiasm.

They clinked cups. "Oh, gee, look at the time. It's six o'clock already. Dennis and Paul are supposed to be here at seven."

Carol stood up. "I guess we should get started then."

Instant hurry and flurry.

Chapter 6

When they were a short distance away from the girls and the pool, Tarla laughed and said, "Whew-w-w, I couldn't have taken too much more of the heat waves you two were broadcasting."

"I'm not even telepathic, and it was almost too much for me." Jorl wiped his forehead.

"Tch, tch. You poor, empty husks. The flames have faded. Nothing left but pale embers—faint memories," Sarn said.

"Yes, old empty shells," Khair agreed. "Nothing left."

Sarn put his hand partially over his mouth and loudly stage-whispered to Khair, "From now on, I guess we'll just have to ease off when we wrestle with him—let him win, maybe. What do you think, Khair?"

"You're right," Khair said and nodded. "Yes, you're definitely right." Exaggerated concern was written all over his face.

"That does it. That's the neutron that broke the star's core." Jorl made a good-natured lunge at Sarn who leaped out of his reach.

All of them were well-trained athletes; their bodies were honed to a high degree of physical fitness. Sarn, at six feet three inches and two hundred and twenty pounds, had to give two inches and twenty-five pounds to Khair and Jorl, but he more than made up for it in agility. Sarn, Khair, and Jorl immediately took a wrestler's stance, knees bent, arms out, and bodies circling, teasing each other with outrageous remarks.

Jorl and Sarn leaped and feinted, circled and taunted. "I get the winner," Khair shouted, for the moment acting as referee.

Tarla, in the middle of a laugh, suddenly became aware of a small cloud of thoughts and looked around. She spoke in a low, urgent voice, "A lot of people are gathering."

Immediately, the four became a watchful, single entity, aware of their vulnerability. They decided to leave at once. Without haste, they walked away.

They left behind them sounds of disappointment.

They reentered the hotel and headed to their suite. When they closed the door, they relaxed.

"Now, we can talk. What went wrong, Tarla?" Jorl asked. "Were they suspicious?"

"No," Tarla shook her head, "not suspicious, more like curiosity that could lead to suspicion. Evidently, we make a . . . a striking-looking group with something foreign about us. Not ordinary. They seemed to be admiring us."

"Great. That'll make everything easier, eh, Khair?" Sarn was pleased.

"Not really," Tarla said. "Think about it. Curiosity will make them ask questions that we can't answer. If we told them the truth, most people would become frightened at what the thoughts of having aliens among them could mean."

"And usually," Jorl said, "anything that people can't understand frightens them. Their fright usually turns to violence. Then their first thought is to kill it."

"And that would mean," continued Khair, "that we would have broken the first and most important directive as it's applied to non-federation civilizations. Remember, suspicion is quite often the other side of unsatisfied curiosity. We'll just have to be more careful."

"Suppose so," Sarn agreed.

Khair nodded to Sarn. "Yes." He began to roam around the suite, taking note of the well-appointed furnishings and decorations that quietly spoke of money. "Also, I think we'd better get some more money. This place looks expensive."

Tarla took a closer look around the suite. "You're right, Khair. We will need more money. And another thing, I think we'd better agree on some sort of a story to tell people. You know, where we come from and why we're here."

"Now, where could we come from? Let me think." You could almost see the wheels turning in Sarn's busy brain. "How about . . . Raffinsten? The University of Raffinsten."

"Very good, Sarn. We can expand on what Tarla told old Bill about how we want to study the desert and all that stuff," Jorl said.

"Raffinsten. It's a very small country in Southern Asia. We could have a lot of desert around us that seems to be spreading into our valleys and threatening our towns," Khair added.

"Okay, that's our broad story line, but we'll go easy on the details," Jorl said.

"I like the story. It's simple and believable." Tarla started to tick off items on her fingers. "But there are some things that we must find out. Most importantly, we need to know which star system we're in and which planet of it that we are on so we can get home. Also, we must find a knowledge center, or a library, as they are known here." So saying, she picked up the phone and asked the deskman for the address of the local library. When she hung up, she said, "I'll take a taxi to the nearest one and load the language converter. I shouldn't be too long."

"I'll come with you, Tarla. I don't think it's wise for you to go out alone. Sarn and Khair can start work on getting some ideas for putting a plan together to get us out of this, eh, difficult situation."

"Difficult situation? Blazing spinning suns, sounds like it's in the same category as, as . . ."

With a small smile, Khair asked, "which brand of toothpaste to buy?"

All of them laughed.

"Anyway," Tarla said, "I would prefer to have Jorl come with me, so come on Jorl, let's go. Bye, guys," she waved, and they left for the library.

"Blazing suns, put a plan together? That's a bit of a challenge. We need more than what the local hardware store is apt to have in stock."

"It all depends on where this civilization is on the scale of technology. We don't even know that," Khair said.

"Well, they must have places where you can find that information. Maybe even where Tarla just went. We already know that they know how to have fun, and I'm sure they must have a lot more knowledge than just that."

"Even if we find out where their technology centers are, there is still the problem of them giving us what we need for our repairs," Khair said. "And that creates another problem. We're aliens. The Federation's directive. That brings us right back to the beginning."

"Blasted spinning comets, I hate going in circles. We'll have to find the technical center, and if they have one that's any good to us, we'll have to find a way in through the back door."

"Hardly any problems at all," Khair sighed.

They mulled over the situation.

Tarla and Jorl were back within two hours and pleased with the results. The discussion between Sarn and Khair as to how to solve their problem was still going on.

"... won't solve the communication problem, but maybe if ..." Khair heard the door open and turned to see Tarla and Jorl in the doorway. "Good, you're back." Khair walked across the room to greet them. "Did you find what we need?"

"Yes, we did. Sorry to interrupt your discussion, but let's do this now." Tarla gave each one an AES that fitted into their ears. The audio ear speaker would set up an immediate link to their brains. When the four of them were comfortable, she activated the transfer code. In fifty-three minutes, the control light lit up.

"There, you now know English, but we'll have to practice the vocals. You shouldn't find it as difficult as some of the languages you've had to learn." She gathered up the AES's and packed the unit away.

"Thanks, Tarla. You and this transfer business always did amaze me," Jorl said.

Tarla smiled at him as she unfolded a rather large piece of colorful paper. "This is a picture and some of the details of this solar system." She laid the picture on the table, and the four of them gathered around.

"It has eight planets in orbit around its sun." She leaned over and pointed to one of the planets. "There's Earth, the third planet from the sun and the one that we are now on. Earth also has its own moon. There's quite a lot of detail printed on the back of this sheet. She flipped it over. "I think it will tell us the most important things we need to know about Earth."

"This is great, Tarla," Khair said. As they were all involved in space exploration, they naturally found it extremely interesting. Khair, still reading, said, "You know, this seems to be a great little planet. I'd like to read more of its history."

All of them took the time to absorb the details printed on the sheet.

Afterward, Sarn sprawled into a large chair and looked more closely around the room. "Hey. What's that unit over there?" He jumped up and went to inspect the long, low cabinet standing against a wall. He discovered a panel and slid it open. It exposed a dark, glass-like surface. "Looks like some sort of a scope. I wonder what it measures?" He started pushing buttons.

"Be careful, Sarn. You don't have any idea what it is," Tarla said.

"I don't think it could be anything dangerous, Tarla. After all, they rent this room to the public." Khair bent over to have a closer look. "What do you suppose it is, Sarn?" Khair laid his hand on the unit. "I can feel a little warmth and hear a faint hum. Hear it?"

"That means it's active," Sarn said. He picked up a small unit that lay on the unit's top and that had many little buttons. "What do you suppose this thing is?" He pushed a couple of them.

Suddenly, a loud, discordant sound blasted out, and a scrambled color design flashed on the screen.

"Hey, this control is an interface for the unit," Sarn yelled with pleasure. "It has audio and visual information."

"Of what, I wonder." Khair was intrigued.

"There, blazing suns, look, everybody—glorious color of moving pictures."

"It's video info, that's for sure." Jorl had come over to see what all the noise was about. "Maybe something like news bulletins to the populace from the government, or something."

"Maybe they're information transporters, similar to the ones we have at home and on board the ships," Khair said.

"Or maybe just plain entertainment." Tarla pointed to the screen and laughed.

"Blazing comet tails—about how to brush your teeth?" Sarn was incredulous.

The picture of the foamy-mouthed family faded, and suddenly they were watching a wild car chase with appropriate audio.

"It certainly could be just entertainment—similar to our own Tri-Di," Jorl said.

They watched, fascinated, for a few minutes. Then, right in the middle of a soaring crash over a bank into a river by one car, and the other car, tires screaming, headed sideways down the road straight for a high-bodied truck—a woman started doing something or other to her armpits.

"A bit basic, isn't it?" Tarla said, her winged eyebrows rising.

"Slightly," Jorl said.

"I wonder what she's selling—sex, armpits, or the stuff in the container?" Sarn laughed.

"Oh, Sarn," Tarla said.

The story came back on the screen, and the cars finished their crash.

"You know," Jorl began, "since we did not, eh, come equipped with the proper federation exploration briefing and kit . . ."

Sarn slapped his forehead. "How could we have been so stupid?" Sarn started to laugh. "My, oh my. Shame on us. How could—we forget to file—a-a—flight plan—noting that we planned a crash-landing—not even—not even—in Federation jurisdiction? My, my, my. And we . . ." Sarn laughed till his stomach hurt.

The other three couldn't help but join Sarn in the laughter.

"That's true, but as I was about to say, the language converter has given us a good knowledge of English, but this Tri-Di, or, as we now know, television, will be an excellent way to learn the vocals and get a good idea of the local slang and dialects," Jorl said.

"Excellent idea. Probably we can learn enough of the local customs to keep us out of trouble," Khair said. "Also, it would be interesting to know something about the conditions here on Earth."

"That's a drag. I hate all this learning, especially local customs." Sarn heaved a huge self-pitying sigh.

"You just hate doing anything you don't want to do," Tarla said.

When he was hit by a sudden thought, Sarn snapped his fingers. "But I know how to make a dull situation slide along a little more easily." He headed for the communicating device, picked it up, waited for the voice, and shouted into it, "Beer. Eight." He heard the customary squeaks and yelled the order again.

"Sarn, don't shout. They're not deaf." Tarla had her hands over her ears.

"We'll soon be, though." Khair had also put his fingers in his ears.

"Besides, you'll be a bunch of boozers by the time we blast off," Tarla warned and playfully tugged at Sarn's brush of red hair.

When the beer arrived, they settled down and seriously watched the scope for a few hours. It wasn't long before the local customs started to stick in their minds.

"You know, this is a lovely planet. Parts of it remind me so much of our own home." Tarla felt a sudden stab of homesickness. "Do you really think we'll get back?"

"Sure we will, sweetheart, sure we will," Jorl comforted her.

"Just leave it to us, Tarla. We'll get you home. But first things first, and right this minute, I'm hungry." Sarn rubbed his belly and tried to look pathetic.

"For once, I absolutely agree with you. Let's get ready and then find a dining room and have some supper." Khair got up and stretched.

Sarn crossed the room and put the interface control back on the set. His curiosity got the better of him, and he pulled the machine away from the wall, pulling out the plug in the process. He took the back off the machine and looked inside.

"Sarn, what are you doing? Stop. Don't take it apart now. Wait till later. Right now, we want to eat."

"Don't fuss, Tarla. Just having a look. Hum-m, it's basic. No wonder it has only two-dimensional capability instead of three, but it's quite good. Good thing to know about." He hummed as he snapped it back together.

"Come on, Sarn," Jorl said.

Sarn put the machine back against the wall and plugged it in. "Really weird power supply. Wonder what it is? I've never seen one like it. Maybe this hm-m . . . curious . . . could we go out a little later?"

Tarla turned off all the lights.

"Hey-y," Sarn yelled.

"We're all hungry now, and you can take a look at it later." She hurried Sarn toward the door.

Chapter 7

"**I** really enjoyed that. How about the rest of you?" Jorl asked the group.

All of them agreed it was a delicious, enjoyable dinner. They got up from the table and made their way out of the dining room.

Just outside the dining room doors, a group of excited men and women caught their attention. The people were walking down the short hall toward tall double doors. When the doors were opened, the group went in, and bright lights, the sound of tinkling glass, and the hum of many voices poured out. The happy noise filled the hall. The doors closed and shut off all the happy lights and sounds.

Jorl, nodding in that direction, whispered in Tarla's ear, "Wonder what's in there?"

She looked inward for a moment. "I think it's a gambling room."

"That's for us," Sarn said. He rubbed his hands together and immediately turned to follow the strangers.

"Sarn. Wait a minute." Jorl yanked him back.

"What? What's wrong? Wait for what?"

"We have to use some caution," Jorl said.

"Have no fear, old dear. I want to get home every bit as bad—well, look who just came through the main doors, Khair. It's Eloise and Carol. Come on."

Sarn seemed to quiver like a compass seeking north. He yanked on Khair's arm. "Come on."

"I'm coming, I'm coming." Khair went more than willingly.

Tarla and Jorl looked at each other, smiled, and shrugged in resignation. They watched the excited foursome greet each other and then Sarn and Khair led the two girls over to where Tarla and Jorl waited.

"Look who we found," Khair said. He smiled down at Carol—admired her almost exotic, calm beauty.

Sarn's green eyes glowed above a wide, happy grin. When he looked at Eloise, an expression of pure pleasure, almost of awe, swept across his face.

"Blazing suns, I feel like I've just been hit in the stomach by a pile driver. She's gorgeous. I love her hair—sort of darkish-blondish and shining—like the Elson moon—I'd love to run my hands through it—just feel it. And that face, smiling."

"It's a good thing you're not using English. She'd probably run away screaming," Jorl said.

"Blazing suns and spinning comets, her body—poured into that gown. I think I—don't even think about it. But . . . blazing suns, I . . ."

"Gee. Hi there, Mr. and Mrs. Sandu." Eloise held out her hand. "We were hoping that we could see you—all of you—all day."

"We wondered if you had checked out of the hotel." Carol spoke more quietly and also held out her hand.

Tarla smiled at both girls. "We stayed in our rooms most of the day." She realized what the extended hands meant and shook them. Jorl followed her lead.

"What are you people planning to do now?" Eloise's wide pansy eyes sparkled. In fact, all of her little voluptuous self, hugged by the shimmering white gown, seemed to quiver with a barely contained bubbling excitement. She never took her eyes off Sarn.

Carol's gown was much more sophisticated, one that loved her tall, willowy body. It was strapless, made of emerald-green velvet, elegantly formfitting and with a knee-high side slit lined in white satin. Her only jewelry was a small medallion on a fine gold chain, which accentuated the almost daring neckline, and a pair of dropped gold earrings. Her gown showed another dimension of her dark-haired, creamy-skinned beauty. She shook hands languidly and looked intently at them with her almost amber-colored, almond-shaped eyes.

Khair, in his own quiet way, was as entranced as Sarn.

"We thought we'd try our luck in the gambling room," Tarla said, aware of Carol's deep scrutiny. "Would you care to join us?"

"That would be very nice indeed. Thank you. But first, Eloise and I need to notify some people that there will be a change in the plans of a previous engagement. May we meet you here in a short time?"

"Of course, Carol," Tarla said. "We'll be close by."

About twenty minutes later, Carol and Eloise rejoined them. There were pleased and happy greetings all around.

Sarn's face was one big smile as he gave Eloise an exuberant hug. "Now, we must go and gamble," Sarn said, in English, to Eloise.

"Gee, Sarn honey, you're speaking English already."

"Anything for love, baby, anything for love." He sang the words to the tune of the song. Then he gave her a quick hug.

"Gee. Did you hear that, Carol? That's good, Sarn." She clapped her hands, pleased and proud.

"Sounds more like a soap opera scene to me," Carol said and smiled, "but it's a start."

"Thank you, Carol." Sarn's eyes shot pleased sparks. He took Eloise's hand and tugged her toward the open double doors. "We should gamble now." He looked from Jorl to his doctored wristwatch.

Tarla laid her hand lightly on Sarn's arm and said in their own language, "Sarn, be careful—the girls are with us this time."

"I will be the soul of discretion, I promise."

Tarla gave him a look of pure disbelief.

"I promise."

"What kind of game do you like best, Khair?" Carol's voice was low and soft as she moved closer to Khair and looked up at him. Her amber eyes looked deeply into his.

"Games? Oh, games." He was momentarily lost in those eyes. "Oh, ah-h," A momentary shortness of breath. "Oh, favorite game. Well—gambling games."

"Which one?" Carol smiled up at him. That almost did him in. He opened his mouth, but nothing came out.

Tarla, aware of Khair's temporary loss of cool, saved him. "About how many games are there, Carol?"

Carol seemed to be suffering a little loss of breath herself. "Oh, quite a few, I think."

"Oh, lots, just about anything you could want," Eloise said. "Let's see now. There's roulette," she ticked them off on her fingers. "That's my favorite. Dice, poker, twenty-one, and lots of slots and . . ."

Sarn had his arm around Eloise's waist. "Let's get going now." Eloise glowed.

The group moved slowly down the hallway. When they came to the tall doors, the porter opened them and ushered them in. They entered the huge exciting expanse and stood inside the doorway just looking.

"What a lovely place, Jorl." Tarla marveled at the sight of the huge, beautiful room that seethed with bursts of color and movement.

"Even I can feel the excitement. And, as you know, I'm not even a bit telepathic," Jorl said. He put his arm around Tarla's waist and watched the action all about them.

"Blazing suns! Just look at it, Khair." Sarn's eyes gleamed as he took in all the sights.

"Almost worth the detour. For all sorts of reasons." Khair smiled down at Carol.

They were slipping in and out of Zalleellian and English.

Dozens of men and women walked around, or sat beside, the gambling tables. Nimble waiters passed around trays of drinks. Laughter, groans, tinkling glass, sparkling lights, flashing eyes, and hands—hundreds of hands, taking and giving—and above and overall a palpable feeling of excitement and the hot urge to win.

"Great blazing suns," Sarn's mouth opened in happy amazement.

"Where do we start?" Khair was as overwhelmed as Sarn. He scanned the room, trying to take it all in at once.

"Damned if I know," Jorl said and shrugged his shoulders.

"Gee," Eloise squealed. "There's a crowd around that roulette table. Let's try our luck, Sarn honey." She tugged gently at Sarn's arm.

They followed her to an empty space on one side of a long table that was marked with a design of squares and with numbers assigned to each of them on a red or black background. A disc spun in a well that was also marked off in numbered and colored compartments. People around the table put markers on numbers. Suddenly, a man said something and spun the wheel. This started a little white ball bouncing around in the wheel. It also started a lot of talk, calls, orders, and groans. The wheel stopped, and the little ball dropped into a slot. The man standing beside the wheel spoke and then used a rake affair to scoop all the markers his way, except for some that he pushed to two other places. One stake went to a short, fat woman. All she did was blink. The other woman, much younger, laughed with delight as she picked up all the markers in front of her and left the table.

The four watched and listened.

Tarla sampled a few minds and then quietly said, "It's a game of pure chance." Tarla spoke in her own language.

"High odds for the house, too," Jorl said.

"The magnetic sender won't work on that." Sarn was disappointed. "Unless, under that wheel, there could be . . ."

"Forget it, Sarn."

"Gee, let's place a bet." Eloise jiggled up and down.

"How?" Sarn asked. His eyes, almost snapping sparks, were doing their best to watch everything at once. "Eloise?"

"We buy chips from the croupier," she said and pointed. "He's the man with the rake."

A waiter held a tray of drinks in front of them. They all took one.

"Um-m. I like that much better than beer," Tarla said.

Khair and Jorl sniffed theirs first, sipped it, and immediately agreed with her.

"I still prefer beer." Sarn grabbed a second one from a passing tray and continued his intense study of the game. Sarn turned to Eloise. "Chips. Where?"

"Right here, Sarn honey. Give the man some money, and he'll give you chips. Better get them in fives. You can try your luck without losing too much all at once.

"Come on." Sarn headed straight for the croupier.

Tarla looked at Jorl, her eyebrows raised in a question.

"Might as well," Jorl shrugged and gave the man three hundred dollars and got sixty chips in return. "We each get fifteen." He doled them out.

Eloise and Carol had already got stakes for themselves.

"Gee, what'll I bet on?" Eloise wrinkled her smooth forehead and pouted in thought.

Sarn studied the roulette table for a minute and said, "Lots of choices."

"I know what." Eloise's face lit up. "Today is August 1, and I found you today, and it sure is a red-letter day for me—so I'm going to bet on number one red." She put two chips on the number and crossed her fingers.

The man at the wheel spoke so quickly that they had trouble understanding what he was saying. With a flick of his wrist, he set the little white ball in motion. Eloise never took her eyes off it. The little white ball bounced around and around and finally found a home.

Eloise screamed a small scream and bounced up and down. "I win. I win. See? I told you it's my lucky day."

Sarn enjoyed her excitement and aimed to kiss her lips but missed. It landed on her ear when she stood still long enough.

Khair, the mathematician in the foursome, had computed the odds against the player. "The mathematical probabilities against winning are extremely high. I would much rather be running the game. However, it's amusing." He placed a small bet. "Great space, I won. I'm amazed."

"It'll be fun for a while," Jorl said. He placed a bet, and the croupier spun the wheel. The little ball bounced into the number right next to Jorl's. "Well, that's not fair."

Khair clucked at him. "What's fair? You gamble, you take your chances. You win, you lose. That's life."

"Well, thank you, Professor Sandu, for sharing that slice of life with me." He lightly punched Khair on his shoulder.

All of them entered into the spirit of the game. When they decided to quit, they had been playing for about an hour, and all of them had won something, which, counting the fun, satisfied them fully.

Sarn said, "Wonder what's going on over there?" He made an instant beeline to the other side of the elegant room where six people sat at a round table playing with small, rectangular pieces of shiny, stiff paper. There was a fair-sized pile of chips in the middle of the table, and the players hardly spoke. There were people at three other tables apparently all playing the same game. With single-minded intensity, Sarn watched every move he could.

He tried to figure out the principles of the game, the relation between the markings on the papers, and who got the pile of chips. He watched for a few moments longer then looked up to see where the rest of his group was. He spied them across the room, and when they saw him, he motioned for them to hurry up and come over to where he was.

"It appears Sarn is excited about the game over there," Khair said.

They made their way through the shifting, laughing crowds.

"Sarn, how did you disappear so fast," Tarla asked when they came closer to him.

Ignoring her question, he asked, "What are they playing, Tarla? Eloise?" Sarn watched the complete concentration on the faces of the players of this strange, but somehow familiar, game.

"That's five-card stud poker," Eloise answered.

"How to play it?" Something regarding the game fascinated him.

"Gee. My goodness. You never heard of poker? Can you imagine, Carol?"

"After today, I can imagine anything, and anything is possible," Carol said with an expressive shrug of her bare, smooth shoulders.

Sarn held his arm up for silence. "Watch," he ordered.

Jorl, Tarla, and Khair watched closely.

"Can you get it, Tarla?" Sarn turned to his sister and watched her as she lightly probed the minds of the players.

"Yes, it seems to be quite simple. I see their hidden cards in their minds and how they are thinking. They bet on each card and hope to improve their hand. The best hand for that round wins the pot, which is all the money in the center of the table."

"Let's get a package of those card things and ask Eloise to teach us," Jorl said.

"Yes, this game has possibilities," Khair agreed with Jorl, "and the stakes seem high enough to make it worthwhile."

"And we always have blazing sevens and things to fall back on," Tarla laughed at the memories.

"Come. Cards. Teach." Sarn's English was rudimentary but explicit.

"He certainly is a bundle of energy," Carol sighed. "Just watching him tires me out. Very much like Eloise's first graders."

Khair smiled at her, put his arm around her waist, and they followed at a more leisurely pace. They made a handsome couple, and many glances followed them out of the room.

"Eloise. Need cards."

"Okay. They sell them in the tobacco store. Come on." She hurried down the hallway to the lobby, Sarn in hot pursuit.

"Now Eloise is catching it," Carol remarked to a smiling Tarla.

"Two alike, I think," Tarla said.

They caught up with Sarn and Eloise in the convenience shop. Tarla and Jorl were attracted to a colorful display of booklike paper sheets. Tarla whispered to Jorl, "I sensed the word 'magazine' from the lady standing next to me."

Tarla picked one up, a picture of a house on the front cover, and leafed through the pages. Such an abundance of printed words and pictures fascinated her. "You know, Jorl, I think our civilization is missing quite a lot by not having things like these."

Suddenly, Jorl whistled. "Blazing sex, yes."

Tarla looked up at him in amazement. "What in suns have you got hold of?" She looked at the cover first. It showed a reproduction of a voluptuous female more out of, than in, her extremely brief clothing and with a rather peculiar furry hat on her head that supported what looked like two long, furry ears. She glanced at the pictures that had forced such a sound from Jorl.

"Good blazing suns, indeed." She shook her head in disbelief. "They certainly seem preoccupied with reproduction."

Sarn and Khair came over for a look.

"Maybe that's to stimulate wish fulfillment for the dreamers," Khair said in their own language.

"Thank the blazing suns I'm a doer." Sarn grinned and turned to less erotic books. "Hey, look at this. They know something about space travel. Great." He quickly leafed through the magazine.

"Oh, Sarn, are you interested in space stuff?"

"It's my hobby. I collect everything about space travel." He quickly scanned through the rest of the magazines, found some others on the same subject, and added them to his stack.

"Gee, Sarn, it'll take you hours to read that great pile," Eloise said. "Do you really want to? Spend that much time, I mean?" Eloise spied one she really liked and showed it to Sarn. "Here's a great one on automotives. That's my hobby. I get one a month of these. And here are the cards and chips. Now what?" Eloise looked brightly from one to the other.

"To our rooms, Eloise." Tarla gave her a warm smile. "Time for school."

After Jorl paid for their purchases, the whole group headed for their suite.

"Gee. Oh, gee." Eloise looked around the spacious suite like a curious kitten. "First class, and that's for sure. And look at the view. You can see almost the whole strip. It's gorgeous."

Carol also took note of the decor. "It's lovely. Beautifully decorated."

"Oh, gee. It must cost a mint a day, I bet."

"Mint?" Tarla asked.

"Gee, yes. At least a thousand a day, I bet."

"You don't get rooms like these in the Dunes for peanuts," Carol said.

"Peanuts are money?" Sarn asked.

"Nope, elephant food," Carol replied. She noticed his puzzled look. "It was a joke."

"Joke?" Sarn still looked puzzled. "What is joke?"

Carol sighed. "I guess you had to be there. A joke is—"

"Oh, don't tease him, Carol," Eloise said. "He's trying to learn our language. It's hard."

"I'm sorry, Sarn. Really, I am. It wasn't nice of me to tease you."

Sarn smiled at Carol. "Wait for me to learn more. I will joke back. Worse."

Jorl had finished sorting the chips into twenty per pile. They put the chairs around the table and sat down ready to learn this stud poker.

"We're ready, Eloise," Tarla said.

"Well, as you know, this game is called five-card stud poker. It's a good game. I really like it." Then, Eloise, breathing a big sigh, said, "I love it, actually, but I'm not smart enough to be very good at it. That's why I play roulette mostly, because it's fun and you don't really need to be smart, just lucky." Eloise looked a little forlorn.

"I'm sure that isn't true, Eloise," Tarla spoke in her defense.

Sarn caught enough to get the gist of Eloise's self-condemnation. "Blazing suns. You are smart and beautiful, Eloise baby."

"Oh, Sarn." Her pretty face lit with pleasure, and she patted his cheek. She broke the seal on the new pack of cards. "Now." She began to deal with aplomb and competence, explaining the game as she did.

Within the hour, they had a clear understanding of the game and were able to reason logically well beyond the level of Eloise.

"Gee, I've never seen people learn so fast. You must play a lot of cards. I thought you didn't know how?" Eloise was puzzled, half suspecting that they had been fooling her.

"Dear Eloise, maybe we don't know your poker, but it's similar to many games we know well. And you're a good teacher." Tarla felt somehow gentle toward the warmth of Eloise and, after giving it a little thought, almost protective.

During one hand, Jorl, Khair, and Sarn were left to battle it out. Finally, Khair folded and Jorl, covering the bet, said, "I'll see you."

With a high level of panache, Sarn fanned out four Jacks on the table. "Read 'em and weep." Grinning from ear to ear, Sarn scooped in the pot.

Eloise listened intently to the sounds of it. "Gee, I love hearing you talk in your own language. It sounds so, so—like it's a cross between Italian and Estonian, you know—warm and clean and cool all at once. Where is your country, anyway?"

Tarla permitted herself a small peek into Eloise's mind to understand her use of the foreign words. "Our country is a long way away in Southern Asia. We're in the mountains, but there's a lot of desert building up in the valleys. That's the reason why we're here—to study the best way to cope with it.

"But you must forgive our rudeness. We shouldn't talk in our language in front of you when you are unable to understand it. All four of us are brushing up on our school English, but as that was a long time ago, we have forgotten so much. Maybe we can teach you some of our language someday, Eloise." Tarla was thoughtful for a moment. "Funny your name should be Eloise. I have a cousin whom we call Elly. You remind me very much of her.

"Do you? Do I? What's her name?"

"Her given name is Elaz-leela. We always called her Elly for short."

"Will you tell me about her sometime?"

"Maybe sometime when . . ."

"Play poker. Blazing suns, let's get at it," Sarn said. "I've got to get the rest of my money back from Jorl."

"Try and get it," Jorl said. "But maybe you need to be a little smarter—"

"Oh, oh. Fighting words," Khair said.

"Deal, Tarla," Sarn said.

They now had an exceptional grasp of the game. Tarla didn't even have to mind read to play her cards. Of course, it was almost impossible to get past the conditioned shield of her three men. People of her world were trained to protect their minds from probing. Besides, it was considered bad manners to intrude into someone's mind unless expressly invited.

Carol looked at her watch. "It's almost 11:30. Do you want to go back down to the games room?"

"Yes, let's go," Jorl said.

Once more, they entered the excitement of the huge games room. The crowds and the noise had increased tremendously. They wove their way to the poker tables.

Eloise turned to Sarn and said, "Carol and I are going to play roulette, Sarn. Carol prefers poker, but she knows I can't play with people of this level. Anyway, it's so serious, and I feel like having fun tonight. Okay? Sarn, will you come and get us when you've had enough?"

"Okay," Sarn agreed and dropped a light kiss on the end of her short, pretty nose. Her whole little person glowed.

"Good luck, Khair." Carol's smile was elusive. "Hope you remember your lessons." She put a light kiss on her fingertips and laid it softly on Khair's chin.

Carol and Eloise disappeared into the crowds. The four Zalleellians watched them go, then turned toward the excitement of the poker table. Fortunately, two couples were leaving the table, and the four took their places. The other two men at the table gave them a calculating once-over but didn't grunt more than the barest minimum of greetings.

Serious poker is a quiet game.

The four soon discovered that the stakes were high. After a few hands, they were playing competently and began to win.

Jorl, Khair, and Tarla played the odds. Sarn had a natural instinct and an easy insight into the whole structure of men and cards. Soon, he understood poker faces, bluffing, and double bluffing, and wholeheartedly joined the ranks of serious poker players. His pile of chips grew steadily higher as he began to win hand after hand.

Tarla knew she could easily win as much as she wanted to by slightly probing the two Earthians' minds. She had already done a gentle probe and found that there wasn't any protection against any kind of mind probe. She considered it would be totally unethical and also would spoil the fun of using her intelligence against others.

All four of them thoroughly enjoyed pitting their skills against one another as well as the strangers.

After a couple of hours, Jorl said, "Well, that's enough for me. How about you, Tarla? Had enough?"

"That's it for me, too."

Carol and Eloise had just come back to the table to find them.

Carol stood beside Khair's chair. He took one look at her and said that it was enough for him, too.

"Aren't you coming with us, Sarn? Eloise is waiting for you," Tarla said softly. Sarn looked up again and beckoned to Eloise. Her face lit up as she hurried over and stood beside Sarn.

"Yes, Sarn honey?"

He reached up and pulled her face close to his. He kissed her lips lightly and said, "Tomorrow, baby. Okay?"

"Gee." Eloise's lips drooped like a disappointed child's. "Oh well." Then she smiled, hopefully, and said, "Tomorrow for sure?"

"Tomorrow for sure." He gave her soft face a gentle pat. "I promise."

"Okay, Sarn honey." A happy smile lit her face once more.

Tarla, Jorl, and Khair exchanged knowing glances. "There's little or no hope of budging Sarn when he's engrossed in something," Tarla said and sighed.

The other people at the table were getting a little impatient. "I must go now. See you tomorrow." Sarn turned back to the table and said, "Sorry. Deal."

Khair and Jorl laughed and totally agreed with Tarla. Jorl said, "He'll join us when he's had enough. Let's go."

On the way to the big doors, Eloise turned and waved, but Sarn's attention was riveted to the table. Eloise heaved a sigh and caught up with the rest of the group.

Again, they were in the lobby. Carol said, "Eloise, I think we should go home now. It's been a long day."

"Shall we get a taxi for you?" Tarla asked Carol.

"Gee, no. Carol has a car parked outside."

"Car?" Jorl's eyes lit up.

"Yes." Tarla noticed the sudden light in Jorl's eyes and the thoughtful look in Khair's. "Not now, you two. One lost is enough." She had spoken in her own language.

"I wasn't planning anything—not right this minute." Jorl quickly pasted on an innocent expression.

They walked with the girls to where Carol had parked her car. Khair said a tender goodnight to Carol as she opened the car door.

"Carol and Eloise, why don't we all meet here tomorrow afternoon? About two o'clock? Maybe you'd be kind enough to show us a little of the city, Carol."

"I would be only too happy to do that, Tarla," Carol said. "Two o'clock would be a perfect time.

Jorl watched Carol's every move as she started the engine of the big, sky-blue Olds. Tarla knew that he fought to control his mad itch to get his hands on the machine.

They all called goodnight and waved until the car pulled away.

Chapter 8

The stars glittered brilliantly, hanging like beautifully fashioned ornaments from the blue-black sky. They seemed to issue an invitation to join them in the heavens.

The three aliens to this world stood there looking up at the velvety night, breathing in the clear, cool air, each in their own thoughts.

"It's a beautiful night," Jorl said. "Let's walk for a while." He reached for Tarla's hand. "Okay?"

"Very okay," Tarla said. She took his hand.

"Good idea," Khair said. "Let's have a look around."

"And look at those stars," Tarla pointed upward and then sighed. "Oh, dear. Millions of light years from home and a broken, buried ship. It's a little—a little daunting."

Jorl stopped, turned, and gently cupped her face in his hands and dropped a small kiss on her lips. "I promise that somehow, some way, we'll get back up there."

They rambled slowly down the paths and enjoyed their walk in the clear night air.

"The Earth's moon is one of the loveliest I have ever seen." She spoke softly, dreamily. "It makes everything look magical."

"And it sure beats the moon arrangements around some of the other planets," Jorl said. "Remember the red moons of Zorna? Made the night look like a blood bath."

"Or how about Leeta?" Khair said. "They don't have even one—and not many stars. The nights are as black as a Surnainian's soul."

"Surnainians? Khair, I even hate the word."

"Sorry, Tarla, I forgot."

"Oh, that's all right, Khair. It's just that the memory is still so real to me." She thought for a minute, then said, "We had picked up a repeating urgent signal from a planet named Yundar in the Prilzor Spiral asking for immediate help against the invaders. Unfortunately, the message was weak and misdirected. When our ship arrived, we discovered a dying planet. It had already been totally stripped of what the Surnainians wanted—and took—with absolutely no regard for the planet's survival.

The Surnainians had drugged the populace to make them almost zombie-like and then used the inhabitants—even women and children—as hard-driven slaves. There were only a few natives left alive, and they were dying from some sort of a lethal gas residue.

The few people that were barely alive told us as much as they could before they also died.

The devastation was terrible. The result was the death of all life. They had said that the invaders were Surnainians."

Tarla's eyes welled up with unshed tears. "My telepathic skills were untrained then, so I was unable to fully turn my memory off, but even then too much terrible misery came in. I've buried it somewhat, but it's still there."

Jorl gently wiped away the tears. "Think about 'now' and let's enjoy it. Come on, let's meander."

All three smiled and continued on their way. They soon found themselves at the edge of a deserted swimming pool. The water looked fresh and inviting.

"Shall we?" Khair asked.

"No reason why not," Jorl said and pulled off his tunic and boots.

Khair's usual laid-back expression cracked with a happy grin. He quickly did the same. He dove into the water right after Jorl did. When he surfaced, he said, "Now that's what I call . . ."

Jorl popped up beside him, "Me, too," and pulled Khair under the water.

When they surfaced again, Jorl looked up at Tarla who just stood there. "Come on, sweetheart, nothing like a moonlight swim after being cooped up all day."

"I know. But . . ." she gestured toward her clothes, "I can't swim in all this. I need an outfit like the women were wearing this morning."

"There's a couple of stores in the hotel that had swimming clothes in them, and probably at least one of them is open," Khair said. "Why not run in there and get something?"

"You could change in that building over there," Jorl pointed to a small cabana.

"I'll be right back." Tarla hurried off to find the store.

"Race you to the other end and back, Khair."

"You're on."

Standing on the edge of the pool, they both dove in and swam as if a shark was swimming along beside them and more than ready to eat the loser.

When Khair touched the edge of the pool first, he yelled, "I win."

In what seemed to be only a few minutes, they heard Tarla call. They looked up.

"Oh, by all the suns in the heavens," Jorl could hardly breathe.

She was barely but beautifully contained in a white bikini. It showed off her five foot eleven, golden-skinned beauty to perfection. The moonlight made shining glints in her long golden hair that flowed around her shoulders. Jorl stared at her in awe—felt the perfection of this woman he called wife—hit him like a blow in his gut that left him breathless. He had difficulty speaking around the lump in his throat.

"Sweetheart—beloved—my wife—you are the most beautiful woman in all the galaxies." Jorl spoke in a whisper.

It was one of those moments in a woman's life when she feels absolutely perfect in her own womanhood and knows the strength of her man's love for her—loved utterly. Beyond words.

"My dearest Jorl." She threw back her head and laughed with the pure joy of living. "Here I come. Watch out!" She leaped into the air and made a clean dive into the water. She swam with a smooth, strong grace.

They splashed, swam, and played like a trio of happy otters. They gloried in the feel of their bodies, the fresh coolness of the water and the brilliant, star-studded moonlight. They lost track of time and place, and all their problems had, for this timeless moment, ceased to exist.

Tarla happened to look up in time to see Sarn tugging off his boots and tunic.

"Hurry, Sarn. It's wonderful."

Sarn took a running leap and splashed ungracefully into the pool, swam underwater, then popped up beside Tarla, shaking water from his head like an excited pup.

"Hey, Tarla, I won a bundle. I put the money in the rooms. I didn't know where you went. I thought you'd abandoned me." Sarn laughed at his own joke.

"As if I ever could." Tarla said. "But there are times . . ."

Sarn let out a monstrous war whoop, which would have struck terror into the heart of the most hardened barbarian, made a lunge, leaped on Jorl's back, and drove him underwater. Khair jumped on Sarn, and that was enough to touch off a rough and tumble game in which not even Tarla was spared. Finally, they were winded and tired but wet and happy.

"That was absolutely wonderful," Tarla said. She was trying to wring her hair dry and to put it into some sort of order before they headed back into the hotel.

Once back in their rooms, Tarla tried to smother a yawn, "Sounds silly, but I'm tired out. I think I'll go right to bed."

"I guess the day has just caught up with us." Jorl yawned and stretched.

"We'll think about tomorrow, tomorrow," Khair said and headed for his bedroom.

They had all figured without Sarn.

"Oh, no, you don't! Blazing suns, I want to tell you all about my spectacular playing. And look at all the money I won." He fanned out a rather large stack of bills. He started to dissect and discuss the hands he had won. The three listened as politely as they could, but after an hour they were almost asleep where they sat.

"Come on, Sarn, turn it off now and get to bed. We've all had enough for today," Jorl said.

"What? Now? I worked my poor brain almost to its boiling point. Just for you guys." He fanned out the respectable stack of bills again.

"And, of course, you didn't enjoy the game. I'm sure it was torture for you to sit there all those hours and play poker," Khair said and tch, tch, tched at him.

Sarn hid a grin.

"We appreciate it, Sarn. It was clever of you to be so good." Tarla meant it. "But now it's time for bed."

"I don't think so. I'm not . . ."

Khair sneaked up behind Sarn, made a lunge, got a good grip on his arms and shoulders, and said, "Gotcha."

Jorl grabbed his feet, and between them they wrestled the laughing Sarn to his bed and dumped him on it.

"Is this a polite way to treat your provider? Hey, let me tell you about the last hand." Sarn started to get up again. "Now, that was . . ."

"Go to sleep." With a laugh, Khair bounced Sarn back down. "Now, stay there and go to sleep."

"But I'm sure you'd love to hear all . . ."

"See this pillow?" Jorl held it in front of Sarn's eyes. "If you don't put a plug in it right this minute, I'm going to put it over your head and sit on it."

"But, kind sir, sweet captain, woulds't thou murder me in my bed?" Sarn sobbed dramatically.

"Anywhere, just as long as 'the great thunder mouth' is stilled," Jorl said.

"Okay, you can get off me, Khair. I guess I'm tired out, too." He yawned widely enough to spring a jaw. "But I do wish all of you noisy people would go to bed so that I can get some sleep. I think it's very inconsiderate of you to keep me awake until all hours of the morning." He opened one glittering eye to see the reactions. Jorl threw both arms in the air and turned to leave the room.

Khair said, "Well, at least, you don't have to share a room with him."

Sarn smothered a grin in his pillow.

Chapter 9

$\mathcal{N}$ext morning, the same sunshine, giggles, and squeals woke them. Jorl knocked and came into Sarn and Khair's room. "Time to get up, guys. Lots of learning to do. It's day three already."

"We're up, Jorl. Won't be long," Khair answered.

"I hear them." Sarn jumped out of bed and almost ran to the balcony for a quick look. "What a great day. It even smells good. Come out here for a minute, Khair. Enjoy a few minutes while you can."

When Khair leaned on the ledge beside him, Sarn said, "I know what I'd rather be doing."

"What?" Khair asked.

"Anything outside."

When they met a little while later in the living room, Tarla said, "I ordered a meal to have up here. Is that okay with you two?"

"Great idea. We can get to the television and the magazines right away." Khair picked up a magazine that interested him and made himself comfortable in a big chair.

"Oh, groan." Sarn said.

"I know, I know—it's a wonderful day, and you'd rather be out in it," Jorl said. "So would I. So the sooner we start, the sooner we'll get home."

"Our security and hopes of escape demand the discipline." Khair smiled at Sarn. He knew a pontificating tone was like fingernails down a blackboard to Sarn.

"Blazing suns and spinning meteors okay. Okay? I know all that, and I agree. Now, where's the food?"

When the expected knock sounded on the door, Jorl answered it and let in the waiter who set up the table. When the waiter finished, he turned around and expectantly had his hand half up.

Jorl was ready with the tip.

"Wow, looks like a great meal." Sarn set about enjoying some of everything on the table.

"Good thinking, Tarla. What would we ever do without you?" Jorl said as he beat Sarn to the last little sausage and laughed at Sarn's expression.

"I'm sure of one thing. None of you would go hungry," Tarla said. "You'd soon figure it out."

They settled down to television and magazines.

About two o'clock in the afternoon, when all four of them were deep in their learning, the phone rang. The unexpected noise startled them. Sarn was closest. He picked up the receiver and hollered, "Yes?" He recognized Eloise's voice. "Hello, Eloise. How are you today? Lovely as ever, I bet."

"Oh, Sarn, you really do say the nicest things to me." She giggled with pleasure. "Oh, why I called, you said you would meet Carol and me here today. Are you coming down?"

"How about both of you come up here first. Then we can make some plans."

"Okay. We'll be right up."

"Sarn, Khair—I'm a little worried. We're letting Eloise and Carol come too close. They'll soon start asking questions and then what? What about the answers? What about the council?" Tarla's expression mirrored her concern.

The three men faced the cold reality of Tarla's questions.

"Well, let's not worry about it yet—we can lose them in words. Besides, Eloise is too happy a person to be suspicious," Sarn said.

"But Carol has a cooler mind, and she doesn't miss a thing," Khair said.

"If the worst happens, you'll have to set up mind blocks and erase their memories of us."

"Jorl, you know that it would be a dangerous thing for me to do to them. If they have any mental flaws at all, it could drive them insane."

"If you edit the memory just enough, it should be mentally safe for them. Don't forget, you're much more experienced now."

The worst had happened once when circumstances had forced Tarla to try the same procedure. "I was only first level at the time, that's true, but even so, my conscience still bothers me."

"I said, if the worst happens, and it won't, Tarla, you're third level now—one from the top, and that is almost due."

"When I marry Eloise, there won't be any trouble, not even with the council." Sarn looked up at the three of them to see how this latest bombshell would strike them.

All three looked a bit stunned.

"Blazing comets, why shouldn't I?" Sarn laughed at their expressions. "I think it's a great idea." He jumped up out of the chair, too excited to sit still.

"You, Sarn? You, married?" Jorl said. "The worst womanizer in the whole fleet?" He laughed until the tears came to his eyes.

Khair and Tarla were both speechless—thunderstruck, even.

"Sarn, that's great news, I think, but it's not like you. I mean, you're . . ." Tarla searched for the right word.

"A dedicated ladies' man best describes your little brother, Tarla, and a first class enjoyer of freedom and good times," Khair said.

"But seriously," Sarn said, "there comes a time when a man needs a legal mate. And I want Eloise for mine."

They heard the expected knock, but before Tarla went to open the door, she said, "Sarn, I have no idea what's going on under that red thatch of hair, but do not drop even a hint of this plan until we talk it over. Promise?"

"Anyone would think I want to shoot down Space Command. Or at least give old Admiral Emslin a hot foot, or . . ."

"Promise?" Tarla pressed for his answer.

"Oh, for—I promise."

They tried to equate this latest, totally unforeseen, piece of news with the Sarn they knew well. Or thought they did.

"In a four-man space racer?" Khair was thinking ahead.

"You know it was designed to carry five," Sarn reminded Khair.

Khair slowly smiled. "What about Carol?" he said softly.

"What? Khair! Wonderful! So we squeeze a little." Sarn gave Khair a slap on his back and a bear hug. They grinned at each other like two fools.

"Don't you think that it might be a little too soon to make such a serious decision?" Jorl said.

"No, I don't. Blazing comet tails—when you know—you know. You agree with me, don't you Khair?"

"Yes, I do."

The knock came at the door again. All of them looked at it but wanted to finish what they were saying.

Jorl came and stood between them, an arm over each of their shoulders. "Remember your promise, Sarn. And that goes for you, too, Khair." He smiled warmly at the two men. "Congratulations. And good luck."

"Well, I give up." Tarla threw her arms up in resignation, opened the door, and greeted Eloise and Carol with a smile. "How nice to see you again. Please come in."

Eloise said, "Hi, everyone. What a lovely day." She beamed at everybody, especially Sarn, and practically bounced into the room. Carol, a little more reserved, entered a little more quietly and just smiled slightly at all of them. "Hello again. I hope we're not disturbing you." Her eyes went almost directly to Khair.

"Never," Khair said and went over to her.

Carol smiled up at him and took his hand. "But you did say that you would like to do a little exploring."

Sarn greeted them both exuberantly. He then grabbed Eloise by the waist and spun her around once. "How's my beautiful baby doll?"

A fair amount of confusion reigned until the first wave of greetings subsided.

"We thought you might like to go for a drive and see some of the country," Carol said when things had quieted down.

"Gee, yes. There are piles of mountains and miles of desert. But the car is air-conditioned, so you won't cook or anything," Eloise said. She almost bubbled with excitement.

"Cook?" A mental image of a piece of meat being turned on a spit immediately leaped into Sarn's mind. "Blazing suns, what . . .?"

"You know, get too hot. It's very hot in a desert," Eloise explained.

"Eh, yes, we gathered that."Tarla smiled at Eloise as she remembered their first experience of Earth land.

"Let's get going."The fire of a vehicle jockey burned in Jorl's eyes.

Khair turned his eyes heavenward. "May all the great gods of the galaxies save us." Khair knew that Jorl would somehow maneuver things so that he would eventually get his hands on the vehicle. They crossed the parking lot to the big, gleaming car. Sarn hurried ahead of them and circled the car curiously.

"Where's the pile?"

"The what?" Carol asked.

"Tarla, where's the pile?"

"I don't know. But Sarn"—she slipped into her own language—"You have to be careful. We're supposed to know what cars are—how they work—and . . ."

"Okay, okay." He switched to English. "This year of Olds is my favorite. Haven't seen one for a long time. Where's the—?" Sarn gestured violently to Carol.

"Where is the what?" Carol asked, confused.

"Power," Sarn almost yelled, "Runs it."

"Oh, he means the motor,"Tarla said. "We still don't know English too well."

"Under there." Carol pointed to the hood.

"Show me." Sarn searched for the way to open it.

"Not now, Sarn."Tarla hoped to deflect him.

Sarn gesticulated madly at Carol, who sighed deeply and reached under the dash to pull the release. Sarn threw open the hood and stared in disbelief. Jorl and Khair crowded around, too.

"Explain, please." Sarn shouted to Tarla and Carol.

"How should I know."? Carol almost shouted back. "You put in gas, and it goes."

Tarla whispered to Sarn, "Basing the technical operation of the vehicle on the knowledge in Carol's mind, the thing should not even start."

"Gee, Sarn, Carol, don't get all mad and everything. I'll tell you how it works," Eloise said.

"You?" Sarn smiled, amused with the idea of Eloise being anything but lusciously sweet and lovely.

"Why not? My dad was a mechanic, and I practically grew up in a garage." With a minimum of fuss and words, in clear and concise order, she explained the motor's operation from the ignition key to the tailpipe. The three men and Tarla were as much stunned by the extent of Eloise's knowledge as they were over the archaic method of producing power.

"Tools." Sarn snapped his fingers at Carol.

Carol's eyebrows climbed up far enough to hide under her hair, and she looked at him as if he were more than half mad. "I beg your pardon." Anger rose with her eyebrows, and in a low and icy tone of voice she said, "And don't you dare snap your fingers at me. Ever."

Eloise interrupted, "Gee, Sarn, not now, not here. Quick, Tarla, explain to him that we will go to a garage soon, and then I'll help him strip down a motor."

Carol controlled her anger and spoke quietly, "I should hope not now."

Tarla hurriedly told Sarn what Eloise had offered. Sarn hugged Eloise and smiled down at her. "You're my amazing Eloise."

The small crisis narrowly averted, they all got into the car.

"I'll sit next to Carol," Jorl said and got in before Khair had a chance.

Tarla, Sarn, and Eloise settled themselves in the backseat.

Carol neatly backed the car out and headed uptown.

Jorl watched every move she made and asked questions through Tarla when his English failed.

"Now, you know the three main things," Tarla said, "brake pedal—stop, power pedal—go and hold on to the steering wheel to steer. Now, relax." Tarla patted his shoulder.

They drove down the main street enjoying all the sights as they headed out of town.

"Look over there," Khair said quietly and nodded to the building where they had eaten their first meal.

"Only three days ago." Tarla shook her head in disbelief.

"Then we must be on the same road that we came in on. Blazing suns, yes. There's where the old coot dumped us."

"Careful, Sarn," Tarla said in their language. She switched to English and said. "Where does this road lead to, Eloise?"

"To Boulder City, I think about fifty miles away. I'm not sure. But you should see the great big, huge dam there. It's huge. You can't imagine how huge it is until you see it. And further on is the Grand Canyon. That is a truly awesome thing to see.

Soon they were out of town and driving along a familiar road.

"There's the dirt road." Jorl didn't point, not wanting to make the girls curious.

"Yes, it is. I wonder how our little ship is?" Tarla suddenly felt weighed down by the almost impossible odds against them. It made her sad.

Sarn noticed her look and patted her hand. "Don't worry. It'll all work out. Blazing suns, I just know it will."

Tarla smiled at Sarn. "You're right."

They drove along the road for a while longer, Carol speaking quietly about the country and Eloise chattering away about everything.

The Zalleellians' thoughts were with the little ship, broken and cold, covered with sand, on an alien world. They were a long way away from their home planet, Zalleellia, in more ways than miles.

Suddenly, Jorl said, "Please turn around—there." He pointed to a service station.

"But we thought you might like to see the big dam outside Boulder City," Carol said. She had planned an orderly afternoon.

"We would love to next time, Carol," Tarla said. She was sure she knew what was on Jorl's mind—on all their minds.

"Well, if you really want to," Carol said. She turned the car around.

Jorl, watching intently for it, saw the dirt road again.

"Turn down there please, Carol."

She looked at Jorl for a second. "You really want me to?"

"Yes, please." Then Jorl, excited, said, "I drive, you teach me. Please?"

"But . . ."

"Please, Carol?"

When they came to a stop, he changed places with an unwilling Carol.

"Explain, please," he said. He was holding the steering wheel tightly in both hands while his eyes dashed all over the control panel.

"But you're supposed to have a license. Do you?"

Tarla spoke quietly, "We don't do much driving at home—too many mountains, and our licenses would not be any good here, anyway."

"Oh, I guess not," Carol said.

"Jorl, I thought you wanted to find the crash site," Tarla spoke in her own language.

"I do, Tarla, but I must learn to drive a car first. How else can we get here alone if I don't?"

"Tarla laughed. "You always make everything you want to do sound so logical. Anyway, Carol says you have to have a license before you can drive." She switched back to English. "Are they hard to get here, Carol?"

"Not really. All you need in the United States is your birth certificate and have proof of insurance and, of course, pass your driver's test."

"Well, anyway, don't worry," Tarla said to Carol, "Jorl won't go out on the highway. It would be impossible to come to any harm here. If he does happen to ruin your car, we'll give you enough money to go and buy a new one. We have our travelling papers and everything else we need."

"Fair enough, I guess," Carol agreed with a shrug. She explained the basic operating procedures of the automatic drive car to Jorl who didn't miss a word.

"Okay, start the car," Carol said and tried to be calm. "Just do everything slowly, okay?"

"Okay," Jorl said. He turned on the ignition, put it in drive—and tromped it. They were off in a cloud of dust and nasty remarks.

"Hey! Gee! Cowboy!" Eloise squealed as she and everyone else were thrown back in their seats.

"Slow down," Carol screamed as they flew over another bump.

"Blazing suns," Sarn howled. "The old coot drove like an old lady compared to this."

The car went into a deep hole, then right away into a big bump. "Cut it out, damn it," Sarn yelled.

Khair braced himself and said nothing, even when Carol landed in a muddled heap in his lap. He simply smiled, helped her to sit upright, and said to Jorl, "I believe, if you take your foot off the fuel supply, the mechanism will slow down."

"Step on the other pedal," Carol shouted.

Jorl turned to look at her and hit another bump square on.

"The brake, you idiot. The brake!"

"Oh." Jorl nodded and stamped on the other pedal.

After they peeled themselves off the dash and the back of the front seat, there was a dead silence. The dust settled down gently with not even a motor noise to disturb it. No one said anything.

Jorl felt he should really say something. "I, eh, am not used to the idea of using my feet to drive with."

"What do you usually do then, swing from trees?" Carol felt a little snappish as she tried to pat herself back into well-dressed order.

"Gee, how can anyone drive without using their feet?" Eloise asked. "I mean, a person has only two hands, and you need them to steer with—and things." She didn't want to make Jorl feel any worse, so she patted his shoulder and said, "You did very well for the first time. At least, there aren't any other cars to worry about on this little road." Eloise smiled brilliantly.

"A little less force exerted on the fuel injection should smooth things out, Jorl. Try it again," Khair said.

Jorl started up once more and gingerly used the accelerator. In a few minutes, he said, "It's beginning to feel right." He smiled with pleasure and started to feel pretty good about it. "It handles very well. I'm getting the feel of it. Nice." He settled into a sedate pace.

"Would you look at that! He didn't even hit that big bump, and blazing suns, look, he missed those rocks completely. Why, he'll be a champion in no time at all."

"Easy, Sarn," Khair said quietly and held out his hand in a "stop" position.

Carol, who had smoothed her ruffled feathers, said, "Well, I suppose it's time to learn about the rest of it."

"Such as what, Carol?"

"Oh, reverse, parking, and other general maneuvers." Carol tried to recapture her good manners and a pleasant attitude. She was as highly annoyed as much as she had also been scared almost out of her wits. "Now, Jorl, this is the gear shift. When you put this lever to this mark," she pulled the lever down to the R, "the car will go backward. Make sure your foot . . ."

"Oh?" Almost before Carol could finish, Jorl had pushed down the gas pedal.

"Stop!" Carol yelled.

Jorl stamped on the brake pedal.

". . . is on the brake pedal."

"It is definitely an animated ride." Khair had only just managed to save his head from the windshield.

Once more, all of the passengers in the backseat had to recover from the whiplash effect and had been able to sort out their own limbs.

They spent about a half-hour on intense practicing.

"I don't think I like steering in reverse very much," Jorl said.

"It does seem to cause you the most trouble but, in all fairness," Khair said, "I must say it doesn't seem quite the best kind of place in which to learn to drive, especially when in reverse."

The ground itself was full of unexpected surprises. Jorl found a few of them. The last one was the worst—an unexpected trench. He had backed into it.

Khair broke the heavy silence. "You're doing very well, Jorl. A little more practice is all you need."

"A little? Blazing suns, spinning comets are less dangerous."

"Sarn, give him a chance."

"Seeing as how the front end is in the air and the back end is in a ditch, I would say he's had enough chances."

"Is everyone all right?" Khair turned his head to see the rest of the group.

"And on its side," Sarn added.

"I'm inclined to agree with Sarn," Carol said through clenched teeth and tightly-balled fists.

They had some trouble getting out of the car because the two doors on the one side were jammed in the ditch and the other two were up in the air.

With the combined strength of the four Zalleellians, and with Carol and Eloise to help guide them, the car was soon on flat ground again.

"Not even to mention all the dents and scrapes, I just hope it will start," Carol said, her lips still a little clenched.

"Don't worry, Carol, if it won't start, I can probably fix it," Eloise quietly assured her.

Carol straightened her clothes, smoothed her hair, and regained her cool, competent self.

When the car was on the level again, Jorl, with single-minded tunnel vision, quickly got behind the wheel and tried the engine. It started with only a slight cough and an explosive backfire, but it continued to run smoothly. "Everybody in? Let's go."

Many different expressions were on everyone's faces as they more or less settled themselves.

Jorl drove down the dirt road for a while longer. He had not forgotten the ship and went further up the track, hoping to recognize the spot where the jeep had picked them up. Khair, Sarn, and Tarla realized what was on Jorl's mind, and all four of them were quietly intent on watching the road.

Tarla switched to her own language. "I think it's just ahead—there, to the left." She held her hands in her lap, knuckles white, hardly daring to hope.

"We were picked up right there," Jorl said. He pointed to a fair-sized cactus tree.

"Next time, I'll bring the transceiver. Then, we can easily home in on the signal," Sarn said.

Suddenly, without warning, a shiver ran through Tarla—an inexplicable feeling of utter coldness. "If it's undisturbed," she said.

The other three looked searchingly at her. Jorl asked, "What happened, Tarla? What's wrong?"

She shook herself. "I felt . . . something . . . nothing, I guess." She smiled, tried to throw off the hateful feeling, and put it down to tiredness or imagination. "I think we should go back now," she said in English.

Jorl got her unspoken message and turned the car around and headed for the highway.

"Remember, stop before you get on the pavement," Carol said. "You aren't exactly what you would call ready for traffic, especially without a license."

"I plan to," Jorl said and turned to look at her for a second. "Don't worry, Carol, I definitely plan to. And I can't thank you enough for all your patience and help."

"Well, I guess that you are very welcome," Carol sighed. "But—oh-h, well."

Jorl looked at her.

"Mind you, you're doing well." Carol tried to make him feel better, but she had reached the limit her nerves would take.

Neither she nor Eloise had caught the undercurrents that troubled the four Zalleellians.

They saw the highway up ahead.

Jorl came to a smooth stop. "There, how was that?"

"All things considered, pretty good," Carol said.

Jorl, a bit reluctantly, got out and let Carol take the wheel.

When they got back to the hotel, they decided to meet later in the evening and try a few of the other casinos.

Once more, alone in their rooms, Jorl put his arm around Tarla. "What did you sense out there, Tarla? What frightened you?"

Sarn and Khair also waited for her answer, concern wiping the usual good humor from their expressive faces.

Tarla tried to pin down what had caused the sudden, deep fear; a fragment of time so unexpected and sudden that it had left before she could examine it. "I'm not sure that I know. It was a flash of utter coldness as if I were in, and of, the heart of a glacier. As if my subconscious mind had touched something—or something touched it. Something alien." She distractedly ran her hand through her hair, taking the long, golden strands away from the high cheekbones of her lovely face.

"Aliens." She laughed with a rueful tone. "What are we here on this Earth but aliens?"

"All we want is off. We're not here because we want to be," Sarn said.

"Are you reasonably sure, Tarla? About it being aliens?" Jorl asked.

"Yes, I am."

"We'll have to be more watchful from now on," Khair said. "Anything is possible. Hopefully, it was some sort of a strange memory that surfaced—something you had forgotten about."

"Come on, Tarla, forget it for now, and let's get in some homework." Jorl smiled as he hugged her, and turned on the television. They settled down to watch the transmissions.

They waded through a few unimportant programs, well larded with blurbs, when they suddenly realized they were seeing an information broadcast.

"Look!" Sarn jumped up to get a closer look. "Blazing suns, they really do have some sort of a space program. That's what was in those magazines. That's a space vehicle. And they're launching it. Blazing comet tails, do you know what that means?" He could barely control his excitement.

Jorl nodded. "It means that their technology is far more advanced than we thought."

"Yes. And it'll be easier to convert components designed for space to our own needs. Blazing suns, what good luck." Sarn was thrilled.

The scene had changed to a room that was vaguely familiar to all of them.

"That looks a little like a shore side communications control room," Jorl said.

"They call that mission control," Tarla translated it back into their own language so that they wouldn't get lost in the fast, excited words of the announcers. "They seem to be in the middle of a countdown."

"They launch by remote control? Maybe the crew is already on board ready for launch." Khair was disappointed. "I would have liked to see them."

The scene flashed back to the launch site.

Tarla concentrated on the announcer's voice as she translated. "Evidently, that vehicle is called 'The Seeker Satellite,' and it carries six telescopes. They're launching it into an orbit eight thousand miles out. It'll be used for studying the ultraviolet light issuing from the stars and stellar clouds without any interference from Earth's atmosphere."

"Great suns. Then, that's the reason why it's not manned. They're using it for scientific purposes only," Khair said.

"But have they sent up manned vehicles?" Sarn leaped up and scattered magazines from wall to wall looking for the one he wanted. "There's a magazine here somewhere with a picture like that launch on it. I thought it was a kid's book. Here it is." He ran back to show them.

They all took a look at it. "Now, all we have to figure out is how to get our hands on some of the material."

"From the looks of the uniforms, I would say that anything to do with the installation is heavily guarded," Jorl said.

"There's always a way. You've only got to find it." Sarn refused to have his enthusiasm dampened.

"Liquid fuel? Look, liquid fuel." Jorl pointed to the picture on the television as the rocket began to ignite, sending out clouds of flame and smoke. "It's . . . unbelievable. They have actually managed to make it work," Jorl said with wonder coloring his words.

"Now, that takes real ingenuity. What a pity that they're following a dead end in their technology," Khair said. "I wish we could show them our method of using pulse waves. But they'll probably discover it for themselves sometime down the road."

"You're right, Khair. If the Earthians are clever enough to get that far with space vehicles, it won't take them long to find something like ours," Sarn said.

They watched the program until the rocket was a small flick of light in the sky.

Tarla and Sarn settled down with the magazines.

In a few minutes, Sarn looked up and spoke to Jorl. "You're still as rough as an unhappy asteroid, but what shall we do about a car?"

"I've been giving that a lot of thought, wondering the same thing." Khair put down his magazine.

"We need one. We must be able to get to the crash site whenever we need to," Jorl agreed.

"How can we prove we were born on this planet?" Tarla mused. "Of course—we need birth certificates."

"Somehow, we'll have to get the papers we need," Jorl thought out loud and began to pace around the room, thinking. "And we have to be able to give them back whenever we've finished with them."

Sarn, only half serious, suggested, "Let's sort of borrow them. You know how much I like the direct approach."

"Forget that one, Sarn," Jorl shook his head, disagreeing. "But we need papers that will stand up to a reasonable check. They must have a pretty good system of checking papers, or no one would need to bother with them."

"Now, as I was saying about sort of borrowing . . ."

"I said, forget that one, Sarn," Jorl repeated in no uncertain terms and continued to pace.

"Borrow a set and have copies made then," Sarn said.

"Humm-m," Khair said thoughtfully. "I suppose it must be the same here as anywhere else in the galaxies. For every legal way to get something, there are people who make a living getting it by illegal methods for people who don't qualify for legal."

"Right you are, Khair. Contact the outworlders." Sarn rubbed his hands together in glee.

"How?" Tarla asked.

"Is that the only word you know?" Sarn threw up his hands in mock despair.

Khair smiled, "You must admit that it's a good one."

"Still, for every result, there has to be an answer to the 'how,'" Jorl said.

"How about Eloise and Carol?" Sarn said.

"We shouldn't involve them in anything. Especially something evidently against the law," Tarla said.

The myriad problems related to transportation were still unsolved when the phone rang. Sarn lunged for it.

"Maybe I should be the one to answer it, Sarn." Tarla held out her hand for the instrument.

"Come up here, Eloise," Sarn shouted into the phone before he handed it to Tarla. He had recognized Eloise's voice.

Eloise explained to Tarla that they were still home. Some friends had delayed them, but they were ready to leave now.

"That's fine, Eloise," Tarla said. "We'll meet you and Carol in front of the hotel. Is an hour all right?"

Right on time the big blue car, only a little dented and scratched from its last journey, drove up, and the four went outdoors to meet the girls.

Jorl didn't mention driving, and neither did Carol. They got into the car and headed for the bright lights.

The six of them spent about four hours gambling in the casinos that crowded up and down the main drag.

"Look at this," Sarn said with pleasure. "Lots of money." He folded it up and put it away. "How did the rest of you do?"

"I won some, and so did Carol." Eloise was still slightly quivering with excitement.

When they compared notes, all of them were ahead of the games.

"That's about enough gambling for one night," Jorl said. "What do you think, Tarla?"

"I agree. But now I'm hungry."

"So am I. Let's eat," Sarn said.

They stood on the sidewalk, among the people and the lights and the excitement, and tried to decide which restaurant they should pick. The choices were almost limitless.

"There's a new place that just opened down the road. Carol and I went there a few nights ago," Eloise suggested. "It's only about a twenty-minute drive from here, isn't it Carol?"

"That's about right, and unless the chef is having a tantrum, I recommend the food. And I really enjoyed the atmosphere."

They agreed to give it a try and headed for the car. On the way to the restaurant, they came to a long, dark stretch of road. Suddenly, outlined in the white splash of the headlights was a figure waving his arms and weaving around in ever-increasing circles.

"He appears to have a problem," Khair said, straining to see past the glare of the lights.

Carol slowed the car to a crawl.

"There's his problem—nose first in a ditch." Jorl pointed to the back end of a car sticking straight up in the air.

"A few more lessons, and maybe you'll turn out to be as good a driver as he is." Sarn jabbed Jorl in the ribs and laughed.

They got out of the car and rushed toward the accident.

"Are you all right?" Jorl asked. "Are you injured?" He grabbed the unsteady little man and, as he held him up, tried to see if there were any apparent injuries.

"Is there anyone else in the car?" Sarn asked.

"He looks as if he could be suffering from some form of brain damage—he's apparently unable to control his muscular coordination." Tarla tried to examine him more closely.

Carol, who was one step behind Tarla, caught one whiff of his powerful breath and remarked, "It's brain damage all right. He's loaded." She wrinkled her nose in disgust.

"Whew," Tarla agreed, "you're right." Tarla also wrinkled her nose. "Pretty much the same on . . . um-m, anyplace."

"Loaded? Whosh loaded? It's my bad car whosh loaded." He began to giggle. "She just can't take that high tsht gash—drove her sloppy shelf right shmack into the bloo'y dish—dits—hole." He hiccupped.

Naturally, it struck Sarn as hilariously funny, and he laughed till the tears ran down his face. Jorl and Khair joined him.

Tarla, Eloise, and Carol found nothing funny in it at all.

"Wha's sho funny? Nothing funny about a drunk car—it will get me into trouble. If that bad car won't come home with me, my wife will kick me in the tailpipe." The big smile left his cheerful, pudgy little face. He suddenly looked perturbed. "I betcha she will, anyway." Large, extra wet tears began rolling down his face. "You fellashs gotta help me. Will you, fellashs?"

"Of course, sir. First, we'll get your, eh, bad car out of the ditch," Jorl, with a bit of affection for him, said. He couldn't help but smile at the little guy.

"Gee . . . thanksh." His eyes forgot to cry as his mouth broke out into an ear-to-ear grin.

"Have you a driver's license?" Sarn asked, his eyes gleaming.

"Driver'sh licensh? Shure, in here shomwhere." He fumbled and weaved through every pocket. "Shomewhere, offisher. Shay. You fellas cops? Wha's—uniform?" He looked blearily at the three men and then at Tarla. "Phew. It loosh better onna lady."

"We are not police. Papers, please," Sarn said.

"Oh." Eventually, he pulled out a card case and unsnapped it. "Wha' card you want? I got hunnerds. Help yourshelf." He let the case unfold, and every slot was filled with some sort of a card.

"Here, let me help you," Sarn said.

The other three suspected what Sarn had in mind and distracted the chubby little man's attention by walking him over to his definitely stopped car. They considered the angle of descent.

"Tarla," Jorl called, "you come down and help."

"Between the four of us, we should be able to push it back on the road," Khair said.

Jorl nodded. "Eloise and Carol—keep the little man away."

The four Zalleellians put their strong bodies to work, and within a minute the car bounced back up on the road.

"Jeesh! Tha'sh mushles. Never saw anything like it." The drunk wobbled toward his car and patted it. "Good girl—but no more high tesht until you learn how to hold your liquor. Thanksh, everybody—now, gotta get home." He attempted to crawl behind the wheel.

"Tarla, he'll be back in the ditch in three minutes. Tell Carol to get his address and lead the way. I'll drive this car and follow her," Jorl decided.

Tarla relayed the message to Carol, who raised her eyebrows. "I suppose Jorl's driving is the lesser of two evils."

"Gee, Sarn. Jorl might get hurt—or the police might stop him . . . or . . ." Eloise worried about the whole situation.

"I'll go with him," Sarn looked unconcerned.

Tarla spoke in her own language. "What can you do, Sarn?"

"Besides annoying any mentors that might stop you, that is," Khair smiled, thinking of the Enforcementors on their planet—mentors for short.

"A lot. I brought a stun pack this time." Without letting Carol or Eloise see him, he pulled up his sleeve and showed them the small weapon that he had strapped to his lower arm.

The stun pack's technology transmitted neural impulses of ascending intensities contained in a narrow field of emission. The lowest setting could temporarily erase a small portion of memory from a person's brain—the highest could kill.

"Don't use it if you can possibly avoid it, Sarn."

"I'm not a complete idiot, Tarla," Sarn replied and chucked her under her chin.

"Of course you're not. But sometimes, you act first and think later."

"Damn fine idea anyway, Sarn. Let's get started," Jorl said, impatient to get underway.

"Be careful." Tarla lightly kissed Jorl.

"Bet on it." He smiled tenderly at her, running his hand down the back of her head to cradle the nape of her neck in his strong hand.

Between them, Sarn and Jorl bundled the helpless little drunk into the backseat.

"Jeesh, there'sh lottsha room back here. Never been here before. Shay, where am I anyway?"

Jorl got behind the wheel, and Sarn sat beside him. Jorl turned the key, which was already in the ignition, and the motor purred to life.

"So far, so good," Sarn said. He sat straight as an arrow and ready to leap from the bow.

"Sarn, don't worry. There's not much of a trick to it." Jorl grinned in pleasure. "Did Carol get the address?"

"Yes. They're turning now."

Jorl made a slow U-turn on the deserted highway.

"Hey, up there. Talk a little shlower. I can't undershtan a word you're saying. Mush be m'ears." He let loose a loud hiccup, closed his eyes, and fell sideways on the seat.

"Out cold," Sarn told Jorl, "just like home." Sarn and Jorl smiled at each other, remembering a few of their own celebrations.

Carol set a prudent pace, and Jorl kept his distance.

"Not much traffic anyway," Jorl said.

"Thank the stars for that."

Because the traffic was almost nonexistent, they came to the outskirts of the town in less than twenty minutes.

"She's slowing down, Jorl. Watch it, she might . . ."

Carol abruptly slowed down and made a sharp right-hand turn that caught Jorl off guard. He overcompensated for the turn, squealed the tires, and nearly dumped the car.

"Blazing suns, Jorl." Sarn rubbed the spot that had bumped the doorframe.

"Take more than that to dent that skull," Jorl said.

The two cars twisted and turned through a maze of streets.

Carol slowed to a stop in front of a rather long driveway that led to a neat white house. Jorl pulled to a stop right behind her. Tarla ran lightly to Jorl's side of the car. "Khair and I think it would be wiser to park his car just a little way down the driveway and leave him there. Besides, he looks comfortable."

Jorl parked the car about halfway down the driveway. "Come on, Sarn, let's go. Hurry up before someone sees us."

Tarla was beside the car to see if the little man was okay to leave alone. "Best to leave the keys on the seat instead of in the ignition."

Sarn had been rummaging through a little cupboard on the dash of the car. "I agree. Let's go." He jumped out and took his find with him.

"Hey, where'sh everybody goin'? Hey! Thash home. Come in and meet Jenny—my wife, you know. She won't be mad if shomeodysh with me." He struggled and hiccupped his way out of the backseat. "Jenny can get awful mad, you know."

"Sorry, old fellow," Jorl said, "no time."

"Maybe if you are as quiet as a bank of sea fog, she won't wake up yet," Tarla suggested. She helped steady him and pointed him toward the house.

"She'sh got earsh on her like a hungry hunting dog, my Jenny hash."

"Here's your keys. We have to go now." He and Tarla left him standing unsteadily beside the car.

They looked back at the little man, who wobbled a little bit and looked sort of sad.

"Oh, dear," Tarla said.

They both hurried back to Carol's car and got in quickly.

Carol hastily pulled away. "Phew. I won't relax until we're ten miles away from here. What on earth will you get me involved in next, I wonder? A highjacking? Rum-running?"

"Gee, Carol, all we did was help the poor man." Eloise found Carol hard to understand sometimes, even though Carol was her honorary sister and best friend.

Sarn gave Eloise a hug, and Tarla patted her hand and smiled at her. Eloise snuggled into Sarn's shoulder and breathed a contented sigh.

They all agreed, for different reasons, that it was time to go home.

It wasn't long before they pulled up in front of the hotel and said goodnight to each other.

Chapter 10

The four Zalleellians gathered around a small table, and Sarn spread out the pilfered heap of documents and cards. They poked through the pile.

"Can you make any sense of them, Tarla?" Jorl asked, baffled.

"Some of it, I think." She spent a few more minutes examining them. "Here it is. Just what we want—a driver's license." She held it up to show them.

"Let me see it." Sarn took it from her and inspected it closely.

Tarla riffled through the rest of the cards. "I think this is the insurance card that Carol mentioned. And here is a certification of birth. We have them all." She smiled, pleased.

Sarn, examining them, said, "I don't think we can make up dummy ones that would be any good. Do you Jorl—Khair?" He passed them to Khair.

Khair looked closely at them. "No, too many numbers, different fingerprints, special inks, no. But now we at least know what we want."

These others seem similar to our interplanetary money cards, and some are evidently memberships. Our man seems to be a very solid citizen—well, most of the time, anyway," Tarla said with a smile.

"We have to send these back to our happy friend somehow," Jorl said. "I wonder if there's any kind of a delivery service we could use?"

"Since they do all this writing, there must be," Khair said.

"Blazing suns! Just imagine the millions of people on this world—all writing things on paper—no communicators. All the paper and books. There must be billions of tons of the stuff on the move every day." Sarn's mind almost boggled at the thoughts of the sheer volume. "Unless they convert to micro storage soon, they'll paper themselves right out of orbit."

Khair's facial expression was in thinking mode. "Seems to me that since they have been able to put up some kind of a spaceship, they must have some sort of an information exchanger, either connected or wireless, means of communication. We just haven't seen enough of their technology to make any sort of a judgment about it yet."

"Well, I still say that they should do away with some of the volume. Ah-h, who knows. There are always rights and wrongs of anything." Sarn shrugged and continued looking at all the papers.

"Maybe they convert most of the used stuff to some other form of material, or remake it into more paper," Tarla said.

"'Maybe' to everything just said, but right this minute, we have to get this batch back to our little man," Jorl said. "Maybe you could ask Eloise or Carol about it tomorrow, Tarla?"

"I've been thinking," Sarn said.

"Oh, that is good news," Khair said and smiled at Sarn.

"Don't interrupt me when I'm about to expound great thoughts." Sarn assumed an orator's pose.

With exaggerated gestures, Jorl shushed them. "Listen closely, everybody."

"Thank you. Anyway, I was about to say, since Earthians seem to need so many papers to live, what if they did lose all of them. Does the person just—disappear into thin air—cease to exist, just like that?" Sarn snapped his fingers.

"That really is a deep thought to ponder, I must admit," Khair said slowly in his pleasantly deep voice and smiled slightly.

"I hope our friend would sober up first," Sarn said, "and when he did, what a shock that would be."

"I suppose if the person's file was somehow removed from all official places, he probably would be dead as far as the government was concerned. Maybe it would be better for him to just stay the way he was—not sober," Jorl added. "Okay. Back to business. Now that we know what we want, how do we get it?"

"We've got to find the equivalent of an outworlder," Tarla said.

"Right. Now—where?" Jorl said.

"And, Tarla, don't say 'how,'" Sarn said.

"Usually, it's by contacts," Khair said.

"On top of all the other things we have not got—we have not got contacts." Sarn slammed his fist into his other hand. He jumped up and began to pace, muttering under his breath.

"Consider it logically," Khair said. "In the other galaxies, there are always people on the fringes of the outworld, but in contact with both worlds. For instance, public conveyance operators, or service people on worlds without automatic systems. All we need is to find a comparable type around here."

"The workers in the casinos. The gambling must attract the outworld type as a moneymaking proposition," Jorl said.

"But if you approach the wrong ones, they'll call the mentors," Sarn warned.

"That's where Tarla comes in. She can narrow down the field so we don't have to spend the next few months waiting while she samples everybody in the city," Jorl said.

Sarn slapped himself on his forehead, and his eyes lit up, "Blazing suns, I forgot, Tarla. Let's start probing right now."

"Who?" Tarla asked.

"With that sneaky-looking outworlder who carries up suitcases and beer and always has his hot hand out."

"Mmm-m, he could be a contact," Khair said.

"If he can get us what we want, how should we handle it? Pay him, or stun pack him?" Sarn asked.

Jorl thought for a moment. "We should pay him a fair fee. Then you can erase that part of his memory, Tarla."

"Yes. Then I'll plant a memory of how he got the money."

"Plant a gambling win." Sarn suggested. "He works in a casino."

"Good, Sarn, a gambling win would account for the extra money," Tarla agreed. "That way he won't go insane worrying about where he got it."

"Perfect," Jorl said.

"Order some beer and food, Tarla. Get him up here." Sarn handed her the phone, and it started to squeak like a rodent right on cue. He rubbed his hands and grinned.

Twenty minutes later, the bellhop arrived with a tray full of beer and sandwiches. For once, Sarn smiled at him and motioned him in.

The bellhop went warily past Sarn and put the tray on the table and fussed with it. He turned around in time to see Sarn smile wolfishly right back at him as he laid a twenty-dollar bill on the extended palm. The bellhop whistled through his teeth.

Tarla nodded and pointed to the bellboy. Sarn took the surprised man's arm, led him to the sofa, and motioned him to sit beside Tarla. The bellhop looked from one intent face to the other, plainly nervous.

"Don't be afraid." Tarla gave him her beautiful smile and thought soothing thoughts at him. "What is your name?" She already knew it was Johnny, but she wanted him to relax.

"Johnny Dill, ma'am." His beady little eyes, under a floppy forelock of mousy-colored hair, brightened in his narrow, ferret-like face. He suddenly realized that these big people wanted something, and no doubt there'd be a few bucks in it for him.

More sure of his ground, he said cockily, "What d'ya want, people—sex, booze, drugs, or weapons—name it 'cause Johnny Dill's your man—eh, for a price, ya unnerstand."

"Those are the only things you can supply?" Tarla asked, disappointed.

Johnny raised his eyebrows. "Oh, innarested in heavy stuff, eh? Look, lady, I can get anything you want, or else I know who to ask. But the price goes up accordingly. Unnerstand? Okay, what'd ya want?"

"Papers—like these—for each of us." Tarla fanned out the three important pieces.

Johnny Dill whistled. "Oh, one of those deals, eh? It's hot stuff messing with the Feds."

Tarla watched his mind clicking over like a cash register. He sorted through the names and prices and wondered how worried and gullible these four were. Tarla gently, but firmly, planted the thought in his mind that he had better not try any fooling around with them.

"Okay," Johnny Dill said, "gimme an hour to track down someone, and I'll get back to you. The going price these papers cost is a mint—I'll have to split with at least two other guys."

"How about . . ." Tarla saw two thousand dollars in his mind. "How about four thousand dollars for first-class service?"

Johnny's eyes glittered. "For four thousand smackers, I would personally lose your mother-in-law." He scurried across the room to the door. "I'll get back to you."

After the door closed behind him, Sarn asked, "What do you think?"

They discussed the conversation with Johnny. Tarla also gave them a picture of the hot little rodent thoughts going through Johnny's mind. "It was like being in a sewer. And a third-rate sewer at that." Tarla shuddered.

This was the part of her gift that she hated. All the minds she entered left the memory in hers. Even though she was able to sink it to the depths of her subconscious, the knowledge, whether good or ugly, stayed there ready to reach out into her conscious mind. She had refused to be mind-blocked because she knew that then she would always worry and wonder about what was behind the block.

"If he gets us what we want, it'll be worth it, Tarla," Jorl said tenderly.

"Let's eat." Sarn reached out for a sandwich.

"I didn't know I was so hungry," Jorl said.

It didn't take long to reduce the food to a few lonely crumbs, and it wasn't quite an hour later when they heard the knock they had been waiting for. They let a craftily smiling Johnny into the room.

"Well, folks, it's all fixed. Get a cab and go to this address. He handed Jorl a folded piece of paper. The Pen will tell you as much as he wants you to know, so don't ask me any questions. Pay me one thousand dollars now. Pay The Pen two thousand when he agrees. He wants cash in advance. As he says, who's to say the Feds won't pick you up before morning, and then where would he fit?" When you get the papers, you pay me my other thousand. Here." Johnny handed Tarla the slip of paper with the address written on it. "You'd better get goin' now. His prices go up if he's kept waiting."

"Eh, thank you, Johnny," Tarla said. Things seemed to be moving a bit too fast for her to catch her figurative breath.

Jorl counted out ten one hundred dollar bills into the quivering hand. When Jorl reached ten, the hand snapped shut and disappeared into Johnny's pants pocket.

"Nice doin' business with you folks. See ya later." The door shut behind him once more.

"Whew! Well, that seems to be that," Tarla said.

"Let's get over there right now. Come on." Jorl hurried them out the door.

When they reached the lobby, they asked the man behind the desk to get a cab for them.

It drove them to an increasingly shabby part of town, far away from all the bright lights and glitter.

"I don't think I like the looks of this part of the town," Tarla said.

"Probably it's in keeping with our type of business. Dark and underhanded," Khair said.

The taxi driver pulled to a stop on a dark street in front of an ugly brick-fronted house. A vacant warehouse leaned into each side of the sullen old house and a dark, narrow alley bracketed both the vacant buildings. A weak light burned over the peeling paint on the door showing the number 73.

They paid the cabby his fare and realized that the dirty look and outstretched hand meant he wanted a tip as well. They obliged.

When the taxi drove away, the four stood in front of the door and checked the address. The night was dark and cold—the street empty and silent. Evil, somehow.

"It definitely is the right one," Tarla whispered. She checked the address again against the one Johnny had written down. "I don't like the look of this place at all." She took Jorl's arm. "It gives me the creeps."

"Now what?" Khair also looked around.

"Pound on it. Maybe someone will open it before it collapses," Sarn said.

"Just ring the doorbell. It won't make as much noise," Tarla pushed the button. They could hear a faint buzz inside the old house. "Someone's coming—he apparently is expecting us," Tarla whispered.

"Must be The Quill," Sarn said.

"The Pen," Khair said.

Sarn shrugged, "What's the difference?"

"Not enough to bother about, I guess," Khair said.

They heard a scuffling noise through the door and then a rattle of chains. A locking mechanism clicked and the door opened. Slowly.

"Security-conscious buzzard, isn't he?" Jorl said.

Finally, the door squealed open enough for them to see a long, wrinkled, ugly face with a thin, beaked nose curving down to almost touch a narrow, mean mouth. Wispy gray hair and a sour smell completed the portrait.

"Who sent you?" His voice was thin and high.

"Johnny Dill, sir," Tarla answered.

"Come in, come in. I haven't got all night." He turned and started slowly down a long, gloomy hallway. He seemed to be almost painfully pulling himself along.

They pushed open the door and entered the hall. The rank smell hit them like a blow.

"Blazing suns, what some people can do with perfectly good air. Phew!" Sarn was disgusted.

They hurried to catch up with the bent old man who had scurried into a room. "Hurry, hurry. I haven't got all night."

"I believe you have two thousand dollars worth of night for sale." Jorl allowed a shiver of steel to show in his eyes and his voice.

"Humph. Don't get uppity with me, youngster. You need me worse than I need you." He climbed up on a stool in front of a slanted desk and snapped on a powerful, narrow-beamed light. He settled the folds of his long, rusty-black coat that flapped around his bony ankles. He picked up a pen in a surprisingly clean and elegant hand and said, "What do you want?"

"We want one each of these for each one of us," Tarla replied politely. Sarn put the little drunk's papers on the desk.

"Humph." The old man fingered them. "Where did you steal these? Never mind. Don't tell me. It's none of my business anyway."

"Can you do as we ask?" Tarla said.

In a harsh and rude tone of voice, he said, "That's why I'm called The Pen, and that's what you're paying me for. What are your names?"

"I am Tarla Sandu . . ."

"Spell."

Tarla spelled.

"Him?" the old man pointed.

"Jorl Sandu."

He wrote it down. "Him?"

"Khair Sandu." Tarla spelled it before he could bark, then quickly pointed to Sarn, "Sarn Dreela," and spelled that.

"Humph! With names like that, you'll be Estonians with passports and papers to prove you are landed immigrants. Much safer."

"No, no, Mr. Pen, it must show us as being from Raffinsten, in South Asia." Carol and Eloise had been told the Raffinsten story.

"Spell."

He mumbled to himself as he rummaged through the drawers and came up with a sheaf of different blank forms, all in different sizes. He opened another drawer and brought up a strange device and pointed it toward them. "I need pict . . ." Before he finished the word, all three men grabbed it and the old man.

"It's a camera! It's only a camera." The old man was more than a little shaken up by the suddenness of the attack. "I need your pictures for the papers."

The three men slowly let him go.

"That will be another thousand dollars. Call it fright pay. Three thousand dollars, right here and now." His black, beady eyes had lost their fear and glittered at them. Hunched over on the tall stool, with the fingers on his hand tautly outstretched for the money, he gave the impression of a small, vicious bird of prey.

Jorl counted out the required amount. The man began to recount.

"It's all there, Quill." Sarn, lip curled in disgust, was close to the end of his patience.

"Sarn, forget it. We need him," Tarla said softly.

"My professional name is The Pen, cockerel. Hold your tongue, or leave with, or without, what you came for. It's all the same to me." He turned back toward his desk, mumbled, "Humph, idiots," and pulled a paper form toward him and started to write.

"Blazing suns, I'll pound that hateful bag of dirty bones to a more polite pulp."

"That's enough, Lieutenant," Jorl ordered.

The lamp over the desk did little about the darkness of the rest of the crowded, musty room. In the dim light, they looked for something to sit on, and in the process, one of them bumped into a high stack of books, and before they could catch them, it wobbled and crashed to the floor bringing the stack next to it with it. Books fell with a variety of loud noises and slithered everywhere. Great things to be hit with and tripped over. Dust that evidently hadn't been disturbed for years, rose up.

"Blazing bloody suns." That, plus sneezes, were only some of the sounds coming from the dust cloud.

"Stop the noise, you imbeciles. How do you expect me to work in such an uproar?"

"If we could turn on another light?" Tarla asked quietly.

"I have enough light. I am comfortable. I advise you to be careful of my comfort."

They heard the pleasure of power, the thinly disguised threat, in the shrill, cracked voice. He turned his back and began to work, mumbling bad-temperedly. "I don't know who the hell you foreigners think you are. You are as bad as that last . . ." The old man paused, perplexed. "Humph," he huffed and then shrugged, "what is it that—why can't I remember—strange."

Sarn snarled, "If he threatens us once more, I'll twist the old vulture's neck."

Jorl held up his hand to Sarn and shook his head. "Wait awhile," he whispered. "There's some kind of a mystery here—and we want those papers."

"You're right, Jorl," Tarla whispered. "Something isn't right. It's almost as though he's been mind-blocked."

"I hope the old man is done soon." This is a really horrible old house, and I can't wait to get out of it. I think I'll just lightly touch the old man's mind again and see if there's anything there that might account for that bitterly cold and awful feeling I felt before. I'll go in slowly and—oh, great heavens, there it is again—the utter cold. "Jorl, I'm scared." She grabbed Jorl's arm and whispered to him, "Jorl, he's been heavily mind-blocked."

"Scan again and make sure."

She did. "I'm absolutely sure. It's a strong, deep one. Probably will cause a lot of damage. Cruel. Jorl, who would do . . .?"

Khair and Sarn heard what Tarla said. They were alert for any physical signs coming from anywhere.

"Can you get through it?" Jorl whispered. He tried to penetrate the dark edges of the room.

"Not like this. It will take time, unless you want me to blow his mind completely. He's already suffering from anxiety acute enough to drive him mad."

The waspish old voice lashed out at them. "Will you people shut up? All that hissing and whispering is annoying me and could ruin my work. And I happen to take great pride in my work."

"Sorry, sir." Tarla spoke as sweetly as she could.

They went quietly out into the hall and took a good look around.

"Now . . . Tarla, could you find out who put the block there? I mean, a native of this planet, or someone from . . .?" Jorl hated to give voice to the other alternative.

"Jorl. Maybe it's someone from Space Command looking for us."

Sarn's face broke out into a smile that nearly lit the dim hall.

All but Jorl smiled in pleasure, contemplating the happy thought.

Tarla's smile faded. "But why the memory block without a message?"

"That's what I thought. That's why I don't think it's about a message for us. It's about something else entirely. See if you can get at least a hint of what it is," Jorl said in a soft whisper.

Tarla found her way back into the old man's mind and spoke quietly as she explored, "On the surface, he's professionally engrossed in the job he's doing, and he's really finding pleasure in creating good work. He loves what he does. I guess they don't call him The Pen for nothing." Tarla slipped further into his subconscious as gently as a sweet thought.

Tarla went into deep concentration. There's the area of the block. It's as solid as a—hmm-m, where's the way through? Which path? Which way? Maybe I'll cross over this synapse. It could lead to a chink in the armor—no. Up this path? What was that? Felt like a faint echo of the mentalist. She probed as deeply as she dared. Suddenly, she felt the same blast of utter cold she had suffered hours ago.

"Tarla, Tarla!" Jorl put his arm around her, comforting her. "Sweetheart. What's wrong?"

"The same as before. It was . . . was so . . . brilliantly cold. Jorl, it's alien. There are others here."

"You mean there are more of us stranded here?" Sarn was stunned at all the possibilities.

"No, not ours. But I almost recognize the echoes. Somewhere, sometime—there's not enough to trace, but it gives me a terrible sense of fear." Tarla was pale with the effort to pin down the memory and the chilling fright of the encounter.

"Are there any other signs close to us here?" Khair asked.

Tarla forced herself to scan in every direction. "No. But then, whoever established such a block would effectively shield themselves from any interference."

"We should remove the block from the old man now," Jorl said, "before something else happens."

"He could die," Sarn added.

Jorl agreed. "Tarla, you'll have to do it right away and hope for the best. We've got to know if they are enemies."

Khair pointed to the closed door. "We should go back in there."

Poised for any situation, they went quietly back into the dank and dark room. The old man sat at the desk as before—his back to them, thin shoulders hunched—and the pool of light shone on four neat stacks of papers. He was still. Too still.

Immediately, they sensed something terribly wrong. Fearing what she might find, Tarla scanned ahead anyway. "He's dead, Jorl. The neural charges have faded."

Jorl quickly covered the distance to the old man's body. He made a cursory examination.

"It might have been heart failure. No signs of a struggle. And we were right outside the door and didn't hear a thing."

"If so, what caused it?" Sarn asked.

"A stun pack produces the same result," Khair reminded them.

"So could a strong mind blast," Tarla whispered.

"Natural or not, let's get out of here now," Sarn said. "Here are all the papers. Find something to put them in."

Khair looked over the desk. "Here's a big envelope. Must be the one he planned to use."

"Good idea. Gather everything up, and we're out of here."

Without warning, a sudden cold draft blew through the room, and the door slammed shut. They jumped, startled.

"What the black damn hole was that?" Jorl said. He almost leaped across the room and, standing to one side, tried to pull the door open. It was locked. He pulled the knob until the rusty lock let go with a screech, and the door opened.

Khair bent over, looked around the corner, saw nothing, and ran down the hall. Sarn and Jorl were close behind him.

"Too late," Khair said as the front door snicked into place.

Sarn, close behind Khair, said, "There could be something else hiding by the door."

"Or just on the other side of it," Jorl said.

They had to waste another few seconds unlocking the front door.

Every sense at full attention, Khair looked around the door to the street. He was just in time to look down the poorly lit block and to see a flicker of someone disappearing around the next corner.

The distance was too great and the light too dim to get any more than a vague impression of movement.

"No point chasing them now," Jorl said. "Let's get back inside." They turned to go back to Tarla and the corpse.

"Whoever it was sure moved fast," Sarn said.

"Too fast for any ordinary person," Jorl agreed.

"Blazing suns and damn black holes, how could anyone have got close enough to reach in and shut the door without any of us hearing it?"

"That's the part that scares me," Jorl said. "We'd better get off the street before someone sees us."

Once more in the room, they stood looking at the old man who now looked pathetic and even more frail in death.

In a calm, low voice, Khair said, "We have the papers, so before someone comes and demands an explanation, we should leave."

"Right. Come on," Jorl said.

Sarn paused for a minute; a brief look of compassion for the old man crossed his face. "What a hell of a way to end a life even if the old vulture probably deserved it." Sarn turned toward the door with the others.

"Jorl, they came right up to the door, yet I didn't feel their presence." Tarla shivered at the thought and what it could mean.

"I've been thinking the same thing. Let's get moving."

They hurried down the hall again.

"This place feels like a trap," Sarn said. He looked around, ready for trouble. They stood on the sidewalk and looked both ways on the empty street.

"Now what?" Sarn asked.

"We'll try to retrace the route the cab used," Jorl said.

They walked at a good clip, their senses alert and ready. After many twists and turns, they came to the lower end of the main street. Sarn flagged down a cab and they headed for the hotel. At 4:30 in the morning, the streets were still jammed with crowds of people, but no one seemed unduly interested in the four of them.

They gained their rooms and locked the doors, relieved.

"Seems we have a mystery on our hands," Khair said.

"It's not my hands so much as my neck that bothers me," Sarn said.

They barely had enough time to catch deep breaths when they heard a knock on the door. They looked at each other in alarm.

"Not the mentors already. Can't be," Khair said.

Sarn hid the brown envelope under the sofa as Jorl crossed the room to the door.

Tarla whispered, "It's only Johnny Dill wanting his money. He knows nothing about the dead man."

Sarn pulled his sleeve back down over the stun pack.

Jorl nodded and opened the door. In slithered Johnny, greed glittering in his small eyes. "Get what you went for, folks?"

"Yes Johnny, thanks to you. Now, come and sit down while Mr. Dreela gets your money for you." Tarla led him to a chair and sat opposite him. Jorl stood behind him and nodded to Tarla. Khair, doing his part, engaged Johnny in conversation about the papers in particular and Johnny's sideline in general.

Sarn walked over and stood in front of the seated Johnny. "I guess this is what you want, Johnny." Sarn counted out ten more one hundred dollar bills.

"Oh, yeah. Come to daddy, my babies." His little beady eyes shone as he lovingly counted the bills again and put them in his pocket so fast that it seemed like a magic trick.

Tarla put Johnny into a light sleep, then slid softly into Johnny's mind. She began to build a block to hide the knowledge of their papers and to implant the idea of a gambling win. "There, I'm sure that's done well enough not to hurt the little guy, but I might as well scan for any indication of previous mind-tampering." Tarla concentrated as she gently explored Johnny's mind. She never ceased to wonder at the volume and content of the brain. "Something is going on around Johnny's life. He's a little troubled at some things he seems to almost know. I'll probe a little bit deeper."

Tarla felt Johnny's psyche twitch and warned her to back off. She did so immediately before any damage could be done. "Anyway, the results are negative. There is nothing even faintly resembling the poor old Pen. Johnny contacted him through a middleman and has no real knowledge of the old man." Tarla left Johnny's mind with a smooth and gentle thought.

Suddenly, Johnny looked around the room in surprise. "Holy cow! What am I sitting here for?"

Jorl laughed. "We met you in the hall and you were so excited about your big win at the slots, that you . . ."

"Yes, so happy that we invited you in to tell us all about your big win at the slots and how lucky you were." Tarla used a soft voice to test the suggestion.

"Yeah." He sounded doubtful. All at once, his face broke into a happy grin. "Yeah! A little better than two grand. Five wins in a row. Nothin' but jackpots. Never saw the like. Thanks for listening."

He got up and walked across the room. He opened the door, paused for a moment, a slightly puzzled look on his face, "Nope. Never saw the like." He went out and shut the door.

They all said goodnight as the door closed behind him.

"Good job, Tarla." Jorl praised her and gave her a hug. "There was nothing in Johnny's mind resembling that of the old man's?"

"No, not a trace."

"They, whoever they are, must have gone to the old man first, before they even knew about us," Khair said.

"Well, they sure know about us now," Sarn said.

"True. And we have to find out who they are. Also, I suggest that we go on mental guard as well as physical," Khair said.

Blazing suns, who in a black hole can they be?" Sarn slammed one fist into the other, voicing everyone else's thoughts.

"We need sleep now," Jorl said. "We'll try to pick up some answers tomorrow."

They agreed with him on all counts and took off for their beds.

Chapter 11

At noon the next day, Tarla called room service. The four of them had lunch and spent time discussing what was uppermost in all their minds—the strong evidence of other aliens.

"I don't know whether to be glad or frightened," Tarla said. "Glad because it may mean the way back home, but frightened because they might be causing the terrible coldness." She was pensive. "I know there's something I should remember."

"I bet it's right on the tip of a synapse." Sarn laughed at his own joke.

Tarla laughed, too, and said, "You're right . . . now, to find the right one sometime."

"To quote someone, and I don't know who, 'sometime, when you least expect it' . . ." Khair smiled.

"Sounds like a bit too much television to me," Jorl said. "However, it must be working if we can even start quoting television programs."

They sat around, watching the television, each in their own thoughts that churned around in their own minds.

When the phone rang. Sarn sprang to answer it and heard Eloise on the other end.

"Gee, Sarn honey, I waited as long as I could to phone. Carol thought that maybe later we could all go out somewhere—or something? Carol had to go out for a while, but she said that she would meet us at your hotel . . . is that okay, Sarn honey? Is that . . .?"

Sarn's eyes lit up with pleasure. "Where are you?"

"I'm home."

"Where's home?"

She gave him the address of her apartment. He memorized it and said, "One hour. I will take a taxi." He hung up and let out a happy yell and headed for the shower.

The other three looked at each other, not knowing what to think.

"I don't like the idea of us being split up. It might be . . ." Jorl said. "I don't want to sound paranoid, but it just seems a little . . . peculiar

"Planned?" Khair said. "The thought has already crossed my mind."

"Not Eloise, Khair, I would have sensed something."

"How do we know? There's been enough time for whoever it is to get to her. To Carol, too, without them even being aware of the change."

"That would mean that we are being watched." Tarla, unhappy with such thoughts, shuddered.

"We have to consider all the possibilities," Jorl said.

"I'll do a soft probe the next time we see them. But I can't believe that I wouldn't have sensed something before now." Tarla thought back to the different times she had been with either of the girls.

"What's the deep discussion all about?" Sarn, half-dressed and toweling his thick red hair, suddenly laughed. "I am of age, you know. And I do know about the . . ."

"Oh, none of us have any doubts about that." Jorl smiled.

"Sarn, you've got to bear in mind that Eloise and Carol could have been—directed—used as a trap," Khair said, "and you know that you have a tendency to jump in feet first and ask questions later."

The realization of the possibilities of treachery hit Sarn hard. "You mean, maybe we were set up? That our meeting wasn't accidental? I don't believe it." Sarn thought for a moment . . . "I just don't believe it."

"But it could be," Jorl said. "Did Eloise mention Carol at all?"

"Only that she had to go out for an hour or so and would come over here later," Sarn replied. "Anyway, I don't believe either of them is of any danger to us."

"You don't have any more evidence, one way or the other, than we do, Sarn. It would be better if you didn't go out alone," Jorl said. His serious expression lightened, and he smiled. "And not because you're a babe in the woods, either—that you definitely are not. But, nevertheless . . ."

Sarn thought about what Jorl had just said. "Look, I promise I'll be totally on my guard. I'll watch for signs, for any change in their attitudes, for anything the least left of centre."

"Unless there are physical signs, how could you tell?" Jorl asked.

Sarn shrugged, thinking fast. "I'll know by any suggestions they make. If it strikes me as phony, if I think that either one of them is trying to set me up somehow, I promise I'll blast off immediately."

"I suppose that as long as you stay on your guard, you should be okay." Jorl was still dubious. "Pain in the neck that you can be, I really don't want to lose you." Jorl gave him a quick hug. "You'll keep your guard up—don't let it down for any reason—and I mean for any reason?"

"I promise."

Tarla had the phone book open. She scanned down a page and said, "Here's their address and the phone number—it's the same."

"If you find out anything, or if you need me, phone, or else come and get me," Sarn said.

"Sarn," Tarla said when she put her arm around his waist, "I'll leave my mind open for a few seconds four times an hour. If you send a concentrated thought pattern, I might be able to catch at least an echo of it."

"That could be dangerous for you, Tarla. It would leave you vulnerable to whatever is out there," Jorl said.

"I can manage, Jorl." She gave him a loving hug." Really, I'll be fine."

Irrepressible, Sarn agreed to the plan. "If, for any reason, I can't phone, write, or get a taxi, I'll send out one of my most powerful thoughts." He saw the three faces, the concern and the love for him showing behind their eyes—his family. "Look—people—I know I'll be fine. I promise that I'll keep my guard up. I won't take any chances. Please don't worry about me."

"When you say 'don't worry about me,' my little brother, that is when I worry the most." Tarla smiled at him.

Sarn suddenly realized that their concern for him was real, that he might be going into a dangerous situation by himself, and they cared about only his safety. "I know how you feel. I know that I probably shouldn't go alone. But, at the same time, now that you've made me aware of the possibilities, at the first sign of anything, anything at all, that doesn't seem right, I'll head for home. I promise."

"Are you carrying a stun pack?" Jorl asked.

"Right here." Sarn patted his forearm.

When he and his beaming smile were ready to leave, he kissed Tarla good-bye and threw a salute to the two men. He and his almost ear-to-ear smile just about bounced out the door.

"Ah, love. It burns with a brilliant flame," Khair said softly. "Or, sometimes, even as a quiet flame that warms deeply."

"He'll be all right, Tarla. Don't worry about him. He's a lot smarter than we sometimes give him credit for." Jorl gave her a reassuring hug.

"That's true, I guess. He's always turned up before. Worrying about it serves no purpose," Tarla said firmly to herself.

"I wonder where Carol is?" Khair said, "I find it strange not to have heard from her. Anyway, let's have a look at our new identities. Where are they?"

"In that drawer." Jorl got the envelope and gave it to Tarla. She emptied the papers onto the table and started sorting them out.

"These are great. That old Quill, I mean, Mr. Pen—I like Sarn's name better—certainly did an excellent job," Khair said. "Good pictures, too."

They were more than pleased with the documents. Jorl separated them into individual piles. "Put these in our small carry cases. Keep them with us." He put Sarn's papers into Sarn's carry case.

"I'll put all the borrowed papers into this one envelope," Tarla said. "We'll get Johnny Dill to mail it later. For a tip, of course."

The three of them laughed.

"What about the dead man?" Tarla asked.

"First, we have to decide how to start," Khair said. "Do you think we should . . .?"

Jorl interrupted him and pointed to the video machine, "Listen."

The news announcer was speaking about the increase in strange, unidentified flying objects, or, at least, glowing balls of light, spotted recently in the sky by the populace.

"The switchboard is jammed with calls from people asking questions. Why, only four mornings ago, at least six people reported a shining object traveling at an unheard-of speed. The object seemed to disappear right into the desert.

And only three nights ago, a brilliant blue light hovered in the same vicinity. As if that wasn't enough to cause great speculation, only last night, at least three people swear that they saw a brilliant orange light. It, too, covered the same general area of sky as the other two, and it, also, disappeared into the desert.

The armed forces weather station, when questioned this morning by yours truly, said nothing appeared on any radar screens. They assured me that the bright lights were due to atmospheric disturbances and also thought that overactive imaginations played a big part in the sightings.

But this announcer wonders, folks. If they are aliens, there seems to be a bunch of them gathering. Maybe they've heard good things about the bright lights of this fair city and decided it's as good a place as any to hold their annual convention—and maybe indulge in a little good old-fashioned gambling on the side.

Well, that's all the news for now, folks, and remember, if you see any little green men wandering around, you should either change your brand of liquor, or else lead them to the nearest casino—their money is as good as anybody's.

"If he only knew." Jorl laughed at the announcer's closing remarks and shut off the set.

Khair suddenly snapped his fingers. "The shining objects—the first one—could have been us. The pile was inoperable and dead when we entered Earth's atmosphere."

Jorl began to pace back and forth. "Different sources of propulsion power produce different colors in the atmosphere. That could mean that two other ships have landed. Our burn-off is almost white, but I've seen greenish-blue—they're the fourth galaxy arm from ours—and orange could be either a slowing down of the drive, or a burn-off—I've seen them around different spaceports, but brilliant blue . . ." Jorl continued to pace, deep in thought, casting his mind back to all the ships he had ever seen landing or flying.

They were still mulling over different ideas when someone knocked on their door. Tarla crossed the room and opened it.

"Hello, Carol. Please come in." Tarla greeted her with pleasure.

"I hope Eloise told you that I would meet her here. I'm a little late. I went to my office to check on two of my accounts, and they're still in the pending file. On my way back through the shopping center, I couldn't resist this." She handed Tarla a large and quite heavy package.

"For me, Carol? How thoughtful. I can't wait to see what it is."

"Hello, Carol. I've been wondering where you were." Khair smiled and lightly kissed her lips.

"Hello, Khair." She smiled with quiet pleasure and returned his light kiss.

"Hello, Jorl. Been in any good ditches lately?" Carol teased.

"No. I've been waiting for you. I wouldn't want you to miss the thrill of it all." Jorl came over to her and gave her a light brotherly kiss on the forehead.

"Look, everybody." With a wide and happy smile, Tarla unwrapped the final piece of fancy paper and took the lid off to see a layer of dark, beautifully decorated chocolates.

Everyone gathered around, and the layer began to quickly disappear with noisy appreciation.

"Did Eloise call Sarn?" She looked from one to the other.

She called about an hour ago, so Sarn took a taxi and went over to your apartment," Tarla said.

"That will certainly make Eloise happy." Carol smiled at the thoughts of the high excitement that Sarn and Eloise would share.

"Oh yes, I totally agree with you." Tarla smiled with Carol.

* * *

But I think I'll just lightly scan Carol's mind. No, I can't sense anything to indicate that she was the dupe in any plot. She's genuinely happy to be here and to see Khair, and Khair her. It's really time Khair got over the death of Mara. It's now about five years since the accident. Carol seems to be the one for him—she's a little bit of the same kind of personality. Anyway, no one has tampered with her mind. That's a relief.

* * *

After a four-way discussion, they decided to go for a drive. Jorl privately hoped that they would be able to spot anyone watching for them. He had to start something moving. Inaction, and the not knowing, annoyed him and made him restless.

The three Zalleellians and Carol walked toward the car. They had not spotted even a strange glance on their way through the crowds in the lobby.

Carol drove expertly through the traffic. Jorl, acting as an interested tourist, suggested directions. Tarla suddenly realized that he was directing Carol to the street where they had been earlier that morning. Only two or three people were about, with no evidence of trouble or excitement. When they drove past Quill's door, Jorl asked Carol to stop for a moment.

"Why?" Carol asked. "This isn't the best neighborhood to spend time in."

Jorl had his explanation ready. "Because the bellboy told me this address is where I could find a man who had a car for quick sale and that he wouldn't ask too many questions."

"You mean it might be stolen? Jorl, you'll get into trouble with the police." Carol had a great respect for the laws of the land and wanted nothing to do with breaking them. She believed that if you had a reason to not agree with a law, you should use the proper channels to change it.

"I didn't say anything about buying it, only that I wanted to talk to him."

"You don't even know if it's some sort of a scam to rob you, or worse." Carol was horrified.

"I'll know. I'll be on my guard. Don't worry, but thanks for worrying."

"Suit yourself," Carol replied and shrugged. "The whole thing sounds fishy to me, but it's your neck in the noose."

Jorl smiled. "Don't worry. I can look after myself." Jorl got out of the car, and so did Tarla. "Where do you think you're going, sweetheart?" Jorl spoke in his own language.

"With you—no argument."

Jorl knew from experience that he could never hope to win an argument with her when she had her chin set in that particular way. "Khair, stay with Carol and stand watch."

Khair nodded in agreement.

Jorl tried the street door. He looked closely and saw that the door was wedged.

"Someone broke the door," Tarla whispered.

Jorl nodded and slowly opened it just far enough for them to enter. They stood still, listening for the slightest sound. They heard nothing.

"Tarla—anything?"

"No."

"Come on, then."

They went lightly down the long, dim hall to the room they had been in before. Jorl, his thumb on the stun pack trigger and motioning Tarla to stand behind him, cautiously pushed open the door.

A man, his back to them, bent over the body of the poor old man that now lay flat on the floor, pathetic in nakedness and stiffened death. The stranger, searching through a pile of clothes beside the body, suddenly felt their presence. He jumped to his feet, turned, and reached for his tunic pocket in one fast, smooth motion, all without a sound.

Jorl and Tarla leaped into the room, one to the right and the other to the left. Jorl fired a blast of neural charges that spun the tall, muscular man around and sent him crashing to the floor, unconscious.

In case anyone else was in the cluttered, dim room, Jorl and Tarla spared a quick look about them.

Tarla quickly shut the door while Jorl, stun pack still aimed, bent over the man he had hit. The stranger was at least six foot six, and the shirt that clung to his torso accented his muscled body to perfection. His bronze skin and thick, blue-black hair added to a strikingly handsome face. His tunic pants and boots were lustrous black with crimson flashings on the tunic and a narrow side stripe on the pants. Tarla also bent over him as Jorl lifted the man's eyelid and looked for signs of returning consciousness.

His mouth hardened into a thin line.

The eyes—the hated eyes.

The eyes of the unconscious man gave away his identity. They were as golden as a hawk's, but instead of the pupils being round and black, they were glittering greenish slits.

Tarla was horrified. "Surnainians! Jorl, this means that . . . this means that Earth could be on their list. That's the reason for the awful cold I felt. Oh, Jorl."

"Filth." Jorl stood up. He stood over the hated symbol of death and destruction. With lips pulled tight against his teeth, eyes that shone with utter loathing, Jorl fired a lethal blast at the unconscious man.

Surnainian!

Execution!

Tarla shuddered, hating it, but knowing that the execution was more than justified. "Jorl, why do you think he was searching him? What possible interest could the Surnainians have in this poor old man?"

"We'll search the place and see if we can find out."

"Now, there are two bodies to worry about. What should we do with them?"

"Leave them here for now, and we'll figure it out later."

They began a systematic search. Tarla started with the old man's clothes while Jorl searched the Surnainian.

"Look what I found," Jorl said, "There's a case attached to his belt." When he opened it, he pulled out a smaller metal case. "I can't see how to open it."

"Here's one just like it hidden in the folds of poor old Quill's coat." Tarla looked at the face of The Quill and shook her head. "This old man just can't be one of the Prophets. He must have been involved with the Surnainians, whether he knew it or not."

"Probably the Surnainians had no more need of him and killed him with a mind blast. Come on, Tarla. We've got to get out of here and collect Sarn—there must be more than one, and they'll kill us before we can say jackpot, let alone have time to interfere with their plans. Come on, Tarla."

They closed and wedged the door shut behind them and ran for the car.

"Quick, Carol, to your apartment. Sarn and Eloise could be in danger." Tarla controlled her urge to panic. She and Jorl hurried into the backseat and slammed the car door behind them.

"What? Danger? What do you mean?" Carol, who liked things to be smooth and peaceful, didn't appreciate such urgency and confusion in her life. "Now what, for heaven's sake. You'll be the death of me yet."

"I hope not, Carol." Jorl's serious tone got through to her.

"What on earth do you mean? Are you telling me that there really is some actual danger? Here?"

"Please hurry, Carol. It's urgent." Tarla prodded.

Carol, in spite of all the prodding. was too scared to attempt dangerous driving, breaking the traffic laws, or maybe killing someone.

Khair raised his eyebrows at Jorl, silently questioning.

Jorl switched to their own language so as not to upset Carol even more than she was. He answered with one word, "Surnainians."

Khair whistled at the startling information. "And the old man?"

"I think he was somehow involved. I killed the Surnainian and left them both in the room. We'll figure out what to do with them later."

Khair turned to Carol and firmly ordered, "Carol, hurry."

"Not you too." Carol, with her heart in her mouth, speeded up and did a fine job of weaving through traffic and cutting every corner that she could.

She parked in front of her building. They rushed out of the car and into the lobby. Carol had her key ready. Like a tidal wave, they burst into the apartment, Jorl in the lead and stun pack at the ready.

Jorl saw no signs of anyone, good or bad. "Sarn," he bellowed.

"Blazing suns, what?" Sarn's voice, edged with annoyed disgust, came from behind the closed bedroom door.

Jorl flung it open, and it banged into the wall with a crash, setting everything that was loose tinkling and rattling.

Jorl, Tarla, Khair, and Carol stood grouped just inside the room, and all of them reacted to the tableau that Eloise and Sarn presented.

"What the blazing and bloody sun goes on now? Are all of you suffering from a dose of space frenzy?"

"Sarn, get out of that bed," Jorl ordered. "Now."

"Why?"

He turned to a blushing, happily smiling Eloise who was cuddled up next to him under the jade green silk bedspread. She modestly tucked the spread around her, but one pretty, rounded globe peeped out from under the covers. They made a happy picture together in the big bed—red hair, white linen, green silk, and smiling faces mixed together in cheerful disorder.

Sarn, with total aplomb, put one arm around Eloise and the other behind his head and yawned. "You ever hear about the social nicety called knocking on a door before you open it?"

Tarla tried to hide her smile.

Jorl covered his feelings with a captain's stern command. "Out of that bed on the double, Lieutenant."

"Gee, Sarn honey, are you an officer, too?"

"Out." Jorl snapped out the order.

Eloise immediately started to jump out of bed, but Sarn held her back.

"Would the captain and his trusty crew at least turn their backs so I can put on my pants, or shall I leap to attention in my bare skin?"

Carol, thinking over the latest set of circumstances, tried to put the facts into some sort of order. "In whose army, for goodness sake? Will someone kindly explain just what is going on? You may exclude the obvious scene in here—I fully understand that."

"Two minutes, Lieutenant." Jorl, gesturing to the others, turned to leave the room.

Sarn threw him a salute and said, "Yes, oh mighty captain of the galaxies. Two minutes, sir"

"Gee, Sarn honey, it sounds important. You'd better hurry up."

"Come to think about it . . . blazing suns, it must be serious. You wouldn't have come to get me if it weren't. What's it all about, Jorl?"

"Surnainians," Jorl answered succinctly, turned, and closed the door behind him.

"Blazing, bloody suns!" Sarn leaped out of bed and grabbed his pants.

Eloise sat up, a puzzled look on her pretty face. Her long hair tried to cover what the spread fell from, but it only became more provocative.

Sarn paused, appreciating the total look of her. "You are beautiful," he said and continued his fight with his pants, "and I love you, and that's the first time I ever said that and meant it."

"Oh, Sarn, I love you more than anything, too." Eloise blushed happily and then asked, "What is a Sur—whatever Jorl said?"

"Trouble," Sarn answered. "Lots of trouble." His eyes glittered as wolfishly as the leader of the whole wild pack. "Get your clothes on and come out—hurry," Sarn, dressed, said over his shoulder as he left the bedroom.

Oh, gee, I wonder what the serious trouble could be. I wonder if it's dangerous, or maybe . . . oh, gee, I hope it will come out right. I know I love him, and just think, he said that he loves me, too. Nothing can be really bad, can it? I guess I'd better hurry—where's my . . .? Here it is . . . but I can't help being happy, and no matter what's wrong, it'll come out right. There, I'm ready to face things, I guess.

Chapter 12

When Sarn joined them in the living room, they brought him completely up to date—from the television announcement right through to the poor old dead Quill and the Surnainian.

"What's going on, Sarn honey? I don't understand. Are you in trouble?" Eloise asked.

"I, too, would appreciate some sort of an explanation," Carol sniffed, "especially as Eloise and I seem to be involved."

The four Zalleellians looked at each other, wondering about the wisdom of explaining. Finally, Jorl nodded to Tarla.

"Yes, Carol, we owe you much more than that, and Jorl, as captain of our crew, has decided that we should take you into our confidence."

"First of all, we come from a place much further away than Southern Asia."

"Gee, what can be further away than that place? Gee, you don't mean Russia. You aren't Russian spies, or anything bad like that, are you?"

"Whatever that is, no, we aren't," Tarla said.

"We come from further away than that—beyond your solar system." Tarla paused for a minute, thinking how best to explain something probably beyond their wildest thoughts. "We are officers in the Universal Federation of Space Command. We were sent on a routine mission. When this was completed, we were then free to begin our vacation. Our ship malfunctioned, went out of control, and we crashed in your desert four days ago." She waited for the two girls to grasp this startling information.

"You mean to say," Carol's usually controlled emotions got a jolt, "you're telling me, you mean that you, that all of you are . . . aliens, from way out there?" She pointed to the ceiling. "From the stars?" Her chin dropped in proportion to her widening eyes.

"Gee, you're not green, or anything. Oh, gee, excuse me. I mean, I don't mean to be rude but—well, you look just like us. How far away from home are you?"

Sarn laughed and hugged Eloise. "We are exactly two thousand thirty-five light years and forty-seven and one-half miles from home."

"Gee, Sarn, how can you laugh? It must feel awful to be so far away and have a crashed plane, or rocket, or whatever you call it. How will you ever get back? I don't think our government has anything we can lend you. Oh, what will you do?" Eloise's smile turned to concern.

"Don't know yet. But something," Sarn spoke with conviction.

"But now," Tarla continued, "to add to our transportation troubles, we have discovered that there is another faction of aliens here. It seems that we have accidentally landed in the middle of some sort of an invasion by the Surnainians. They are evil people, and somehow we have to stop them. It's an important part of our duty as officers of Space Command."

Carol jumped up, agitated, and paced the living room. "I simply cannot believe it. I'm hearing it, but I don't believe it. It's straight out of a science fiction novel."

"Gee, yes. Only better. This is real." Eloise put an arm around Sarn's waist and looked meltingly into his eyes.

The four Zalleellians laughed with warmth at Eloise's evaluation.

"Eloise," Jorl patted her head, "you're a loyal little thing with a one-track, all for the best, mind."

Tarla explained the chain of events that led up to the present moment.

Eloise and Carol were shocked, especially at the news of the two dead men.

"But why did you have to kill the Sur—what's his name? What makes them so bad? And what gives you the right to be both judge and jury?" Carol asked. "And what is all this talk about the Old Prophets? What if the police come? What if . . .?"

"One thing at a time, Carol, one thing at a time." Khair tried to stem the flow of questions. He put his arms around her and gently hugged her.

Carol, overwhelmed with too many thoughts, pulled away from Khair. "It's like standing on shifting sands—can't depend on any firm ground being under your feet. I don't like the feeling."

"Carol, lovely Carol, please wait until you hear the whole story before you judge. I know you believe in fairness. Please." Carol agreed with the "fairness" remark and allowed Khair to put his arm around her again.

"Gee, Sarn honey, are you married on your star?"

"When we're not serving on the Federation Star ship, we live on a planet," Sarn said with a laugh. "Stars are like your sun—too damn hot. And no, I am not married—on any planet. I was waiting for you." He gave her a hug.

"Gee, I am so totally glad, Sarn honey." Her face broke out into an all—over, brilliant smile.

Now that their immediate danger was past, Tarla remembered a few things. "Jorl, even though we found the case in his clothes, we now know that the old man wasn't a prophet. He couldn't be an Ancient because, when I did a probe, there was nothing in his mind that should have been there if he was. The Surnainians were using him for some other purpose. They also would have known that he wasn't an Ancient as soon as they probed his mind, and they would have mind-blocked him. That's why he was mumbling about not remembering something."

"I think you're probably right, Tarla, but the third sighting in the desert could have been one of the old prophet's ships, which would mean that they are after . . ." Jorl slammed his fist into his open palm. "That's what it was. The blue burn-off is the Surnainian's ship, and the Prophets were hunting it down."

"Logical." Khair nodded in agreement.

"Blazing suns, that means there should be two other ships close by. Think of all the spare parts." Sarn whooped in joy.

"Now, you've got me totally confused. Will you, for heaven's sake, explain about these different people." Carol, hands on hips, demanded an answer.

"Gee, yes, I want to know who are the bad guys and who are the good guys—so I know who to root for and who to boo at."

The four Zalleellians laughed at Eloise's unerring skill of reducing any situation to its absolute basics.

"We will have to go back to Quill's place and get the Surnainian's body. If the police and medical experts of this planet examine him, they'll soon discover he's not of this world. The eyes, for one thing, will give him away," Khair said.

"Why would that matter?"

"Because if the inhabitants of this planet had solid proof that an alien was among them, they would panic and start a search for others. They might notice us. It's very hard to convince frightened people that you mean them no harm," Khair said.

"Also," added Tarla, "it's against the laws of the Federation to make an unauthorized contact with life forms of any planet."

"Gee, Khair, Carol and I aren't frightened one bit, and we're people," Eloise said, puzzled.

"But you are Eloise. And you and Carol don't make a mob, either," Tarla said and smiled at both of them.

"What in heaven's name are you going to do with a body? With two bodies. How will you get them away without being caught? What is a Surnainian? I would really appreciate some answers."

"Gee, Carol, don't get all upset. They're going to tell us all about it—aren't you?" Eloise looked from one to the other.

"Yes, we are, Eloise. I was just trying to think of the best way." Tarla turned to the men. "I think it would be simpler and best if I spoke mind to mind with them."

"What? Mind to mind? What are you talking about?" Carol said. "I'm beginning to feel like Alice in Wonderland and that I'm having a talk with the Mad Hatter."

"I'll explain what happens," Jorl said. "Tarla can read minds and can transfer her thoughts to your mind."

"Gee, you lost me. Do you mean that Tarla can think thoughts at me and I will see them?"

"That's it." Sarn laughed with pleasure. "I think you're a whole lot smarter than you think you are."

"Will it hurt?" Eloise asked in a small voice.

Tarla felt a strange lump in her throat. "Not even a little bit," she said and smiled. "That could have been Elly talking," she said to the three men.

"Gee, that's your cousin, isn't it? I don't care if it does hurt—a little. Send me some thoughts. I'm ready. Especially about Elly."

"I absolutely do not like the idea of someone messing about in my brain." Carol wasn't enthusiastic about anything to do with the whole idea.

"It's only so that you may completely understand everything. Just words could cause confusion, Carol," Khair said, and put his arm around her.

Carol thought about it for a minute, came to a conclusion, and agreed, "Very well, Khair, I would like to understand everything, especially about you. Go ahead, Tarla."

Tarla smiled and began to speak in a soft and gentle voice. "I will start with the first day that Sarn, Elly, and I were on our way to Jorl and Khair's home and we found the old man."

"That would be the best place to start," Jorl nodded.

"Carol and Eloise, make yourselves comfortable and let your minds relax. I'm going to give you whole pictures of thoughts and impressions. It will seem as if you were actually there watching."

"Will it take long?" Carol asked, settling herself next to Khair on the long chesterfield.

"Only a few minutes. Eloise, get comfortable."

Eloise smiled widely and led Sarn to the other end of the chesterfield and curled up half on his lap. "I'm ready when you are."

Sarn smiled at her.

"Very well, I'll begin." Tarla settled herself for the close concentration she would need.

Jorl, Sarn, and Khair, who already knew the story, relaxed, glad to have a few minutes with nothing to do.

⁕ ⁕ ⁕

Tarla began.

A picture of a lovely summer morning, fresh and clean and sparkling with dew, which gave the look of diamonds, outlined every blade of grass and every leaf. It had rained the night before, and all the world smelled damp and green and living.

Three young people were ambling down a path lined with flowering bushes and delicate young trees. They were a younger Tarla and Sarn. Elly, their cousin, was with them. She was a little shorter and darker than they were and warmly lovely.

They were carefree and pleased with life. Laughing and teasing each other, they were on their way to the home of Jorl and Khair. Together, they had planned a lovely day. Suddenly, as happens to all young, healthy creatures, and for no particular reason, a surge of delightfully high spirits hit them. They jumped a hedge and raced off across a field toward a stand of trees, their young adult dignity forgotten. Hair flying, eyes flashing, they chased one another to the edge of the wood.

Tarla burst out of the trees and was the first to see the ancient figure sitting cross-legged under a huge old tree. He was more than motionless—he was utterly still in a pool of utter stillness.

The other two joined Tarla, and the three edged closer, poised for instant flight. I bet he's one of those old prophets that the Enforcementors are trying to suppress," Tarla whispered.

"Yes, they're supposed to be crazy, and they preach madness," Sarn added.

"Oh, do you really think so?" Elly shivered in excitement mixed with fear.

"I imagine the mentors are hunting for him now, but he had to stop for a rest," Sarn said.

"Really, Sarn? Oh, poor old man. Why does he not just . . . disappear like they are supposed to be able to do?"

"Don't be stupid, Elly," Sarn said.

"What's stupid about that? Everyone knows that's why they're hard to catch . . . don't they?" Elly asked.

Sarn, whose curiosity usually overrode his caution, and always driven by the need to know, went closer to the Ancient and said, "Will you speak with us, Old Prophet?" He stared intently at the strange old man.

"Oh," Elly scarcely dared to breathe, "do you think he really would? It is forbidden, you know."

"If you would keep quiet long enough, maybe he would."

"Oh, Sarn, you're always so cross with me," Elly said. She was close to tears.

"Listen, listen!" Tarla grabbed an arm of each of them.

All three held their breaths as the old man's lips began to quiver. Then, in an unbelievably sweet voice, he said, "Once upon a time, when our world was dying . . ." His huge black eyes, surrounded as they were by long, silky, white hair of head and beard, widened.

Silence.

Then he began to speak again. "Hundreds of years ago, when our world was dying—and men and women died—and the waters were without life, and life itself was choking . . ." His voice faltered, and a tear welled up in the corner of each now wetly brilliant eye.

"What do you mean, Old Prophet?" The lovely, golden-haired Tarla looked anxiously into the face of the frail old man.

The three young people, no longer feeling fear, gathered close to the old man to offer the comfort of their sympathy.

"Would you like some cool wine?" Tarla asked.

"Or maybe some of my cakes?" Elly offered.

The ancient, strange man stared for a moment into each perfect face. "I will try once more," he said, more to himself than out loud. He reached into a fold of his full garment and slowly brought out a flat, oblong box.

It was small enough to sit in the palm of his hand and was made of a gleaming metal that appeared to have its own inner light. He cradled the box in both hands and then brought it slowly, as if it weighed a world, up to the level of all their eyes.

"I need neither wine, nor food, nor even rest no more—forever." He spoke softly and sadly. "I have these."

He touched the inlaid symbol of the small case, and it opened and revealed hundreds of tiny red spheres. Each small, round bead pulsed with a warm pinpoint of reddish light.

The Ancient appeared lost in thought as he stared unseeing into the glow—and far beyond.

"How beautiful," Tarla breathed.

"Oh-oh-," Elly was lost for words.

Sarn stared, fascinated. "What is their power?"

"Their power?" The old man raised his eyes to Sarn and whispered, "They are the power of everlasting life—paid for by death."

He paused and then began again. "I will explain. I must make you understand." He gestured to the box. "It was these. These softly glowing tiny spheres that cost the life of a beautiful green earth, of many worlds, now threatening your lovely planet.

There was a puzzled silence until Tarla said, "Will you tell us how, please?"

"Oh, dear, is some sort of an epidemic coming? Is it very painful? Do people die?" Elly, upset, asked.

"Elly, you idiot, he means something philosophical. Don't you, Old Man?" Sarn asked.

"Yes, my children, a thing of the mind. The two plagues of mankind—greed for the power that great wealth can bring, and the terrible fear of personal dying."

"Then, what's the connection between what you say and those spheres?" Tarla asked.

"Yes, what?" Sarn added.

"I wish I didn't have to know," Elly murmured.

Sarn snorted with disdain.

Elly looked down at the ground and murmured even more quietly, "Well, I wish I didn't."

The old man looked at them with compassion. "Man seems to learn his lessons too late, but maybe this time . . . I will tell you a story."

Soon, under the spell of the old man's voice, which rose and fell with all the emotional notes of a beautifully played violin, the three settled into the stillness of complete attention.

"Many, many years ago, when the planet of the birthplace of our race was young, and fresh, and green, and . . . clean, strangers from the outer reaches of space came to our world. They came arrayed in beautiful garments covering their perfect bodies. They came like the gods of Ollinzus and offered to raise our people to the same dizzy heights of splendor. They, the gods, seemed happy to live among us, the lowly mortals.

They laid bare for us the secrets of atoms and universes. Man splashed joyously, with no prescience, in the almost overwhelming ocean of knowledge. The new branches of technology they taught gave leisure and wealth to everyone.

Then, the few skeptics among us, the scholars and the scientists, began to have grave doubts. There must always be a price to pay. Even a few of the most powerful leaders became concerned. They began to question, to doubt the goodwill of these strangers. To each of these skeptics, the godlike strangers gave a beautiful box that held the softly glowing red spheres, the giver of eternal life.

The skeptics said no more. That was the final flick that sealed the fate of my world."

The Ancient lapsed into silence. The spell of his voice still hovered—shimmering. The silence pulsed, but just before it shattered, with the consummate skill of a weaver of spells, the ancient spoke again. "Every desire was now in our hot grasp."

"'Surely,' all we men and women of Mostell said with one voice, 'there must be something we can do for you, man's greatest benefactors. There must be some way in which we can show you our gratitude.'"

"It has been our privilege, and has given us the deepest pleasure, to bring such happiness to the people of Mostell," our caring visitors replied.

"But surely there is something," we said.

"Well, if you insist, there is one small thing you could do to . . ."

"Anything," we cried.

"Very well, we would appreciate it if you would begin production of a special alloy, that which we call ULT, and upon which our civilization is based."

"Yes? Yes!"

"It would be an exceedingly great service to us if we could have one-third of your production of this substance for the next twenty-five years. After which time we would consider ourselves . . . overpaid."

"A pittance, a pittance. It is yours," cried all our people in unison.

"We had become their victims, and they sprung their trap. Much like the poor mouse when he tries for the cheese."

The Ancient paused, then continued. "It was—is—a wondrous alloy. From it, man fashioned everything for his every need—starships, buttons, clothing, food—this little box is made from it.

Some of us, who had been given the red spheres, began to feel another worm of doubt beginning to form—that maybe the price we were paying for life's pleasures was too high. So, to calm us, the aliens gave us, the skeptics of our world, the secret of replenishing the miraculous red spheres. The fear of the aliens refusing us more of them was now removed, forever.

Ah, my children, I see that the fundamental horror of my tale has begun to leap to your faces. Man, in his great greed, never asked, *Why?* No one asked the kind and generous aliens why they did not do their own manufacturing. After all, given the proper equipment, manpower, and the acres of land, it was really a simple process. No one asked them until it was too late.

This wondrous alloy, extracted from the earth, altered with their secret chemicals and by a simple process, caused the planet to be gradually stripped of its goodness and to be replaced by a virulent waste. Also, a strange kind of sickness developed for which there seemed to be no real cure. Over the next few years, the birth rate dropped alarmingly, and the few babes that were born were pitiful in their deformities.

Man, as seems to be usual, pretended not to see.

When the question was finally put to the aliens, the smiling gods merely pointed in all directions to the dying earth. "We value our own planet and people much more than untold wealth and everlasting life . . ."

"Oh, oh, the horrible . . . the terrible . . ." Elly was shocked by this tale of subtle horror.

"How wicked!" Tarla, full of cold anger, clenched her fists.

The Old Prophet paused, looking inward. From the depths of his soul's grief, he spoke softly and slowly—sadly and sorrowfully—"A few of us, each with his own container of Forever, secretly filled three spaceships with as many families as possible and escaped from Mostell.

"We soon discovered that our planet was heavily guarded. The aliens did not wish the word of our planet's death throes to be known by other civilizations. One of our ships was blown to dust. Another was so badly damaged it was captured, but my ship escaped. We have been desperately trying to atone for our crime ever since. And the crime was ours—the blame is justly laid on our heads. We, the most powerful of Mostell's leaders, did not use our power well. We were filled with greed, my beautiful children, greed." The pain and sorrow that filled him showed in his eyes as he paused.

"Our mission is to reach all planets before the aliens do and to warn the people that the price they will pay for their wonderful gifts is ugly death for their race and their world." The Ancient's voice quavered with deep sadness.

"Now, the aliens come by stealth and whisper in the ears of the powerful. The powerful do not want to believe us, so they aid the aliens in their hunt and help to suppress us. They hunt us down and kill us. We can be killed—and without the red spheres, we age and die.

"I have attempted to let myself die for the last seven hundred years. I ache to put down my burden of guilt and duty. I had thought to sit peacefully under this friendly old tree, and in the warmth of the sun, let my spirit leave this weary body." He bowed his head and sighed sadly.

"But suddenly, like an omen not to be ignored, you three, representatives of humanity renewed, gathered around me like a wall of glowing strength. I am given fresh courage and am driven to live still a while longer." He gathered himself up with a stirring of great hope.

"Now, I will show you that for which Man sold his planet, Mostel . . . his birthright . . . his Earth. Maybe you will be better able to understand his weakness." With a hand that shook, he slowly put one pulsing sphere on his tongue.

"Oh, Sarn, Tarla, look . . . look." Elly flew into Sarn's arms for protection from things she couldn't understand. Sarn never took his eyes from the old man, but he held Elly tightly to comfort them both.

Tarla was too spellbound to be frightened. Before their awed stares, an amazing transformation took place.

New dark brown hair literally pushed out the white. On his face, he applied a few drops of lotion from a little bottle that he carried that would prevent the growth of facial hair. Lines of age quickly filled, and the old skin began to glow with young health. In the space of five minutes, the frail, old man became one of them. He became one of them in apparent youth, but the soul looking out of his black eyes was one thousand years old.

"Even after seeing it, I think it's impossible." For once, Sarn was shaken.

"No wonder the mentors can't find you." Tarla, too, was beyond amazement.

"To give up such a gift—it's asking man to be godlike. No wonder you're having such a terrible time convincing people that the aliens are wicked," Elly said.

The strange man turned to Elly and gently touched her soft cheek. "You have gone right to the heart of the problem, child." Then, to all of them he said, "Will you help me to bring the truth of the Surnainians to your council of elders?"

"If you can prove to us that what you have told us is really true, then it becomes our duty," Sarn said.

"I agree with Sarn," Tarla said.

"Oh, dear, so do I, but oh, dear, what can we possibly do? What power do we have?"

"You have the power of youth who must think about your future children." The man smiled at the young people. "We must convince the powerful men and women of your world of the horror they would unleash. Then, all the rest will follow easily

"First, we must go and get Jorl and his dad. He will be more help to you than anyone else."

"Jorl?" The man asked.

"And Khair, his brother," Sarn added.

"They're right," Elly said. "Jorl is the man whom Tarla is going to marry someday. He's strong and smart, and he will do more than all of us put together." Elly admired Jorl. "Also, his dad is the president of the Council of Elders. That should help."

"Yes, that should certainly help." The Ancient smiled in full agreement.

"How do you plan to convince the council? Where will you start?" Sarn asked.

"This time, I want to get all the leaders on a starship that is hidden in space and take them to the ruined worlds. Show them. Take them on a tour of the dead things that once were alive and beautiful. Show them. Let them see. Then, they cannot pretend that it could not happen in their world."

"If we have to, we'll kidnap the whole bunch of them," Sarn said.

"I agree with Sarn," Elly said. "And now, what shall we call you? We can't very well call you Old Man anymore. You're much too young and handsome." Elly clapped her hands and laughed with glee.

He laughed and said, "My name is Mosets. Now, lead the way to the house of Jorl and Khair and the president of the council, and let us begin our task."

The three young people jumped up, filled with determined excitement at the adventure to come. The stranger watched them intently, smiled, and then the oldest young man in the universe nodded with an answering excitement and said, "This time, we shall succeed."

The four young people continued across the field and were back on the path that led to Jorl's house.

Chapter 13

The pictures faded from the minds of Eloise and Carol, and they slowly came back to reality.

"Gee," Eloise said, her eyes still clouded with the wonderful pictures. "Oh, Sarn, you haven't changed a bit." Eloise smiled up at him, pleased and content.

"And did you convince the council?" Carol asked.

"Yes," Tarla answered. "Jorl and Khair's father helped us. We soon discovered that the Surnainians, for that is who the aliens were, had convinced most of the remaining council members to not interfere with them, and in return, they were given the secret of the red spheres and the reward of eternal life."

"What did you do then, Sarn," Carol asked.

"What Mosets asked us to do. With the help of Jorl's father and two trusted members of the council, we kidnapped the whole bunch of them and took them for a ride on the spaceship. Believe me, that took some doing." Sarn grinned at the memories. "I can still remember the ruffled feathers and angry threats."

"Gee. I bet there was some mighty loud hissing and spitting."

"At first," Tarla said, "but it didn't take long for their attitudes to change. The dead planets convinced everyone, beyond any bribe, that nothing was worth the horrible death of any world."

"Shortly after our return," Jorl continued, "our planet called an emergency meeting of all the galaxies and made Mosets's crusade public knowledge. From then on, one of the basic duties of Space Command was to stop Surnainian activities once and for all.

"So, your worlds finally decided to help the poor old Ancients instead of hunting them down?" Carol asked.

"The Ancients always found the Surnainians when it was too late. The leaders for the dying worlds had already committed their planets. This action was already taking its toll on people's lives and their planet.

Now, we work together and try to get to the Surnainians before they get to the people," Khair said. "The idea is to remove temptation before it even begins."

"So now we have Surnainians on our Earth? Are they getting set to bribe our, eh, leaders, our authorities?" Carol asked.

"Gee, do the worlds really die from these people? I mean, is it really all that bad?" Eloise was unable to imagine it.

"I'll show you. Then, you can see for yourselves. Both of you close your eyes again, and I will show you the world of Mosets, the Ancient you have already met. a picture of a planet just starting to be sick and destroyed by the Surnainians." Tarla concentrated—put the whole pathetic, heart-rending scene in their minds—a planet full of death. She showed them another world only beginning to feel the first visible impact of the horror that would soon win—the ghastly look of impending death on the face of the population. They saw mothers holding babies that were more dead than alive—deformed and full of rotting sores. She moved to another planet even more advanced in sickness and death.

"Stop! Stop the pictures! Stop them, please." Eloise hid her face in Sarn's shoulder and sobbed.

"It's okay, Eloise, it's okay." Sarn held her close.

"Oh, my dear Eloise, I'm so sorry. I forgot that both of you are not as mentally conditioned as we are." Tarla gave Eloise a strong hug. "I'm sorry, I'll erase some of it."

"No, I mustn't be a coward. I need to remember." She cried into Sarn's shoulder. "The terrible, the evil, the, the . . ."

Carol had turned almost deathly white. Then, her eyes turned as hard as the line of her mouth. "How can we help stop the filthy creatures?"

"My dearest Carol," Khair held her close. "I think that you're the stuff from which Space Command officers are made." He felt a quiet, proud pleasure as he held Carol closer.

Carol sat up straight. Her eyes almost sparked with a burning light of realization. "But it's obvious that the Sur-What's-it-Names were more than smart. They bribed the rich people and the government with promises of eternal life. That was the truth, but, and there's always a but, they didn't tell them the whole story—that by the time they had mined the stuff for their reward, they and their whole planet would be dead from the terrible gases released from the making of it. Consequently, the secret of Forever would die with the planet, and the Surnainians would get what they had wanted.

"Gee, I wish I was as brave as Carol," Eloise sighed through her tears.

"You're perfect just the way you are, and I'm officer enough for both of us," Sarn said.

"But, Sarn, I will help you. I'll be scared, I guess, but I will help all of you any way I can." Eloise sat up, almost quivering with the desire to convince them she could, and would. "They are such, such, sneaky people."

"We know you will, Eloise," Tarla said. Compassion and warmth tinged her voice.

"All right, where do we begin? What tipped you off, anyway?" Sarn asked. "Was it only the eyes?"

"No." Jorl reached into his tunic pocket and brought out the small, shiny metal box. Without a word, he touched the inlaid symbol that opened it.

There they were, the greatest temptation to any man. The tiny beads of soft red light glowed, gently shimmering with the promise of something wonderful. The six people were deep in their own thoughts. A palpable quietness entered their room.

Eloise slowly went over to where Jorl sat, afraid of things that she could scarcely imagine. "Gee, that looks like the same kind of little box that the old man had. Is it?"

Carol went closer too, as if mesmerized, a hot look in her amber eyes. "Do you mean that those little beads can really keep you from aging? To stay young and never wrinkle, or sag, or be sick?" Her voice sank to an almost hoarse whisper, "Never get old—never die?"

Jorl heard something in her voice and looked up right into her eyes. He saw the glow of the spheres ignite an answering flame from deep within her.

She suddenly realized that Jorl might see her hunger and lowered a curtain of bland indifference over her 'windows of the soul'.

It was too late. Jorl knew that Carol burned for "Forever" and might not be able to resist the lure. He felt compassion for her, deeply understanding her need. Much stronger and much more brilliant people than she were unable to conquer their lust for a never-ending, healthy life.

Carol saw the look of understanding and knew what it meant. She knew in that fleeting second that there were no secrets between them.

"Gee, Jorl," Eloise said softly, "Do you mean that those pretty little things could make me live a long, long time? I don't have to be an old Ancient?"

Sarn put his hands on her shoulders and said, "There are enough spheres there to keep you just as you are now for ten thousand years."

"Really?" A look of pure wonder lit her whole face.

"Really." Sarn laughed and ruffled her hair.

Eloise thought for a minute, trying to crystallize a sea of emotions. "Gee, I don't think I would want to live that long. All your friends would die—and, and people would talk and say you were different, so you would have to keep moving away, and—well, I don't think I would want to. I read a book once called *The Wandering Jew* in which a man had that same problem, and I don't think I want that."

Carol's hands clenched and unclenched at her sides.

Tarla reached into her tunic pocket and then showed them an identical box. When she opened the lid, it, too, was full of Forever spheres.

"This is why Jorl and I first thought that the old man, The Quill, as Sarn insists on calling him, was an Ancient. I found this in his coat.

The Surnainian was going through the old man's clothes when we went in. Evidently, he was searching for the box of Forever. I wonder where the old man got it?"

"Pity you killed the Surnainian so fast. We might have been able to get a few answers from him," Sarn said.

"No." Tarla shook her head, "My mental powers wouldn't have been any match for his."

Suddenly, Carol leaped up from the chair where she had been sitting quietly and ran to the bedroom and slammed the door.

Everyone but Jorl was surprised.

"What happened?" Sarn asked.

Jorl spoke sadly. "How could you not feel it, Tarla? She's burning for these." He held up his box of spheres.

"Poor Carol," Tarla said. "I'll go to her mind—try to help her." Tarla looked inward and reached out to smooth Carol's troubled thoughts.

In a few moments, Carol came back to the living room calm and cool once more. "Sorry, people, I was overcome with the idea of never growing old. I've always hated the thoughts of it. No matter how much make-up you plaster on your face, you would still look wrinkled and ugly. And I hate make-up in wrinkles." She crossed the room and sat beside Khair. He put his arm over her shoulders and pulled her closer.

"Carol, you could never be ugly. You'll always be beautiful in my eyes.

With a small smile of love to Khair and in a faint tremor, Carol asked. "Okay, now that the, eh, mind bending is over, what's next on the agenda? Do you have a plan, Jorl?"

"Yes. I think we'll borrow your car, if we may, and get the corpses out of the old house and bury them in the desert," Jorl said.

"I agree," Khair said. "The sooner the better."

"May we borrow your car, Carol?" Tarla asked her.

"Why, yes. Eh, do you want Eloise and me to go with you?" She was absolutely horrified at the thoughts of the irregular burial—of any burial.

"I think it would be best if you stayed here. If anything goes wrong, you can report the car as stolen," Jorl said.

"Smart," Sarn agreed. "Let's get going."

Her expression of utter relief was intermixed with one of trepidation—no burial detail, true; but Jorl would have to drive her car. Carol handed the keys to Jorl. "You're not ready for the road yet, Jorl. I mean . . ."

"Hey, don't worry, Carol." In spite of the seriousness of the mission, it struck Jorl funny that Carol held such a low opinion of his driving ability. "Don't you have any faith in me? After all, I drove millions of miles to get here."

"And you crashed."

"Gee, Carol, be fair," Eloise said.

Jorl, momentarily taken aback, roared with laughter. "You can't hold me responsible for a malfunction."

"I suppose not." Carol's mouth twitched a little at one corner when she tried to hide a smile.

Sarn grabbed Eloise in a quick hug. "Expect us when you see us, baby, it might take a few hours."

"Oh, Sarn honey, be awful careful." Eloise hugged him, worry in every well-formed line of her.

"Blazing suns, it'll take more than a ship full of Surnainians to keep me away from you."

"You really must cut down on soap operas," Carol murmured.

From the doorway of the apartment, Carol and Eloise waved good-bye to the four of them.

"Oh, Carol, I hope they'll be safe. I hope nothing bad happens. I couldn't bear it."

"Don't cry, Eloise, please don't. They're trained officers, and they know what to do. They'll be fine, I promise."

Chapter 14

With the customary jolt of a too rapid acceleration, the four were off. The situation hovered between hairy and horrendous, especially through some of the more complicated intersections.

Jorl had somehow developed the knack of picking the wrong lane. He left a stream of bad-tempered, terrified motorists in his wake. Flocks of pedestrians also felt threatened. It was pure blind luck that the police weren't around to stop them.

"Blazing bullfrogs . . . what did I say? . . . I mean . . . galaxies. Will you quit trying to launch a land vehicle.

Look out for that—you nearly—damn!" Even Sarn, occupying the passenger's seat, felt his usually unflappable nerves twitching.

Jorl disregarded all comments and plowed on. They finally squealed to a bumpy stop in front of the seedy old house.

Sarn let out a huge breath and made a big show of unhooking his fingers from the door handle "Draw your stun packs," Jorl ordered.

They quickly scanned the street for any signs of life. Jorl, satisfied, said, "Okay, let's go."

They opened the car doors and got out.

It was a dark and sullen-looking street with only a couple of dim light poles that seemed to make it feel even worse.

"Tarla, sense anything?" Jorl asked quietly.

"Not yet."

Carrying the two blankets they had borrowed from Eloise, the four entered the sinister building.

On full alert, they went down the long hall. All their senses were tuned for the slightest irregularity. They came to the shut door of the familiar room.

They stood close to the wall, and Jorl reached for the knob—gave the door a push—and it slowly opened. Nothing happened. He looked around the doorframe. His eyes quickly raked the interior, and he went in, motioning the rest to follow.

The two bodies were exactly where Tarla and Jorl had left them.

"Poor old Quill," Sarn said. He stood looking down at the skinny, wrinkled body of the old man. He took one of the blankets and wrapped him in it. "There, that will at least give the poor old vulture back some dignity."

Jorl and Khair rolled the other blanket around the Surnainian.

They made a quick search of the cluttered room, but they found nothing that helped to increase their knowledge of the situation. At least, there were no signs of anyone else having been there.

"I think we should take them to the car one at a time—start with the Surnainian," Jorl said.

He stood over the two bundles. "If there's any interference, we'll at least get away with him."

The massive Surnainian made an awkward cargo for the three men as they wrestled him down the hall.

"He's a heavy son-of-a-space rat," Sarn said.

"Hunh," Khair grunted.

"Tarla, see if you can put that arm back under the blanket," Jorl said.

"Oh, damn, now the blanket's coming off." Sarn tried to make a grab for the loose blanket, but the Surnainian was too heavy to hold with one hand.

"Put him down for a minute. We've got to rewrap him." Jorl half turned to Tarla and pointed to the door. "Tarla, have a look outside."

She opened the front door, looked up and down the street, and scanned the windows. "It's clear."

They carried their unwieldy bundle toward the car and hurriedly tried to lay the Surnainian on the floor of the backseat. He was too tall and too big.

"We'll have to sit him up on the seat next to the door," Jorl said.

Even then, it was a tight fit, but it worked.

"Sarn and I can manage the other one, Tarla," Khair said. "You wait here with Jorl. It might be a good idea to start the car, Jorl."

When they reappeared a few minutes later, they laid the smaller bundle on the floor of the backseat.

"I suppose I get to ride in the back with the bodies," Sarn said. He climbed in with some difficulty, wondering where he should put his feet. He didn't want to step on, or sit too close to, either of the blankets.

Khair got into the front seat with Tarla and Jorl.

Jorl at least knew the way to their dirt road and headed in that direction. His driving was showing signs of improvement and soon, after a reducing number of near misses, they made it to the turnoff. They bumped along the dirt road until they arrived at the spot where the jeep had picked them up.

Jorl pulled to a stop. "Tarla, scan around—see if there's any trace of Surnainians."

After a minute of deep concentration, Tarla said, "I can't sense anything."

"Good. We don't need any more complications."

"I wish we had brought the transceiver to be sure of our directions," she added.

"Consider your wish fulfilled," Sarn said. With a smug expression, he pulled the small receiving set from his tunic pocket.

"Bless you, Sarn," Tarla said. "When did you think of that?"

"As soon as we got home the last time. I didn't want to get caught out here again without it." Sarn adjusted the set to pick up the homing signal. "Okay," he said, "take a right bearing."

Jorl left the road and drove the car in the direction that Sarn indicated. Sarn watched the direction needle. A few minutes later, he said, "Okay, bear a little to the left—a little more—good. Hold that heading."

They came to a place where they recognized the terrain.

"Full alert," Jorl said. "It could be a trap set by the Surnainians."

Even so, they felt a rising excitement—to see their ship again. Their hopes that they might be able to get home. Somehow.

Jorl stopped the car again about a mile from the crash site. "I think it would be wise to bury the bodies before we get any closer. Leave us free in case of trouble."

The other three agreed.

They got out of the car and began a search for a safe burial ground.

"There's an outcropping of stones over there and a bit of a hill." Khair pointed to his left.

"Okay, let's have a look," Jorl said.

"There's already a sort of a depression in the rocks," Tarla said.

"We can laser a bigger hole," Sarn said.

"Good idea. Get out your stun packs and set them on neutron laser," Jorl said.

Jorl and Sarn burned a larger crypt into the base of the exposed rock formation, and between the four of them, they placed the two bodies in it side by side.

The three men dragged over a large, loose boulder and melted it solidly into the opening in the stone face. Then, they pushed all the loose sand and rocks from the layered hole back to the original level and made it look as natural as the surrounding ground.

"I think we just might have found another career—terrain manipulation." Sarn laughed at the thought. "We're getting pretty good at hiding things in it."

All four of them laughed and then stood back, satisfied that they could see no telltale signs of any tampering with the land.

They got back into the car, and Jorl drove over the rough ground toward the crash site.

"There it is," Tarla said.

They recognized the large boulder that marked the opening to the buried space racer.

When Jorl stopped the car as near their buried ship as possible, he said, "Okay, I know I don't need to tell you to keep a sharp lookout. But, until we know more, we'll have to assume that we, or this planet, are under attack. Let's go."

They walked slowly toward the foot of the bluff and the boulder that covered the cave mouth, stun packs out and ready. They systematically scanned the ground and hills in all directions searching for the slightest indication that the site had been visited.

"Let's have a look around a wider perimeter. I'll take this section. Khair, you cover that one, and Sarn, you go up there on the bluff above the racer. Tarla, you wait here and scan in all directions."

In a short while, they met back at the entrance.

"No sign of any disturbance on the bluff," Sarn said.

"Nothing on this side," Jorl said.

"How about you, Khair?" Jorl's eyes were still on the move.

"No, nothing the least out of context," Khair answered. "Nothing that even faintly suggests a trap."

"I sensed nothing at all. I sent my mind searching in all directions, even into the ship."

"I hate this feeling of fighting with shadows," Sarn said.

"So do I," Khair said. "Help me wrestle this rock away from the entrance, Sarn."

"Actually, there's no need to enter the ship," Jorl said.

"Blazing comets, maybe not, but I, personally, want to see if I was dreaming. Maybe it's gone, or maybe it was never there. Maybe we're all hallucinating." Sarn was agitated as he violently helped Khair to move the rock.

The other three laughed, but underneath the laughter, they felt the same way. The need for reassurance was too strong for them to ignore.

They ducked under the low entrance and cautiously went down the narrow, short corridor to the open lock of the ship. It was as dark as a mineshaft. They had to feel and fumble for the switches that would turn on some of the auxiliary lights.

"Blazing suns, if there is anyone else here, we've totally lost the element of surprise." Sarn's disembodied voice echoed around in the total darkness.

"Especially after a bellow like that," Jorl said.

Khair found the switches, and the lights came on. "There, that's better."

In silence, they each looked around the interior of the ship, and they each felt the same tug on their emotions. This broken, small craft was their only link with their own lives.

"I guess we're hanging our hopes on a pretty thin string." Jorl's remark endorsed the thoughts that had crossed everyone's minds.

"I'm going below and having another look at the pile. Maybe it's not as bad as I thought." With that, Sarn disappeared down the hatch.

Tarla inspected her navigational console while Jorl tried the pilot's controls. Khair inspected the areas where the hull indents were.

After hard work and a lot of time, they had nearly completed their in-depth inspection. Some of the components didn't look totally useless. They still had a slight reason to be hopeful. Parts of junctions 2 and 3 didn't look too bad. The last and most important control—Section 1, Junction A—would tell the tale.

Finally, by using all of their combined strength, Khair and Sarn had a section on the rim of controls around the pile pulled partially open. Now, they could get enough of a grip to make the last attack on the cover. Under this cover would settle all the questions.

"This alone is not a good sign," Khair said. He grunted with the effort needed to remove the cover.

"You are so right. Blazing suns . . ." Sarn gave one last heave, and the panel cover flew off and landed with a loud clang.

All four of them just stared at the charred, fused, and melted components.

After a short, sad silence, Khair said, "I would hazard a guess and say that home is still a rather long way away."

Jorl poked at some of the charred ruins that Sarn held in his hand. "That's a damn black hole of a mess," he said. "I don't suppose that you've got any replacement parts for any of it, Sarn? Khair?"

"I think that's what they call =black humor in the face of the impossible. Anyway," Khair said, "all we carry on a space racer are for simple repairs, not for major burnouts like this."

"So, all we need to repair is what is almost beyond repair—junctions 1, 2, and 3, which then brings us to a totally useless drive. So, our only real problems are the whole compromised hull and the mostly destroyed drive . . . I guess we can't class them as minor."

Tarla's distress showed in her expression as she started up the companionway. "Oh well, we'll think of something." She smiled a small rueful smile. "Hey, at least we have some things to be glad about—we have lights and food." She continued on toward the main cabin. "Come on up now and let's make a cup of something."

The others followed her, equally sad, but just as determined to be as cheerful as possible about their situation.

"Yup. All we need is an army of trained technicians, a factory, some spare parts, and a good supply of tools and equipment—all of which, incidentally, I do not seem to see around here," Jorl said.

"Sarn's eyes began to glow with a sudden thought, and he hooted with laughter.

Jorl watched him with raised eyebrows and suggested, "The youngster appears to have been hit by an Earth bug."

"No. But all of you have forgotten the most beautiful thing on this earth."

They watched the cavorting Sarn, more or less suspecting temporary insanity.

"Don't you remember? Blazing suns—the Surnainians!"

Jorl pounded one fist into the other and said, "Of course. They got here by space vehicle."

"And if we can find it, we'll fight them for it." Sarn smacked Khair on the shoulder and continued his wild little dance.

"Beautiful. Just beautiful." Khair laughed and hugged Tarla and Jorl.

"Okay, we have lots to shoot for." Jorl suddenly thought about what he had said and grinned. "Pardon the pun." Jorl rubbed his hands together, glad of the prospect to have something constructive to think about.

"And, don't forget, there is still a good chance that Space Command picked up the trail we laid," Tarla said.

"I think we had better leave now before someone wonders why a car is parked out here in the middle of nowhere," Tarla said. After a short pause, she patted the bulkhead nearest to her console and said quietly, "I know I'm being silly, but I hate to leave her out here all alone."

"I know what you mean, but our first and most important job is to find the Surnainians. So come on everybody, let's get going," Jorl said.

Much as they almost hated to, they prepared to leave the little ship once more for an indefinite amount of time. Before they left, Jorl said, "Wait a minute. I think we'd better deactivate the positioning device. The danger of the Surnainians finding it far outweighs the hope of being traced by Space Command."

"You're right. I'll do it," Khair said.

When they turned into the dirt road, the car began spluttering and coughing, finally died, and coasted to a stop. Jorl was nonplussed, to say the least.

"Okay, Captain. Now what have you done?" Sarn said.

"Nothing. Not one damn thing." He tried turning the ignition key on and off.

No good. Dead car.

"Blazing suns, with the cooler off, it's getting hotter than a nova in here," Sarn howled. "What in great black holes is wrong?"

"Have you checked the fuel supply?" Khair asked. "I remember that Eloise said something about a fuel tank."

"How do you do that?" Jorl asked. He pushed and pulled every lever and knob he could find. "We never had to worry about a liquid fuel supply before, so I didn't pay too much attention to what she said. Do you remember anything about it, Khair? Sarn?"

Khair shrugged. "No."

"Me neither," Sarn said.

With their heads under the hood and totally involved in their mechanical problems, they failed to hear a motor noise until a vehicle pulled up in a cloud of dust beside them.

"Wal, now, having trouble?"

They looked up, startled.

"That's the same old coot that nearly broke my spirit along with my damn tailbone," Sarn shouted in his own language.

"Can't understand a word you're sayin', young feller." He spit, and then he looked closely at them.

"Say, you're the crazy furriners that got lost here three, four days ago. What in tarnation ya done now? Why, hello again, beautiful lady, you still mixed up with these dang furrin fools?" He got out of his jeep and said, "Mebbe I can help."

He got behind the wheel of the car and, about to turn it on, he noticed the gas gauge. "Wal, fer dang's sake. Yer outta gas." He pointed to the needle. "Empty as last year's birds' nests."

"How extremely clever of you." Tarla gave him her high voltage smile along with the praise. As usual, it melted the heart of the crusty old man, and he smiled back.

"Wal, get in the jeep and come back to my place. I got gas, but I ain't got all day."

"Thank you for your trouble," Jorl smiled at the old coot.

"Learnin' the lingo, eh?" He didn't feel any need of apologizing for his remarks. He still thought they were crazy furriners and didn't mind saying so.

Sarn looked ready to snarl when he hesitated before getting into the jeep.

"Maybe you would rather walk, Sarn," Khair said and smiled slightly.

"Huh, some choice—broken tailbone or parboiled. Blazing fireballs . . ." Sarn's expressive face showed that he hated the thought of that worse than the prospects of a ride in the jeep.

"Just get in, Sarn," Khair said.

"All in? Okay, here we go." The old man did a tight U-turn on the road and took off as if he had a JATO rocket stuffed up the tailpipe.

Jorl and Khair, not appreciating the bouncing any more than Sarn, at least tried to ride with the movements and thereby cut down on the bump effect.

Sarn tried to do this but, without fail, met the jeep seat on its way up just as his was coming down. "I'll kill that old bastard." He lunged for the old man's neck, both hands curled to grab it.

"What yer sayin', young feller? Ya gotta talk U.S. of A. if ya want an answer."

Khair grabbed at Sarn before he could clench his hands around the old man's neck, only half believing that he would never do such a thing.

The jeep viciously hit a rut, and as Sarn was half on his feet, it threw him back into the seat with a crash and made him bite his tongue.

"That does it. I swear I'm going to murder the old buzzard. Squeeze him to a pulp." Sarn howled, almost beside himself in anger. His hair stood up on end, as wild as his eyes.

Jorl sat on him, not quite on purpose, and began to laugh. He laughed till his stomach hurt. Khair joined in.

"Blazing bloodly suns, what's so damn funny?" Sarn yelled. "Ow-w." He tried to see the blood on his tongue by sticking it out, nearly rolling his eyes out of their sockets in the process.

All Jorl could do was point at Sarn before he dissolved into laughter again.

Tarla looked over her shoulder and said, "I don't think any one of you is behaving like an officer and a gentleman. Shame on you," she hissed as she smacked Sarn's hand when it tried to make another grab for the old man's neck. "Sarn, either cut it out, or get out and walk." She reverted to a sister's stern command.

Between the heat, the ride, and their laughter, Jorl and Khair were nearly helpless.

Sarn was saved from committing an unsocial act by the slowing down of the jeep as it turned into a vague driveway beside a cabin.

Even though the building was small and weathered, it presented a neat and functional appearance. An outbuilding, with a small corral in front of it, and a chicken coop were to one side and toward the rear of the cabin.

They jumped from the jeep with the same speed they would have used if they had to escape from a burning building.

Safely on the ground again, they tried to settle their various bones back into their proper joints.

Jorl caught sight of a bunch of bird things that clucked and pecked all around the place. "What are those? Pets? Or . . ."

"Them's chickens. Eggs for breakfast and roast for supper."

"Interesting," Khair said. He watched them for a few minutes.

"They're food? Alive?" Sarn could hardly believe what he saw. "You eat them?"

"Yup, food on the hoof, so to speak. Here comes the king of the flock now."

A large and magnificently colored rooster moved through his harem, conscious of his kingly grandeur and, head bobbing and wattles waving, came over to inspect the intruders. His beady eyes looked over all of them but seemed to make a beeline for Sarn.

"Don't come near me you bird, you," Sarn said. He kept backing up, but the king kept coming. He moved closer to Sarn and clucked in a friendly way.

Suddenly, they were startled by a loud, strange noise.

"Blazing suns, what's that?" Sarn nearly jumped out of his boots.

"Them's my two best friends," the old man told them. "Jessie and Tessie, the best donkeys a man ever had." He called out to the animals, and they answered back with happy braying. "We go out prospectin' together—come on over and meet the girls."

They followed the man over to the corral and gingerly stroked the animals.

"Oh, come on Sarn, they won't bite you," Jorl said.

"How do you know?"

"Well, you're bigger than they are—bite them back."

Sarn put up a tentative hand to stroke one. "They don't feel too bad," Sarn said.

"That's Jessie, and I think you have a friend."

Sarn tried to move away but Jessie came with him. She tried to nibble his hair and breathed on his neck. As he backed up, the rooster was right behind him. Naturally, he tripped and landed on his rear. "Blazing bloody suns!"

Then Tessie came over to see what was happening and suddenly let go with a loud bray. Jessie echoed it.

Jorl and Khair were practically doubled over with laughter. Tarla tried not to but couldn't help it.

Total noise and confusion reigned.

Sarn gave up and just lay there and laughed when the rooster almost sat on his head. The donkeys looked down on him, their faces nearly in his. Out came a big tongue and licked him, "Jheesh," Sarn said. He made a half-hearted attempt to wipe the lick off his face and push away the Girls.

The old man did his best, but the slapstick scene did him in. His head back and mouth wide open, he roared with laughter. He pulled out a handkerchief to wipe the tears of laughter away.

When things got a little bit back to order, the old man said, "You've got a way with you, young feller. The animals sure seem to like you."

"That doesn't make two of us." Sarn dusted himself off as much as he could.

"Admit it Sarn, you liked them as much they liked you," Jorl said.

They headed toward the cabin.

"'pears as how you folks don't know too much 'bout everyday things, though. City folks, I guess." He looked at them closely, his blue eyes much sharper than expected.

"We have been too close to our studies for too long, I think." Tarla quickly explained.

"S'pose so," he said and spit a good distance. "By the way, my name's Bill Bent." He stuck out a gnarled, strong hand. They introduced themselves and shook hands. "Well, nice names, different. Tarla, that's nice. So you're married to Jorl, and Khair is his brother, and Sarn is your brother. So, you used to be Tarla Dreela—hmm-m. Nice. Well, come in the place for somethin' to cool you off before we get the gas." He led them to the front door of the cabin and opened it for them.

Inside, it was sparsely furnished but clean and neat. Old Bill went into what they took to be the kitchen. He leaned over, pulled up a trap door, and started down the ladder.

The four watched him going down, not really understanding.

"The engine room, maybe?" Sarn whispered.

"Wait and find out, I suppose," Jorl answered.

Bill saw their puzzled looks and said, "Ain't you ever heard of a root cellar, either?" He shook his head. "Come on." They leaned over to have a closer look. "Come on down, dang's sake, you can't see much from up there."

"I don't detect any kind of a trap, Jorl, "Tarla whispered.

Jorl gave the okay sign to Khair and Sarn.

Not knowing what to expect, they slowly went down the ladder. It was at least forty degrees cooler. After the heat, it was like finding a heaven, and the final touch, to make it perfect, were the bottles old Bill took from an ice chest.

Sarn's face broke out into a smile big enough to light a room. "Beer." He rubbed his hands together. "Blazing icebergs, cold beer."

Old Bill quickly opened some bottles and passed them around. For the next few seconds, the only sounds were gurgles and deep sighs of contentment.

"Nothin' like a cold beer on a hot day, I always sez."

"You sez right, Bill." Sarn grinned at him.

"This room is a good idea in this country, Bill," Jorl said.

"Wal, when you haven't got electricity for to run an air conditioner, and your generator quits, you need one," Bill said.

They were in the middle of a light and friendly conversation, feeling safe and peaceful, when Sarn shot forward, lost his beer, and smacked into a wall. He let out a combined yell and howl when he fell and landed flat on his back.

A big canine grin with a sloppy tongue licked his face.

"Now what! What the blazing sunballs is it now?" Sarn struggled to sit up and to push the great, furry, slobbering face out of his. "What the great, bloody, blazing, damn suns is it now?" He caught a glimpse of it.

Sarn had drawn his stun pack. Khair had assumed a fighting stance, and Tarla tried to believe what she was seeing.

Bill helped Sarn to right himself.

"Great fireballs, what is it?" Sarn stared at the huge animal.

Attached to the dopey grin outlined by large, loose jowls and wrinkly skin over its eyes was a huge, reddish dog. He had a bit of white on his massive chest. He sat back and looked Sarn in the eyes, the long, red tongue lolling out one side of the silly grin.

Old Bill had hold of the dog's collar. The animal wriggled loose and went as close as he could to Sarn, obviously thinking Sarn was a long-lost friend. He kept putting his big sort of shaggy head under Sarn's hand.

"Seems as if you've got another friend, young feller. He don't usually take on so to strangers." Bill took a long pull of his beer. "Matter of fact, he usually bites first and thinks about it later." Bill kept looking at Sarn. "You do seem to have a special way with animals."

The other three patted the huge dog and generally made a fuss over him. He loved being patted, right enough, but he never stopped giving Sarn soulful looks and getting as close as he could to him. He would not leave Sarn's side and that, as far as the dog was concerned, was that.

They went back upstairs and found something to sit on.

"Sarn, be nice to him," Tarla said. "He really likes you."

Sarn gingerly patted the huge head that brought an immediate doggy sigh of pure contentment.

"Where did he come from anyway?" Sarn asked.

"'bout six months ago, he wandered in here, half—starved, and scared out of his wits. I reckon as how someone lost him. I never heard of anybody looking for him. Maybe the bastid lost him on purpose because of what old Doc. Mac said. The girl in the post office said that he was a real special breed of dog—very expensive—and sorta rare. She found his picture in a book she had. He's French. From France, and he's a—I'm not sure how to pronounce it but here's how it's spelled. Old Bill wrote it on a piece of paper—Drogue de Bordeaux, and it sounds sort like drogdabordoe."

"Old Doc. Mac said that there was a whole lot of somethin' else that warn't so highfalutin' in the mixture, that with a square snout like that he warn't no high-class anything. And I said, 'so what?'"

"What's his name," Sarn asked.

"Rusty," Bill said. "He can go up and down ladders slick as you please. Real smart dog. I never worry about any animals or men with him around. He can even be sitting down and, in a flash, make a six-foot jump straight up.

Rusty sat at Sarn's feet with his big head on Sarn's lap.

"Seems as how you now own a dog," Bill said. "I wouldn't let him go to just anybody."

"But I don't want a dog. What'll I do with a dog? Go away."

Rusty was hurt to the depths of his doggy soul and slinked a few feet away and lay down with a thump. Big brown eyes watched Sarn's every move. And he moaned, and he groaned—louder and louder.

Everyone tried to comfort him. He just groaned louder.

"Poor Rusty, come here by me," Tarla said. Rusty looked at her for a moment, but then let out another long drawn out moan and thumped his head back down on his paws and moaned.

Both Jorl and Khair coaxed him to come to them.

Same result. He raised his big head, looked at them, then thumped his head back down, and groaned and moaned in an ever-rising volume. He wouldn't even go to Bill.

Sarn couldn't take one more groan. "Come here. Blazing suns. Come here, Rusty."

Like a shot out of a cannon, Rusty plunked down beside Sarn and leaned heavily on him, the dopey grin pasted back in place once more. All was well in his doggy world.

When Sarn absentmindedly scratched him between his ears, Rusty's sigh of pure joy made everyone, including Sarn, laugh. "Well," Sarn said and smiled, "guess I'm stuck with you."

"Yup, seems so," Bill said as he lit his pipe.

"Kinda strange the way things happen. Matter of fact . . . seems like there's all kinds of strange goin' ons lately." For all the country drawl and bland expression, a feeling of tension entered the room. Old Bill's eyes were as bright as polished stones, and a greater intelligence than his general appearance would indicate shone through.

The four, still smiling and chatting, were suddenly wary and on guard.

"Really? What sort of going ons do you mean?" Tarla asked.

"Why . . . I almost expect to hear that Russians have landed in some kinda newfangled machine." He struck another match and sucked noisily on his pipe.

"What sort of machines—and why always Russians?" Jorl asked.

"Hum-m," Bill shrugged. "Russians seem the most likely, but I guess Arabs are just as likely, but who knows?"

"What have you seen, Bill? Anything interesting?" Khair spoke in a slow and apparently disinterested tone of voice and lounged back in the big old chair.

"Wal now, let me think." He paused, and his bright eyes, under bushy eyebrows, moved from one to the other. "About four, mebbe five, days ago, I was out in the barn feedin' Jessie and Tessie. In the morning it was, when a sudden strong gust of whooshing wind passed overhead and kicked up a mess a sanddevils. By the time I got outside to see what it was all about, there warn't nothin' there and no more wind. Just a smell, like after lightning hits—ozone, I think they calls it." He pulled a couple of puffs on his pipe. "Mighty strange, I said to myself."

The four didn't look at each other, afraid of giving themselves away, but they knew that the old man had described exactly the conditions that would have resulted if they had passed low overhead just before they crashed. And it was logical to suppose that this area had been in their glide path.

"And on the next day, as I was on my way to town, I picked up you folks on the road. Eh, you fellers Russians, or Arabs by any chance?" He took his pipe in his hand, pointed, and cast penetrating looks at each one of them.

"No," Jorl shook his head, "we ain't—aren't Russians or Arabs."

"But you're strangers to this country," old Bill bored in.

"Yes, we're strangers, but no one has anything to fear from us. We will do no harm and will soon be gone away again," Tarla said.

"I reckoned as much on all counts, so there ain't any need for you to tell me more. But that ain't all." He paused again, getting up to open more beer. "About three, mebbe four days ago, in the middle of the night, I get woken up by a queer sound, sorta like a swarm a bees, only louder. I got up and went out that door there and looked all around. I could hear Jessie and Tessie yellin' and tryin' to kick out their stalls. Somethin' sure scared them. Suddenly, danged if I didn't see a ball of blue light floatin' low overhead. It zoomed around a fair bit, then lit off toward the east. Then, be danged if the next night it was the same again, only the ball of light was more orangey and it went more south. I tell ya, folks, I'm sorta waitin' for one to land in the west, then I'll feel real surrounded."

The four just looked at each other without a word.

"That was certainly a lot of strange happenings," Khair said.

"Yup. Friends of yours, mebbe?"

"Have you spoken of this to anyone?" Jorl asked.

"Nope. They don't ask. I don't tell." He rocked the big rocking chair, and smoked his pipe, and drank his beer.

The four looked at each other and seemed to come to an agreement.

"The orange one might be a friend, but the blue one is not. If we come back sometime, will you tell us if you have noticed anything else different, or strange?" Jorl asked.

"Important?" old Bill asked.

"Yes," Jorl answered.

"Then, come back whenever you like."

"Thank you for everything, Bill," Tarla said.

"Yup." He got up again, stretched, and said, "Sure hope they stop comin' around. It's beginnin' to feel a mite crowded around here. Now, let's get the gas and get you back to your car." He went outside, took a gas can, and walked toward a tank on the far side of the cabin. The others followed, not knowing quite what to think.

They were waiting for the container to fill when Jorl spoke. "Do you travel much? I mean, out that way?" He pointed toward the east.

"Yup. Me and my two girls range all over prospectin'. Why?"

"If you discover anything strange, stay away from it. Danger." Jorl, afraid of saying too much, nevertheless felt duty-bound to warn old Bill.

"Dangerous, eh?" Bill spat.

"Maybe. If you see anything, get away instantly—tell us when we return."

"Shotgun any good?" Bill looked squarely at Jorl.

"No," Jorl said.

"But you would kinda like to know to the east? The blue one?" Bill said softly.

"Yes, but without harm to you," Jorl said. "Don't take any chances."

"Then me and the girls will play Indian—careful and quiet."

"You're a fine man, Bill." Tarla laid her hand on the old man's arm. She realized that he, without even knowing how dangerous it might be, was unconditionally offering his help.

Khair heard what Bill had said. "You must understand, Bill, that the danger is real. We do not want you to be destroyed because of us."

Bill and Khair looked into each other's eyes, reading below the surface. They both understood without a word being spoken. They shook hands on a pact between them.

"Shucks, me and the girls were going that way anyway. Time we had another little trip."

When the gas can was full, they headed back to the jeep. Rusty tried to sit in Sarn's lap.

"This will never do. Tarla, let me sit in front. Rusty wants to sit in my lap, and he's too blasted heavy." He heaved Rusty off him and jumped into the front seat. Rusty followed Sarn and claimed the middle of the seat, sat up, tongue hanging out, his bright eyes fixed on the road ahead.

Sarn watched Rusty, heaved a sigh, and followed Rusty in. "Move over, you big lump."

Bill got into the driver's seat. Sarn looked at him and said, "Can you go a little slower? Wouldn't want Rusty to bounce out." Sarn smiled around clenched teeth.

"Slower? Yup."

Soon, they saw Carol's big blue car just where they had left it.

"There it is," Sarn said, "looks okay."

Within a few minutes, it had water and gas. After a short session of priming the carburetor, it started. The air conditioner began to labor, clearing out the heavy heat.

Jorl said, "Well, Bill. We can't thank you enough—for everything." He shook Bill's hand. Tarla, Khair, and even Sarn politely shook hands, and they thanked old Bill.

Sarn suddenly noticed Rusty's strange behavior. "What's wrong, Rusty?" Rusty sat on the ground and howled. He kept turning his head from Bill to Sarn. "Oh, I know. He doesn't know what's happening, and he has to choose. Poor old Rusty. But I guess you should come with me. Say good-bye to Bill."

Bill came around the car and stood beside the unhappy dog. "It's okay, Rusty boy. I know you won't forget me, and I'll be seeing you soon. Go with Sarn," he said and turned Rusty's head toward Sarn.

"Come here, Rusty. We'll look after each other." He patted the big red dog and gave him half a hug. Sarn opened the back door for him to get in.

Rusty looked at Sarn and the back door, then went and stood at the front door and barked once. He looked from Sarn to the door. There was no mistake as to where Rusty wished to sit.

Sarn smiled ruefully and did as the dog demanded." Move your big rump over. I need some room, too."

"We'll see you in a few days, Bill. In the meantime, be careful," Tarla said and waved good-bye.

"Yup."

Khair looked out the back window as they drew away. "Good. Bill is back in his jeep and turning around."

"I hope that he'll be careful and not try to do anything by himself," Tarla said. "What a nice man he is."

"Yes," Jorl agreed, "he is. And a lot smarter than he lets on."

Chapter 15

They reached the main highway, relieved that everything had turned out well.

"Jorl, I feel we should hurry," Tarla said. "I have a sense that something's wrong."

When they got to the apartment building, they parked the car and took the elevator up to the apartment. Jorl knocked. No one answered.

"That's odd," Jorl said quietly. He started to unlock the door with the key that Carol had given him. "It isn't locked. Stun packs out. Stand back." He slowly pushed the door open.

They stood in the doorway and they could not believe what they were seeing.

They entered the apartment prepared for anything.

"Great blazing suns, what happened? What . . . where are the girls?"

Tarla said, "They're not here. Jorl, there's trouble.".

"Can you sense anything, Tarla? Anything at all?" Jorl asked. He, Khair, and Sarn ran to check out the rest of the apartment.

"The place looks as if an angry solar wind just went through it." Kair said.

"Oh, Jorl, nothing is left but a strong feeling of . . . of fright, almost terror. And that same frightening cold." She shivered violently.

"What if Carol and Eloise were kidnapped by the Surnainians? Blazing suns, why? Why the girls? Oh, great heavens, what if . . .? Sarn was horrified at all the possibilities—of harm coming to his dearest Eloise and to Carol.

"They must have seen us with them," Khair said with pain deep in his eyes. "That would mean that we are being watched."

"Surnainians on our trail?" Jorl said. "How would they . . . how could they know about us?"

"They were looking for something. And something quite small, or else why slash the furniture?" Khair said. "Even the cushions."

"Surnainians," Jorl said. "Has to be."

"I think that they must be searching for the Forever spheres," Khair said. "But how . . .?"

"No matter what, the girls are gone. Let's get to the hotel, fast. Maybe Carol and Eloise got away and went there." Sarn turned and ran for the elevator. Rusty was nearest to him. The other three were moving fast. They scrambled into the car and headed for the hotel.

For the last hour, the sky had been heavily overcast with racing, sullen clouds that had been let loose as the heavens were ripped and torn with thunder and lightning. Rain fell down hard enough to jump six inches when it hit the pavement. Visibility was reduced to almost nil, and Jorl was forced to drive at a crawl—the wipers hardly cleared the windshield, and the lights glared into his eyes. Tarla, beside him in the front seat, tried to help navigate through the storm and traffic.

"Well, I thought that it didn't rain and storm in a desert," Tarla said. "What's going on?"

"If conditions are just right, it can, but it's rare," Jorl said.

Suddenly, Khair shouted, "Look! Over there. I think I see them." He rolled down the back window to see better and squinted through the curtain of rain that immediately pounded into his face.

"Where? Where?" Sarn slid across the backseat to look out the window. He also caught sight of them and yelled. Rusty barked his loudest. They were screened from a clear view by lights and traffic, but Khair saw one of the figures turn her head for a second, then quickly follow the other further along the street.

"There they are. Turn around, Jorl," Khair said, "quickly."

"Black bloody holes. I can't turn here. There's too damn much traffic."

Vehicles rushed past them. Across the next intersection, Jorl found a side street and turned to his right. He quickly made a U-turn in the narrow dark street by bumping up and down over the curbs.

"At least you missed the lamppost," Sarn said. "But that garbage can might not recover. Get back out on the main street, Jorl. Come on."

"There's too much traffic," Jorl said. "I have to wait for an opening."

"We'll lose them. Hurry up, hurry up, Jorl," Tarla said.

"Carol would launch me if I smashed up her car."

At last, there was a momentary lull in the traffic, and he hit the gas. He made a wide left turn across two lanes of traffic. Brakes screeched, horns blared, and confusion reigned supreme for a few seconds.

"You're going too fast," Tarla said and held on for dear life, doing her best not to panic.

"Can't hurry and go slow." Jorl had a tight hold on the steering wheel.

The wet pavement was slippery, and the car fishtailed when Jorl tried to cut into the far lane.

"Stop the yaw," Sarn shouted. He sat bolt upright, white knuckled hands on the doorknob. Rusty tilted into him and breathed in his face.

Jorl tried to compensate. He did, nicely. Unfortunately, an old truck, loaded with crates of something or other stuff, tried to occupy the same spot that Jorl was heading for.

"Hang on," Jorl warned.

The four of them were absolutely quiet, waiting for the inevitable. It was like watching a study in slow motion. Jorl rammed the truck broadside, slewed it around, and it promptly tripped over the curb and laid itself neatly on its side. It was now raining chickens and vegetables along with the original rain.

They sat in silence—watched with a dreamy, detached interest—like it wasn't real—more like a silly movie, perhaps.

Sarn shook himself and said, "Congratulations, Jorl. You have perfected your ramming technique to an unbelievable degree."

Khair kicked Sarn on the ankle and gave him the sign to shut up and don't touch off a volcano.

They sat where they were for a minute longer—watched the mayhem and the traffic pile up noisily in all directions. They got out of the car. A disgusted, disgruntled cop showed up. The truck driver jumped hysterically up and down as he screamed and yelled between wild grabs for loose, squawking chickens.

Sarn watched the farmer catch a hen and put it in a crate. Since the crate had one side broken out of it, the chicken walked right back out and rejoined the fray. "At that rate," Sarn whispered to Khair, "he'll get a hundred in that one case, easy."

Even though Khair felt pangs of sympathy for the farmer and some concern for the dangerous situation that they were now placed in, he couldn't help but chuckle, quietly so that Jorl wouldn't hear, at Sarn's observation.

Rusty evidently thought it was a new game and loudly helped the man gather chickens. The chickens didn't like it very much.

Meanwhile, Jorl and Tarla tried to explain things to the policeman.

The violent storm, sheets of rain, blaring horns, and yelling motorists made enough confusion and noise to nearly drown out a howling dogfight. Rusty and the farmer's dog took an instant hate to each other.

"This is too much." Sarn held his hands over his ears.

"Do you think the car will go, Jorl?" Tarla whispered to him when the policeman turned his back to deal with the irate farmer.

All of them were soaked to the skin. Sarn's hair was plastered to his skull, but suddenly, in the midst of loose chickens, dogfight, yelling, and thunder and lightning, Sarn whooped with laughter. "So much for Federation rules and . . . he laughed even harder, "wait until Admiral Emslin . . . this is too much. Oh, my stomach."

"Put a lid on it, Sarn. We've got to get out of here, right now." Khair turned to Jorl and said quietly, "See if the car will start, Jorl."

Jorl got behind the wheel and turned the key, and wonder of wonders, it started and ran as smoothly as ever. Jorl nodded with relief.

"Good," Khair said, "let's leave. Sarn, go get Rusty. Hurry."

Sarn ran over and forcibly broke up the dogfight, pushing chickens left and right in the process. "You crazy dog." Sarn grabbed Rusty's collar.

"Sarn," Jorl said quietly, "stun the whole crowd with the lowest charge—give us time to get out of here."

Sarn sprayed a mild beam in a complete circle.

Jorl backed the car away from the truck. That caused a stray, soaking-wet chicken, which had perched on the roof of their car, to slide off and land with a splash and a thump on the hood with an annoyed squawk and face-to-face with Jorl. It startled Jorl. "Get off. Damn bird. Go away."

Rusty's tongue lolled out one side of the grin that was wider than ever. He looked up at Sarn with bright-eyed excitement and licked him.

"You enjoyed that, didn't you, Rusty?" Sarn bundled Rusty into the backseat and squeezed in after him. "You smell like a wet dog, or a wet something. Get off me. Move over. You idiot dog." He threw back his head and roared with laughter at the whole situation. Tarla and Khair couldn't help but agree. Jorl remained unsmiling.

Jorl inched the car through a narrow opening, being fair in his paint exchanges as he wove his way clear of the tangle.

Sarn sprayed the stun pack as they went.

Tarla, looking back, said with sympathy, "They'll never know what happened—won't know who to blame. What a mess!" She felt sorry for the farmer. "Sarn, give me an extra minute. Jorl, stop the car. I'm going to leave some money in his truck." She took some bills from Jorl and ran back to the overturned vehicle. She hurried back into the car and shut the door. "There, I feel better for that. It still means a lot of trouble for him, I know, but that should help to soothe him somewhat."

Jorl agreed as he began weaving his way out of the traffic and chicken jam.

Finally, they were travelling back up the street. "It was right about there that I saw them." Khair pointed to a neon sign.

"I'll find a place to park the car along here somewhere, and then we'll do a thorough search of all those buildings. They can't have walked far in this storm."

When Jorl parked, he said, "Search as fast as you can. Meet back here in half an hour and don't miss a place."

"They must be terrified," Tarla said.

Through the driving rain, they hurried off in different directions.

Chapter 16

Meanwhile, after the four Zalleellians had said good-bye to Eloise and Carol and were on their way to the old house to complete the burial detail, Carol slowly closed the door of the apartment behind them.

Carol and Eloise were quiet, each lost in their own thoughts.

"Gee, Carol, I hope they don't get into any trouble with the police, or anything. What if they get stopped, and the policeman sees the two—oh dear—two corpses in the car?" A frown of worry wrinkled Eloise's smooth forehead.

"Them! What about us, for goodness sake." Carol paced back and forth, her agitation showed in every lithe movement.

"But we're sitting here all safe, and they're the ones in danger. They could get caught or killed by those awful people."

"What about danger by association? Don't you realize that by law we are accomplices? We are aiding and abetting a crime. Eloise, sometimes, you really are almost too much." She was annoyed and somewhat confused by the whole situation. She continued to pace like a caged panther. "Why did we ever get mixed up with them? Why? Strangers from the sky, for heaven's sake."

Eloise, even in the face of all that Carol had said, giggled. "Well, maybe not from heaven, probably not angels."

Carol stopped pacing for a second to look at Eloise. Then she just relaxed and laughed. "But why not a nice dentist, or an accountant, or even a lawyer from New York? Someone with a stable, safe future?"

"Oh, Carol, we already agreed about dentists and accountants. Don't you like Khair a whole lot? And what about the others? I know you have feelings for Khair. I know he thinks a lot of you."

"Where's the future? Off into the sunset—to another planet? It's ridiculous. It's . . . it's . . ." She threw up her arms in frustration and couldn't think of a word to describe the situation. She continued to pace.

"Gee Carol, I don't understand you. They're wonderful people. Besides, I'd be happier than I have ever been in my whole life to follow Sarn anywhere, to any weird place."

Carol stopped her pacing right in front of Eloise and looked at her. "Just what do you mean?"

"I mean . . . I mean that I love him." Eloise's eyes glowed softly, dream-filled.

"You surely can't be serious, for goodness sake. It's . . . the whole thing . . . it's . . . totally impossible. Think about it. They're not from just around here. Not from another country. Not even from this planet. According to them—from another planet! Do you really understand that, Eloise? You'll get over it." She continued her nervous pacing.

"I will not. I love Sarn. And I will, forever and ever. And please, Carol, please, please sit down."

Carol stopped in mid-stride. Her amber eyes glittered with swirling thoughts. Forever—forever and ever.

"And I mean it," Eloise said.

Carol turned quickly. "I mean the red spheres. They have two full cases of them." Her voice turned soft and dreamy. "Two full cases—twenty thousand years—just think . . ."

Her tone of voice upset Eloise. "Carol, we already agreed to forget those. Carol? Carol?"

"What?" Carol snapped her mind back from her dreams. She barely concealed a cunning look.

"I've never seen you like this before. You act as if you have a coiled spring inside you. Like you might explode any second. Carol, please stop. Let's make some tea. Carol, you're scaring me." Eloise watched her. She caught a faint glimmer of what was in Carol's mind, and it horrified her.

Carol slid back into her thoughts. The remembered gentle, soft glow of the red spheres suddenly exploded into a fiery, scarlet flame that filled even the tiniest space in her mind. Only brutal self-discipline stopped the hot rush of wanting that nearly choked her, and she forced it down deep, away from anyone's sight. "Silly Eloise, what we need is a drink. Come on." Carol led the way to the kitchen and made two tall, cool, gin drinks. They took them into the living room and relaxed. Carol listened as Eloise chatted away about Sarn and everything to do with him.

Carol listened on the surface, but her inner self was lost in thought. Her mind was racing. I can't stand this Forever thing too much longer. Red spheres. Never die. Never grow old. I can't sit still a second longer. It's too much—too much to think about. Damn. Damn. Damn.

"Come on, Eloise. Let's go out for supper. We'll go to that little Italian place on the corner. You know how much you love the mushroom and chicken cannelloni with lots of sauce. Come on. I'll even treat us to some Chianti."

"Gee, that would be fun." Eloise jumped up, ready to go out. From habit, she crossed the living room and looked out the window. "Gee, the sky looks sort of weird. I've never seen it like that before. Come and see, Carol."

"Never mind the sky, Eloise. We'll be in the restaurant in five minutes, so come on, let's go."

It was getting late in the afternoon when they left the cozy restaurant. They walked slowly toward the apartment, enjoying the cooler air. Carol, more relaxed after a pleasant meal and a drink, even felt a little tenderness toward Eloise's constant, cheerful chattering about Sarn. They got out of the elevator and walked toward their door. Carol had her key out to unlock it when she noticed that it was open a fraction.

She and Eloise looked at each other, startled.

"I tried the door when we left. It was locked," Carol whispered.

"Do you think someone's in there?" Eloise whispered too. "Oh gee, Carol, I've got a nervous, shaky lump in my stomach. Maybe . . . maybe Sarn and the others have come back?"

"I don't think so. Something's not right." Carol opened the door an inch at a time and tiptoed into the apartment, with Eloise staying close behind her.

It took a few seconds for them to assimilate the fact that the room was in shambles. Eloise's mouth and eyes made silent, round O's. Carol realized the place had been ransacked and was about to let loose an angry torrent of words when the bedroom door suddenly opened wide.

A huge man filled the space. For a split second, the stranger did not see the girls.

Carol's instincts for self-preservation were immediately aroused.

She spun around, pushed Eloise ahead of her, and hissed, "Run! Run!" She slammed the door behind her, and they flew off down the hall like a pair of frightened gazelles. "In here." Carol slammed Eloise through the fire door and pushed her toward the up flight. Carol, even though frightened, and as her impression of glowing, hypnotic eyes grew larger and larger in her brain, still reacted smoothly in the emergency.

Eloise, a step ahead of her, suddenly froze in her tracks. She clutched at her head—covering her ears—her mouth open in a silent scream.

Carol felt the same sudden jolt of a mental command to "halt". She instinctively set up a mind block, even though it wasn't nearly strong enough to stop the blast. She screamed at Eloise as she shook her and yelled, "Think hard about something! Think about cake! Say cake! Cake! Cake! Run, Eloise! Get going!"

Eloise made a supreme effort to throw off the paralyzing command in her brain. She took a few jerky steps and half-whimpered, "cake, cake, cake—chocolate cake." Trembling with the effort, she tried to move her legs faster.

"That's it, Eloise. Try! Cake, cake, chocolate cake!"

They ran up the stairs fast—faster to the top floor, screaming the words. They went through another fire door and found the freight elevator at that level.

"Cake, cake, chocolate cake!" Eloise continued to scream.

"Whipped cream, calories, fat, cake!" Carol screamed in concert.

They were still moving like puppets but gaining some control of their minds. They rushed into the elevator, winded and frightened.

Carol pushed the basement button. "Keep yelling, Eloise." She gasped for breath. "Keep your mind too busy to let him in!"

Eloise, near collapse, her hand to her throat, whispered hoarsely, "I'll try." Faintly, she cried, "cake—cake—chocolate cake." As her voice weakened, the command in her brain grew more intense.

"Scream it out, Eloise!" Carol shook her—hard.

All the way down in the elevator, they screamed their chant. The doors opened into a dim and, thankfully, empty basement. They ran for the garage door. When it opened, they were hit by a high, screaming wind. Frantically clutching their clothes and squinting their eyes, they ran up the street, their screaming drowned in the violence of the wind and street noises. They came to a corner and leaned against a building to rest. Their breaths came in hot, ragged sobs.

After a few minutes, the terrifying panic and exhaustion began to ooze out of them. Carol held her head up and listened inwardly. "I think he's gone, Eloise." Carol clutched Eloise's arm. "How about you? Has the voice gone away? Can you still hear it?"

"No, not anymore." Eloise was close to tears. "Where's Sarn? Who was that awful man? What's happening, Carol?" A faint note of hysteria tinged her voice.

"Get a grip on yourself. Come on, we've got to get further away." She tugged at Eloise.

Heading for uptown, Carol set a fast pace. Eloise clutched her hand and stumbled along behind her. Neither of them could resist looking backward every few seconds.

"Now we know how a poor, dumb, hunted animal feels." Eloise was close to tears of exhaustion and fright.

"It's worse for people—they can think," Carol answered. "Now, come on."

Fighting the high wind, they soon neared the business district and felt better on seeing lights and people.

Suddenly, there was a frighteningly loud clap of thunder, and the sky darkened to an alarming degree and added an even darker shade of a sinister-looking color. The heavens opened up, and down came a torrential downpour accompanied by dazzling, flashing bolts of lightning.

"Carol, what's going on? What's happening? I'm scared. It's not supposed to rain in a desert." Eloise was still shaken from their escape from something frightening.

"It's only a storm, Eloise. It happens sometimes. Keep running. Come on."

The rain roared down harder than ever, and they were now soaked to the skin.

Eloise thought she heard someone call her name and tried to peer through the curtain of rain. "Did you hear that, Carol?"

"No. I hope that damned stranger hasn't found us again."

"But I thought I heard Sarn, Carol. Oh, Carol," Eloise wailed.

They stopped for a moment to catch their breaths, looked at each other, and felt the wave of panic threaten to rise again.

"Carol, do you think that terrible man can pretend to be someone we know? That it could be a trap? Oh, Carol," Eloise tried hard to not be overcome by another whole bunch of horrible ideas.

"Could be. But blubbering won't help, so stop it. Come on."

They hurried a little further down the street.

"Look, there's the bus station. We'll go in there, dry off a bit, and call the hotel," Carol said.

"And h-have s-some coffee. But I absolutely won't ever, never want a piece of cake again." Eloise's chin wobbled. "Never."

They pushed through the door into the haven of the depot with its shelter and bright lights. They found a warm corner and fell into the seats with heartfelt thankfulness. Neither of them spoke for a few minutes.

Eloise's pansy eyes were far away in thought. "Carol, isn't it funny how things you always thought were so important, aren't—and how other things are?"

Carol sighed. "Now what confusion torments your poor little brain? Just relax. I need to think of what to do next." Carol leaned back with her eyes closed. Like any sensible animal, she took advantage of every moment to rest.

Eloise, pensive, wrestled with hard-to-express ideas. "But yesterday, Carol, we thought we needed our pretty apartment, closets full of clothes, and everything else we have, and tonight, this noisy, warm, dry old depot is heaven."

"And if we were in a jungle, all we would need would be a few branches over a pole and a fire to keep us warm and to scare off wild animals. That's just the law of survival, Eloise. Everything is relative."

"Is it? Well, it sure proves what's really important. Oh, I wish Sarn was here." Eloise leaned back in the chair, an unhappy, wet little bundle.

"Come on, Eloise. Let's go to the washroom and make ourselves presentable." Carol had looked in her mirror and was disgusted.

"Okay. But—but what does it really matter how we look? Any minute, that awful man might show up, and we would have to run in the rain again."

"It matters a lot. It always matters what sort of a face you put on. Come on, my dear Eloise, philosophizing is hard work. Leave it to the ones who love to spout it. And we both look a mess." Carol headed for the washroom. "Come on. We'll get coffee when we come back."

Eloise shrugged and followed.

They came back to their seats in a more presentable condition.

"There, that's better. Now, we don't look so much like poor little waifs. And the coffee is good. How's yours, Eloise?"

"Good. At least I've stopped shivering."

"Let's go sit at that table over there. Then, we can see the door and the street."

Now that the fright had almost gone, they were able to discuss matters. There had been no answer when they called the hotel room.

"I wonder if that big brute is out looking for us?" Carol said.

"Oh gee, Carol, I hope and pray not. I don't think there's any run left in me."

"I wonder where Khair and the rest of them are?" Carol said. "Some answers would be good."

"Do you think that awful man could have people working for him? What's so scary is, it could be anybody, in here or out there," Eloise said. "I just felt a shudder that went from my toes to my head."

They both looked out the window and watched the heavy rain being thrown about by wild gusts of wind. It made a black and unhappy night.

"Carol . . ." she clutched Carol's arm hard in a convulsive wave of fright. "Out there. I saw something."

Carol peered into the storm. "Where?"

"There—across the street. See it?"

In the darkness, Carol saw a flicker of movement across the edge of the asphalt. "I see something, and it's coming closer. It's an old man."

For some reason, the old man gave the impression of furtiveness, the feel of a sly, emaciated bird of prey down on his luck.

He came toward the big double doors and, wrestling with the wind and the weight of them, managed to get inside. He stood there in the bright lights of the bus station, a scrawny, unkempt old man.

Carol and Eloise never took their eyes off him. He pulled his battered hat further over his eyes and sidled, rodent-like, into the room. His shabby, rusty-black overcoat flapped around his legs. Either by accident, or design, he stood directly opposite the girls.

He was dripping wet, and a pool of rain formed about his feet. His ferret's gaze slid over and around everybody and seemed to come to rest on the tensely watchful Carol and Eloise. Instead of evoking compassion, his seediness brought a shiver of disgust and fright as if in the presence of a meanly evil spirit.

"Carol, what was it they said about old men? Do you think he's . . .?" Eloise's purple eyes looked huge with fear in her pale face.

"I don't know, but if he comes near us, I'll make him wish he hadn't. I'll hit him. You be ready to run." Carol's dark amber eyes burned fiercely.

The old man edged over toward them. Carol and Eloise were frozen to their chairs, hardly daring to breathe. When he was about five feet away, he held out a dirty, claw-like hand and opened his mouth full of snaggy, stained teeth to speak.

Like an over wound spring, Carol leaped to her feet, blazing with anger and fright. Eloise shot up too, ready to help.

The big doors burst open, and Eloise screamed, "Sarn, thank heavens! It's you." She burst into tears.

Carol, ready to spring at the old man, made a cornered animal sound that chilled to the bone.

Sarn leaped across the room and grabbed the old man. A huge, rusty bundle helped.

"Oh, Sarn, Sarn. I—we—we were so frightened—so—oh, Sarn." Eloise collapsed into her chair, huge tears rolling down her cheeks. Rusty licked her face for attention. Eloise hugged him. They became immediate friends.

"What do you want, old man." Sarn bared his teeth and kept a strong grip on him.

"F-fer Chris' sake, all I wanted was a handout. What's the matter with those women? They crazy? L-let me go."

Carol, too, collapsed into her chair. Sarn freed the old man who immediately ran for the door, terrified. Rusty bounded after him and added to his terror and speed.

Sarn put an arm around each of the girls and hurried them toward the door.

"Oh, Sarn honey, where were you all this time?"

"Come to the car first. Then, we will talk."

The three, and Rusty, scrambled into the backseat. Sarn blew a few short blasts on the horn. Soon, the Zalleellians had the full story.

"Now what?" Khair asked.

"Back to the hotel," Jorl said. "They may have traced us there before they found the girls." It wasn't long before he pulled up haphazardly in front of the hotel.

The door of their suite was closed. Jorl motioned them to be quiet, held his weapon at the ready, and slowly pushed the door wide.

The same untidy cyclone had hit their rooms. Everything was thrown everywhere.

"Look over there." Sarn pointed to the chesterfield cushion that partially hid a tray, which, when Sarn lifted it, had in turn hidden broken glasses. Sarn smelled the familiar odor. "Well, that's what all these wet spots are—spilled beer."

"I'm so glad it's not blood," Eloise whispered.

"That means that Johnny Dill was here," Khair said. "I wonder why?"

A pathetic groan quivered in the air.

"Great blazing suns." Sarn leaped to the overturned chesterfield and righted it with a quick flip.

There lay Johnny Dill, still semi-comatose.

Tarla knelt beside him. "He seems to be all right. He's almost conscious."

"Mind-blasted?" Jorl asked.

Tarla gently probed Johnny's mind. "Yes, but lightly. The poor little guy was terrified out of his wits."

Then, whoever it was, was in too much of a hurry to do the job right," Jorl said.

Suddenly, Johnny's eyes snapped open, and his wiry little frame went tight with tension.

"Everything's all right now, Johnny. You're safe." Tarla soothed him with a quiet voice and peaceful thoughts.

Johnny, in a state of nervous shock, and evidently terrified of what he might see, scanned each of their faces and then all around the room. Jorl and Tarla helped him into a chair, and he leaned back, visibly trembling.

"Who—what—were those b-b-big guys? What happened?" He groaned, then said, "Jeez, I was conned."

"They're gone now, Johnny. Relax, relax." Tarla continued to soothe him. Poor Johnny's mind was still a chaotic jumble of frightened thoughts.

Sarn found a bottle of beer still half full. "Here, Johnny, have a couple of mouthfuls of this." He passed the bottle to Johnny who took a couple of large swallows.

"Tell us what happened, Johnny." Tarla spoke softly as she gently probed into his mind.

"Well—well—umm," Johnny gathered his thoughts. "I guess—well, I'd sneaked out a side door for a smoke, and I see this gorgeous chick I'm after, so I walk her a little way down the street. There I was—tryin' to get this little gal talked into a date for tomorrow night, and she's givin' me a hard time, when I trip over something. So there I am, flat on my can and suddenly I'm lookin' into the face of some old guy, all wet eyes and white hair, sitting under a tree. He looks awful sick and sort of . . . tired out. I'm about to yell at him, but he looked too bad. Anyway, it started to rain, and he says how sorry he is and wants to make it right for me if I will talk to him for a minute—that maybe I could help him." Johnny finished the beer and suddenly felt the total and undivided attention of his audience.

They could almost see the avaricious little wheels begin to turn in Johnny's mind.

"Continue," Jorl ordered.

"Okay, okay. Well, from what he said, I knew it was you folks he was innarested in. So I told him your suite number. He asked me to help him get into your rooms, and I told him that was against the rules."

"And you would never, ever break the rules," Sarn said.

Tarla shushed him.

"Well, I could lose my job, and that's what I told him. Anyway, the old guy said he would make it worth my while, which he hasn't done yet, and I did him a big favor."

"Continue," Jorl ordered.

Johnny sighed. "Well, since the chick had already got snooty and left, I said okay. I figured he was too old and harmless to cause any trouble anyway, so I brought him here. Jeez, I thought he was goin' to kick the bucket any minute, so I said to wait—that I would get back to him as soon as I could. I helped him to the sofa and asked him if he needed a doctor, or anything. And he said something about—well—that he would be all right if he found Forever. I said that you can't find forever, and he said that all he needed was one. I didn't know what the hell he was talkin' about. I think he was a little off his nut."

Johnny paused to think. "About an hour later, your call came into the desk. I brought up the sandwiches and beer you ordered and knocked on the door, and the old man unlocked it."

"I ordered?" Sarn asked.

"You phoned room service and asked for the usual, didn't you?"

"Mind probes, I suppose," Khair said.

"Yes, I bet they called the desk and waited for the bellhop to show up and open the door," Jorl said.

"Anyway," Johnny continued, "just as I opened it, these two huge guys jumped me from behind and shoved me inside and threw me across the room. One grabbed the old guy by the throat and the other big bastid started tearing the place apart. I started yelling when, all of a sudden, there was nothin' but—but—eyes. Yellow eyes with shiny green slits. And my head hurt so bad and . . ."

Tarla saw the kaleidoscope of confused scenes in Johnny's mind—could see the terror and the horror.

Johnny put his head into his hands and moaned. "And that's—that's all I remember until you woke me up. Who were they? What happened to the old guy?" Johnny's fright was gaining ground again.

"Relax, Johnny, relax. I'll help you." Tarla started a gentle job of repairing the mind probe, fading the terror from Johnny's thoughts. By the time she finished, Johnny was his usual greedy, cocky self.

"What're ya gonna do about the old geezer? Will he be okay?"

"Yes. We'll find him and help him—and thank you for looking after him. He's a very old and dear friend of ours," Tarla said.

Johnny's beady little eyes opened wide. "What is that, fer God's sake?" He pointed to Rusty who was busy gulping down the sandwiches he had found under a cushion. "You ain't allowed to keep dogs in the rooms, and that's one big, wet, dog-smelly mess."

"Pretend you don't see him then," Sarn said, half disgusted.

"I should also pretend I don't see two soaked, scared chicks. Not to mention that the rest of you look like drowned rats. What's with you people anyway?"

"Don't give it another thought," Sarn said. He led him to the door.

Jorl passed Johnny a hundred dollar bill. "For your good deed to our friend."

Johnny grinned at the money and spirited it away into a pocket. "Will I send a maid to clean up the mess?"

"No. And don't mention this to anyone," Jorl said. "You never know what might be needed in the future, and you're the one we'll call."

"You mean . . ." Johnny made the age-old sign of money changing hands. He rubbed his thumb over the ends of his fingers.

"That's what I mean."

"Good-bye for now, Johnny. We'll call you when we need you again. Okay?" Tarla eased him to the door.

"Okay, I guess." Johnny was a little doubtful if he could take too much more involvement with these big, strange people. "Oh well, the money's good. See ya." He waved as Sarn closed the door behind him.

"Blazing suns, the devils have taken Mosets," Sarn said. "We've got to get to him right away. How?" Sarn paced and thought. "How?"

While putting the room back in some semblance of order, they discussed the situation.

"To sum up," Khair said, ticking off on his fingers, "we have been in contact with the Surnainians in three locations—here, the girls' apartment, and the old house."

"Right. And they might reappear at any one of them." Jorl paced the room, thinking. "Tarla, you and the girls stay here. Sarn, you check out the apartment and surrounding territory. Khair, you and I'll search the old house."

"I don't like the idea of splitting up," Tarla said.

"Neither do I, Tarla, but the situation is urgent. The girls need some rest, and I don't think it would be wise to leave them alone. We must find Mosets." Jorl took the pair of intricate boxes from a pocket. "One of these must be his."

"Do you think that's what the Surnainians are looking for?" Tarla asked.

"And Mosets," Jorl added. "I think the old man that Johnny helped was Mosets. I think it's safe to assume that they now have Mosets and that there's something big going on, and we've stumbled right into the middle of it."

"Then they ran across evidence of another batch of aliens—us," Sarn said.

"Gee, Sarn honey, please let me go with you. I can't bear the thought of losing sight of you again. I can help you look."

"No, Elly, it's not safe. Stay with Tarla and Carol. I'll be back before you even have time to miss me." He cuddled her to him and pushed damp tendrils of hair away from her anxious face.

Carol tore her gaze away from the tantalizing boxes. "Don't be dumb, Eloise. By the way, Jorl, do you think it's wise to take both boxes with you? Why not leave one here in case you get caught. Or the old man gets back here." Her tone of voice was offhand—just offering some sensible advice.

Carol held her breath while the eternity of a few seconds of silence ticked by.

"Carol is right, Jorl." In a soft voice, Khair agreed with her. "Mosets might escape and return here, and from the way he apparently looked, he will need one of the spheres immediately."

Jorl hesitated for a second longer, then passed the second box to Tarla. "Guard it well, Tarla, but not as well as yourself. Now, check your weapons, and let's go." He kissed Tarla and turned to leave.

Sarn hugged Eloise and whirled her around, making her laugh. Rusty bounced around both of them, barking and grinning.

"Oh, Sarn." Eloise giggled and gasped.

Khair put his hands on Carol's shoulders and looked seriously into her eyes. He gave her a soft kiss on her forehead and a light one on her lips. "Be careful, lovely Carol. There's always a price to pay," he whispered.

Carol said nothing as the three men and Rusty left.

"Oh, they're gone again. I'm scared Sarn might get caught, or hurt, or something." Eloise felt a tremble in the pit of her stomach.

"It won't be too long before they get back, Eloise. And when they do, maybe we'll be closer to getting home. Let's order food, and then you two can rest awhile." Tarla kept her misgivings well hidden.

Chapter 17

On their way down the hotel hall toward the elevators, Jorl said, "Full alert from now on—'til we know if we're the hunters or the hunted. Sarn, scout the apartment. If you don't find anything, come straight to the old house. If we're not there, it means trouble, so get back to Tarla and the girls.

Sarn nodded in agreement.

"And remember, Sarn, if you do find any Surnainians, come for us first. Do not, and I repeat, do not tackle them by yourself."

Sarn made a noncommittal noise.

"That's an order, Lieutenant."

"Aye, Captain." Sarn threw a snappy salute.

Outside the hotel, Sarn, with Rusty at his heels, flagged a taxi. Jorl and Khair pressed Carol's car into further service.

Sarn had the taxi drop him a block from the apartment complex. Rusty helped Sarn do an intense recce of the area as they gradually worked their way toward the girls' building. He and Rusty entered the lobby and took the elevator to the girls' apartment. He listened at the door, heard nothing, and cautiously let himself in. The hair down Rusty's back bristled, and he growled low in his throat as he sniffed from room to room.

"You remember that scent, Rusty. It's bad." Sarn squatted on his haunches and rubbed Rusty's big head.

"That's who we've got to find—and kill."

Rusty understood.

Sarn stood up and prowled through the apartment once more. "Come on, Rusty, let's go."

Out in the hall, he found the flight of stairs that the girls had described. He continued on up and forced his way through the door to the roof. It was dark and still drizzling. They did a quick tour of the roof but saw nothing out of the ordinary.

"Come on, Rusty. Let's find the other elevator."

When they got into the freight elevator, Rusty sniffed and growled. "Yes, Eloise and Carol were here." Sarn patted Rusty's head. In the short while that Sarn had known Rusty, he had come to have a deep affection for the large reddish dog.

Rusty continued to sniff and growl all the way down to the basement.

When they left the elevator, Rusty circled ahead and had plainly picked up the scent of Eloise and Carol. He ran for the garage door with Sarn right behind him. When it opened, Rusty bounded up the driveway toward the street. Suddenly, he came to a stiff-legged halt and growled.

To Sarn, Rusty's actions made a plain diagram. Carol and Eloise had run for the street just as the Surnainians had come up from the direction of the terrace.

"Follow Surnainians, Rusty. Track."

Rusty, hackles raised and casting back and forth to pick up the scent, started down over the terrace toward the rear of the next building. Sarn followed quickly and noiselessly, holding his stun pack ready.

Soon, the alley led to a dark, paved lane that he could see would eventually come out on the street at right angles to the one he had been on. Even though it was no longer raining, everything was dripping wet, and the damp, dark night seemed to muffle the very air.

Slowly, with all senses alert, Sarn and Rusty started down the alley. They passed two closed doors and looked behind the untidy rows of trashcans, prepared for a possible ambush.

They both sensed the sudden danger at the same instant. Out of nowhere, two hurtling Surnainians landed, one on each side of Sarn and Rusty.

Instinct fired Sarn's weapon at the nearest one as the other smashed a hard blow on Sarn's head.

Rusty turned into a raging beast, went for the second Surnainian's throat while Sarn, down on one knee, fought for consciousness. Through blurred eyes, he saw two more figures, one at each end of the alley.

"Bushwhacked, by the gods." A fragment memory of television homework.

Searing white pain started at the base of his skull when he felt the beginning of a mind blast. With all his mental strength and training, he tried to ward it off by sending strong mental calls to Tarla.

Rusty had the second Surnainian down but, even so, was absorbing terrific punishment from the Surnainian's fists and boots.

Sarn sent a wide hard blast of the stun pack to one end of the alley, but the fourth man was already on him.

Rusty ripped out the throat of his enemy and turned to help Sarn. At the beginning of the fourth man's onslaught, the stun pack was lost in the darkness.

It was a silent, brutal fight. All the training and tricks of both strong men were brought to bear. They injured each other badly, but neither could gain the advantage. An unlucky slip on the wet pavement brought Sarn down. His head hit the concrete with a sickening sound. Blood ran from a gash on his unprotected head. Sarn stayed down, limp and apparently dead. Some kind of a sharp weapon had ripped his side, and wetness oozed on the black pavement.

Rusty, himself almost unconscious, feebly harried the enemy who had got to his feet and was bracing himself to kick Sarn's head to make sure of his death. The Surnainian kicked Rusty instead, and a wide gash opened on Rusty's already bloody head. One ear now hung lower than the other. Rusty collapsed.

The last Surnainian, bent over with pain, thinking everyone else was dead, slowly made his escape.

With just enough strength to bare his teeth and growl, Rusty slowly and painfully dragged himself over to Sarn's side. He licked Sarn's face—and cried. He laid his big sad face on Sarn's chest and cried as if his heart was broken. Losing consciousness, his crying turned to whimpering—then silence.

Slow dripping water made the only sound.

Once more, dark wet, quiet settled over the alley.

Chapter 18

*orl brought the car to a slow stop a hundred feet away from the front door of the old building. They intended to reconnoiter the whole surrounding area.

Jorl touched Khair's shoulder. "Look," he said softly.

From nowhere, two tall, fast-moving figures had almost disappeared down the poorly lit street. "That looks like a pair of them."

"If it is, we'd better find out where they're going."

Jorl nodded in agreement and, without putting on the headlights, he slid the car into gear and slowly followed.

The two hurrying figures set a fast pace and seemed to know exactly where they were headed.

"I'm sure they're Surnainians," Jorl said. "They're big and fast enough."

"I think you're right."

Forced to keep a good distance to prevent suspicion, they lost sight of their quarry. When Jorl came to the corner, the Surnainians seemed to have disappeared. Between the darkness and the rain, it made it impossible to see far enough down the street to be sure.

"Not a sign . . . damn," Jorl spoke quietly as his eyes tried to search all the dark places.

"I suggest we track on foot," Khair said.

Just then, a car drove toward them. The headlights partially lit the dark street.

"Look. On the left—about halfway down," Khair pointed down the street. The lights of the oncoming car silhouetted a movement for a second. Jorl and Khair both strained to see past the headlights. When the car passed, there was nothing left to see.

"Maybe they crossed to the right side and went down an alley. "There," Khair pointed. "There, Jorl. See that?"

"Just for a split second. Let's go."

They both drew their weapons and left the car where it was.

They walked the short length of the twisted, narrow, dark street. It entered into a wider one at right angles.

"There's no sign in either direction," Khair whispered.

"Across from us—there's another alley. Come on."

They ran across the street and stood flat to one side of the alley mouth. Cautiously, they looked in. No apparent sign of trouble in the dark maze. The further they went, the more backyards and alleys they found.

"Great black holes, it's like a damn rabbit warren," Jorl said. "We can't be on the right track. There's not one sign of them." Jorl scanned around, looking for any sort of a clue. "And, I keep thinking . . . I have a feeling of—danger—urgency—there's trouble. I must have made a mistake. Damn it." He felt a towering sense of frustration.

"No point cursing yourself. You made logical choices. They've got to be here somewhere."

"We've got to hurry . . . or . . . we'll be too late." Jorl spoke with quiet desperation.

Khair, even though he was Jorl's brother, did not have the intuitive sensing that Jorl had, but he had long ago learned to trust it.

"I knew it. I took the wrong turn. We're right back where we started. Blazing fireballs. That's the same alley. Come on, Khair, let's go round again."

They started off at a fast pace, and finally they came to the spot where Jorl decided he had taken the wrong turn. "This is the way we should have gone, Khair. Come on."

They kept up the grueling pace as they traveled down another narrow lane and came to a wider street. Across this street, and a few feet down, they saw yet another alley opening.

"That's the one, Khair," Jorl whispered.

They shot across the street and stayed to one side and listened. They were about to enter the mouth of the alley when Jorl held up his hand for quiet and said, "There. Hear that?"

Khair listened. "Sounds like someone's dragging himself along." They heard a muffled groan. "And hurt." They froze where they were and waited as the blurred steps came closer. Out of the mouth of the alley staggered a big man. He saw them the same second that Jorl and Khair knew that this was a badly wounded Surnainian.

With no hesitation, Jorl gave him a lethal blast with his stun pack. The Surnainian caved in and instantly died.

The two Zalleellians rushed into the alley, stun packs out and ready for battle.

They saw a darker mound in the gloom.

With superhuman effort, Rusty rose up, straddled Sarn's body, and growled viciously at the approaching figures.

"Rusty," Jorl shouted as he ran up to the dog and the body it guarded. Rusty collapsed from the effort. Jorl praised and patted him. Rusty raised his injured head and gave Jorl a small lick on his face, laid his head back down on Sarn's chest, and whimpered.

Khair knelt on the other side and examined Sarn with a small, but intense, light.

Jorl looked into Sarn's face. "Is he still alive, Khair?" Pray God he is."

"Just barely. We need help." Khair checked Sarn for broken bones and did what he could to stop the bleeding.

Jorl, while he was kneeling beside Sarn's head, shone his light on the surrounding area. "That's four more dead Surnainians—a four to one fight."

"Two to four—Rusty had a lot to do with it." Khair pointed to the throat of the nearest body. He made a hurried examination of Rusty's wounds.

"I'll try to send a message to Tarla," Jorl said. He and Khair were about to pick up Sarn and Rusty to carry them to the car when they heard running steps in the alley.

"Jorl, Jorl," Tarla shouted. She and the two girls were running in from the opposite end. "Is it Sarn?" Tarla knelt beside the unconscious body of her only brother. She cried and was heartbroken at what she saw. "I got weak messages from him that led me here. Oh, Sarn. Oh, Rusty."

Eloise and Carol rushed up to the group. Carol was shaken at the sight she saw in the small light's beam and knelt beside Khair. He raised his eyebrows in pleased surprise when she asked specific medical questions about the injuries and helped to temporarily bind the wounds of both Sarn and Rusty.

Carol saw the look and said, "First Aid course, okay?"

"You never cease to amaze me, my lovely Carol."

Eloise knelt by Sarn's side and spilled hot tears on both Sarn and Rusty.

Carol gulped back her own tears and said in a nearly firm tone, "All tears do is make your eyes red and your nose run, and they don't help anyone, Eloise. Hold this pad over that gash." Eloise steadied herself and did as Carol ordered. "We need a hospital. Now."

"We can't Carol—too many questions. Can't go to the hotel, or your apartment, either." Tarla had a tearful, frustrated edge to her voice. "How about the old house? Maybe we could go there."

Jorl said, "That may be the best idea."

"Well, we'd better do something quickly before Sarn and Rusty die, and this place fills up with policemen wanting to know what kind of a party we're having," Carol said.

Jorl snapped his fingers when he made his decision, "Carol, you come with me—get the car." Jorl took her arm. "Tarla, do what you can, and, Khair, guard them. There's probably more of them. Eloise, you help Khair." He hurried Carol back down the alley.

Within ten minutes, Carol and Jorl were back. They got Sarn and Rusty into the car as carefully as they could, trying not to do more harm to the already badly wounded bodies.

"Now, what do we do with these four bodies?" Jorl said. "His mind searched for a quick and simple solution. "We can't leave them here for the authorities to find. They're aliens."

"It'll be daylight soon," Khair said.

"This building looks like an old warehouse." Eloise pointed to the building on her left. "Why not just hide them in there for now?"

"Good idea. Find a door!" Jorl quickly scanned the side of the building.

"Hurry," Carol said.

"Here's one," Khair called softly from further down the alley. A hard shove by Jorl and Khair together sprung the lock.

"Hope there's no alarm." Carol quickly looked for any sensors.

"Get the bodies and put them in here," Jorl said and pointed to a large, empty bin.

It took only a few minutes to stack the bodies and for everyone to find old sacks and wooden crates and bits of other junk to cover them.

"That should be okay until we can get them buried in the desert. It looks like part of the general scenery," Khair said. "We just have to get back before, eh, they start to, eh . . ."

"Say it, Khair. Decompose," Carol said.

"Yes." Eloise agreed

As soon as they were settled in the car, Jorl started off.

"Are you heading for the old house?" Khair asked

"There's nowhere else for all of us in the condition that we're in. And Mosets might be there."

"True. Surnainians there, or not, it's the only choice," Khair agreed.

Jorl parked in front of the old house. "Khair, we'll do a quick search first and then bring in Sarn and Rusty. Tarla, you sit in the front seat beside Eloise—and draw your stun pack. Carol, move behind the steering wheel and be ready to drive away."

Jorl and Khair disappeared through the front door of the old house.

In about five minutes, they reappeared. "As far as we can see, the place is empty," Jorl said. He gently lifted Sarn and carried him toward the entrance. Khair brought Rusty. They trooped into the silent, surly house.

Tarla kept her weapon at the ready.

They entered the same room where they had first been only four days ago and laid Sarn and Rusty on two hastily cleared sofas. They found the lights, and the garish glare showed the awful extent of the wounds on the two unconscious bodies.

Tarla, within the limits of the small medical kit she carried, went to work on Sarn.

"I'll help you clean the wound and bandage it after you close it, Tarla," Carol said.

"Thanks, Carol. I need to look at his head wound."

Carol went to the other sofa to help Khair with Rusty.

"Oh, Tarla, is my Sarn going to live? I couldn't bear it if he . . . he . . ." Eloise tried her best not to break down, but tears wet her pale cheeks.

He's going to be fine," Tarla said. "Don't worry. Would you bring Sarn's case over to me? I need the medical kit from it." Eloise brought the case to Tarla. "Thanks, Elly. Why don't you see if Khair and Carol need any help with Rusty?"

Tarla opened Sarn's case and gave him another needle. She kept her finger on the faint pulse in Sarn's neck and waited. The pulse, although still weak, began to strengthen. Finally, she called out, "Yes, Elly. Yes." The two women looked at each other, and as the terrible tension left them, fresh tears of deep relief started down their faces.

The two men and Carol smiled, misty-eyed, and hugged each other in pure relief. They huddled around Sarn, touching him and whispering their thanks to whatever gods there were.

Jorl prowled around the room. He had a feeling he was missing something and began searching every inch of the wall and floor space.

Khair had closed and bandaged Rusty's wounds. Khair had also reattached and bandaged Rusty's ear, which gave him a rather rakish look. There were many little cuts and scrapes but no broken bones. Soon, the big, heavy head tried to lift. Rusty opened his eyes.

"Good boy, Rusty, it's all right now." Rusty gave Khair a lick on his hand. Then he began to fidget and tried to get up. He moaned and whimpered. Khair suddenly realized what was bothering him and said,

"See, Rusty? There's Sarn. He's safe."

"Oh, Rusty." Eloise gently hugged him, trying to avoid hurting any of his wounds, and some of her tears spilled on him. Rusty licked her face and whimpered. "Khair, help me pull this sofa over by Sarn so Rusty can see him." Khair did, at once understanding.

Rusty raised his head to look at Sarn's unconscious body. He sensed that all was well and let his bandaged head fall back down.

"I'll give him a sedative so he won't try to get up for awhile." Tarla measured out a dose from a different container and injected Rusty with it. Within seconds, Rusty was under and gently snoring.

Khair had been watching Jorl. "What's on your mind, Jorl?"

Now that the emergency was over, Tarla, too, became aware of her surroundings. "What are you worried about, Jorl?"

He didn't answer for a minute. "I'm not sure. I . . . Tarla, see if you can find anything."

Tarla looked inward for a few seconds. "There's a weak pattern close by. It could be . . ." she listened again. "It is. It's Mosets. But he's almost finished. He seems to be close to us. Have you checked the other rooms? Where . . .?" Tarla got to her feet, circled the room, and tuned into the fading neural impulses. They led her to a corner behind a ceiling-high bookcase.

"What else?" Carol spread her arms and looked toward heaven.

"What do you mean?" Khair asked.

"The usual old saw of a revolving bookcase that hides the entrance to a hidden room, or tunnel, or something. Regular Hollywood."

"Secret room." Jorl ignored Carol's sarcasm. "How do you open the door, Carol?" Jorl ran his hands over the surfaces of the bookcase.

"Oh, you usually push a knot in the carving, or pull out a certain book—any one of a hundred different ways."

"Everyone, come help," Jorl said.

After pushing and pulling innumerable spots and things, with no results, Jorl slipped on one of the dozens of books they had pulled to the floor. Trying to save himself, he accidentally pulled down on a short section of the top shelf. Instantly, the bookcase slid to one side, revealing a well-lit metal staircase.

Tarla, about to rush down them, felt Jorl grab her. Whispering, he said, "Tarla, wait. You stand guard here. Khair," he motioned Khair to his side, "follow me." With quiet caution, the two men started down the stairs and disappeared into a doorway on the right.

"Mosets," they heard Jorl shout. Instantly, Khair and Jorl appeared at the bottom of the flight of stairs. Jorl, carrying a frail old man, rushed up the stairs with Khair on his heels.

Tarla dumped the books out of a big armchair, and Jorl gently placed the ancient one in it. "Red Sphere, Jorl—quick."

The Ancient, barely conscious, managed a small nod. Jorl put one of the red spheres in the old man's mouth.

Carol and Eloise didn't say a word—just watched.

In a few seconds, the marvelous transformation they had seen through Tarla's mind began to take place in front of their own eyes. Their mouths opened in silent awe as the evidence of old age fell away. Finally, a strong young man sat in front of them.

"Thank you, old friends. My total death was a near thing." He suddenly jumped to his feet and hugged a still worried Tarla.

Then, a general hugging, backslapping, laughing reunion took place.

"Old friends, it is many years since we last met. And once again, just in time to avert sure disaster. Now, what is wrong with our youngest?" Mosets knelt beside Sarn and examined the still unconscious form. He asked Tarla some explicit medical questions and nodded with approval.

From a small pouch under his loose midnight blue jacket, he took a vial of pale red liquid. "As you know, I am not permitted to give him a Forever sphere. He is much too young, and it would throw him out of step with his peers, but this liquid will hasten the healing process." He held the unit on the pulsing neck artery and pressed a button. It injected a few drops. Immediately, Sarn's color improved, and he began to look only asleep. "And I gather this fine animal is no less deserving of the best the universe can offer?"

"Oh yes, Mr. Mosets. He saved Sarn's life." Eloise's pansy eyes filled with a fresh lake of tears.

"And, may I ask, who are these two beautiful maidens?" Mosets smiled sweetly and softly at the two girls. He radiated compassion and took even the practical Carol under his compelling spell.

After a vivid mixture of thought transferences and rapid words in two languages, they had given Mosets a detailed and up-to-date chronicle of events from their mad rush through space to this room, at this moment.

"Now, most venerable of the Ancients," Jorl said, "explain your part in this."

"Ah yes, my story will complete some of the gaps in yours. About two weeks ago, Earth time, I was . . ."

"Blazing suns—bushwhacked. Blazing damn suns!" Sarn had started thrashing about on the sofa, still unconscious.

"Sarn. He's back. He's coming round." Tarla rushed to his side, as did everyone else.

Sarn had begun the swim back to consciousness. He tossed, and turned, and mumbled.

"Take it easy, Sarn." Jorl grasped his shoulders. "It's all over. You're safe and almost sound."

Eloise was on the floor by his head, smoothing his hair, brushing small kisses on his forehead. Everyone gathered around. In a minute or two, his eyes blinked open, and he silently looked into each face surrounding him. "And Rusty?" His voice was still weak.

Tarla stood aside so he could see the sofa facing his and the snoring occupant. Sarn reached his arm over to touch the matted coat, winced with pain, but managed to curl his fingers gently in the short fur before he let his arm drop. Tarla placed it back by his side.

"Blazing suns, I'm weak."

"Not much wonder—four against one man and one dog. Between the two of you, you got them all, and both of you are still alive," Jorl said.

"I walked into that trap like a raw recruit." Sarn was disgusted with himself.

"Don't be so hard on yourself, dear Sarn," Tarla said. "You had no way of piercing a mental blanket. And how could you possibly know that you were under surveillance?"

Sarn's strength was returning fast. "Help me sit up."

Khair helped him sit up. "Lean on me, Sarn, and be careful. Just take it easy—don't make it bleed again."

Rusty began to wake up too, and his joy was complete when he heard Sarn. Rusty made small sounds in the back of this throat and tried to get up. Nothing was going to stop him from being at Sarn's side. Nothing.

"He won't stay still until he's beside Sarn," Jorl said. "Come on, Khair, help me move him over."

Khair obligingly helped Jorl pick Rusty up and lay him on the other end of the sofa with his head in Sarn's lap. His grin reappeared. He heaved a great loud sigh, and with pure contentment, dozed off again.

All of them arranged themselves in a close circle and laughed with sheer happiness. It was the kind of laughter that is founded in love and nearly touched by soft tears. They told Sarn the outcome of his fight.

"Blazing stars . . ." Sarn's mind had connected all the dots.

"Now what?" Jorl was puzzled.

"Another trip into the desert with four more bodies to bury." He suddenly realized he was naked from the waist up. "Where's my tunic? I can't go anywhere like this. I'll burn to a crisp. To a potato chip. I'll . . ."

"Hush, hush, hush, Sarn, calm down. We'll bring your case back when we go to the hotel, there's a change of clothes in it. Actually, all of us need some cleanup time." Just relax and finish getting better." Tarla patted him. "Now, behave."

"And yes, Sarn, another trip into the desert will be necessary, and quite soon, too," Jorl said. "Now, Mosets, continue with your story."

"Ah yes. I will go back a little further. About fifteen months ago, Earth time, I came across a strong indication that Surnainia had decided on this arm of the galaxy for their next operation. By using every avenue of detection, I knew that two advance parties had begun their preliminary work and that a third would shortly join them. But which solar system?

I cast back and forth . . . back and forth . . . across the arm, searching for even a faint spore that would mark their passing. Finally, I found the guiding trace that led me to this solar system. There being only one inhabited planet, I knew I had found their new base. But where on this orb would they go to ground? I patrolled and monitored for weeks and weeks, searching to find them before their filthy deed could be done.

And then, during a wide swing round this lovely, blue planet, I caught sight of what I thought could be a ship emerging from subspace. I went closer and picked it up in my scanners. I knew beyond any doubt that it was my elusive prey. Taking every precaution to prevent their knowledge of me, I followed them. I had plotted their course, and they seemed to be heading straight for what appeared to be their rendezvous point on Earth." Mosets paused dramatically, dropping his voice lower. "Then, it happened."

Once more, Mosets had cast the spell of the storyteller on his audience.

"I was rounding your Earth's moon, when, with nerve-twisting shock, the wild screaming of the alarm system warned of impending disaster.

"The sensors had picked up the track of what could only be a ship zeroing in on me. I took immediate evasive action and hastily scanned the area. Sure enough and to my total surprise, another Surnainian ship was nearly upon me.

"We joined in battle. It was a twisting, turning battle of wits.

"The Surnainian scout ships are larger and more heavily armed than ours, but we even the odds of firepower by having the mobility of mercury. It was a long fight, but I finally maneuvered into position to launch two direct hits at the enemy. Just before the ship disintegrated, one of their guns did damage to my ship that made it difficult to maintain my previous course behind the original Surnainian ship.

"The accuracy of my sensors had been impaired by the Surnainian blast, but I still had the coordinates of their landing site. I marked it on the map and decided to wait until the following evening to follow them to land. I headed away to a safe orbit and effected some necessary repairs to my poor ship.

"On the following night, I came down to complete my own landing. With great misfortune dogging my footsteps, the repairs to my ship were not sufficient. The feeders to the pile were unstable and caused a meltdown.

"Again, unfortunately, I had a rather bad crash landing, and my ship is beyond repair, but at least I wasn't injured beyond self-help. The Surnainians probably monitored my descent, so I held myself on full alert.

"When I had recovered sufficiently, I made ready to find the Surnainian headquarters. Before leaving, I set the emergency call system for help, so, hopefully, another ship will be coming for me. I expect the Surnainians have, by now, alerted their home base, and the possibility of the two opposing forces meeting close by appears inevitable."

It took a minute or two for the group to shake off the spellbinding ability of Mosets.

"We also sent out a call for help," Jorl said. "If Command received the message, it's also probable that they will send a ship."

"And neither one of them will know anything of the Surnainians," Khair added.

"Blazing suns. And no way to warn them," Sarn said.

"But if Command receives either message, they will know that they are emergency signals and will go to full alert," Jorl said.

Tarla laughed.

"What's so funny, Tarla?"

"I suppose it isn't really, but what bothers me, among lots of other things, is how do we ever explain how badly we broke the iron-clad directives governing 103AZ? Not only smashed them to smithereens, but, so far, are bringing back two aliens and a dog. And I have a peculiar feeling there could be even more to come."

"Blazing suns, Jorl, you, being the Captain, will have to write the report for old Admiral Emslin explaining it." Sarn laughed at the thought. "Man, you'll sweat stars." Sarn was almost his old self again.

"Believe me, Lieutenant," he smiled at Sarn with affection, "you'll do your share of star-sweating. You'll be right there on the bridge with the rest of us."

Sarn's mobile face screwed up with a frown of distaste. "If there's one thing I hate, it's watching an admiral having a star-spangled rage—they are so damned icy and quiet it freezes you to the boots."

"At least, the freezing is a good anesthetic while you work your way up from private again," Khair said and smiled.

"Oh, Sarn honey, will I cause you that much trouble? Maybe . . . maybe . . ." Eloise was distressed. "Maybe we shouldn't . . ."

"Forget that nonsense, Eloise. You're worth a whole world more to me than a dressing down from an admiral—freezing or not—private or not." He gave Eloise a small hug and dropped a light kiss on her soft, damp cheek. "But two girls and a dog are a dead giveaway, however . . ." Sarn's mind was busily clicking out a plan. "We'll say that we had to either break the directives, or be forced to watch the two girls be destroyed. It was our humanitarian duty to save both of you and Rusty from the Surnainians . . . actually, that's really true anyway." Now, a brilliant smile replaced the frown of distaste, and he hugged Eloise again. He suddenly turned to Jorl with a flood of excited questions. "Jorl, did you check out the whole place downstairs when you found Mosets? Is it a headquarters? Is it some sort of a control room? Is it . . .?"

"I didn't have time for more than a quick glance. It appears to be some sort of a control room."

"Help me up. I want to go down right now." Sarn struggled to stand up.

"No, Sarn. Wait until you're a little more mobile," Jorl said.

Carol had been thinking about what she had heard about the future with an admiral involved. "Wait a minute, I don't know about . . ." Carol stood up, perturbed by the twist in the conversation.

"That's enough everyone," Jorl spoke with authority. "We have a real situation here. We now find ourselves in the middle of a dangerous problem, which we must solve, and that will take us to the absolute limit of all our skills. However, I'm sure we will find the solution. Anyway, Mosets, what happened? How did the Surnainians find you?"

Mosets continued with his story. "I knew that this was the city where they had their base, and I prepared for the trip. I reached a paved roadway that led to the city. A young couple picked me up, anxious to help a solitary old man. You see, for that purpose, I had allowed myself to age. An old man is less noticeable and also is inclined to cause sympathetic vibrations from others, which in turn makes them more than pleased to help in any way that they can. That is a good quality in a race. I asked them to let me out in the middle of the main street.

"I stood in a dark doorway and activated my receiver. I searched the bands for the Surnainian emitting station. I began following the directional signal. As I got closer, the volume increased. I was too intent on it. From out of nowhere, two monstrous Surnainians grabbed me, and with a minimum of fuss, and since I was now too old to have much strength, they hustled me through dark alleys and finally into an old house—this room.

"There was an old man in here that looked very much as I did then—on first glance. One of the Surnainians searched me and took my receiver and my box of Forever. He handed the container of Forever to the old man who grabbed it and hid it away on his vile person. They had literally taken my life without striking a blow. Thank the stars they left me with my health unit."

"I wonder how they found you so quickly?"

"That is what amazed me, Jorl. Must be something new. Then, I heard a signal bell that sent both Surnainians running to that bookcase and on down to their command station. This much I had now learned, but, at the moment, the knowledge seemed useless, as there was nothing I could do about it.

Within a few minutes, the two Surnainians went barreling back out and told the old man to guard me well. I mentally rubbed my hands—I might be old, but the old man would be no match for me. I was about to put the creature to sleep, take my Forever, and destroy their headquarters when the door burst open. The Surnainians must have suddenly realized their error in thinking me harmless. With unnecessary roughness, they took me with them. I gathered that even another strange ship had been sighted, and since their new methods now seemed to be stealth and personal contact with important people, they had to stop any form of publicity at once."

"Then, they did sight our ship," Sarn said.

Mosets nodded agreement. "Yes, and I imagine they thought you were the scout for the whole fleet that they thought was planning to attack them.

"They were now heading for their ship in the desert. Because I pretended to be utterly helpless and half in the world of death, they didn't think to bother with bonds. They bundled me into the backseat of a car and headed out. When we became stalled in a traffic jam, I lunged for the door and rolled out onto the pavement. Well, suffice it to say that in the middle of the altercation I had started in the midst of a group of people, which immediately turned into a much larger group, I made my escape. The Surnainians did not want to be noticed and continued on their way without me.

With the time left to me, I waited to seek out the new aliens. I had neither the strength nor the equipment to reach my ship and, without my directional receiver, I could not find my way back to the old house.

I sighted all of you at different times but got to the apartment and the hotel too late in both cases. Also, I assumed the Surnainians were hot on my trail, and I had to be careful not to put you in direct danger.

Finally . . . was it only early this evening? . . . I collapsed under a tree by your hotel."

"And that is where the redoubtable Johnny Dill found you," Jorl said. "And then he took you to our room in the hotel."

"Yes. And that is also where the Surnainians found me, in your hotel room. Then, they brought me here again to do a mind probe and then to probably kill me. They never did either because they saw Sarn and Rusty on the scanner apparently tracking the scent of them from the apartment to here. I heard them contact another party, and they decided on Sarn's capture as well. They seemed to be a little unnerved about the disappearance of the old man and one of themselves. They threw me into their control room downstairs and left.

And now, my extremely dear people, here we all are with a big job to face and not much more than our wits to face it with." Mosets leaned back in his chair, his story finished.

"Mosets, about how many Surnainians are we talking about?" Jorl asked.

"There were four ships, eight men to a ship. I disintegrated one ship, which leaves twenty-four men and three ships. We know where one ship is," Mosets answered.

"We know where five dead are—that leaves nineteen loose ends plus two ships to locate," Sarn said. "Blazing suns!"

"If we can help Mosets finish this job, it may be the flame that'll warm up our esteemed admiral." Khair smiled his slow, small smile. "After all, searching out and destroying Surnainians and their plans is one of the most important duties of the Federation."

"Blazing comet tails, yes. We'll enjoy doing our duty. Blow them all up." Sarn's grin went almost from ear to ear.

Jorl got up and stretched. "Right. But for now, we need sleep. We'll make our plans in the morning."

"It's already morning. It's half past five in the morning, and it's getting light now," Carol said.

"Then let's get to bed fast," Jorl replied.

They scouted the house for usable blankets and bedlike furniture. They locked and blocked the door of their room and booby-trapped the bookcase. Sleeping in the headquarters downstairs wasn't an option, not only because of the lack of room, but also because there could be another concealed entrance. In any event, they agreed to post a guard, each of the five taking a one-hour shift.

At last, they were all settled down on a variety of makeshift beds.

Khair took the first watch.

Chapter 19

"Up everybody," Jorl called. "It's almost noon, and we've got a situation that must be solved today."

With the help of an ancient bathroom, everyone managed to pull themselves somewhat together.

When they were sitting around the dusty old room and still on full alert, Jorl said, "We need to come up with a plan. At the moment, this situation appears to be a little beyond our control. We've got to get control, and we've got to find the best way to do it."

Rusty stretched, snorted, got up, and put his head on Sarn's lap. He moaned, wagged his tail, moaned some more, and looked into Sarn's eyes with a deeply concerned expression.

"First things first, I think," Khair said.

"Oh gee, yes. Rusty needs to go out, Sarn."

"Take a stun pack with you. Here." Khair held one out to Sarn.

Sarn took the weapon that Khair handed him and held it. "I can't go out without a shirt. I'll freeze."

"Here, Sarn, drape this around your shoulders." Carol handed him an old black sweater that was on the back of a chair.

"That works. Come on, Rusty, let's go." Sarn was still too weak to move at his usual pace, but he gave Rusty a hug, and they headed for the door.

"Gee, I'll go with you, Sarn honey." Eloise, concerned about Sarn, went to his side, and the three of them left.

When they came back, Sarn said, "Not a soul around. No sign of anything to worry about." He stretched out on the chesterfield. "What I wouldn't give for a cold beer."

"It would seem that you are well recovered, Sarn," Mosets said with a laugh.

"And starved." Sarn got up and slowly paced the room. "I need food. And a shirt." He stopped pacing for a minute and yelled, "Hey!" A light had dawned on Sarn's face. "Blazing stars. Of course. Call Johnny! He'll know how to organize it."

"We can't very well do that, Sarn," Jorl said. He thought about it for a moment. "But when you think about it, why not? He knows all about food, and all of us can't very well go trooping out to an eating-place. Eloise, everybody, find a communicator—a phone."

"Here it is," Carol said as she pulled a phone up from behind the desk and listened for the dial tone. "It's connected."

"Good. Call Johnny, Tarla." Sarn's eyes shone as he rubbed his hands together and contemplated his hunger problem solved.

Eventually, Tarla had Johnny on the phone and explained what she wanted and where to bring it. Johnny put up an argument.

"But, Johnny, surely they wouldn't fire you. You wouldn't be gone long."

Carol listened to Tarla, realized Johnny was being difficult, smiled, said, "May I?" and took the phone from Tarla. She then proceeded to squelch Johnny's arguments with cold determination. She gave him a large order, including, at Sarn's shout, lots of dog food, and also he was to pack all their cases and bring them, too. You could hear Johnny's raised voice gabbling and arguing.

"If you do this quickly and quietly, within the next two hours, Mr. Dill, you will be well paid. If, by any chance, you disappoint us, Mr. Dill, you will find yourself surrounded by big, bad men with yellow eyes. Do I make myself clear, Mr. Dill?"

Johnny's arguments died. He promised to be there within the allotted time.

"There," Carol said as she hung up the phone.

"Thanks, Carol. Well done." Tarla smiled at the "high command and will brook no arguments" tone of voice Carol had used.

"Hear that, Rusty? Food is on the way." Sarn laughed when Rusty tried to get on the sofa with him.

"See? He understood the word food." Rusty started to fidget and moan a bit. "What is it? What's the matter, Rusty?" Sarn knelt down to look him in the face, worried.

"I should imagine he wants to go outside again," Carol said.

"But—oh well, come on Rusty, let's go." Sarn started for the door with him.

"You stay here, Sarn," Jorl said. "I'll take him."

"And I shall accompany you," Mosets said.

After Jorl, Mosets, and Rusty left, Sarn prowled the large cluttered room. He found a small television set and turned it on.

Khair settled down with a stack of books, and Carol, who loathed clutter and mess, began to straighten up the piles of loose books and junk.

A news broadcast was playing on the television. It told of a famine, a flood, more racial riots, the smashing of another dope ring, political scandal in high places, an argument as to whether or not three factories were adding to the pollution of the environment and, while the argument dragged on, another piece of the tortured earth dies—a murder—a daring daylight robbery—and on, and on, listing one instance of horror after another.

"By the heavens," Sarn whispered. A mixture of sadness, and anger, and compassion flickered across his mobile face. "By the celestial heavens, what are they doing, Khair?"

Khair had come over to watch the broadcast. He shook his head and spoke sadly, "I don't know. It almost looks like a mass suicide attempt—taking their earth, and everything in it, with them. No wonder Surnainia decided on this planet."

"And yet, it can't be all bad," Tarla said. "Look at Carol, and Eloise, and old Bill, and some of the wonderful art and writings . . . and music . . . it's only since their technical knowledge improved so much. Maybe too much, too soon."

"All intelligent races find and use technical knowledge. It's man's nature to explore. They have done some wonderful things such as fighting disease and trying to mend damage done by their machines, and without that drive, they would remain placid animals little better than their cattle herds. And they do have a higher plane—a godlike touch. Otherwise, they couldn't have produced all the wonderful things they have. But they do need some sort of guidance," Khair said.

"But how could you give it to them?" Carol asked.

"Unless the Federation decides to step in, we can't," Khair said.

"If all the good men and women and all their separate gods can't prevent the carnage, I don't think the Federation could. And just what could your . . . Federation . . . do except set itself up as a dictator, or worse, make us feel that it is the benevolent keeper of a funny farm. Either way, we would fight them." Carol stood straight and proud, ready to defend her race no matter how dumb or cruel it was.

"Neither one, Carol," Khair said. "One of the Universal Federation's main goals is to preserve the race of man and not to let any branch of it die out. That would be a terrible loss. We are spread so thinly over the universe now."

"Just as a matter of academic interest, why would it be so terrible if man died out? Why?" Carol asked in a cold tone of voice. "I'm quite sure all of the animals, in fact, all of nature would almost be glad we were gone."

"Because, my dear Carol, then there wouldn't be anyone to enjoy the beauty and joy and love of this whole creation and to be alive and to wonder at its final meaning. And anything in nature, animals and vegetation, has only one driving force—survival. But man, I think, has a small layer of God on the top of his brain, and a thin layer of evil on the bottom of it, and everything in between is a mixture of both. That is why he is capable of so much that is good and so much that is evil. But most people are usually somewhere around ninety percent for the good and usually try to appreciate the one and to fight the other."

"Go beyond that. What's the ultimate point of it all?" Carol waited for the usual religious platitudes. Scorn showed on her beautiful face as she stood there, taut and waiting.

All of them waited, each one thinking of an answer. Each answer that occurred seemed too puny, too close to the immediate.

After a long pause, Khair replied, "Taking that question to its ultimate limit—past all everyday things, past all thoughts, past all knowledge—there is no point, Carol."

Carol's expression showed her surprise at the unexpected reply. "Well, thank you for an honest, unhypocritical answer." Carol relaxed her challenging stance a little.

"But," Khair steepled his fingers under his chin, then smiled and said, "We're here, now, in this universe, and here we're all going to stay in the best way possible. We'll worry about ultimate reasons, if the need ever truly arises, later."

"Fair enough, I agree to that," Carol said. She went to Khair, and he took her in his arms.

Eloise had been listening closely to the whole exchange. Her face was clouded with a troubled expression. "But, gee, don't you have any religions in your worlds? Like ours—it says when you die you go to heaven, or hell, depending on how you lived your life that was given to you." Eloise twined her fingers in and out of each other.

Khair replied, "Yes, Elly, but it's more of a philosophy of living. There isn't any formal worship. We do believe in a Supreme Being and that we shall join with Him when we die. And we have tapes, much like your Bible, that every child is taught about from an early age. It's a code of ethics and morals by which everyone lives.

"We have lots of the same things, but not enough of us try to live by them. Or they only obey the parts that suit them." Carol dismissed it all with a wave of her hand.

"But in our worlds," Khair said, "we don't have the pressures of an overwhelming population with its inevitable consequences—the masses of the poor, the famine, the unhealthy, and the lack of education."

"And just how do you get away from those consequences—massive welfare?" Carol asked. Her tone of voice was tinged with truculence.

"No, Carol, welfare is the wrong end of the stick," Khair said. "On our planet, we believe that every man, woman, and child is entitled to a good place to live, good food, excellent education, and good health. This leaves people free to follow their chosen paths and to earn their living as they wish."

"That sounds like a page torn right out of the fantasy book of Utopia and just as far-fetched." There was a sound of a faint sneer in Carol's voice. "Anyway, as long as man is man, it's fantasy."

"Because of our advanced medical knowledge, we are genetically and physically sound and in perfect health. The amount of population is controlled by choice. Therefore, as we are all genetically sound, and since we are always finding new planets to inhabit, everyone satisfies their desire for children. Since all the children are wanted, therefore, they are all loved. And they are taught when growing up to want and to love their children."

Eloise sighed deeply. "That's the way I always thought it should be." Her eyes and her mouth turned sad. "I can't bear to hear some of the things I have to know as a teacher of small children. How could anyone do such things?"

Sarn put his arms around her. "As Khair said, too many pressures, too many untaught."

"I agree your ways are right, Khair, but by the time those methods would have any effect on our world, it would be too late," Carol said. "You'd better tell your Federation to get here—right away."

"They may not want to interfere yet," Khair replied.

Carol shrugged. "Tell them it's too late if they arrive only in time for the Earth's funeral." Carol turned back to an untidy pile of books. She left an ocean of silence behind her—everyone quiet and each one lost in their own thoughts.

Eloise's soft voice broke the silence. "Gee, I know I must be dumb, but I find it really hard not to have some reason for going through life. There just must be a . . . a reason for living."

"There is, Elly dear. It's to have people around you who love you—who care whether you live or die—and for you to care about them," Tarla said softly. "Live your life as well as you can, and then you'll be prepared for whatever, if anything, comes after."

Sarn, more like his old self, jumped to his feet and snapped his fingers. "I made a poem once."

"You, Sarn?" Tarla smiled.

"Yes, me. Why not me?" Sarn challenged her doubt.

"I'm sorry, Sarn, go ahead. I'd love to hear it."

"Well, anyway—it's called 'Living Time.' Wait a minute while I remember it. It'll be a bit hard to put it into English as I go, but here it is." Sarn took up a stance in front of them and cleared his throat. "Are you ready?"

"We're ready," Khair said.

"Remember, you have to think 'Clock.'"

Sarn paused for a moment and then repeated the title, 'Living Time.' All jokes had fallen from him, and seriousness shone through—these were personal thoughts from his own soul.

Tick . . . . Tock . . . . Tick . . . . Tock
Waiting for borning.
Tick . . . . . Tock . . . . .
Tick . . . . Tock . . . .
I am born . . . Tick . . . Tock
I live! . . Tick . . Tock . . I am Me!
Wondrously.
Tick . . Tock . . Tick . . Tock . .
Growing, learning, laughing, playing
Joyously.
Tick. Tock. Tick. Tock.
Time flying faster with pulsing living days
Tick. Tock. Tick. Tock,
Star-flecked nights,
Damp earth smells, sunlight touching colors,
Flowers in cool, shady places,
Warmth . . .
Loving faces.
Tick. Tock. Tick. Tock.
Tick. Tock. Tick. Tock.
Laughing, weeping, eating, sleeping,
Working.
Strong touch of Man,
Warm breath of Woman.
TICK. TOCK. TICK. TOCK
Gloriously higher my living soars.
Touching, tasting, smelling, seeing,
Hearing.
Family, loving, crying, caring. . . .
Creating.
Faster and faster the years fly by
TICK TOCK TICK TOCK

Growing older . . . gently; maturing, teaching . . .
Remembering.
Tick . . Tock . . Tick . . Tock . .
Life has been wonderful . . .
Glorious . . . still is . . .
As the clock slows . . .
Tick . . . Tock . . . Tick . . . Tock . . .
Life's lessons . . .
Wisdom, knowledge . . . seeing the miracle
You helped in
By creating life.
That created life.
Tick . . . Tock . . . Tick . . . Tock . . .
I am . . .
Fulfilled . . . . . . Tick . . . . . . Tock
Tick . . . . Tock
. . . . Beyond time . . . .
To . . . .
My . . . . Infinity . . . .

When Sarn finished, they were quiet. Sarn looked at each of them. "Well? Blazing suns, it can't be all that bad."

"Sarn dear, that was so . . . unexpected . . . so . . . I still can't believe you wrote it. I mean, it was . . ."

Tarla had difficulty speaking around the huge lump in her throat. "It was beautiful."

"Oh, Sarn honey," Eloise threw her arms around him, almost in tears. "That was so true, so lovely. It makes me want to cry." And she did while Sarn held her tight.

"Very good considering," Khair said.

"Considering what?" Sarn asked.

"I only meant that it was so unexpected—coming from you. I guess there are depths in you that I didn't know."

Sarn had his mouth open to challenge that remark when they heard a commotion in the hall. Tarla ran to open the door. In came Jorl and Rusty, a loaded-down Johnny, and Mosets bringing up the rear.

"Food," Sarn yelled and hurried to help unload the boxes.

Looking around the strange room, Johnny said, "Jeez. What kinda spooked out place is this?"

"It's our home away from home, Johnny boy," Sarn said. He snapped the top off a bottle of beer.

Everyone helped themselves to the food, and they settled Johnny down with a beer.

They each took their cases, and Sarn immediately pulled a tunic out of his and slipped it on.

"That feels better," Sarn said. He pulled the shirt up again and looked down at the bandage still on the side of his body. "Tarla, blazing fireballs, is that blood?"

Tarla looked at the dressing. "It's probably just a bit of leftover seepage."

"Well, take it off, take the bandage off. Have a look anyway." Sarn didn't like anything to do with blood, especially on him.

"Okay, but it's apt to hurt a little." She started to pull off the dressing as carefully as she could, but Sarn yelled anyway.

When the dressing came off, the wound looked practically healed. "There, you're almost as good as new."

Sarn risked a look. "Good." With relief, he let his shirt down.

"How did you get here, Johnny?" Khair asked.

"In my car," Johnny replied. "The bill for the food was a hundred and thirty-five dollars and sixty-three cents." Johnny turned around and held the bill out to Jorl with an expectant look.

Jorl smiled and gave the little guy three hundred dollars. "That should cover it, and a little extra for all your help." He handed Johnny the cash, and Johnny slid it away more quickly than the eye could see.

"A car?" Khair asked. "Jorl, maybe it would be a good plan if Tarla went back with Johnny, picked up the rest of our stuff, and checked us out of the hotel."

"Good idea. Okay with you, Tarla?"

"Eloise and I'll go with you. We should go to our apartment and see if we can straighten it out at least a little bit. It's going to need a major overhaul. What a mess those big goons made." Carol was still highly annoyed. "We also need fresh clothes and baths. Oh, how I crave a tub filled to the brim with hot, soapy water."

Tarla nodded in full agreement. "I'll go to your apartment with you. Even though we haven't seen another sign of Surnainians, there's still no need for you to take chances. Agreed?"

"I totally agree," Carol said.

"Oh gee, so do I. I don't want another time like the last one—I think I'll hate cake for the rest of my life."

"We'll go to the hotel first, and I'll finish my business there. Then, we'll head over to your apartment. What do you think?" Tarla asked. Carol and Eloise agreed that it was the best plan.

"It's time to get back to business," Jorl said. "Tarla," Jorl took her aside and spoke softly and rapidly, "Here's money for the hotel. Mosets, Khair, and I'll leave now in Carol's car to get the bodies. You and the girls take a taxi as soon as you're finished and come back here to Sarn. We'll also come back here as fast as possible." He held her close for a moment. "Where's your weapon?"

Tarla pulled up her sleeve far enough for Jorl to see it. "It's fully charged."

"Good. You'd better be going now." Jorl tightened his arms around her. "Take very good care of yourself. Don't let your guard down." He held her tightly for a second longer and then let her go.

"Jorl, I'm a trained officer in the Universal Federation. I do know how to look after myself," Tarla said softly. She understood his worry.

"I know, Tarla, but you are also my wife, and I love you very much," he said quietly. He lightly kissed her good-bye, and she and the two girls left with Johnny. "Sarn," Jorl spoke seriously, "I hate to leave you here alone, but you need the rest, and maybe you can figure out something from the control room down there. Don't touch any strange controls. Also, there's a chance that the Surnainians might come back before we can get out of here. Check out the exits and be ready to move. We'll get back as soon as possible.

"I would rather do that than sit on a pile of corpses. It's almost worth getting wounded to get out of that job," Sarn said. "Mosets, my good man, you may have my ringside seat with pleasure." Sarn made a sweeping courtly bow.

"Thank you, dear boy. Your kindness is exceeded only by your blatant bumptiousness." Mosets returned the courtly bow. "Sarn, all joking aside, I have a decided feeling that there is more to this old edifice than meets the eye. On our dog walk, we looked over the building as much as possible. One thing caught my eye." Mosets frowned in thought.

"Oh? What?"

"It seems unnecessarily taller than the original design would have called for. Not quite right, somehow."

"I'll give the whole place a thorough search." Sarn's eyes almost glowed with excitement at the prospect of the job at hand.

"Do you understand any Surnainian?" Mosets asked.

"No, I've never had any reason to have it transferred to me."

"Pity. All the controls are marked in that language. I suggest you be most careful before you touch any of the panels."

"You mean as in a self-destruct control and such other cheerful things?"

"Eh, yes. It seems logical they would want to prevent tampering."

"Don't give it another thought, Mosets. Machines and I are like that." He put his hands palm to palm.

"Oh, youth," Mosets sighed.

"Sarn, just be extra careful," Jorl said. "Don't take any chances with anything."

"I will. I won't. Now, hadn't you better get started on your burial program?"

Chapter 20

Sarn walked to the front door with them, anxious to begin his explorations. They took affectionate leave of one another, and Sarn and Rusty watched the three men drive away in Carol's car. "Come on, Rusty, time to have some fun, and work, of course."

The man and dog hurried down the hall to the large room, crossed to the bookcase, and clattered down the stairs.

"This looks like the main control room, Rusty." Sarn's eyes lit up like a child's in candy land. He rubbed his hands together and quickly scanned the banks of controls, trying to feel the use of them.

Rusty stood still, teeth bared, stiff legged, hackles up, and growling deep in his throat.

Sarn squatted down to be face-to-face with him. "It's all right, boy. They're not here. Relax for now." He hugged Rusty and stroked his back and patted his head. "Come on, let's investigate. Have a look at the rest of the place." Rusty relaxed. He padded after Sarn and helped explore the rest of the underground rooms. In short order, they were finished with the inspection.

The rooms were comfortable, unadorned, and with adequate eating and sleeping quarters.

"The whole layout reminds me of something, Rusty. It's almost familiar." He thought about it as he sat at a console.

"Blazing suns!" He slammed a fist into his other hand. "It's laid out like a scout space vehicle. He banged on all the walls and the ceilings. "It's all metal. I wonder . . ."

A wild thought crossed his mind. "Blazing comets, Rusty, maybe the whole house is metal, and they left the outside sheath in place to disguise the fact."

Rusty watched Sarn, his big head going from side to side as he listened intently to him.

"No, they couldn't put it all back on the inside the way it was . . . is. Blazing fireballs, I'm missing something, Rusty—something obvious. What?" He paced around the quarters again. "I guess that bang on my head shook something loose." He looked at the ceilings again.

A brilliant light dawned.

Rusty's intelligent eyes never left Sarn's face, and he woofed in all the right places.

"Hey, Rusty, that must be it. Of course. A whole new floor on the roof. That's what Mosets noticed." He tore back up the stairs to the big room with Rusty close on his heels.

Suddenly, he grabbed for the back of the chair and leaned on it. "Whew, I'm dizzy." He winced as a sudden sharp pain stabbed his side. "I've got to sit down, Rusty." Rusty sat as close as he could to Sarn's knees and woofed a little woof.

Sarn held his head down in his hands. "I guess I'm not quite back to normal yet."

Rusty watched him closely and let it be known he was worried.

"I'm okay, boy, really," and he patted the big head.

Soon, the sharp pain and the dizziness went away. "Okay now, let's go. Come on." He continued his search of the whole main floor.

"Here's just what I need, Rusty—a hefty piece of metal pipe."

Sarn sounded all the walls at intervals and found a few places where the quality of the sound was different. Rusty watch his every move. "Come on upstairs, Rusty. We'll bang some walls up there—see if what I'm beginning to think tests out." A wide grin and a large charge of excitement sent him around the rest of the walls. "Sure enough, Rusty boy, it fits my theory."

"That's exactly what we have here, Rusty—supporting pillars. Four to a side and four internal. Sixteen pillars. That's enough to support a tremendous weight. Now . . . there should be stairs to another floor . . . but there aren't."

He began to knock away the plaster where he was sure one of the supporting pillars would have to continue from downstairs.

Chunks of plaster fell with their accompanying clouds of drifting dust. Between sneezes, Sarn and Rusty finally heard the sound they searched for—metal on metal. Sarn scraped off some disguising paint, and there it was, the dull gleam of construction alloy.

"I was right, Rusty. Blazing suns, I think we've found a—pardon my pun—homemade spaceport."

He made a couple of joyful jumps, curly red hair and glee swirling about. Rusty sat there grinning and making the occasional conversational woof.

"If I'm right, Rusty my friend, anywhere I knock away the plaster on the ceiling, metal should show because . . . that's the floor of the hangar!"

He pulled a wobbly old table to the center of the definitely unused room, jumped up on it, and started banging plaster with determination.

Soon, big chunks began to fall, and smothering white dust drifted down. One fair-sized chunk caught poor Rusty on his sore head. He yelped and backed away. Sarn jumped down and knelt on one knee beside Rusty, petting him. "I'm sorry, boy. You okay?" Rusty licked him affirmatively. You get under the table." Rusty wholeheartedly agreed, and Sarn went back to chipping.

Within the space of a few minutes, the sweet sound of metal on metal made Sarn laugh with pleasure.

He jumped down from the table. From his red hair to his black boots, he was now a dusty white—

Rusty's red coat was an almost perfect match.

Sarn was forced to detour into the bathroom to shower before he could continue. Then, he put Rusty into the stall and turned on the water. Rusty was more than a little apprehensive, and, when he escaped, he shook off the water in a wide, wet circle while snorting like a steam engine. Sarn quickly dried him off, anxious to get on with his exciting discoveries.

"I know there must be some kind of an elevator down here—there's no way to get to the hangar from upstairs. Something in one of these rooms is not what it looks like."

He decided to sound the walls of all the places that could conceivably hide an elevator shaft. By checking the layout upstairs against the wall arrangements in the control room, he eliminated a lot of guesswork. That left him with a limited number of possible hiding places.

"Well Rusty, I can't even find an entrance to a cellar that would show where the foundations are and where the elevator shaft ends. Blazing damn suns. I wish you could smell something."

After another hour, he had to give up. "I know there has to be an elevator shaft to go up and that it's got to be here, Rusty, but I just can't find it. Blazing, spinning comets, where is it?" Rusty listened and commented with more of a grunt than a woof. In frustration, Sarn threw down his improvised tools.

"Let's head for the control room, Rusty. Change of pace is always good."

Bearing Mosets's stern warning in mind, he studied each of the banks with only his eyes. He kept his itching fingers away from the switches. He began to feel a familiarity with the banks of keys—noticed that six of them were in banks of two. They were complete with what appeared to be scanner screens and all of them were identical.

"Strange . . . why six?" He left those controls for a minute to puzzle out the other four.

"Well, Rusty, these two can only be regular communication sets—this must control the hangar. And this one—it looks dangerous. I'd be willing to bet it's a destruct panel—for here, and maybe for remote vehicles." He rubbed his hands together and sat in front of one of the matched six.

"Let's see, now . . . this should be the ON control." He pushed the toggle upward, and immediately the screen activated and a picture snapped into focus.

"Blazing suns, what've I got here?" He studied the still picture intently. "It's a view of a street. Hey, Rusty, that looks familiar. By the comet's tail, that looks like . . ." He sat forward in his chair for a closer look. "That's the building across the street." He studied it for a minute longer. "I think it is. It is! One way to find out for sure. Come on, Rusty."

He bolted upstairs with Rusty right behind him. They opened the front door and looked across the street. "I knew it." Keeping a keen watch, Sarn slipped across the street and looked upward to the top of the old house, scanning for anything that looked out of place. "I don't see anything, let's get back."

He ran back to the doorway and noted points of reference.

"Come on, Rusty." He charged back to the control room and sat down in front of the activated screen. He studied the panel of switches even more intently—bringing all his engineering training into play.

"Well, Rusty, I'm pretty sure I know enough to say this control is safe. But, in case it isn't, I'll say good-bye now." He gave Rusty a pat and kept his hand on Rusty's head. Rusty seemed to understand and gave a big lick to Sarn's wrist.

"I'll choose this one for starters." He held a small lever, color-coded blue, and set it in a perpendicular slot. He gingerly pushed it upward, mentally braced to maybe meet the end of his world.

The picture blurred with the speeding change of perspective. Sarn realized he was a long way up and looking down on the whole city.

"Blazing suns, will you look at that, Rusty?"

Sarn's grin of amazement spread from ear to ear. He eased the lever back slowly, and the screen showed a coming down effect. When the switch was fully back where he had found it, the view was almost the same as before.

"Okay, Rusty, if whatever it is can go up and down—I'll lay you six beers to a new soup bone that there must be some way to make it go back and forth." He reached for another lever—color-coded in yellow—with the slot running horizontally. "This time, I'll take it slow." Tongue between his teeth and with deep concentration he carefully moved the lever to the right. He saw buildings to his right zipping under him—reversed to the left and saw buildings to his left.

"This is definitely some kind of a surveillance device. Wonderful. Well, now . . . that's up and down, and back and forth . . . then this green knob should control the direction of the lens." He turned it and got a complete 360-degree turn of view on the screen.

"What a great surveillance tool. We have a remote control camera, Rusty. I wonder what it looks like?" With great care, he manipulated all the controls and set whatever it was in front of the house. On the screen, he saw the front door getting closer. Within a few seconds, what could only be a portion of the bottom panels filled the screen.

"Rusty boy," Sarn whispered, "I hate to admit it, but I'm almost afraid to go up there and open the door." He got up from the console, slowly. "But I have to go." Upstairs they trooped, and down the hall. Sarn paused with his hand on the doorknob.

"Rusty, over here, behind me." For some reason, which annoyed him, he felt the need to whisper. "It could be a booby trap."

Sarn slowly opened the door and looked down in awe. Rusty sneaked a look, yelped, and jumped back so hard he tripped over his back feet and sat down with a thump that made him yelp louder, which evidently embarrassed him.

"Don't feel bad, Rusty. If I were you, I would've yelped even louder."

Sarn shook his head in disbelief. "Blazing suns, I see it, but still I don't believe it."

There on the step stood a three-foot-high bird, complete with feathers, talons, hooked beak, and almost glowing red eyes.

"It looks like an, a, well—a bald eagle—this country's national emblem. Rusty—look—at—that."

Rusty ventured a slightly closer look at the apparition that stood as still as stone in the doorway.

Sarn stared for a few seconds longer, then booted off down the hall to the control room. He wanted to examine this . . . bird? . . . more closely.

Rusty won the race. No way was he leaving his tail end exposed to anything that looked like that.

Manipulating the switches gently, Sarn controlled the bird's trip down the hall, through the big room's door and down the metal stairs, until he saw his own back on the screen. The effect made the hairs on the back of his neck stand on end. Rusty knew all about the hairs on his back. From his ears to his tailbone, each one stood tall.

Sarn quickly shut off the controls. He got down on his knees and delicately examined the strange sight. He noticed that the wings seemed to be hinged and, on a hunch, activated the screen. There were three controls in a small section by themselves that he hadn't tried yet.

"This one. It's color-coded green—shouldn't be dangerous. The green one on the other panel wasn't. So we'll try this one, Rusty. Now, let's see what will happen." Rusty watched Sarn, his eyes never left Sarn's face."

Slowly, Sarn pushed the control up. As he did so, the wings of the bird began to lift.

Rusty crowded behind Sarn and sat there watching from between Sarn's legs. He growled in the back of his throat at the thing. Sarn's jaw dropped as the wings lifted and spread to a span of about six feet and stayed in the gliding position. When Sarn returned the lever to its original position, so did the wings return to theirs.

Sarn switched off the set and continued his examination. He felt the metal framework and marveled at the perfect job of feathering it. It looked real.

"Those eyes are the lenses, Rusty. I wonder why the beak is hinged, though?" He sat back on his heels, thinking.

"There are two controls left. One is red, and that's danger in most languages. The last one is a black push button. Rusty, I bet the red one fires a small missile of some sort through the beak, and the black button destroys the whole bird. It has to be. What an invention. It's ingenious. And who would tamper with a wild and protected bird? No one. And that means there are five more of them scattered around. Perfect mobile observation posts."

Sarn jumped to his feet. So did Rusty. "Do you know what I'm going to do now, Rusty boy?" Sarn chuckled at the idea that he thought of and grinned. "I'm going to fly this thing out into the desert and have a look at the Surnainian ship, and then I'll take a peek at Jorl, Khair, and Mosets and see how they're doing slugging it out in the heat and the desert." He sat down at the console to begin the maneuver of getting the bird to the front door.

He was so intent on his new toy that he didn't notice Rusty get up and listen and didn't hear any footsteps. The first he heard was the clatter on the metal steps. He jumped to his feet and whirled to face the door as he drew his stun pack. The noise had been so sudden that sweat popped out on his forehead. Rusty barked and wagged his tail.

Tarla, her stun pack out, ran down the steps, turned into the control room and stopped in her tracks. She stared in silence at Sarn and his weapon—then at the huge, feathery thing. Eloise bumped into her and she, too, stood and stared at the weird tableau.

"Whew," Sarn whooshed when he put his stun pack away and wiped his forehead. "You shouldn't sneak up on a person like that . . . especially someone in my weakened condition."

"The front door was wide open. I saw big chunks of stuff and white dust all over everything. I thought you were in trouble, or . . ." Tarla's voice shook a little. She put her stun pack away with a slight reaction shake in her hand.

Eloise ran to him. "Oh, gee, Sarn honey, you look so pale . . . and," she pointed at the bird, "and . . . what's that thing. Is it real? Is it dangerous?"

"I'd like to know, too," Tarla said. She knelt down to examine it with a delicate touch. "It's beautifully made. What does it do?"

"It's a perfectly disguised mobile observation post. It has fantastic speed and fire power to an unknown extent." Sarn craned his head to look at the door. "Where's Carol? Is she upstairs?"

Tarla shook her head. "When I was having my shower, she came into the bathroom for something or other. I couldn't hear her because of the running water, but I suddenly felt her thoughts. She couldn't fight herself any longer. The red spheres were there in my pocket. She took them and ran."

Eloise started to cry.

"But, blazing suns, why didn't you grab her? Why didn't you stop her?"

"All of us knew the temptation was deep in her from the very beginning, and we all hoped she could overcome it. But, in the end, her drive for her own preservation overcame every other consideration. Khair, us, Eloise, everyone . . ."

Sarn nodded.

"I could have stopped her but, why? She was free to choose, and one box of Forever won't change the Earth."

"What will Khair say . . . how will he feel?" Eloise sobbed.

Tarla patted her shoulder. "Khair knew she wanted them but hoped she wanted life with all of us more. He'll understand. That's why I let her go."

"You were right, Tarla. But it's really sad for Khair. Maybe she'll change her mind and come back," Sarn said. He turned around to face the controls. "Well, on with my project."

He quickly told them the story of finding the secret hangar and the consoles. "I was just about to send Number 5 Bird out to scout the

Surnainian ship and then drop in on Jorl to see how they're getting along without me. Tarla, you run upstairs and open the door so it can get out."

Tarla did. When she came back, she and Eloise pulled up chairs, one on each side of Sarn, and were as enthralled as he was.

Rusty had sniffed the whole place over thoroughly after the bird left. He sighed in relief and thumped to the floor just behind Sarn for a well-earned rest.

Sarn quickly became adept at handling the controls and was soon able to show them some fancy televising. He swooped and dipped all around the city and on out toward the desert.

"There's the highway down there," Sarn said.

He started the big bird on its way again. He swooped and zoomed all over the desert playing, along with his searching. All three were fascinated by the amazing travelogue.

"There they are," Sarn said. He brought his camera down close.

"Jorl—Khair—Mosets!" Eloise squealed.

The three men stood around the front of the car, almost disappearing in clouds of vapor. Jorl bent to open the hood.

"The car must have broken down," Tarla said. "Can you tell where they are?"

Sarn drove the bird in a wide circle around the car. "Yes. See? They're almost to the main road on their way back here. I wonder what they'll do. Get to the main road and flag down a vehicle?"

"Gee, Sarn honey, should you try to tell them where they are, or something?"

Sarn, with an impish grin, zoomed the bird straight down and landed it gently on the roof of the car. It visibly startled the three men. Sarn kept the wings slowly flapping. The two girls and Sarn watched the conversation their bird had started. They saw Khair coming closer to have a good look. Sarn zipped the bird straight up and landed it right behind Jorl who jumped quite high. Then, Sarn landed it as quickly right behind Mosets, who also rewarded Sarn with a quick leap to one side. Sarn kept the bird going up and down in front of and behind each of the men till Jorl drew his stun pack, whereupon Sarn lowered the wings and stayed very still in front of Jorl.

Jorl came closer to the bird again, made motions with his hands, and mouthed a sound.

"It looks as if he's trying to communicate, but what's he saying?" Sarn asked. "All he does is open his mouth like a fish and hold up three fingers."

"He's saying 'Sarn,'" Eloise said, "look, watch my mouth when I say Sarn."

"It could be, but why would he think it was me? And why is he waving three fingers?"

"Maybe if you flap the wings three times, it would mean 'Yes, it's Sarn,'" Tarla said.

"Maybe." He quickly raised and lowered the wings three times. The actions seemed to satisfy the three men, and Jorl shook his fist at the bird and then laughed.

"I think he's telling you that he's somewhat annoyed with you and the way that you startled them," Tarla said.

Sarn grinned and shrugged. "Hey, watch—Jorl is trying to tell us something." By motions they understood that the car was useless, but old Bill's place was over there. Try and get him to bring back his jeep to get them.

Sarn flapped his wings three times and took off.

As the bird flew, it was a matter of only a few minutes before they saw Bill's homestead. Sarn swooped down and sat on the porch. There was no sign of life.

"Can you make the bird peek in the windows, Sarn honey?"

"Sure." Sarn looked through every window and found no sign of Bill anywhere.

"Look in the barn—see if the two burros are there," Tarla said. After a thorough search, they knew beyond a doubt that Bill, Tessie, and Jessie were gone.

"He must have gone out prospecting," Sarn said. "I bet he went looking for the Surnainians."

"I hope he hasn't found them," Tarla said.

"So do I."

Sarn sent the bird in the direction he guessed the Surnainian ship almost had to be in. The terrain quickly turned from sand to rocks, with higher and higher outcroppings. It was wild, empty, but somehow a beautiful sight.

Then, Sarn sent the bird in wide, looping, searching arcs looking for some trace of old Bill and his burros.

"It's getting late. It'll be dark in a couple of hours. Then we won't be able to see any movement—that'll make it harder to spot him," Sarn said.

They searched in different directions without any luck. They were a long way from Bill's homestead.

"Old Bill must have left home the next day to have covered so much ground," Sarn said.

"There." Tarla pointed to the bottom left of the screen. "I thought I saw something moving."

Sarn swung the bird around and down a little. In a second, they saw what could only be Bill, Tessie, and Jessie.

Sarn dropped closer, and a peaceful scene filled the screen.

Bill and his two girls had made camp on a small level shelf protected by rocks on three sides. They saw Bill sitting beside a small fire holding a pan over the embers and a pot sitting on a rock beside it. The two burros were standing quietly close by.

Sarn, unthinkingly, got close enough to make Jessie and Tessie restless. Tarla put a restraining hand on Sarn's arm. "Don't disturb them, Sarn. If the Surnainians are close by, they might pick up a strong signal and destroy them before we could get there."

Sarn nodded agreement and gained altitude. This gave him a sudden view over the ridge and into a small, natural valley. "Blazing suns and big black holes, there they are. That's the Surnainians' ship," Sarn whispered. He felt a small lurch in his stomach, maybe a small advance signal of things to come.

Tucked away in the middle of the surrounding small hills that were dotted with sparse vegetation, the ship was almost invisible.

"It won't take Bill more than ten minutes to come across it," Sarn said.

"Somehow, we've got to stop him." Concern and urgency colored her voice.

"If Jorl could get to Bill's jeep and take it as far as possible, and then if they run like speeding comets, the three of them might get there before Bill makes a move. Maybe," Sarn said. He flew the bird directly back to the car.

"How will you tell them what you want them to do, Sarn honey?" Eloise twisted her hands in worried excitement.

"I'll think of something. There they are. I'll land the bird in front of them and flap the wings."

Sarn swooped in for a perfect landing, then, going as fast as possible, began to start off in one direction, come back to the men, and repeat the moves. The three soon got the idea that Sarn wanted them to follow the bird.

"There, they understand. There're going to follow me." Sarn set the course in a direct line to Bill's place. By the speed of the bird's comings and goings, the three watching the screen could tell that Jorl guessed it was urgent.

The three men opened up and ran. They were in perfect physical condition to begin with, and that allowed them to reach, and maintain, a running speed that would leave most people in the dust.

Sarn made sure they could see the bird at all times, but it was still almost an hour before they raced up the roadway to Bill's front door.

The heat of the August sun, added to the physical exertion of running, left them almost winded and breathing hard. They sat on the steps for a rest.

"Here," Mosets said, reaching into his pouch, "take one of these." He handed them a very small white pill for energy and took one himself.

In a matter of a few seconds, they felt an upsurge of strength and well-being.

Sarn perched the bird in front of them and bounced it up and down to show his impatience and the need to hurry.

Sarn led them around the side of the house to the jeep. He perched on the hood and flapped the wings.

Sarn, Tarla, and Eloise watched as Jorl got behind the wheel and Khair sat beside him. Mosets got into the back. Sarn lifted the bird a little way up and hovered over the vehicle.

Jorl turned the key and looked puzzled at the extra pedal and the rod coming up from the floor. They saw him shrug his shoulders and prepare to drive the normal way. He didn't go anywhere.

"Oh, Sarn, that's a standard shift. Jorl can drive only an automatic. He's" . . . Eloise put a hand on each side of her face and desperately wanted to cover her eyes.

Jorl stamped on the three pedals and jerked the stick. By accident, he hit the right combination of clutch and shift and roared off—backward—into the chicken house.

"Not chickens again." Sarn began to chuckle, then leaned back, and roared with laughter till tears ran down his face. "B-blazing suns, I know it's a matter of life and death but . . ." He wiped the tears from his eyes. He quickly moved the bird out of the way of the oncoming cloud of dust, chickens, and a violently jerking jeep.

Tarla and Eloise were unable to help themselves—their peals of laughter joined Sarn's.

Jorl stalled the jeep. He pushed pedals and moved the stick and jerked along with violent jerks. He finally hit the right combination and moved forward, erratically. Khair and Mosets held their hands over their heads whenever they were not trying to save themselves from being dumped from the wildly cavorting vehicle.

Jorl tried his hand at circles, squares, and triangles but steered very few straight lines.

"That utterly damned chicken yard, and those equally damned occupants, are continually in the damn way," Jorl yelled. "How do I get out of this damn place?"

It wasn't hard to tell that Jorl was employing every swearword he had ever known. He took one hand off the steering wheel long enough to shake a hard fist in the bird's face.

"Sarn, he's mad at you," Eloise told him. Quite unnecessarily.

The bird flew a jerky course because every time Sarn tried to control himself enough to work the controls, he went off into fresh gales of laughter. "Oh, my sore side," he gasped, holding his almost healed wound tightly.

"Oh, my poor darling Jorl," Tarla said. She also had to wipe laugh tears from her eyes.

"There. He's getting the hang of it now."

Sure enough, Jorl had the spirited beast under some sort of control and had it turned in the right direction.

"It's going to be dark soon. That's going to make it harder to lead them," Sarn said.

"Gee, Sarn, the moon is supposed to be full tonight and should come up soon. Most of the time, you can almost read by the light of it."

"They've got a long way to go, Sarn. Can you think of any way that you could tell them to take food and water with them before they start out?" Tarla asked.

"I could try." Sarn landed the bird in front of the jeep and flapped the wings three times in order to get the men's full attention. Then he pecked the ground, then flew toward Bill's house. The three men watched the antics for about three repeats. Puzzled. Then, Jorl pointed to himself and pretended to peck the ground, put something in his mouth, rubbed his stomach, and licked his lips. Sarn jumped the bird up and down, flapped its wings three times, and then headed for the front door of the cabin. Came back to the jeep and went back to the door. The three got the idea. They carefully opened a window, and Jorl got inside and opened the door to let Khair, Mosets and the bird in.

Sarn bounced the bird to the kitchen and pointed to food. Then he bounced it over to the sink and pecked the tap.

"Pretty smart, Sarn," Jorl said.

Khair stood in front of the eagle and, in mime, indicated eating and drinking.

Sarn bounced the bird up and down. "He's got it. Eat and drink. I'd better make sure they take it with them, not just eat now." Sarn jumped the bird up and down for attention, then quickly pecked the food and the tap and the front door. He repeated the actions twice. "They get the message," Sarn said. "Khair is looking for containers."

Sarn got the bird rushing about the living room until the men got the message to hurry. They went outdoors.

"Look, Sarn, the moon is rising. You should be able to see well enough quite soon," Tarla said. "So should Jorl."

In a short while, the desert landscape was bathed in the soft light of the rising full moon as she rode into the night sky from between two hills.

Sarn set a course for the jeep. Finally, it became too rough even for the jeep, and its three passengers left it where it was and followed their guide over the increasingly rocky terrain.

It was a hard run, and the three men took rests when needed. At least, it wasn't hot.

Sarn, running on pure adrenaline, continually flew to Bill's camp and back.

The sun is beginning to come up," Tarla warned. She stifled a yawn and stretched. Both she and Eloise had fallen asleep in their chairs.

"Yes, and Jorl is still about a half hour's travel away from Bill. Let's hope the old guy sleeps late," Sarn said. He put his arm around Eloise who was almost awake now. "Morning, sunshine."

Eloise smiled sleepily at him.

"He won't. Look." Tarla pointed. The bird made another pass over the campsite and they saw old Bill stand up and stretch.

"He's only got to look over the ledge to see the ship. I hope he'll be content to watch awhile and leave it alone," Tarla said.

"There he goes," Sarn said.

Bill, evidently enjoying the feel of the morning, ambled over to the lip of the ledge to get the benefit of a full view. They watched him scan the panorama, then suddenly drop to his belly, and cautiously look over the edge, lying as still as the rocks.

"Too late," Tarla sighed. "Now what? What should we do?"

"Just hope Jorl gets there before Bill figures out a way to attack it," Sarn said.

"Do you honestly think he would? Attack it, I mean?" Eloise asked. Sarn nodded.

"Oh-h," Eloise sighed.

His mind busy with ways and means of protecting old Bill from the possible results of his undoubted courage, Sarn was momentarily inattentive to his controls.

"Sarn. Look out!" Tarla pointed to the screen.

The big bird was heading straight for a cliff face. It was too late to gain altitude as a ledge was above him. He slowed down enough so that he didn't hit hard, but the bird was tightly wedged into a crevice.

Sarn slowly, and carefully, manipulated the controls, afraid of damaging the mechanism, but nothing budged. The big bird was stuck tight.

"Didn't you say that maybe the beak fired a missile?" Tarla almost whispered.

"Blazing suns, that's right. And that sure would alert the Surnainians." Sarn's frown of concentration deepened.

The edges of three big rocks with a tiny chink of light on the high right side filled the whole screen. Sarn gently used the controls much like someone with a land vehicle stuck in the mud—reverse, forward, turn, reverse, forward, turn—"It moved a little, I think," Tarla said. She pointed to the rock edges as reference points.

"How long have I been?" Sarn asked. He had started to sweat from the extreme concentration.

"About fifteen minutes," Eloise answered.

Sarn grunted.

With abrupt suddenness, the entire screen filled with daylight. Sarn shoved the attitude control, ramming it straight up. The bird passed a huge jagged rock going in the same direction.

"What happened?" Tarla asked.

"Gee-e-e . . ." Eloise's eyes were round with wonder.

"I'm not too sure," Sarn said. He flipped the bird to look down. "Looks like an explosion. Explosion?"

He zoomed straight for the campsite. They were dismayed at what they saw.

The Surnainians must have come out of the ship, and old Bill opened fire on them with his rifle. Looks like Bill shot—" Sarn counted, "three of them before they fired the missile that brought down that piece of the hill. Now they're coming up on Bill."

Two of the remaining five crew members of the eight-man Surnainian vehicle were on the ramp. The other three were armed and closing in on the unseen enemy. One, with drawn weapon, worked his way closer to the bottom of the ledge where Bill had camped. They could also see the two burros bucking and kicking, evidently terrified. Dust still rose from the blasted-out rock from two of the walls close to the campsite.

Sarn brought the bird to the ground, which added to the terror of the two burros, and skimmed it over the freshly turned rock looking for Bill. They found him, still lying by the lip of the shelf, his rifle aimed at the advancing Surnainians. He was covered in rocks and rock dust. One huge slab had his legs pinned to the ground.

When Sarn put the big bird beside Bill, he, evidently in great pain but still game, turned his rifle on it. Sarn bounced the bird out of the way but tried to show Bill it was friendly.

They watched old Bill shrug and accept the fact that a raggedy-looking eagle wanted to befriend him.

"Quick, Sarn, see where Jorl and the others are before Bill fires again," Tarla said.

Seconds later, they found them. Within a few minutes' climb, they would be at old Bill's side. Sarn bounced the bird three times in front of them and showed them the way up.

Jorl, Khair, and Mosets were sweating and dusty. They had put on an even greater burst of speed after they heard the explosion.

Sarn breathed a huge sigh of relief as the three men climbed on the ledge and ran toward old Bill. They looked over the edge and saw the whole picture.

Suddenly, Bill's face convulsed, and Sarn, Tarla, and Eloise watched the silent scream.

"Mind blast," Tarla said. "Can you do something, Sarn?"

"Hope so." He drove the bird toward the nearest Surnainian. He reached for the red push button. "I don't know what this does, but I hope it fires a missile."

The Surnainian disappeared in a blue flash. When the noxious cloud dissipated, so had the Surnainian, completely.

The remaining two Surnainians ran for their ship. Sarn fired a missile at the next nearest one. When it was done, the last Surnainian had disappeared into the ship, and the port began to close behind him.

Sarn drove the bird at full speed and made it inside just as the hydraulics slammed the port into place. The third Surnainian, at the console preparing for lift-off, turned around when he heard a strange sound and looked with almost frightened puzzlement at the invader.

Sarn wasted no time gloating over his first sight of a self-acknowledged master of the universe suffering from the human emotion of fear. He headed the bird straight for the hatch leading to the drive and sat the bird on the most vulnerable spot. He reached for the last black button. He hesitated for a second. "I sort of hate to do this."

"What?" Eloise asked.

"Self-destruct," Sarn replied.

"Oh. Oh-h," Eloise said. She had suddenly realized what he meant. "Poor big bird."

"Hurry, Sarn, the dials show 1.130 seconds to the liftoff condition."

Sarn pressed the button firmly. The screen lit for a microsecond with a searing white light—then it went black and dead. "Scratch another Surnainian ship. I forget how many Mosets said there were." Sarn sighed, "Scratch number five eagle. I must say I feel sorry about it. I grew to like that bird." He activated the sixth console. "The bird is dead—long live the bird. Now, let's see where this one is."

Chapter 21

After a hard climb through the rubble and dust of the explosion, the three men finally made it to the campsite.

Jorl knelt by old Bill's side as Khair and Mosets heaved the heavy rock from his legs. They gently turned the old man over, and Jorl cradled his head on his arm. Bill's eyes blinked open. He winced with pain when Mosets examined his legs.

"Wal, now, young feller—Jorl, ain't it?—Seems to have been a busy sort a morning, and it ain't above a half hour old."

Mosets prepared the health box to administer the same liquid that he had given to Sarn. Then he leaned forward to place the box directly on the old man's jugular vein.

Bill gasped with a jolt of pain from his legs. "Hey, hold on there, young feller. I don't reckon we've met."

Khair could hear the pain in Bill's voice that he tried not to show. "Leastways, tell me your name afore you make some kinda pincushion outta me."

"This is one of our dearest friends, Bill. This is Mosets. He will make you well—fast," Jorl said.

"Another danged furriner," Bill said. He smiled. When Mosets retracted the health box, he winced. "Never could abide needles." Bill winked up at Jorl. "He, by any chance, the orange ball?"

Jorl was puzzled for a moment. Then, Bill's earlier description came to his mind. "Right, Bill, and down there are the remains of one of the blue ones."

"Wal, now. Things seem to be movin' right along smartly. Which reminds me, you seen anything of a big, raggedy eagle?"

Jorl laughed. "Yes, indeed. Sarn found that remote control thing somewhere and led us to you."

"Figures. Can't picture him using one a them heleocoptor things, or something simple like that." He looked down at his legs. "Both pins broke, eh?" He looked up at Mosets and Khair.

"Afraid so, Bill," Khair replied, "but they'll soon mend."

Mosets examined Bill's legs and hips more closely.

Khair started to lay the two broken legs straight when Mosets said, "Be careful, Khair." He spoke barely above a whisper. "They feel crushed—not just broken. And so is this hip. We will have to work more carefully." He barely touched a leg when he saw Bill wince and go suddenly pale. "Sorry, Bill, but the pain will soon go away."

"Yup." Bill felt intense pain but the injected liquid had already begun the healing process. "Six months mebbe, if these old bones ain't too damn brittle and dried out."

"By tomorrow, they will be healed, and by the next day, stronger than ever," Khair assured him.

"Yah? Wal, that's as mebbe. In the meantime," Bill had started to sweat, "anyhow, would you fellers catch Jessie and Tessie so I can gentle them down afore they bust a few of their own legs?"

Suddenly, Bill turned deathly white and passed out. His breathing became labored and raggedy. Mosets felt his pulse. "I fear the worst—he has begun a heart attack. Jorl, the injection is not strong enough. He is dying. As a captain of the Federation, will you permit me to administer a Forever pill?"

"I herby give you full permission to save Bill's life. Hurry, Mosets, he looks . . . hurry."

Mosets put a Forever on Bill's tongue and gently rubbed Bill's throat until he felt him swallow it.

Within two seconds, the dangerous, deathly symptoms began to disappear.

Still not quite conscious, old Bill tossed and turned and said, "Need to catch Jessie and Tessie. They're frightened—hurt themselves." Bill opened his eyes and then quietened down some.

"I will bring them to you," Mosets said. He walked unhesitatingly toward the spot where both burros were standing still for a minute, quiveringly ready to run at even an imagined falling leaf.

"It'll mebbe take a mite longer to catch 'em than he figures on, and bringing 'em to me may be rougher than he thinks." Bill's body was rapidly improving.

They watched as Mosets walked slowly and steadily toward both animals, patted them, and started back toward Bill, leading two quiet animals.

"I'll be danged," Bill whispered. "He's sure got a way with him." Already Bill's condition had dramatically improved. "Wal, now, since there's nothing left to be done for a few minutes, Jessie and Tessie gotta be fed and watered. Then, we'll brew us some coffee and have some breakfast."

The three of them carried Bill over to a flat spot, found his packs and blankets, and had their first lesson in outdoor camp lore.

Under Bill's orders, they got a proper campfire going, boiled coffee, cooked beans, and made pan biscuits.

"Wal, now, you've done right well considerin' you're city folks, and furriners, and all." He sipped more coffee. "Right well."

The three of them felt pleased, and then Jorl started laughing.

"What's so funny, young feller?" Bill asked.

"Well, it's only that—well, all three of us," he swept his arm to include Khair and Mosets, "all three of us have our heads stuffed full of technology that is almost unbelievable. We drive interstellar ships, we have been all over the galaxies, and here we are, pleased with ourselves, because we made a prospector's breakfast under extremely basic conditions, after having just blown up a space vehicle. It's, well, it's unbelievable," Jorl said. He was amazed at the reality of the incredulous situation.

"Put like that, it's also ludicrous, to say the least, and totally ridiculous," Khair said. They all had a good laugh.

"Mebbe if more folks would take time out from zappin' around in the sky to walkin' around in the mountains, this world, and mebbe some of yours, might be improved some."

"Yup," Jorl agreed, "and the air sure is nice."

The four men made themselves comfortable and enjoyed the companionable silence. Without meaning to, they all dozed off.

The sudden braying of Jessie and Tessie woke them up with a start.

"Be danged. Here comes another one." Bill pointed.

Jorl, slightly disoriented after such a deep sleep, went for his stun pack. "What? Another what?" He sat up and found himself nose to beak with an eagle-type bird.

"Oh," Jorl relaxed, "he's found another one." He turned to Bill with a smile.

Bill still held his arm out, steady and unmoving, and his face was frozen in a look of startled disbelief.

"It's all right, Bill. It's just another bird."

Bill didn't even hear. He stared, transfixed, at his arm and still pointing finger.

"Bill, what's wrong? Are you in pain?" Jorl moved closer to him, worried.

"Look," Bill whispered. "Look at my hand . . . and . . . arm, and my other—they don't appear to be mine—and my legs hardly hurt."

Jorl patted his shoulder. "That is a little gift from Mosets. He has given you about one hundred good years of life."

Bill looked at all of himself that he could see and wonderingly felt the play of younger muscles under a smooth, taut skin. "You mean to say—that little pill—I'm young and healthy again?" Bill's face slowly filled with a wondering joy as the knowledge settled in.

"Yes, Bill." Jorl gripped Bill's shoulder. "You've been given a second chance to use as you wish."

Old Bill was thoughtful. Finally, he said softly, "Another kick at the can calls for some heavy thinking—yup, it sure does."

Jorl smiled and stood up. "Yup, it sure does."

Mosets and Khair had been busy putting a makeshift stretcher together. They laid it beside a not-so-old Bill, and the three of them lifted him on it.

Sarn kept the whole area under surveillance as the four men and two burros began to pick their way toward the jeep. The sun was now well up in the flat blue sky. It was hot, dusty thirsty work.

They came to the place where the Surnainian blast had started a rockslide that had completely obliterated the trail. The three men could have managed to find their way across, but the two burros flatly refused.

"Nothing to do but retrace and go down and around." Jorl sighed at the thoughts of the long, hard walk.

Sarn, in the guise of Big Bird #6, scouted the area looking for a possible way through the rockslide. He landed in front of them and motioned them back to a safe distance.

"Now what is the youngster up to?" Mosets asked. He kept a tight rein on the two frightened burros.

Sarn had turned the bird to face the slide.

Khair snapped his fingers. "He's going to blast it out. Take cover." They hurried behind a shield of rock and saw Sarn's eagle watching them. Sarn couldn't resist an entrepreneur's bow before he turned back and prepared to blast away the blocking rubble.

Back in the control room, Tarla said, "How do you know that you won't start another slide, Sarn?"

"To backtrack would cost at last three hours. The other Surnainian ship could show up here any minute."

Tarla nodded agreement with the logic, but that didn't lessen the crawl of fear in her stomach.

"Besides, we've had a good close look at the area, and it's only a short distance through the blockage. One well-placed missile should clear it out." He placed the bird in the best possible angle and reached for the red button.

Two seconds later, the sound waves in the area were in a complete uproar, and the hot smell of ozone enveloped them. They had just begun to spit out the dust when Eagle appeared before them. One wing dragged in the dust, and his feathers looked a bit singed; nonetheless, he moved with a definite swagger. He motioned them from behind their cover. The way was clear.

A few hard hours later, Khair pointed. "There it is, right where we left it."

"That certainly is a welcome sight," Mosets said.

In about twenty minutes, they were all loaded into the jeep, and within another two minutes, they knew it wouldn't budge.

Sarn, hovering around, threw up his good wing in disgust. He turned to Tarla and Eloise and said in disgust, "Blazing damn suns."

"Sarn, it's not Jorl's fault," Tarla said.

"I suppose not."

They watched the four men talking to each other. Old Bill nodded, rummaged through his pack, and took a piece of paper and a stub of a pencil from a jacket pocket.

"Look, Sarn honey. Old Bill is writing something." Eloise peered into the monitor.

All three of them could see that Jorl was telling Bill what to write. When he finished, Jorl took the piece of paper and held it up in front of the bird's eyes. To correct the focus, Sarn backed the bird up a little. The three of them read it aloud. In essence, the note said to meet them at Bill's house with some kind of vehicle and to hurry.

Mosets was the only one who could make the frightened burros behave. This left Khair and Jorl to take up Bill's stretcher again. The bedraggled group headed across the desert toward Bill's homestead.

Eagle took off in a hurry to organize transportation from the other end.

Chapter 22

✳ ✳ ✳

arn had just got the bird neatly parked on the roof of the old house when the seventh console burst into loud, bright life. It momentarily scared the wits out of all of them.

"Stay back," Sarn whispered. "We don't know if it's automatically a two-way scan or not."

"Oh—oh-h." Eloise wailed quietly. "What's that awful man saying?"

"Shh-h," Sarn whispered. "I don't know."

The two-foot square screen filled with the darkly handsome head and shoulders of a Surnainian. The small area of background they could see appeared to be a ship's control room.

The three stayed breathlessly still while the Surnainian repeated the same set of sounds over and over. His tone got more and more angry at each repetition. Finally, with what looked like a bad-tempered gesture, he evidently slammed a switch, and the transmission ended. The screen went dead.

"Seems someone's supposed to be on duty here and is in for a chewing out," Sarn grinned, possibly with the memory of a few chewing outs of which he'd been on the chewed side.

"They are probably close and expect to come in to dock," Tarla said, "and, to say the least, we're a little shorthanded. And to say the most, we shouldn't even be here."

"Right. Let me think . . ." Sarn slammed his forehead with the palm of his hand, "And we need wheels. Come on." He ran for the stairs and the telephone with Eloise and Tarla close behind him, and Rusty led the way to wherever it was they were going.

"Eloise. Eloise, get Johnny on this." He thrust the phone at her.

Eloise nodded, reached for the phone book, and began to unhurriedly search for the number.

"Hurry, Eloise, hurry."

"I can't hurry. I'll only get mixed up." She began to dial the number, carefully checking each digit.

Sarn was practically bouncing from foot to foot. "At least, speed up to a crawl. Blazing suns . . ."

Eloise paused—one finger holding the dial from completing its turn and another on the hotel number. "My daddy always said 'more haste, less speed,' and I've never seen a dial phone before—it's always push buttons, so . . ." and, with utter concentration, continued her job of dialing.

"Okay, just try to hurry a little. Hurry!" Sarn tried to control his impatience, but his arms were flying all over the place as he paced back and forth.

"Sarn, Sarn." Tarla held Sarn's arm. "Stop it. Leave her alone."

Sarn jiggled around and tried to control his urge to hurry Eloise.

"I need to speak to your Mr. Johnny Dill, please . . . Yes, it is an emergency . . . a family emergency. Thank you."

Sarn came up close to her and asked in a loud whisper, "What's happening?"

"I'm waiting for him to come to the phone."

"Tell them to hurry. Blazing comet tails . . ."

"I can't, Sarn. No one's there yet. Besides, my daddy always said . . ."

"Damn your daddy."

"Sarn." Eloise was shocked. Her chin began to wobble.

"I'm sorry. I'm sorry." He put his arm around her and dropped a loving kiss on her forehead. "But when you do get hold of Johnny, tell him to hurry up and get here. It's an emergency. Promise him anything. Tarla, I'm going down to the control room. I've got to somehow warn Jorl that there's another Surnainian ship that is probably heading in for a rendezvous with the one we just blew up."

Tarla nodded, feeling the same urgency as Sarn. "I'll make sure that Johnny gets here, Sarn, but you'd better do an extra careful scan of the whole area."

Sarn nodded, threw a kiss to Eloise, and then clattered down the metal stairs. Rusty's toenails clickety-clicked close behind him.

Sarn sat in front of the console, reactivated the eagle, and zoomed it off toward the part of the desert with which he was becoming intimately familiar.

A few minutes later, Tarla and Eloise hurried into the control room. "Johnny's on his way, Sarn honey," Eloise reported.

"Without an argument?" Sarn raised his eyebrows in surprise.

"A thousand dollars cools a lot of disagreement," Tarla replied.

Sarn laughed. "One thing about our Johnny, he stays true to his money god."

Tarla smiled. "That's what makes Johnny our Johnny. He's dependable." She looked at the screen. "Any sign of the ship?"

"Nope, not yet."

Intently, they watched the scenes flashing dazzlingly across the screen.

"Johnny should be here any minute," Eloise said. "Shall I go up and wait for him." Her bravery was patently forced.

Tarla and Sarn both smiled tenderly at her.

"Dummy," Sarn said, a tone of tenderness in his voice. He put his arm around her shoulders. "Tarla will go."

As Tarla headed for the metal steps, Sarn said, "Bring him down here, Sis. I'll show him the way from here."

Eloise cuddled into Sarn's free arm and looked adoringly up at him. Sarn reached over to the switches, hastily landed the bird, and held Eloise as close as he possibly could. A tremendous surge of passion flooded them both.

"I want you in bed—now." He almost growled into her soft hair behind her ear.

"Me, too, but . . . but . . ."

"I know." He loosened his grip and put his two hands on her lovely face. "There will be years of time later . . . whenever we get out of this blazing damn mess." He threw up his arms in disgust.

Eloise looked up at Sarn through her long lashes. "If it weren't for this mess, we wouldn't be loving each other now, would we?" Her wide pansy eyes sparkled with mischief. "Besides, as my daddy always said . . ."

"What did your daddy always say?" Without waiting for her answer, he pulled her close and kissed her, long and deep.

They were oblivious to the whole outside universe and were lost in the wonder of their own.

With nerve-blasting suddenness, the communication set once again blasted forth just as Tarla and a decidedly nervous Johnny rounded the corner.

All one hundred and twenty-five pounds of Rusty leaped to his feet and stood quivering and stiff legged, torn two ways—one at the stranger, Johnny, and the other at the violent noise from the console. *Attack*, he thought, *but what? Which?* and barked as loud as he could at both. He turned to the nervous Johnny and growled deep in his throat with teeth bared. He turned and barked even louder at the communicator with a growl even more hair-raising than the one at Johnny.

Sarn, startled from all directions at once, clamped his hands over his ears and roared, "Black damned holes."

That about took care of the rest of Johnny's fast-ebbing courage, and he turned to bolt back up the stairs. Tarla grabbed him by the back of his collar.

"There, there, dear Johnny Dill. Calm yourself."

"N-not even for a thousand bucks do I wanna get any further into this crazy house act. I'm for out. L-let me go!" His voice slid up to a thin scream as he struggled to get away.

"There, there, Johnny Dill." Tarla crooned as she gently slid into his mind to calm him.

Rusty interlaced his growls with well-placed sharp, deep barks.

Sarn swore at everything.

Eloise timidly tugged at Sarn's sleeve for attention. "Didn't you say it could be a two-way screen, Sarn? Sarn?"

He threw up his arms in pure disgust. "Blazing suns, it's too late to worry about that now. What a shambles. For all we know, they're already on the roof. Rusty, shut up. Johnny, get over here. Everybody—shut up!"

Suddenly, the communications set went dead, and everyone was shocked into silence at the same instant.

Even Sarn was disconcerted by the sudden silence he had commanded. All eyes and attention focused on him.

He broke the silence with a quieter tone. "Well, that's better. Now, let's get things started. Johnny, you need to know a few things, and what it is we want you to do. Come here and sit down." For once, Sarn smiled nicely at him. Johnny, a bit calmer, did as Sarn asked—warily.

In a few minutes, he had heard what had happened, and what might happen, and the need for speed to get Jorl, Khair, and Mosets back here. He also explained about the eagle.

"Jeez." Johnny's eyes got rounder as his chin dropped further. "You gotta be kiddin' me . . . jeez."

"We're serious, Johnny. You have to follow this route to find Jorl."

Johnny tore his eyes away from Sarn and Tarla and looked at the screen. "Jeez. Jumpin' jeez." He watched the screen, fascinated by the bird's-eye view—all the familiar places seen from such an angle.

"Hey, I know that street. And that one. Jeez. Jumpin' jeez."

"Here's the road to the small dam," Sarn said, "and right there is the turnoff you must take. Think you can find it?"

"Yeah. It's a cinch."

"Okay. Leave now and get back here as fast as you can." Johnny nodded vigorously and went a little pale.

"I'll check on you with the camera . . . in case you, eh, get lost."

Johnny's little ferret mind caught that one. "Yeah. For a thou, I'll lug them all back here quick as a flash."

Sarn gripped Johnny's shoulder and grinned wolfishly, "I have faith in you, Noble John."

Johnny paled a few degrees more. He recognized the underlying threat. "I'll be back insidea two hours." He bolted up the stairs as the others called out their good-byes.

Sarn returned to the console and picked up the bird. He flew it to the site of the destroyed Surnainian ship. All was quiet and still in the hot afternoon sun—not a trace of the new threat. He cruised the bird at a high altitude, searching the sky as well as the ground. He passed over Bill's house and on out to the site of their hidden space racer. Not a sign. He dropped the bird down to Bill's cabin and looked in the window.

The four men sat around the small living room, somewhat relaxed and enjoying a cool beer.

"Oh," Sarn sighed, "what I wouldn't give for one of those. Hey, come on, open up. Open the window." Sarn jiggled the bird, trying to attract attention.

He didn't get even a sideways look.

"Try tapping on the window with his beak," Tarla suggested.

Sarn, impatient, tapped too hard and went through the glass. This got all the attention one could ever hope for. As fast as a chameleon's tongue, the three men had deployed themselves and had their stun packs drawn and ready.

Sarn chuckled. "At least they're right on their toes."

Jorl approached Sarn's eagle with some degree of anger evidenced by his outstretched arms and half-curled fingers—not too far from fist mode.

Sarn pushed the bird the rest of the way through the broken window and landed it on the floor in front of the men.

Through a brisk exchange of notes and wing flaps, the three men knew Johnny was on his way.

"Aren't you going to let them know about the new Surnainian ship, Sarn?"

"Not unless I have to," Sarn answered. He walked the bird to the door, which Jorl opened, and cruised it back toward the city. On the way, he looked for Johnny just to see how far away from Bill's house he was.

"There he is—down there," Eloise pointed.

"He's almost to the turnoff," Sarn said.

"Better not get too close—the bird might scare him into a ditch," Tarla said.

Sarn laughed. "You're so right. I wouldn't be surprised if he still has the shakes. Poor Johnny." He took the bird up to a high altitude again and patrolled back and forth between the homestead and Johnny's bright red car. Johnny was now on the dirt road and unwinding a dust cloud behind him.

"I'm going to take another look at the site of the explosion," Sarn said. "I feel a bit uneasy for some reason."

Within a few moments, the camera picked out the hidden depression of their first brush with the aliens.

"I don't see a sign of them," Tarla said, "and yet . . . I sense something. Something isn't right."

"I've got the same feeling," Sarn said.

With the camera, Sarn searched the whole area of ground and sky, troubled by an instinctive feeling of missing something.

All three of them saw it at once—a flicker of movement at the top right of the screen. Sarn turned in that direction, and they were in time to see the Surnainian ship settle to the ground on the high ridge above where old Bill had made camp the night before.

"Don't let them see the bird." In spite of herself, Tarla whispered.

Sarn shook his head and placed the bird in cover, but from a place where they could still see the whole ship.

Suddenly, the blank communication screen activated, and the same Surnainian began making the same query as before. Not bothering to shut off his set, the Surnainian turned away. Immediately, Sarn and the girls could see two other Surnainians. The three seemed to hold a conference, and then they moved out of sight of the camera.

Sarn could not watch both screens at once. "Tarla, you watch that one." He pointed to the large communication set. "I'll watch the outside of the ship."

Tarla nodded and sat in front of the big screen. Nothing happened in either screen.

"I see four of them now," Tarla suddenly reported, "and they're activating some switches."

Sarn nodded and sat in front of the big screen. Nothing happened on either screen.

He nodded again. "Yup, the exit is opening and . . . one, two, three men are coming out."

"There," Tarla said, "the fourth is on his way now. Oh, oh."

"What? What?" Eloise was suddenly scared. She went to stand behind Sarn again.

"They can see there were explosions—and now they see the burnt hollow where the other ship was. They know. They're running back to their ship," Sarn said.

"They're coming back in now," Tarla called. "One of them is sitting at the console."

The air was rent again by the loud calling of the ship. Sarn stuck his fingers in his ears. "I sure wish I dared to try turning the damn thing down. Maybe I should blow that one up now. I wonder if the missiles would destroy it from the outside."

"I don't imagine," Tarla answered thoughtfully.

"Too late anyway. They're lifting," Sarn said.

With the usual abrupt suddenness, the screen went dead.

"They're heading for Bill's place." Sarn rammed the bird to full speed, and thankfully, he saw no immediate sign of the Surnainians' arrival at Bill's.

"There they go," Eloise pointed. The strong sunlight shot a brilliant reflection from the metal hull. "Now, they're heading toward the place where our ship is hidden," Sarn said. "Blazing suns, it won't take them long to locate it with their sensors."

"Or Jorl and the others with their minds," Tarla added. "Sarn, warn them . . . Quick. Quick!" Tarla was more than a little frightened that they would be caught before they could take any steps to protect themselves.

Sarn zoomed the bird straight for a window and splashed his way through broken glass to land on the floor once more.

"Eh-h-, you could have used the same window, Sarn." Tarla felt a bit guilty when she chided Sarn because she, too, watched the four men try to jump clear of their skins.

"No time for niceties," Sarn mumbled through his grin.

By the wild gyrations of the bird, Jorl, Khair, and Mosets knew there was danger and trouble on the way. They followed the bird outside, and Sarn indicated the direction of the alien ship.

Sarn and the two girls could see that Jorl was deep in thought, considering the best way to get out of this situation.

Sarn took Eagle up for another look. He was in time to see the Surnainian ship hovering over the site of the hidden space racer. Sarn and the two girls watched as the Surnainian ship shot straight up to about one thousand feet. "They're going to . . ." Sarn shouted.

The ground erupted viciously in a blinding flash. As the vapors cleared, only a charred, smoking, and fused hole remained.

Tarla and Sarn were shocked into silence. Then, large tears welled up in Tarla's beautiful eyes. Sarn's voice was husky with the same emotion. He put an arm around his sister to share their mutual feelings of loss—not only of their own ship but also the frightening loss of their only tangible link with their impossibly far-away home.

"Gee, Sarn honey. Ah gee, Tarla." Eloise put a soft hand on each of their shoulders. "I know how bad you must feel, but you could've been inside it. I mean, at least you're safe, and I know that you'll find a way to get back to your home."

Tarla and Sarn both tore themselves away from their own pain at the sound of Eloise's distress for them.

"As usual, Eloise, you have arrived at the true essentials." Tarla gave her a hug.

"And there are two more star cars around here somewhere," Eloise said and flashed a brilliant smile.

"Right." Sarn agreed with her. He turned his attention back to the screen. "They're starting a search." Sarn watched the monitor intently as he put the bird into full speed to warn Jorl.

Jorl understood the message and began to put into effect his plan of defense. Sarn watched, intent on understanding the orders Jorl gave him. Jorl pointed in Johnny's general direction and held up his hands, palms outward.

Sarn snapped his fingers. "That means stop, Johnny."

Next, Jorl covered his head with his arms and then made circles out of the fingers on both hands and held them to his eyes.

"That means keep hidden but keep watch," Tarla translated.

Sarn nodded agreement.

They watched Jorl motion Mosets and Khair to go to each end of the outbuilding, old Bill to the house, while Jorl hid himself in a thick clump of bushes in front of the house.

"Good thinking—forces deployed and concealed." Then Sarn took the bird off toward the distant dust cloud that they knew hid a diligently speeding Johnny.

Sarn matched his speed to Johnny's and flew along side the driver's window. Johnny looked, couldn't believe his eyes, and looked again. He almost lost control of his car as well as his nerves. Sarn slid Eagle on the hood of the car and blocked the view. Johnny skidded to a stop and just sat there, shaken. Sarn hopped the bird to the ground and stood by the driver's door. Johnny slowly, and with many misgivings, opened the door. He stared at the weird bird that stared back implacably.

"Now, to make him park where I want him."

"He'll stay frozen to the spot if you don't do something," Tarla said.

Sarn nodded, grinning as he lunged the bird at Johnny who immediately slid back into the driver's seat. He stared at the fierce-looking apparition with saucer wide eyes. Even though Sarn had told him about the eagle, he was absolutely not prepared for such a large, scary-looking thing.

Sarn lunged twice more, and Johnny, in spite of his nervous twitchings, got the idea that he was to close the door. Sarn plopped the bird in front of the car and hopped along the track for a few feet, turned, and watched Johnny. Sarn repeated the maneuver and, thankfully, Johnny began to drive the car, keeping pace and a reasonable distance.

Sarn led him to an outcropping of large rocks not too far from the homestead and indicated that Johnny should hide the car as best he could in the few bushes at the base of the outcropping.

Johnny got out of the car and looked around the edge of the small hill. He could see the whole layout about two hundred yards ahead.

Sarn decided that Johnny now understood that he should stay hidden and just watch. The three of them laughed at the look of thankfulness on Johnny's thin face as he hunkered down behind a bush.

Sarn flashed the bird back to Jorl's side.

All of them waited in the hot stillness.

One second, there was nothing new in the landscape. A second later, a metal disc hovered over the house. Its underside was a gleaming, light-reflecting silver, and when it dropped down, the top that showed was a dull, light-absorbing black.

"Well, we're committed," Sarn said softly.

"And we're here, safe, and can do nothing." Tarla controlled her emotions. "Oh, Jorl . . . I should be with him, Sarn."

"I feel the same way, but we aren't, so we'll do the best we can to help any way that we can. Now, give me a hand to use this eagle to the best advantage."

Tarla bit her lip, tossed the long strands of gold hair behind her, and concentrated on the job at hand.

All eyes watched intently as the spaceship slowly descended toward the earth.

Jorl grabbed the eagle by the neck and spun it round to face him.

Sarn found himself looking Jorl in the eyes. Jorl mouthed Sarn's name. Sarn gave the wing signal to indicate he was watching.

Jorl pointed toward the ship, then at the bird, then moved his arm in an arc, pointed at Eagle's beak, and then threw both arms in the air to imitate an explosion.

"He's saying to go around to the rear of the ship," Tarla said, "and stay hidden. Take the first chance to get inside, then blow it up."

Sarn gave the wing signal again.

Jorl blew a kiss, gave the universal "thumbs-up" sign, and grinned.

Eagle gave some sort of a wing salute.

Sarn hurried Eagle behind another clump of bushes to wait. They watched as the ship landed as lightly as a butterfly. Within seconds, the bulkhead opened, and the landing ramp folded down into place. A magnificent Surnainian appeared in the entrance. With weapons drawn, he and two others cautiously, but still as rulers of the universe, descended.

Sarn, meanwhile, had evidently escaped detection and was far enough around the curve of the ship to not be seen by the aliens. He risked a look and watched the backs of three Surnainians as they moved, with powerful grace, down the ramp.

Sarn made his move and managed to get the eagle under the protection of the ramp.

Suddenly, the apparent leader held up his arm to the other two, bringing them to a stop. The Surnainian turned to look in the direction in which Jorl was hidden.

"Mind probe." Tarla's voice shook. "He's found Jorl already."

They watched as the Surnainian put his hands on his hips, and even from where the bird was, Sarn and Tarla could see the cold disdain on the face of the magnificent Surnainian. They watched the clump of bushes, that hid Jorl, shake violently.

"Mind blast," Tarla said. "Oh, Sarn, mind blast."

Jorl rolled out of the bushes. Even from a distance, they could see the agony he suffered. With an almost superhuman effort, Jorl steadied his arm and sent a fatal neuron blast toward the hated enemy alien. Only the edge of the beam caught the Surnainian, and that had allowed him to escape certain death, but even so, that brought him down to the ground, stunned.

The other two were ready to fire at Jorl. They suddenly crumpled, dead forever, as Khair and Mosets began their run toward the ship, firing as they ran. Jorl, the agony gone but not the memory, also ran toward the ship. He paused, took aim, and fired at one of the two more Surnainians running down the ramp. The second man ran back up, and immediately the ramp began to ride back on its hydraulic path, closing.

Sarn only just managed to squeeze the bird inside before the ramp slammed into place.

"I hope they saw me get the bird into the ship," Sarn said. "I'll wait for as long as I dare before I blow it up."

Jorl had seen the big raggedy eagle manage an entrance. He yelled to Khair and Mosets to head for the house.

Extending themselves to their fullest, within two minutes they had crashed into the house, grabbed old Bill, and tumbled into the root cellar and closed the trapdoor behind them.

Things had happened too fast for Bill to ask even a one-word question. The other three laid him on the floor and shielded him with their bodies and their own heads with their arms.

"Any second now," Jorl said.

Sarn rammed the eagle as fast as possible down the companionway, right behind the Surnainian. He saw the last member of the crew, who was sitting at the console, turn to see the other man enter the control room. He evidently sounded the alarm, and the officer at the console reached for the controls. Sarn went full speed to the engine room bulkhead and perched the bird on the most vulnerable spot of the drive.

"It's rather like putting a hen on a nest to hatch the eggs." Sarn felt the terrible pressure. "I can't tell if they're getting ready to launch or to fire. It's been almost two minutes."

"Do you think they're safe yet?" Eloise asked. Worry lines creased her smooth forehead.

With her total attention, Tarla watched the dials on the section of the drive that the eagle could see. "No more time, they're preparing to fire." She felt her throat muscles suddenly tighten.

"Here we go," Sarn said, barely above a whisper, and reached for the destruct button.

"Oh-h-h." Eloise wrapped her arms tightly around Sarn as she leaned into his back and also crossed her fingers.

In a split second, both screens lit with the familiar blinding flash of a violently ferocious explosion.

The three in the control room were silent, each with their own jumbled thoughts.

"There isn't any way for us to know if they're safe until we see them," Tarla whispered. She fought to control herself. Her hands were clenched tight, and her throat felt constricted with fear.

"We will consider them alive and well until we have evidence to the contrary," Sarn said. "Now, I'm going to activate another bird and have a look." He turned to the console and started the activation. "It's not working." Sarn was puzzled. He did the activation procedure again, with the same negative result.

"What's wrong, Sarn?" Tarla looked over his shoulder.

"I don't know. I'll try the other one. Nope, it doesn't respond either. Now what. Blazing suns, what the black hole is wrong?"

Rusty, at the tone in Sarn's voice, got up and put his head in Sarn's lap. He gently snorted and wagged his tail and looked up at Sarn's face.

Sarn looked down at Rusty, smiled, and patted his head. "Sorry to wake you, you crazy dog. You can go back to sleep. It's okay."

Rusty snorted and flopped down on the floor again and dozed off.

Sarn began a careful examination of the whole console.

"Sarn honey, can you fix it? Maybe we could find some tools—take off the face plate—maybe it's a fuse or whatever circuit breaker they use." Eloise examined the controls she could see and was looking it over for some panels that could be removed.

Sarn and Tarla both had a bemused look on their faces—as if a child had suddenly started talking knowledgeably about three-dimensional calculus.

"Well, now. That's my Eloise—full of delightful surprises." Sarn gave her a big hug.

"But Sarn, I told you all about me and my daddy. How we stripped down cars or any kind of machinery, for that matter. I love to see machinery doing its job."

"Then, let's get at it," Sarn said and rubbed his hands together. "We'll make these units do their jobs."

Chapter 23

Like a monstrous hammer, the earth tremor and accompanying concussion battered at the four men. Within a few seconds, it was over.

Atmosphere and earth were almost eerily quiet.

The men raised their heads, looking for any evidence of the tremendous blast.

Mosets gently rubbed his ears. "Except that my ears are ringing like alarm bells just before the battle is joined and I feel as if I had lost a round to a steamroller, I'm fine. How about the rest of you? Khair?"

"I feel about the same as you, Mosets. My head is ringing, and I feel rather like one big bruise."

"Same here," Jorl said. He stood up and stretched. "You okay, Bill?"

"Thanks to you fellers, I feel pretty good." Bill also got up and stretched out some kinks. The two Zalleellians and Mosets had shielded Bill from most of the pummeling effect of the concussion with their bodies.

"I hope it was Sarn who blew up the ship, and not the ship that blew up the house," Khair said.

Jorl looked at him for a moment as the realization of what the alternative could mean. "I hadn't thought of that probability," Jorl said. "I should have. Great black holes, I've got to know." He flexed his muscles to get out the knots and headed up the steps as quickly as he could. He drew his stun pack and inched the trapdoor upward an inch at a time. "I'll find out right now."

With his weapon drawn, Mosets moved to stand at the bottom of the steps ready to follow Jorl up to cover him.

Bill got slowly to his feet and tested his legs. To his astonishment, effortlessly and painlessly, they held his weight. "They're fixed. Wal, what do you know." He stamped his feet lightly. His not-so-lined face broke into a smile fit to dim the sun.

"Don't test them too far yet, Bill," Khair said. He smiled, enjoying Bill's pleasure. He moved to shield Bill from whatever might come at them from above with his steadily aimed stun pack.

Jorl, meanwhile, had opened the trapdoor far enough to stick his head out for a quick look. He was suddenly conscious of the glare of direct sunlight. He looked up and all around. He pulled himself out of the opening and stood up for a comprehensive, 360-degree, look. "You can come up now," he called down the steps. "It was the ship that blew," Jorl said. He took another look around. "Um—m, Bill, be prepared for a, well, there's a few changes."

Mosets, as he got out, turned to give Bill a hand up. "Here, Bill, allow me to assist you."

Bill, still so wrapped up in the miraculous cure of his broken and crushed legs, grabbed Mosets's hand for a pull up and failed to take in his surroundings. "Dang, I can't believe it. What was in that pill thing anyway? Hey, you furriners," Bill used the word with a big smile, "I haven't felt this good for years. Thanks." He was almost overwhelmed with his feelings for the men around him.

The three men stood quietly, waiting for him to focus his attention on the damage.

Bill realized that the three men were quiet and watching him. "What . . . there's, there's no walls. No walls? No damn house." His voice dropped to an unbelieving whisper, "Nothing, in every direction."

And it was as if nothing had ever been built on this piece of land. No trace of anything remained. Only the sand in all directions, and a few wisps of faint, lazy smoke rising into the still air from the places where the sand had fused. It had formed something much like glass. And, of course, the space where the ship had rested had become a large depression that resembled a solid glass basin. The air still held the remnants of the hot smell of burned atmosphere.

"Tessie and Jessie," Bill cried out. He looked from one compassionate face to the other. "Mebbe they ran into the desert in time. Mebbe they're safe." He looked at the men with his eyes full of unshed tears.

Jorl shook his head. "No time. They're gone, Bill." Jorl laid his arm across Bill's shoulders. "I'm so sorry."

Mosets and Khair each gave him a hug, and Khair said, "We know how you felt about them. We're so sorry to have caused you such pain. When all the things you have done to help us . . ."

Bill swallowed his grief. "Oh well, mebbe it's just as well. I reckon I have to plan a whole new life now—to go with the new one Mosets gave me." He tried to smile. "There's not even a board left here of this old one."

"Listen," Jorl suddenly commanded them. All of them strained to identify the faint noise they could now hear. They tensed for a new danger.

"That's a car motor," Bill said.

Around the edge of the still standing rocks poked the dusty nose of a red car.

"It's Johnny," Jorl shouted. They ran to meet the welcome sight.

* * *

Johnny went white-faced with terror at the instant disappearance of what looked to him like a bunch of very solid things.

Even with the protection of massive rock walls, the concussion of the blast had knocked him backward, covered him in powdered dust, and his ears were still ringing loud enough to be heard in Vegas.

When he screwed up enough courage to open his eyes and look again, he saw what appeared to be men pulling themselves out of the bowels of the earth. He had only one thought—get out. Get away! Fortunately, he took one more look and recognized them. So, instead of running away, heroically decided to drive toward them.

* * *

"Never thought I'd be so happy to see you again, Johnny boy," Jorl said. He helped Johnny get out of the car and playfully ruffled his hair. Then, he slapped some of the dust off him.

"It was brave of you to wait for us, Johnny," Khair said.

Johnny puffed up like a sly little banty rooster. "Hey. Yeah. Jeez, I nearly decided to cut out, though. But I didn't."

Johnny suddenly had a small glimmering of what it felt like to give help in the face of danger. It was, maybe, the first time in his life he hadn't thought of number one first—not wholly—and discovered a small kernel of courage that had lain dormant for all these years.

Mosets, who had been scanning the sky and terrain, spoke softly and urgently, "I am of the opinion that we should leave this vector as quickly as that little vehicle will carry us. Even if the remaining Surnainian ship isn't in the immediate vicinity, surely the military or law enforcements of this country will investigate three unexplained explosions."

"Absolutely right, Mosets. Let's go." Jorl paused. "Eh—would you like me to drive, Johnny? Maybe you're still shaken up from your experience?"

Jorl couldn't help it. He laughed at the totally horrified expression that crossed Johnny's thin, ferrety face.

"No. No, I can. I'm okay." Johnny hurried behind the wheel. Johnny's chief joy was his car, and he had the talent of being a fine driver. And no way was he taking a chance on any other driver—especially one he had never seen handle a hot set of wheels.

Khair pretended to wipe sweat from a worried brow. "Whew-w."

Jorl laughed and punched him on the shoulder. "Get in—get in."

The five men, three of them extra large, squeezed into the cramped quarters.

"Do you think your vehicle can manage this much overload?" Khair asked. He surreptitiously put his hand to his head and realized there was room enough to stick only one finger between the top of his head and the roof. He eyed Jorl and Mosets's clearance. "I suggest you miss as many obstacles as possible, Johnny, or your wonderful car will be converted to an open roof model."

"Damn good thing Sarn isn't riding with us on this trip," Jorl said. The three aliens roared with laughter.

Johnny sneaked a worried look at them, not understanding the joke that Sarn suffered volubly over any discomfort.

With three large men stowed into a midsized back seat and Jorl crammed in the front seat, Johnny pulled away.

Bill turned for one last look at the scene of his life to date, and sighed.

Johnny, now in his own element, did an expert job of gearing up and down to get maximum efficiency from his gallant car.

Jorl watched every move, as usual, and his eyes began to gleam with a pilot's delight. He knew that this car was as different from the other vehicles he had mixed it up with, as a slow freight scow was to his space racer.

In between explaining the mechanics of revs and gears with the mounting enthusiasm of finding an interested listener, Johnny passed on the information that Sarn had given him.

During the course of the story, Khair realized that Carol wasn't with them. Jorl put his hand on Khair's shoulder in sympathy. "I don't think you can be too surprised, Khair, even though that will not make you feel one damn bit better."

Khair smiled and said softly, "We haven't launched yet."

"True—true." Jorl grinned and turned around again.

The three aliens were keeping as much of a watch as was possible in the confined quarters.

"A flight of aircraft at two o'clock." Jorl pointed. "A little more speed, Johnny boy—let's get lost in the traffic."

"We should reach the main road in approximately ten minutes," Mosets said.

"Good thing—I think we must be the only vehicle in this particular vicinity—and we sure don't—"

Johnny interrupted Jorl. "There's a dust cloud coming toward us—fast." Johnny's newfound courage threatened to slip through the soles of his feet.

"Gird your loins, fellow travelers, I fear we will once more be in the thick of something," Mosets said and sighed.

"Yup, here we go again." Khair folded his arms to wait.

"Mebbe they're goin' about some other business," Bill hopefully suggested.

"Could be." Jorl didn't put too much stock in that idea. "Don't slow down, Johnny boy, unless they give you a signal."

"Jeez. It's two—no, three, police cars. They're spreading out to block us."

"Weapons on low stun—keep them hidden—follow my lead. Start slowing, Johnny—leave the speech to me." Jorl issued his concise orders in the staccato voice of command.

Chapter 24

Meanwhile, back in the old house and after taking a much-needed rest, Sarn took Rusty out for a run while Tarla and Eloise made a picnic of sorts from the leftovers of the last meal.

Sarn, still worried over the problem with the birds, gnawed on a thick, untidy sandwich and switched on the television.

No one was really listening to it.

Sarn heard something that focused his attention—he shushed the others and said, "Listen."

The newscaster had just finished a sentence with . . . three unexplained blasts.

Sarn grabbed the remote and turned up the volume.

The newscaster continued, "The force of these intense blasts registered on seismographs around the country. The police in the immediate area have been deluged with frantic calls, and as yet, neither the police nor the Pentagon has any explanation.

One of the calls that we have received is from a professor who suggested that it was the "first signs of an imminent volcanic disturbance"—while one of our local, eh, intellectuals thought it "might be something to do with sunspots—that maybe they solidified and fell off the sun, and three of these solar freckles landed near here" . . . Could be, friends, could be. But I can't help but think that our friend, Mr. Walker, had something to do with that last one. However, friends, remember what I said a couple of days ago about little green men—and women, maybe." The newscaster grinned into the camera. "And also remember, dear listeners, you heard it here first. Here's a note someone just handed me. It says that the police department has informed us that they have dispatched a detachment and they are, at this moment, entering the vicinity of the last blast. The Air Arm has also agreed to divert a squadron of jets over the area, and a team of experts is about ready to go in as well. There you have it, folks, that's the latest up-to-the-minute news, so stay tuned, and we'll bring you the latest, the fastest . . ."

Sarn shut off the TV and shot downstairs. Rusty and the girls followed.

"I've got to find out what's going on—I need another bird."

The panel of the console was apart. Eloise and Sarn examined it again. "What are we missing?" Sarn said with frustration.

"Tarla," Eloise said, "why don't you try to do—whatever it is you do—in your, you know, your brain—or your mind. Maybe it'll work this time."

"I've been trying all the time, but . . ." Tarla sat down and concentrated on looking inward. Sarn and Eloise remained quiet; they didn't want to break her intense concentration.

Suddenly, Tarla jumped to her feet and joyfully reported, "Jorl's alive." Tears of relaxed tension sprang up in her eyes. "I can't get much, except that he's alive and cheerful, but he's too far away and not listening inside. But I can sense him—and Khair—and Mosets—and Old Bill . . . Oh, thank the heavens!"

The three hugged each other and wiped away one another's tears.

"Now, blazing suns, I need another camera. Let's put this console together, Eloise, and see what happens."

"Sarn, how about that little black button—right up there?" Eloise squatted down and pointed to an almost hidden spot on the back wall of the console well.

Sarn took a close look. "It's a strange place for it, but it could be a reset switch."

They both helped to put things back together. The second the last piece was in place, Sarn said, "Eloise, push that button now." A loud blast of sound made all of them jump nearly out of their respective skins.

"We did it. Blazing suns, we did it." He grabbed Eloise and Tarla and did a little victory dance. "What would I ever do without you, my dear little Eloise?"

Sarn activated the remaining three eagles.

"Look. Look. That's the White House," Eloise said. "And that's," she pointed to another monitor, "wow, oh gee, that's the Tower of

London—that's in England . . ." She pointed excitedly to the last one, "and that's somewhere in—China, I think because . . . see that cute little building? It's called a pagoda. That's the style they use in China."

"Hmm-m. The Surnainians have built quite a surveillance system. I hope they haven't started actual contacts yet."

"With the mess our world is in, I sort of think the Sur—what's it's—have started working already."

"How far away are those places, Eloise?" Sarn asked.

"Gee, I don't know exactly. Around three or four thousand miles, I guess."

"Damn, I need one of those birds to find Jorl."

"Well, you could fly the bird back here," Eloise said.

"Eloise," Sarn spoke with amused frustration. "Eloise, use your head—I've no maps. No real idea where we are in relation to them, but," he said with firm decision, "I'm going to fly them around just for a look. There isn't anything we can do for Jorl and the others, anyway. Maybe we'll come across something that could be useful."

"Such as what?" Tarla paced back and forth in the control room. Their helplessness made it hard for her to hide her agitation.

"Blazing suns, Tarla, sit down. You'll get all of us pounding back and forth—for nothing—here, take the controls of the bird that's looking at the White House." Sarn demonstrated the controls for her. "Just keep altitude."

Tarla was relieved to have something to do and became thoroughly wrapped up in manipulating the mobile camera.

Sarn caught sight of the wistful look on Eloise's face. "Come on, Eloise," Sarn said and smiled understandingly, "you play with the London one."

"Oh, Sarn, can I? Really?" When she sat in front of the console and began to work the controls, her face broke out all over in a wondrous smile.

Sarn laughed at her and ruffled her thick, soft hair. Then, he turned to the camera that was supposed to be somewhere in China.

"Gain altitude and watch for any signs of another ship," Sarn said and continued doing just that.

Except for ooh-hs and ah-hs and the occasional squeal from Eloise, all remained quiet in the control room. Before long, Tarla and Eloise were as adept as Sarn at flying the birds and began a wide-ranging search.

Even though it was a bright moonlight night, it was still more difficult to see details. Sarn's search had covered miles of empty Asian desert country when he thought he saw the shape that he had been searching for. He circled the spot from a safe height. Then, he risked one low swoop to make sure.

"There it is—the Surnanians' ship. Land your eagles, and come and see."

Tarla and Eloise crossed over to Sarn's screen to have a look.

"Gee, it's still dark. How did you ever find it? It's so hard to see." Eloise squinted into the screen. "I guess it has to be dark in China now—they're on the opposite side of the world."

Sarn nodded. "We have a few more hours of daylight left here. I doubt if they'd come into this hangar in daylight, so we have plenty of time before we can expect them."

"If they come," Tarla said.

"They will." Sarn flew his eagle to a safe distance, but also from where he would still be able to see the ship. He landed the eagle, got up from the console, and paced.

"Now, you're doing it," Tarla said to Sarn.

"What?"

"Pacing."

Sarn, red hair flying and green eyes glittering, suddenly slammed one fist into the other. "Let's go!"

"Where?" Tarla asked.

"Find a car and look for Jorl. Come on."

"But where, Sarn? Where do we look? We can't just go out and run around without a plan," Tarla said.

"Can't we just call a car rental place?" Eloise asked. "I have a license and everything."

"That would mean records," Tarla said.

"Find the address of a rental place anyway, and we'll get a taxi. We can't just sit here." Sarn bounded up the stairs, Rusty at his heels, with the two girls close behind him.

They opened the door to the street and turned toward the far corner that led to the bright lights of the main drag.

"Wait, Sarn, wait." Eloise was nearly exhausted trying to maintain the same fast pace as the Zalleellians without any of their physical advantages.

"Poor Eloise," Tarla said. "We're sorry—we forgot."

"I'll carry her."

Tarla shook her head. "No, that would cause comment." They walked another block. "There's a cab. Quick, flag it down."

Sarn stepped out into the street and waved at the cab and yelled, "Taxi!" He was totally pleased that he had got that part right.

The cab stopped, and they climbed in.

"Where to folks?" the cabbie asked.

Tarla and Sarn looked at Eloise. As the hot heaving of her lungs was finally slowing down, she was able to give the cabbie the address. After a few minutes, Sarn suddenly yelled, "Stop here."

When the taxi stopped, Sarn threw some bills on the front seat, and they hastily got out and regrouped on the sidewalk.

"What happened? Why did you do that?" Tarla asked.

"I'm sure I saw something that might help." Sarn was half running, retracing the cab's route.

Eloise and Tarla followed him, and Rusty was joyfully following everyone. Sarn turned into a small side street, stopped, and said, "What do you see, Tarla." Sarn's excitement was catching.

"Can it be? Do you think . . .?" Tarla caught the excitement.

They came up to the car they'd recognized, not only by the car itself, which was an old bright green, wood-paneled station wagon, but also, by the position of it—hard up against a lamppost—on the sidewalk.

"Jebidiah," Eloise and Tarla both said at once.

They looked in the car to make sure Jebidiah wasn't in it.

"He's around here somewhere, probably in one of the bars," Sarn said. "Let's start looking."

They had looked in four bars and two small casinos and were getting a little discouraged.

"Keep on looking," Sarn ordered.

They turned toward another set of drab-looking doors in a drab-looking front with a couple of dead neon letters in a boring neon sign and made their way through the doors. Immediately, they found themselves in a totally unexpected world filled with lights and laughter and a shifting throng of pleasure-seeking people. In spite of the urgency of their situation, they couldn't help but respond to the excitement of the place.

"Spinning comets and shooting stars!" Sarn's eyes reflected the excitement as they tried to take in the whole scene with one gulp.

It was a shifting, vibrant scene full of color, stage show, laughter, clinking glasses, movement, music—life.

The three of them just stood there recovering from the dark chill night on the other side of the doors.

"I'm sorry, sir, no dogs allowed," a sweet little thing behind the hatcheck counter said.

"He's not a dog," Sarn said. "He's Rusty."

Tarla poked him in the ribs. "I'm sure Rusty would be more than happy to spend a few minutes with this charming young lady."

Sarn obeyed Tarla's logic in not starting anything. "You stay here, Rusty, and watch the people, and be good." Sarn patted his big head.

Rusty sat down in the opening at the end of the short counter. He grinned from ear to ear, and his tongue lolled out and was on the move with every turn of his head.

The girl patted Rusty's head and smiled when she got a big lick on her wrist and then saw a twenty-dollar bill get tucked into her hand.

They went to the bar and scanned as well as they could, searching for little Jebby.

Sarn happened to hear a foursome behind him talking about the newscast. He quietly drew Tarla and Eloise's attention to the conversation.

They listened.

One man in the group agreed wholeheartedly with the "little green men" theory.

His friend said, "Ya don't mean to say ya really think they'd be green, do ya?" He exploded into raucous laughter.

"Maybe not, but it's possible that whatever exploded could have been from outer space." He was a little miffed at his friend for trying to make him look like a fool in front of the women.

"Aw, come on. What d'ya think . . . aliens are invading us, and they're in a shooting war among themselves already? Come on, have another drink, and sober up."

A woman chimed in. "But it could be creatures from another planet."

"You have another drink, too, Agnes. Chris' sake, you're all gonna start seeing little green men."

"But they don't have to be green, you dough head." Agnes tried to remain reasonably even-tempered. "They could look just like anyone in here—or almost . . ."

Sarn had, unknowingly, been staring hard at Agnes. She suddenly became aware of the intense candlepower of Sarn's eyes. Their looks fused.

Sarn broke the connection by turning to Tarla. Agnes, momentarily frozen to the spot, didn't know what to say. She didn't believe what she was thinking. Did not believe it—or did she? So she said nothing, but she watched Sarn shepherd the two girls toward the gaming rooms. She raised her arm toward them but still was unable to organize her chaotic thoughts.

"Agnes. Hey, Agnes. Fer Chris' sake, you in a trance? Wake up."

Now that Sarn and the girls had become aware of that conversation, they began to hear mentions of the explosions and the possible reasons for them in every direction.

"The hounds will not need much more scent to start baying," Sarn whispered to Tarla.

She nodded as they both became wary.

Eloise put a hand on each of their arms and whispered, "Let's say that . . ." A man accidentally bumped hard into Eloise, which made her say out loud, "and we think that they're really bright blue and five feet tall."

Tarla and Sarn looked at Eloise in surprise. Then, of course, it struck Sarn hilariously funny.

"Hey, buddy." A younger man, waving a big cigar, spoke directly to Sarn. "You actually see something?"

"Well, maybe not too blue, more of a greenish-blue." Sarn tried hard to keep a straight face.

"Sort of like a turquoise color," Eloise said

Tarla just looked at both of them as if they had taken leave of all their senses.

"Yeah? Hey, Al, this here big guy says he saw some aliens, and they were made of blue fur and seven feet tall."

"Yeah? Hey, blue fur, eh? I wonder if it would sell."

Sarn tried to politely shut the loudmouthed man up. He knew that people were beginning to focus on them, but the latest rumor spread like wildfire.

"Hey, yeah, but who'd want to buy a blue-furred alien. Maybe they're dangerous."

"Not if the fur isn't still on him, Joey," shouted the unfeeling, bottom feeder, litter liner, Al.

The light dawned. "Hey. The latest style—real blue fur. Al, you're a real go-getter."

Eloise got mad. "You'd kill them for their fur without even giving them a chance to say why they are here? What if they were here to make friends—if there were any aliens? And if there are, they'd be a lot smarter than you could ever be." Eloise had her hands on her hips and was almost nose-to-nose with a startled Joey. "I ought to push that smelly cigar down your filthy throat!"

Sarn lifted her bodily to one side, away from the noxious Joey.

"Hot-tempered little fireball, ain't she? No offense, big man." Joey backed away from Sarn and regained some of his aplomb. "But she sure would look cute cuddled into bright blue fur."

Eloise doubled her small fists and was ready to pound Joey into the ground. Sarn held her behind his back.

Tarla and Sarn were suddenly aware of all eyes on them as a slightly hysterical Agnes pointed in their direction and shouted, "I bet they are. I just bet they are."

"Tarla, do something to her tongue," Sarn whispered.

Tarla nodded.

Within a blink of an eye, good old Agnes began to slowly buckle at the knees. The guy who was with her caught her as she slumped limply, sound asleep.

"Hey, jeez, Agnes. Chris' sake, she's passed out." The other couple helped him cart good old smart Agnes to a quiet place.

Sarn nodded his appreciation of a fast, efficient job.

"Gee, I wish I could to that," Eloise said.

"What? Pass out?" Sarn said, startled.

"No, silly. What Tarla did—does."

Joey and Al, two real hustlers in the garment trade, were each talking out of the sides of their mouths, watching the handsome trio with hot eyes.

"Tarla," Eloise interrupted Sarn. "Tarla, you'd better do the same thing to those two goons." She still felt animosity toward Joey and so caught their heated looks.

Tarla looked inward and into their minds. Almost instantly, Joey and Al looked at each other, puzzled. Both shrugged and turned to their companions.

"I think it's catching, and rumors will run like wildfire. We'd better get out of here. We've got to find Jebby." Sarn started to herd the girls to an exit.

"I can feel the little whirlpools of suspicions all around the room," Tarla said quietly to Sarn. "They're ready to . . ."

"My cop lady. My be-yoo-tee-full cop lady. Jeesh. I knew I didn't con-sh . . . conus . . . dream you."

Approaching with outstretched arms, unsteady legs, and a smile that seemed to cover his total, little, round body was the man they had borrowed the papers from and in just about the same degree of a cheerful alcoholic haze as then.

"That gorgeous dish is a cop?" A man standing near them said in a loud, clear voice. "Omigod, what a waste." A few people near them laughed.

"Yesh. She'sh my favorite cop. I'll let her arressht me—everyday."

"I'm with you, pops," another voice chimed in almost prayerfully.

"It's very kind of you to feel that way, Mr. . . . . Mr.?" Tarla suddenly realized she had forgotten his name.

"Mr. Jebidiah Pickle. At your servish, beautiful cop lady." He managed a bow, which nearly plummeted him into Tarla, who helped him until he regained his almost upright position.

"It'sh Jebby to my friendsh—Shub-Cubby to my long-suffering, but mean, wife.

Even without Tarla's confirmation, Sarn knew that the crowd hysteria had calmed before it had gained enough momentum to turn into an ugly situation.

Sarn gave a sign to Tarla and Eloise to grab Jebby and make their strategic retreat.

Jebby chattered cheerfully on as the three eased themselves, and him, to the door.

Rusty saw them coming and marched out from beside the counter, tail up, jowls flapping, and tongue out.

Jebby rubbed his eyes and looked again at the huge dog planted in front of Sarn. "Jeesh." He rubbed his eyes again and took another look. Jebby weaved up beside Rusty and lovingly patted his big head. Rusty turned on his widest grin, gave Jebby a lick up one side of his face, and he and Jebby were friends for life.

"Let's get to your car, Jebby," Sarn said.

"Oh yesh! Now, le' shee, where did I leavsh, leash, ploush, put her?" Jebby tried to think. "Ooh yesh. I tied her to a lampposht becaushe shesh indish . . . shindish . . . She'sh drunk again. Put me on the wrong stree's, and even down a siewal fer heave'sh shake."

Sarn could not help himself. The situation of pickled Pickle, and his car, tickled his funny bone. He roared with laughter.

Tarla and Eloise smiled politely, still unable to see the slightest humor in anything to do with drunks.

Sarn caught Tarla's look of censure and felt a small squirm of guilt.

"We should hurry, Sarn."

"Right. Come on, Jebby, let's get your bad car and take her for a little trip to teach her some discipline."

"Good idea," Jebby agreed. The four of them and Rusty walked outside.

Jebby, wobbling, pointed a 360-degree turn, unable to decide on any one direction in which to start.

"Let's go this way," Sarn said.

They started off in the direction of the car, and Jebby began to get his bearings.

Two turns and a side street later, they saw the car. It was still up on the sidewalk. She looked sadly neglected and lonely.

"There she ish." Jebby greeted the car like an annoyed parent with an erring child. "Bad, bad car." He patted it.

Sarn rubbed his hands happily. Almost at once, his wide grin collapsed as a problem stared him down. He smacked one fist into the other in frustration. "What's the good of a car—it won't drive itself—and Jebby—well, no thanks," Sarn paced. "Now what?"

Eloise gently tugged at his arm, trying to interrupt his monologue.

"Tarla, you don't suppose you . . .?

Tarla shook her head.

"I could try, I suppose, but—Eloise, what is it?"

Eloise had been trying to get his attention. "Why can't I drive, Sarn?"

"You, Eloise? Do you know how?" Sarn happily grabbed her by the shoulders. "Really?"

"I told you my daddy owned a garage. Why shouldn't I know how to drive what I know how to fix?"

Sarn leaped toward the car door and gleefully shouted "Everybody in. Let's go."

With the sure touch of an accomplished driver, Eloise backed the car away from the lamppost, put her back into the street, and headed for the dirt road.

Jebby grinned with pleasure, cuddled up to Rusty, and promptly went to sleep.

Chapter 25

✳ ✳
✳

Carol, looking coolly lovely, sat at the airport bar. Her plane was due to leave for New York in forty minutes.

She had one elbow on the bar, and her chin rested in her hand. She slowly muddled her drink with a long swizzle stick. Her expression was an inward, pensive look—almost impossible to think about the life-changing thinking that was going on inside her head.

Two or three traveling executives had attempted a conversation with the beautiful woman but had been intimidated by the cold, well-modulated brush-off.

I suppose you can't blame a man for asking. Like someone once said, "If you don't ask, you don't get." Oh, well, I've been sitting here for almost an hour, and I still don't know what I really want to do. I'm not used to this. I always know exactly what I want, what I want to do—and be. Oh, damn. I don't know whether I want to be sad, mad, or glad. I don't even know if it's either me or the Zalleellians. Why did they have to come crashing—crashing? That's almost funny—into my life and confuse everything. I had my life all mapped out—I need more ice cubes—"Bartender, would you freshen my drink, please? Thank you." Ice cubes seem to melt faster when you swizzle them around. Wonder why? Good essay for a high school science paper. Oh, Carol, shut up and be serious. Am I making the right decision or not? I don't know. Well, you don't have much more time. Well, I just don't know. Someone also said, "When in doubt, don't!"

But which "don't" should I not do? Oh, this is driving me . . . Am I throwing away a much better life for the one I'm choosing?

And Khair—strong, kind, steady, and great looking, and yes, extremely, eh, sexy, Khair . . . a man to respect—to trust—to love. Love? I said love?

But to live forever and not grow old and ugly and die, how can I give that up? Explosion? What was that?

She sat up straight, taut as an alert jungle animal, and listened with undivided attention to the broadcaster describing the unexplained explosions in the desert.

Her chaotic thoughts suddenly slid into perfect order. She quickly put money on the bar and stood up. Her elegance masked her determined speed as she left the terminal and headed for her rented car.

Excitement, purpose, fear, and intelligence shone through the now added softness in her eyes as she, too, headed for the dirt road.

Chapter 26

The four police cars, shoving great clouds of dust up from their skidding wheels, formed the classic barricade in front of the sporty red car—two in front and one on each flank.

"Wh—what'll I do now?" Johnny screamed. He fought his vehicle to a slewed stop. He was white-faced with the thoughts of impending doom.

Jorl grabbed Johnny's shoulder and spoke in a tone guaranteed to cut through his rising hysteria. "Just sit there and be ready to drive. Khair, Mosets—weapons on stun. Raise your arms with palms turned in and stun pack not showing. Johnny, when I say go—get."

Four doors at a time, the police cars were disgorging policemen with drawn guns. Some took cover on the far side of the cars while the rest advanced—spread out—on their quarry.

They shouted commands to 'get out of the car with your hands up'. They didn't give, to even the smallest degree, the impression that they had brought cookies and milk for a pleasant picnic.

"You stay right here, Bill. Okay, open the doors slowly—smile—start to get out, then spray the whole crowd," Jorl said. "Now."

The three acted in unison.

Before the policemen could fire a round, there were confused expressions on their faces and they went limp. Some folded gently to the ground while others just stood there, guns falling from nerveless hands—a look of surprise at their surroundings—no idea in the world what they were supposed to be doing here.

At that precise moment, a helicopter had come in fast and low—now almost above them. At the same instant that Mosets noticed the aircraft, a high-powered rifle bullet hit the forward end of the car roof and bored a hole and, as it later became evident from Johnny's outburst of pure panic, right into the seat beside him. Johnny had felt the heat as it passed by.

Old Bill could do nothing but watch the whole scene as it played out. "I can see I must get me one of them there stun things if'n I'm goin' to be hangin' out with you guys."

The three aliens turned their stun packs toward this new obstacle blocking their peaceful retreat. "Don't stun the pilot," Jorl shouted above the noise of the rotors. "We don't want any casualties." He took aim at the rifleman and fired. Nothing happened. "Out of charge. Damn." He shoved the useless weapon back into its holster.

"On t'other hand, there's a lot to be said for an old fashioned shotgun. Don't need to be plugged into anythin'."

Khair disabled the rifleman and the next man who stuck his head out of the helicopter, and then his stun pack went dead, too. The helicopter retreated for a regrouping.

"Into the car," Mosets said. "Let's try for the main road."

Jorl slammed into the front seat and told Johnny, "Go!"

Conquering himself, Johnny reversed out of the police car pocket and took off across the low shoulder to get past the section of blocked road. Mosets leaned out the window to re-stun two policemen who seemed to be coming out of their daze.

They suffered a bone-shattering ride until Johnny managed to get his car back on the relatively smooth road. Johnny kept his foot as hard to the floor as he dared. The car, as well as its cargo, began to feel the results of such hard and unfamiliar usage.

Heat, dust, and sweat mingled hatefully.

Coming toward them, fast, were more pillars of dust that almost obscured the light-reflecting glints of the metal at their hearts. One dust cloud was well ahead of the pack and coming up on the red car at a great rate of speed.

They saw it coming.

Jorl shouted, "Turn off to the right."

"It'll wreck my car," Johnny wailed, but he turned off anyway.

"But think of all the great experience as a driver you're getting," Khair said.

"Yes, but . . ."

"We'll buy you another one, Johnny," Mosets said in a soothing tone of voice. "Maybe an even more powerful one and much, much redder."

Johnny snatched a second to give a happy look at Mosets. "Really? Ya mean it? Wow."

The car coming toward them turned off, too, on an intercepting course.

The sporty red car was being banged to death on the rough ground. The strange car was closing in on them, and Mosets prepared to fire the moment they came within range.

With a bone-shattering crash, the right front end dipped and dragged. They saw the wheel running with ever-increasing speed ahead of them—bouncing higher and higher. Johnny fought his screaming car to a standstill.

"You're a good pilot, Johnny boy." Jorl tapped him on the shoulder. He opened the door to get out.

"Yup." Old Bill agreed. "And we're standin' here alive, I think," Bill said as he tried to unwind some of his muscles, especially at the seat end.

Mosets, with his stun pack aimed at the fast-approaching stranger, said, with a deep sigh, "It does seem to have become a rather fouled-up sort of situation, though, doesn't it. Observe the strangeness of the approaching vehicle," Mosets said.

Jorl and Khair both felt the bubbling up of laughter at the ludicrous understatement by Mosets.

They watched with varying degrees of surprise and dawning joy. As the vehicle closed in on them, they could see hands waving from the windows and hear shouts and what seemed to be a dog's barking.

"It's Sarn! By all the shining suns of the great beyond, it really is Sarn—and Tarla—and Eloise."

The big station wagon came to a skidding stop, and all the doors burst open at once. Jorl let out a great whoop and ran toward the car. Khair and Mosets were close behind, with Bill and Johnny bringing up the rear.

There followed a glorious reunion filled with hugging, laughing, slapping, and barking, all weaving in and out—no beginning, no ending, just one big swirl of deeply grateful and loving people who would remember this moment as one of their lives' greatest.

"Eloise! You did the driving? As one pilot to another, well done." Jorl gave her a great big hug.

"Gee. Thank you, Jorl . . . thank heavens that . . . oh gee . . ." and she burst into smiles and tears.

It couldn't last for more than a few minutes . . . they would have to wait for later, if there was to be a later, because the danger of death, or capture, at the hands of the Earthmen was still a real threat.

"Jebidiah Pickle, our paper person." Khair caught sight of a sleepy, grinning Jebby standing by the car door. He rushed over to shake Jebby's hand.

"So that's where you got it, Sarn." Jorl laughed and lightly punched Sarn's shoulder. "I'll want to hear that story when we have time."

"It will be a most edifying lesson in cargo storage to observe how you plan to stow ten living bodies and one rather large dog into even such a spacious vehicle as that," Mosets spoke quietly.

Jorl studied the situation for a split second. "It'll be a tight fit, but we should be able to manage for a short while. Everybody in. Johnny, you do the driving."

One of the dust clouds on the dirt road swung off and was coming toward them.

"The hounds have the scent again. Johnny, keep the same course. Move out."

"Yes, sir." Johnny was almost in tears . . . to leave the wounded joy of his life, broken and abandoned, in the desert, but nonetheless, he obeyed Jorl's command with full attention and speed.

Between the heat, dust, bumps, and bangs, there was a lot of grunting and moaning going on.

Eloise pointed and shouted, "A car!"

Another car was speeding head on toward them.

Johnny cut the wheels to change course—the strange car altered its course to match. "Jeez. What's the idiot doing! Has everyone gone nuts?"

The distance between them closed fast. Mosets had his stun pack ready.

To avoid a probable head-on collision, Johnny was forced to slew yet another car to a dust-blinded halt. When he stopped, the stranger's car was no more than six feet away from him. Johnny just sat there. Every one of his nerve ends was, figuratively speaking, waving in the breeze.

The dust settled, and the door opened.

Carol got out and stood there, elegantly cool and calm, beside her rental car.

Complete silence.

Everyone got out of Jebby's car.

Still complete silence.

"Would any of you gentlemen care for a lift?"

Khair took the first leap toward her and folded her into his sweaty arms—got dust on her—and tried to brush some off. She pulled him close, her tears ran down Khair's face, and mingled with his sweat and not a few tears of his own.

They used a few of their precious seconds and, with genuine pleasure, welcomed Carol back.

Mosets had also been watching the dust pillars of the police cars as they turned toward them.

"The pack of dogs is closing in for the kill—I suggest, once again, that we bend every effort to gain enough of a lead to, hopefully, elude them," Mosets said.

Meanwhile, Johnny had been scanning the countryside, slightly puzzled. "Jeez. I sorta recognize this place." He snapped his fingers and did a little dance. "Fooled me for a second because I'm on the other side of the property. We're handy a place I know where we can be safe."

"Good," Jorl said. "Bill, Mosets, and Jebby, come with me. Johnny, you drive. Tarla, Khair, Sarn, Eloise, and Rusty, get into Carol's car. Carol, you drive and follow Johnny. Okay, let's go. We've got to lose that pack."

Johnny took the lead and drove the wagon as hard and as fast as possible, slowing only a hair's breadth this side of a crack-up. Carol, without a moment's hesitation, stayed with him.

Johnny drove no more than a half-mile toward the city and then left the highway on the opposite side, following a side road that wound through a small wood. Jorl told Johnny to stop, got out of the car, and flagged down Carol's car. He waved everybody to come close.

"Johnny says that at the end of this little road is a house, and he's pretty sure that they'll be willing to help us. But first, we need to get the bird dogs off our scent. Johnny, here, has a plan that just might work."

Tarla said, "I think we'd best be quick—I hear sirens."

"Okay." Jorl began to speak more forcefully and faster. We'll tie down the steering wheels of both cars, put a weight on the gas pedals, and head them back into the desert. Hopefully, the herd will follow them. Johnny, you drive one car to the highway, and I'll bring the other one. Sarn, you'll come with us—you can jump faster than Johnny. The rest of you head into the woods, stay out of sight, and wait for us to come back. But first, we need something to tie the steering wheels with and something heavy to put on the gas pedals. See what you can find."

"How about this?" Johnny showed him a length of rope and a hunting knife. "They were in the back of the little fat guy's wagon."

"Perfect," Jorl said. He sliced the rope into two equal pieces with the knife. He tested it for strength. "That should do the job."

Sarn and Khair each brought a fair-sized stone and put one on the front seat of both cars.

Jorl drove off in one car, and Johnny, with Sarn, drove the wagon.

When they reached the end of the dirt road, they crossed the highway, went down over the bank, stopped the cars, put the gearshifts in neutral, left the engines running, and got out.

"We've got to move fast," Jorl said.

Sarn and Jorl anchored the steering wheels into slightly divergent straight-ahead positions. The lull in the traffic they waited for came. Jorl and Sarn placed a heavy stone on each of the accelerators, wedged to give them about forty miles an hour. Sarn and Jorl each reached into a window and put the cars into drive. They jumped clear as the cars leaped ahead. Like expert drivers, the cars took off straight and true.

The three ran back across the road and turned to watch their handiwork as the cars, masked by the telltale dust clouds, headed back into the desert. They grinned their pleasure and ran back up the country road to join the rest of their group.

Within ten minutes, they entered a large circular driveway, which fronted a huge, white Southern-style mansion complete with a large porte cochere. All of them were surprised and appreciative of the beauty of the house and grounds.

"Johnny, you're sure you know the people who live here?" Tarla asked. "It looks almost like a mansion."

Johnny grinned and nodded his head—strutted up to the front door as cocky as any banty rooster. The rest of the group shrugged, looked at each other, and followed Johnny up onto the spacious verandah. White pillars—two stories high.

Chapter 27

***

$\mathscr{B}$ig Mama Alice opened her eyes. They were still clouded with her inner thoughts. She then sat up straight and, with wondering eyes, looked at the whole group that sat around her dining room table. Everyone smiled at her and waited to hear what she would say.

"I know—I know zee names—zee—all of you—eez—eez . . . I find me . . ." She was totally lost for words. "You—I eez . . ."

Alice now knew the whole story about these strangers before her.

"I—I eez . . ."

"Dumbfounded," Marion supplied, and held out a glass of wine for her.

"Zank you, my sweet Marion, you always know what it eez your mama needs," and drank it in one long swallow. "Now, eet izz zee time to organize everything." She called for Janice and told her to see to having the kitchen prepare a good meal for their guests.

"I geeve you about an hour to rest and clean up and then come down for supper. I must get hold of Happy Harry and organize zee escape." She clapped her hands, and order soon prevailed.

"Dearest lady," Jebby said. He had been waiting patiently for a break in the conversations. "Even though you remind me of my wife, and she would say no, is it possible to get a drink here in this lovely establishment? I surely would appreciate it, madam. Is there?" He was still a little wobbly, but sobering up was coming too fast for him.

"Sure, dear leetle man, what eez eet that you like?" She pushed a button and half a wall slid back to reveal a well-stocked bar. Three of the girls went behind it and mixed drinks for whoever wanted one.

"Take zem wizz you, and I will see you back down here in about an hour."

"Thank you, madam." Jorl half saluted and followed the parade upstairs.

Johnny shouted back down to Alice, "Big Mamma, if the police come again, there's nobody here but you pussycats."

"You hurry and get right back down here, my smarty leetle Johnny."

* * *

Sarn and Eloise had commandeered a bedroom complete with a luxurious bathroom.

"Eloise, do you love me enough to put up with me and to come home with me?" Sarn asked, for once deeply serious. He stroked her still damp hair.

"There was a discreet knock on the door, and a soft voice said, "Supper in ten minutes, please."

"Oh, Sarn honey, I love you enough to follow you to any star in the sky—and I'll go with you anywhere, as long as you love me." Tears sprang up in her pansy eyes.

"Planet, baby, planet—stars burn." He nuzzled her soft cheek and neck.

Eloise laughed at him, then turned serious. "Oh, Sarn, is getting away going to be dangerous? Oh, that's silly of me—I know it's dangerous—but, but—do we have a chance?"

"Yes, my sweet Eloise, it's dangerous, but we have a good chance." They stood quietly, their arms around each other.

"This will be our last peaceful time together until we're space borne, and no matter how it turns out, remember that I love you more than any other woman in all the galaxies, and I always will. He kissed her tenderly.

"And I feel that way about you, Sarn. And always will and . . . and . . ."

"And let's go to supper and then take whatever comes."

They left the room, arms around each other. Eloise sneaked a peek backward into the room and sighed.

Sarn caught her looking and smiled. "There'll be lots more cozy rooms, my love."

Khair, clean and refreshed once more, knocked on Carol's door and, on her invitation, went in. She sat at a dressing table, still wrapped in a large bath towel, sorting through some makeup that was there.

Khair stood with his back to the door. They looked long at each other without a word.

She smiled and opened her arms wide for him to come closer.

He gently pulled her to her feet and wrapped her in his arms. Carol fitted her body to his. "Easy, my darling, you're forgetting your own strength."

He eased off a fraction. They both felt their physical passion begin to rise. Carol pushed Khair away. "No. No, Khair. Not now, not here."

"Why not? You'll be my wife." He suddenly leaned back to see her face. "You will, won't you?"

"Of course, I will. I've never wanted anything so much as to spend the rest of my life with you. I realized that what I was about to throw away wasn't worth what I thought I wanted."

He relaxed. "Then why . . . bridle our passion . . .?"

"Because, my darling, supper is in twenty minutes, and as this would be our first time together . . ." Carol indicated the whole house with a sweep of her arms, "no matter how lovely, the fact remains that this is a brothel. Also, and just as important, I don't want us to be hurried."

"You're right." He gave her a gentle kiss, "Now, better get dressed."

Carol, getting her clothes on, said, "Khair, do you think we'll be able to beat the Surnainians and get away with their ship?"

"As long as we hold the element of surprise, the odds are very good."

"But we might all be killed," Carol spoke in a matter-of-fact manner, accepting the possible truth.

"Yes, we might be. But then, it's as fair to say that we won't be."

Carol, dressed, came and stood in front of him. "I'm glad you're not the type to feel a woman is too stupid to handle the truth. I'll never disgrace you."

"I know that. Come, my Carol, let's go down to supper and prepare to face a, a . . ."

"Fateful?" Carol suggested.

"Yes, fateful evening." He gave her a quick hug, then followed her out into the hall.

* * *

"Come on, Jebby dear, you've soaked in there long enough. Get out now, and I'll dry you," young Evvy coaxed.

"Just a few more minutes. Just time for one more little drink, pretty Evvy. Please?" For the first time in his life, Jebby had found out how things are in seventh heaven—huge bathtub, steamy hot water, fragrant bath salts, headrest, cold drinks, and best of all, pretty little Evvy to mother him.

"Oh." She shook her head at him, hands on hips, smiled, and then said, "Okay, but just one." She came back in a minute with the freshened drink.

"Here you are. You'll have to hurry, Jebby, supper will be ready in about fifteen minutes."

"Do I hash—have to, Evvy? It's so warm and coshy in here. The world ish gone away." He made a small wavelet in the tub while looking at Evvy with his large, brown, begging eyes.

Evvy, head tilted to one side, looked at him, a soft look in her sad eyes. "Sorry, dear Jebby, time's just about gone. Finish your drink."

As soon as he did, she ordered him out of the tub and swaddled him in a large, fluffy towel.

"You're a lovely lady, Evvy, to do all thish for me. Shay, why are you doing all thish for me?"

"Because you remind me of a fat little cherub that needs doing for, and, thank God, for once there is no 'turning a trick' called for."

"What?" Jebby looked blankly at her.

"Lay a guy—for money."

Jebby still looked blank.

"I'm a prostitute, for Chris' sake."

"A pretty little lady like you shouldn't ush bad wordsh. Shouldn' do such thingsh." He waggled a finger at her.

She continued to rub him vigorously. "In the first place," she accentuated her statement with an extra hard rub, then had to catch Jebby before he wobbled away, "I'm no lady."

"Guesh—guess you're right, Evvy, but to me you're shtill a lady. And, at least, you don't use that real bad word."

"What real bad word, chubby little Jebby? Oh, you mean . . ."

"Evvy! Don't." Jebby sounded close to horrified unhappy tears.

Evvy stopped drying him long enough to look into his face. She saw he was really shocked, even through his alcoholic haze, and genuinely hurt that she should use gutter-type language.

"I'm sorry, Jebby dear, I guess I forgot who I was with. I was taking out my spiteful feelings on you. I'm truly sorry. How I wish I'd had someone like you in my life—life could have been so different."

"Tha'sh okay, pretty Evvy. I would have liked to have you in my life, too." He patted her head.

Evvy gave him a big kiss on his chubby cheek and lightly slapped his round, pink little bottom. "Get in the bedroom, and we'll get you dressed for supper."

When they were ready to leave, Jebby turned to Evvy with an expression that showed he was having a hard time to say what he meant. "Evvy, would it be . . . posh . . . poshible, could we, I mean, can we do thish again . . . shometime? I mean, jusht the same?"

"If you have the money, Jebby, we can spend your time here anyway you please."

Jebby's face lit up with an angelic smile, "Goody."

Evvy guided him downstairs. She had the weirdest feelings—a strange mixture of concern and something like motherhood for this round little person.

*   *   *

Mosets had gently, but firmly, refused any other service from his attractive, willing guide but that of showing him to a bathtub. As he said, "My dear, I have hundreds of years to enjoy the delights of the flesh, so, for the next hour, I look forward to appreciating a smaller delight—a bath and some quiet repose."

"You're sure? It's on the bill already, you know."

"I'm sure, my dove. Enjoy your hour any way that pleases you."

He shut the door.

Later, Mosets, now refreshed and cloaked in his usual calm, was on his way downstairs to supper when he passed an open door and saw Bill sitting peacefully relaxed in a deep, comfortable chair, pulling on his pipe and meditating as he watched the lazy smoke curl around in the air.

Mosets paused. Bill saw him and called, "Come in, set a spell, my friend."

Mosets did, and elegantly sprawled into the companion chair.

After a long minute of silent companionship, Bill said, "Well, no matter how you cut it, 'pears we have a fight on our hands."

"True, Bill. True. But it isn't necessary for you to put yourself into the path of more danger than you have already. Stay here, and know that you will still have acquitted yourself with honor."

"That's as mebbe, but for more reasons than one, I want me a piece of a Surnainian hide."

Mosets smiled. "I understand all your reasons and would appreciate your help, but are you aware of the deadliness of the next few hours? And I can guarantee no safe escape from harm."

Bill shrugged. "Seems there's usually a loophole in them thar guarantees." He puffed on his pipe. "I'll be agoin' with you, Mosets. And if you'll have me, I've got an itch to keep on a'goin'—out to some of those other worlds that're out there—with you. If that's okay."

"It would be an honor, my friend."

They both stood up and shook hands firmly—a pact.

"Now, let's to the delights of supper and Big Mama Alice."

* * *

Jorl and Tarla, lying comfortably on the bed and glad to feel clean and refreshed, enjoyed a half-hour respite from all their hectic problems. Jorl, as captain, knew that the final safety of all the lives, not only those of his crew, lay on his shoulders.

Flat on his back, and hands behind his head, he finally spoke out loud. "You know, sweetheart, this has got to be the most disorganized military operation on record. Space Command, and especially Admiral Emslin, will never believe it—I hardly do myself." He grinned, in spite of the seriousness of the situation, and turned his head on the pillow to face Tarla.

Tarla turned on her side to see Jorl's face. "Circumstances haven't allowed you many choices, my darling."

"I haven't only just bent about every rule in the book, but I've also smashed into atom-sized pieces at least three of the big ones. Never mind how many of the little everyday ones."

Tarla laughed softly, "I'm afraid a cover-up is impossible. For one thing, wherever Sarn goes, so do Eloise and Rusty. And I know Khair won't leave without Carol."

"That's what I mean, Tarla, the whole thing is ridiculous. If it wasn't a life and death thing, it would be funny." Jorl thought for a moment and then began to laugh. "It is anyway."

Tarla laughed with him. "But dear old Jebby won't be going—we'll leave him some money—drop him off at home and report his car stolen before we go near Surnainian headquarters."

"Good plan. What about Bill? I know he'll want to finish the fight."

"True, he certainly will. He loved Jessie and Tessie. I think he's already made his choice, Jorl."

Jorl nodded in agreement, "He'll want to go with us. But Johnny should stay right here when we leave. He's already surpassed himself."

Tarla laughed, "Beyond his wildest, most egotistical dreams."

They heard a knock on the door, and a soft voice told them supper was ready.

They got up at once. Before they left the room, Jorl paused and gently took Tarla into his arms. "I love you, my dearest Tarla."

"And I, you, my dearest Jorl."

"If all goes well, we should be space bound tonight." He gave her a light kiss. "And heading for home."

"Oh, Jorl," Tarla sighed.

With their arms loosely around each other, they went downstairs to join the group in the large, formal dining room.

* * *

Rusty and the two Siamese cats went on a raucous, fun-filled tour of the whole house. In one room after another, they investigated everything. Leaping across beds, over chairs, grabbing a small pillow, or whatever else took Rusty's fancy on the way was evidently not proper behavior.

In some places, there were girls that petted them and thought that they were so cute—in others, it was a totally different story. Words and sometimes things flew after them.

In one of the rooms, Rusty picked up a feathery, fluffy slipper and wouldn't give it back. The girl was highly annoyed and chased Rusty down the wide hall yelling and waving her fist at the three of them.

The unlikely trio, with virtual shrugs and expressions that said, "Oh well—on to the next something"—and they were exuberantly off again.

Suddenly, Rusty came to a full stop and sniffed the air. Only their agility saved the two cats from a humiliating pileup on Rusty's rear end. The cats watched Rusty, and their cross-eyed brilliant blue eyes shone. They looked at each other, then stared at Rusty. They figured there was more excitement ahead.

Rusty was off again—tongue lolling, ears and jowls flopping— following an intriguing smell. The two cats leaped up and ran after him. Rusty's nose led him to a narrow staircase. He ran down the steps and slid into a huge, strange room. He and the two cats just sat and looked for a moment. People and things were everywhere. Rusty was almost overwhelmed by all the different sorts of noises and smells. He couldn't make up his mind which of what he should investigate first. Everywhere the trio started to investigate, someone yelled and even waved a broom at them.

Rusty stopped for a moment, and the cats stayed right beside him. Then, Rusty caught the full force of the tantalizing smell and took off toward a long table that had a big bowl on it.

Front feet upon the table and his nose in the bowl. The cats are on the table having a taste, too. The head cook screamed at them, threatened them with a large spoon. It sort of scared Rusty so that he swiveled his eyes toward her, then jerked his nose around, and down went the large glass bowl. Naturally, it landed partially on Rusty's head—where else—dripping all down his front and also splattering the cats. The bowl broke in three big pieces. Pudding everywhere. The trio pretty much covered in it. The cook and at least three others yelled even louder and threatened them with something horrible.

The trio took off, dripping pudding in all directions. They went into another room. It was empty. Rusty plopped down and started licking off the pudding. So did the cats.

The cats purred, and Rusty looked happy as they licked themselves and even a lick or two on each other.

Peace and contentment reigned.

Chapter 28

At last, the now slightly unwieldy crowd was seated around the oversized, rectangular dining room table. Two maids served the varied and delicious meal.

"Madam," Mosets stood up and toasted Alice with his upraised wineglass, "you are to be heartily congratulated on your housekeeping abilities to have rendered up such a sumptuous banquet on such short notice and for your invaluable help in our time of dire need. Your health, madam."

Everyone at the table heartily concurred and raised their glasses to Alice. Pleased with the compliment, she laughed and said, "I am zee one who taught zee boy scouts everything zey know about being prepared."

Alice raised her glass. "Now, Mama Alice will make zee toasts. I feel mellow tonight. To zee marriage between these two couples. I have never seen such glow coming from anything less zen a big neon sign. May you have zee long and happy life together." Everyone drank to that. "I also drink to zee big fee, and to Happy Harry, who'll be arriving in about an hour, to take you to wherever you want to go." She belted down the glass of wine in three gulps, but with her little finger at the correct and proper angle. Everybody drank to all of that.

Light and cheerful conversation was the order of the day, and they were just about ready for dessert.

"Now eez coming my favorite desert—zee most wonderful pudding in all of zee world." She flung her arms out as wide as they would go.

Janice came into the dining room and whispered something in Alice's ear. She listened to Alice—then whispered something a little louder. Alice said something to her—Janice, apparently thankful, nodded and left the room.

"You will not taste zee best pudding in zee world. Zee big red dog and zee two cats ate it. You will taste the second best pudding in zee world. So everything is under zee control now."

Everybody drank to all of that, too.

They were just finishing a most delightful, puddingy thing when they heard chimes followed by a number of voices.

In a minute, a pretty little maid entered from the foyer door. "Excuse me, madam, but there are policemen at the door, and they, eh, request to speak with you for a moment."

"Humph," Alice grunted. She wiped her mouth daintily, threw her napkin on the table, got up, and pronounced, "local fizz."

"Fuzz," Marion corrected.

Alice looked at Marion. "Oh. Fuzz. Don't make zee move and don't make zee talk." For all her bulk, she walked majestically out the door.

For the span of nine or ten tense minutes, they listened to the rumble of male voices and the booming, only slightly less rumbling, voice of Alice. They heard her raucous laughter, the door slam, and the returning steps of only one person.

None of them had realized that they had been holding their breaths until it seemed that the situation was still under control.

"Well, zat eez zat," reported Alice. She once more took her place at the head of the table. "Now, where was I?"

During dessert, they held a discussion on Harry and all his mysterious ways. Alice told them how she knew all about Happy Harry. "I've known zee good old Harry most of my life. Harry eez a cousin to me on my mother's—rest her rotten old sole—side. Harry's older brother has also risen to zee dizzy heights of zee respect in zee, uh, underzeeworld. He got zo good at his trade that 'The Pen' was well known just about all over zee country. But, you know, eet's funny," Alice mused, "no one's seen him or even heard from him for zee past week or zo."

The five galactic travelers sneaked quick looks at each other. "Poor old Quill," muttered Sarn.

"But I . . ." Johnny stopped, looked puzzled. "Well, I sure thought I talked to him—just a couple of days ago. Didn't I?" He looked at the group. "But didn't I go . . . ?"

Tarla decided to gently reinforce the mind block and also to remove some of the portion of Johnny's part in the Quill's last days from his memory. She also thought it best to block the same portion from

Alice's mind before she could recall the facts surrounding the apparent disappearance of "The Pen."

"Guess I didn't, though. I guess it was longer ago than I thought."

"Don't worry your handsome head, my leetle Johnny. We will now go back to the salon and wait for Happy Harry and hees hearses."

"Horses? Did she say horses? Like the picture of those animals pulling a coffin holder? No motor?" Sarn was perturbed. "What kind of a get-a-way . . . ?"

"Shush, Sarn. Shush. She means hearses—long black cars. Why don't you go and find Rusty," Tarla said.

"Humph. Come on, Eloise, let's go find our bad dog." Sarn laughed. "Blazing suns, I bet he had one great time."

Chapter 29

$\mathcal{H}$arry was expected at any moment.

"Thank you for all that you've done for us, Alice," Jorl said. "We would've had a hard time without your help."

"It eez my pleasure." Alice smiled as her eyes glittered. She counted out the money that Jorl paid her and folded it into her pocket. Almost sleight-of-hand.

"Will you also see to it that Jebby and Johnny get home safely, Alice? And also to protect them when their cars are identified, would you please make anonymous phone calls to the police."

Alice's eyebrows rose. "Of course, of course. Eh . . ." She rubbed her thumb and fingers together in the age-old pantomime. Jorl got the message and handed her a few more bills.

When Jebby swayed past him, Jorl took his arm and said, "Jebby, I'm going to miss you, and you'll never know just how much help you have been to us. Here, take this home to your dear wife and just say that you sold your old car. Tell her she can pick out the new one. Then, maybe, she won't be too mad at you." Jorl smiled fondly at the chubby little man and stuffed a wad of money in his inside coat pocket. "Jebby, our friend Alice is going to see to it that you get home safely. Okay?"

"That shounds good to me." He smiled happily at everyone.

"Hey, Johnny—come over here a minute."

"Yeah, Captain. What can I do for you?"

"You've done more than you'll ever know. Over and above and beyond the call of duty."

"Gee. Yeah?"

"Everybody, gather round. I want to propose a toast to our Johnny Boy for his bravery and help. I, with the agreement of all of us, pronounce you an honorary Zalleellian."

Everyone held up their glasses, said cheers, and drank the toast. Johnny shone with pleasure, and his ego puffed up a little more.

"And here is the price of a brand new car to take the place of the one that suffered destruction in the desert." Jorl handed him a wad of bills that made Johnny's jaw drop. He looked at it for a moment, and then it disappeared into his pocket as fast as Alice's money had disappeared into hers.

Jorl turned to Tarla, grinning, "We'd better get away tonight, or it's back to the gaming tables. We're just about broke."

They heard vehicles crunching on the gravel in the driveway, and then the chimes rang again.

Soon, the same little maid showed a short, slightly round, pink and white person into the salon.

Big Alice had moved toward the doorway. "Harry. Good to see you again." She gave him a rather restrained hug and patted him on his little bald head.

"Hello, hello, hello, dear cousin Alice. And it's good to see you again. Seems to be more of you to see, too. Guess I'll have to reserve a bigger coffin for you."

"What do you mean?" Alice roared with laughter at the grisly joke. "Haven't put on more than zee one pound in zee last year, you gyp artist."

"Don't get me wrong, cousin. You're still a magnificent figure of a woman. Truly." Harry turned to look at the silent crowd gathered in the room. "Are these the friends of our dear departed?" He looked them over with a measuring eye, hands folded in the commiserating pose.

"Dear departed?" Sarn said. "You mean," Sarn walked over to the window and opened the drapes enough to see the big black hearse parked under the lighted porte cochere. He pointed out the window. "You mean there's a body in that thing?"

"Well, of course. Our dear departed cousin got caught with his hand in the till, so to speak, but even so, we must have respect for the dead—see him decently buried. He doesn't have an entourage of his own, so you people will help me to kill two birds with one stone, so to speak," he tittered. "Besides, there's a limit to how far you can push a policeman. If they stop a funeral procession, they should at least see a body if they want to. There's a limit to their, eh, goodwill or their culpability. Now, back to business." He raised his voice and called in another man—taller, thinner, and on the surface, tougher. He carried a big box, which he took to Harry, dropped it at his feet, turned, and left without a word.

The group watched this whole scene with varied expressions.

"Here's the plan. By the way, Alice, is there an APB out on any of them, or a description of them?"

"Not in zo many words." Alice said.

"Well, we won't take any chances. Now, at the end of the hearse is a curtained panel. You two," pointing to Khair and Jorl, "should ride in there. "Under the coffin, but off the floor, is a space big enough to lie down in. You go there." He pointed at Sarn.

"Blazing suns, under a coffin?" Sarn was about to put up a fight, but Jorl shushed him.

"Now, for the close family in the limousine behind the hearse. You will be the bereaved widow. Put this on." He handed Tarla a wide-brimmed hat draped with widow's weeds and a long, black cape that almost touched the floor.

Happy Harry stood back to see the effect. "Good. In the dark, by flashlight, nothing shows. Don't forget to sob a bit if we're stopped. You other two women are the dear departed's sisters. Put these on." The hats and cloaks were slightly different, and all achieved the same effect—anonymity. Eloise and Carol were now suitably garbed and would pass a brief inspection.

"You two men—an uncle and a friend—into the car behind the women. Put these on." He bounced over and handed Mosets and Bill each a black raincoat, snap-brim hat, and a wide, ruffled, black armband. He dusted his hands and was pleased with the results of his planning. "There. Is the bill paid, Alice?"

"Yes, eet eez." Alice nodded and smiled.

"Good." He pirouetted in the center of the salon, regarding each of his charges with pleasure. "Very good." He snapped his fingers dramatically. "Oh, by the way, the dear departed's name was Tony—Tony Goodman—names don't always tell the right story, eh?" He tittered again.

"Well, let's get on with it—come on, come on." He minced from the room.

The group made their good-byes with especially warm ones to dear little Jebby.

"B-but you will call me the next time you're in town?"

Tarla got a lump in her throat when she heard the lost note in Jebby's voice and saw the huge, unshed tears in his eyes. "Of course, we will, dear Jebby. Of course, we will." She gave the little man a big hug.

Jorl shook hands with Johnny. "M-maybe I should go with y'—ya'. Ya might need some extra help." Johnny's newfound courage threatened to drive him a little further than he really wanted to go.

"No, no, Johnny. We need you here—to tidy up any details we may have forgotten," Jorl said. "You help Alice handle the police inquiries."

"Yeah, sure. I can do that slick as a whistle." He strutted a little. "I'll also finish up the packing of the apartment and look after that end for Carol and Eloise, too, like they asked." His feelings of importance were slowly growing. His head was up, and his shoulders were back. He was ready for just about anything—a mental reservation being, of course, if it was within his definition of reason.

Outside, they sorted themselves into their respective vehicles. Harry would have made an excellent ringmaster.

He showed Jorl and Khair how to fasten the false panels from the inside but said they didn't need to shut themselves in unless they heard a signal that the procession was about to be stopped.

Sarn, relieved that he had to slide into his narrow berth only if danger threatened, whistled for Rusty.

Harry was halfway backed out the rear door of the hearse when Rusty came barreling through. The surprise forced a small scream from an off-balanced Harry. He caught himself before he fell into the hearse and was about to straighten up and regain his composure when something furry used his shoulder as a springboard and landed inside the hearse. Harry, as he caught himself from falling, looked up to see a large Siamese cat posed nobly in the midst of the flowers on top of the coffin.

Cat slowly blinked her large blue eyes at Harry, then began to wash her face, slowly, with what she considered deserved majesty.

"But . . . but . . . this will ruin the whole effect if we're searched." He almost sobbed. He hated untidy ends and anything that spoiled the perfect effect of any of his plans.

"If we have to, we'll stuff them in somewhere, but they stay." Sarn's tone of voice brooked no argument.

Harry brushed himself fussily off. "Very well, but one bark . . ." he glared at Rusty, "or one banshee howl . . ." he glared balefully at Cat, "and we are finished." He threw back his shoulders and his head in a dramatic pose.

Rusty, like some smart-aleck kid, sat there grinning at Harry through his clenched teeth. Cat resumed, with great deliberation, to wash her face again. Between wipes, she fixed Harry with her insolent, wide-eyed, cross-eyed, brilliant blue stare.

Jorl told Harry where they wanted to be let out. Harry agreed, took one more look at the animals, threw up his arms in disgust, said "TCH," and slammed the door.

Within minutes, the procession began moving.

The ride seemed to go on forever, but nothing untoward happened. At last they reached their destination, which was one block from the old house.

Harry opened the back of the hearse for the last time, motioning them to be quiet. "No point waking up any nosy neighbors, and leave the clothes there," he ordered.

Jorl, Khair, Sarn, Rusty, and Cat quickly jumped out of the hearse and found themselves beside an alley.

They saw Harry being gentlemanly and holding the door for the three women.

"Leave the clothes in the car, please, ladies. They do serve their purpose at times, eh?" He tittered as usual and then hissed, "But hurry. Hurry."

Bill and Mosets joined the group, and they waved good-bye to the quickly disappearing funeral procession.

Chapter 30

"We have two operable stun packs left," Jorl said. He then gave his orders in a quiet, crisp voice. "Sarn, you use this one, cross the street, take Tarla, Eloise, Carol, and Bill with you. Khair, you and Mosets and I will stay on this side with the other weapon."

"Take it slow—we've got to make sure the Surnainian ship hasn't arrived yet and that they haven't set up a surveillance detail. Okay, move out."

"Wait a minute. Rusty is busy," Sarn whispered. Rusty had already anointed two lampposts and was now busy with a hydrant. Cat, not to be outdone, followed Rusty and put her mark in the same places.

Jorl heaved a sigh and shrugged with resignation. "Somehow, it fits right in with this entire operation."

"He can't help it," Sarn said in Rusty's defense. "Anyway, I wish I had the nerve."

"Be thankful Rusty didn't befriend a horse," Khair said. In the interest of Jorl's somewhat frayed patience, he tried to suppress a grin.

"Come here, Rusty," Sarn ordered in a loud whisper. Rusty, and therefore Cat, obeyed.

"I take it that we are now ready to get on with the business of survival in a hostile situation?" Jorl said. "Okay? Stay close to the buildings and keep watch." Jorl turned to Tarla. "Tarla? Anything?"

"I'll scan the area again." In a moment, she said, "Nothing that has anything to do with us," she assured Jorl.

Sarn and his group crossed the street and moved off in silent single file. They went past where the doorway was.

Jorl, Khair, and Mosets did the same on their side of the street. They reached the front door of the old house first. Careful observations found nothing strange or out of context.

Jorl called out in a soft voice, "Cross the street. Now."

Sarn's group quickly did and stayed in single file against the buildings on the other side of the front door.

"Move up closer to the doorway—stay close to the building," Jorl said and waited.

When everyone was in place, Jorl said, "I'll open the door. Stay where you are." They pressed as close to the walls as possible.

Jorl tried the door. It was as he had left it—wedged shut. He held the stun pack in his left hand and quietly forced it open, prepared for anything. He waited for a few seconds. Nothing happened.

He motioned Khair and Mosets to him and whispered, "We'll go in first—see if the building is empty. Tarla," he called softly and motioned her to him, "if we're not out in three minutes, send in Sarn and Bill. You look after the girls." She nodded agreement.

Quietly, the three men went down the hall, not knowing what to expect, and turned the corner into the familiar room.

The hidden panel was closed. Jorl worked the mechanism and, as it slid open, saw no sign of intruders. He whispered, "Wait here. I'll go down first." He disappeared into the control room but, within the space of a few seconds, stood once more at the foot of the steps. "All quiet. Tell the others to come in, Khair."

Once more, they were gathered in the old room and glad to draw a relatively peaceful breath. Rusty showed Cat around the rest of the place. When they came back Rusty flopped down beside Sarn, and Cat plopped down on Rusty.

Jorl paced the floor. "Now. A battle plan. First, we've got to have the Surnainian ship docked into her berth here." He pointed to the ceiling. "That's the most important part. Second, we must get rid of the whole crew before they can take the ship off again. As you know, most scout ship's personnel have some emergency pilot training, and any one man can operate the ship for a short while. Any suggestions?"

"I believe the answer is that large communication set. I speak some Surnainian, and somewhere in my mind are the call letters of the Surnainian command ship. Let me think." About ten seconds later, Mosets snapped his fingers. "I recall them."

"Great. Then we locate the ship," Sarn said, "blur the transmission so that they can't see us, tell them to get back to headquarters—here—at once—there's trouble—an unexpected problem requiring an immediate meeting of all the captains." Sarn quickly filled in part of the plan.

Jorl nodded. "Okay—so they dock—come down to the control room—and we still don't know where the elevator doors are—then what?"

"Ambush," Bill said.

"Yes, but we must get them all down here together, or we lose our only advantage," Khair said, "and maybe the ship."

"And there's one big factor we're all forgetting," Jorl said. "Their mental powers are greater than ours. If we can barely cope with keeping our mental shields up from a cursory probe, what about Bill, Carol, and Eloise?"

"I can put up a temporary shield for them, but it wouldn't hold if the Surnainians came down expecting trouble. They would scan ahead to find out what it was."

"Then we don't tell them there's trouble—say . . ." Jorl thought for a moment, then snapped his fingers. "Say that Command has issued a new directive and that ship captains are required to report immediately in order to attend a face-to-face conference," Jorl suggested.

Mosets nodded, "Words to that effect should have the desired results. No matter whose army you are in, everybody knows about Command and its directives."

"Good. Let's get down to the control room and start the pile humming." Jorl rubbed his hands together and headed for the stairs.

"Is there a, a watchamacallit, a pile down there that needs to hum, Sarn?" Eloise whispered.

Sarn smiled at her. "No, Eloise, that's just an expression. The same as 'let's get busy.'" He had been rummaging through his case that had been left in the old house. "Here are two more stun packs." He examined them. "And fully charged. Great." He gave one to Mosets and the other to Khair.

"Sure you don't have a plain old rifle, or even a shotgun around here some place?" Bill asked.

"Sorry, Bill," Sarn said, "but maybe we'll have the chance to take a weapon away from a Surnainian before too long."

Everyone started down to the control room.

When Bill turned the corner at the bottom of the stairs, his eyes went wide with amazement. "Wal, would you take a look at that." His keen blue eyes looked at the strange room. "Sorta just like—wal, somethin' right outta television land."

"Those were my exact words a couple of days ago, Bill," Carol laughed. "And it still does."

"Gee, yes, Bill. But you get used to it in a hurry." Eloise assured him with a pat on his arm.

Sarn went to the only operable mobile camera left and began to scan. "The ship has left," he reported. "Blazing suns, they must be on their way here." Excitement quivered in his voice.

"Scan as far as possible, Sarn—see if they're in the vicinity," Jorl said.

Meanwhile, Mosets had seated himself in front of the large viewing screen and began adjusting the controls. Jorl stood to one side and made sure no one was behind Mosets just in case the transmission suddenly cleared.

Mosets called the ship.

Suddenly, accompanied by a blast of sound, the screen filled with a blurred picture of a Surnainian. Mosets adjusted the volume to a bearable level. There followed a five-minute exchange between Mosets and the Surnainian. Mosets switched off.

"What's the result?" Jorl asked.

"Yes, blazing fireballs, are they on their way here?"

The whole group waited impatiently for Mosets to tell them what had been said.

Mosets held up his hands to stem the flow of questions.

He began, "I will abbreviate, but in essence, I said that I, as communications officer on board the command ship, gave their captain the same command as I had been ordered to give every other captain in this operation. That they were to report to this headquarters immediately for an order group re: mining operations—Earth—Top priority—for their ears only. His ship was to use the berth at headquarters, as Commander Xanaeon desired to make an inspection tour. The other captains would use other berthing facilities. Rendezvous time—one hour from—now."

"What do you think, Mosets? Did he believe you?" Jorl asked.

"I heard no sound of doubt in his acceptance but if they try to contact the other ships—who knows?"

"Wait and see is all that's left," Jorl shrugged. "Good work, Mosets."

The hour had almost gone before they decided on the best way to deploy themselves and how to handle a few other technical details that needed attention.

"I wish we dared to attempt to contact our own space command," Tarla said.

Jorl gave her a quick hug. "We don't."

"Sh-h. Listen." Sarn waved them to silence.

They felt, as well as heard, well-oiled machinery start to work. The building shivered with faint tremors.

"They're coming in," Jorl said. "Stations, everybody."

"I wish to black damn holes we knew where the elevator doors were," Sarn muttered to himself.

They took the most central position in the downstairs quarters that they could, and everyone had a section to watch. Jorl posted Carol at the head of the stairs on the off chance that the opening of the elevator was in the upper portion of the old house.

"Don't make a sound, and stay behind your mental shields," Jorl said.

Nothing happened but absolute silence.

About three minutes later, they again heard faint sounds of machinery movement.

"Bay doors closing," Mosets whispered. Jorl nodded agreement.

It was another five long minutes of pulsing silence.

Khair suddenly nudged Jorl and pointed to the large communications set. Everyone looked and tensed. It had begun to open slowly from the wall like a huge door. Sarn and Jorl jumped behind the swinging-out section and pressed themselves flat to the control panels. Mosets and Khair were by the door leading into the room itself—one on each side.

Rusty, stiff-bristled, growled only to himself. He and Cat waited under the chairs to the left of Sarn and Jorl.

Three huge Surnainians entered the room. The last one reached for a control high up on the panel of the communication console.

Sarn and Jorl blasted the three down before their looks of surprise had time to fully form.

Mosets and Khair ran toward them—Jorl leaped around the fully opened door and saw that the elevator cage was empty.

"Sarn, get their weapons. Khair, help him move these bodies to another room. Mosets, did you see how they operated the elevator?"

"I think it should be this lever." He reached up high on the communications panel for the same lever he had seen the Surnainian use.

"We'll try it. Khair, Sarn, and Moset—into the elevator—we'll go up. Tarla, give Bill one of the Surnainian weapons—show him how to fire it, and you and Bill, stay here with Carol and Eloise." He calmly, but with underlying urgency, issued his orders. "Give us about three minutes, then all of you come up. Understood?"

"Understood, Captain." Tarla saluted. She was now a disciplined junior officer following orders.

The four men ducked into the elevator, and Mosets found the control on the inside.

Tarla watched.

As the whole communication panel began to close into position, Rusty and in short order, Cat, squeezed in.

The four men stood braced sideways—their packs leveled at the elevator door—the killing ground to be established the split second the door began to open.

"You be careful, Rusty," Sarn whispered. His other hand rested on Rusty's big head. He could feel how tense Rusty was, but Rusty took time from his single-minded purpose to slap a warm lick on Sarn's wrist. Cat was between Rusty's front legs, her favorite position, poised for action.

They felt the elevator come to a gentle stop, and the doors began to slide into the wall.

Jorl fired the instant there was an inch of opened space, spraying the rays back and forth. As the doors opened further, the other weapons came into play. Rusty and Cat screamed like demented banshees and were out of the elevator in a split second and leaping toward the Surnainian who had turned and started back to the ship.

It was a kaleidoscope of action. The four men soon realized they had totally surprised and killed three of the four Surnainians who were waiting for their turn to go down in the elevator.

Rusty leaped for the back of the neck of the quickly retreating Surnainian and got it in his strong jaws. The Surnainian shouted before Sarn, running toward the downed alien, could get a safe blast away that would avoid hitting Rusty. The noise brought the last member of the crew to the gangway. He took one horrified look and, correctly assessing the situation, headed back into the ship instead of firing his weapon. Once inside, he would be impregnable from small arms fire and could take the ship out by himself.

Jorl saw these thoughts racing across the last Surnainian's face. "Get to the ship before he has time to close the gangway and blast off," Jorl shouted the order.

Sarn was nearest, but Rusty had already decided to pick another fight and was, at that moment, ready to leap through the opening with Cat behind him.

"Get him, Rusty. Kill." Sarn ran toward the gangplank.

Tarla, Bill, Carol, and Eloise had just arrived, and as the elevator doors opened, they watched helplessly as the whole tableau unfolded.

The tremendous thought struck all of them at once.

Everything they wanted and hoped for—going home—everything—now depended on the delaying action of an Earthian dog and cat.

After a century of slow motion, Sarn leaped through the fast closing port, prepared to either finish off the last of their enemies before he could activate the takeoff or die in the attempt.

There wasn't much left for him to do except pull the trigger. The ferocious attack by the two animals had fatally injured the last Surnainian.

Mosets got to the outer port control and, just in time, had stopped the port from closing.

The others rushed up now—witnessed the end of resistance in silence.

Jorl heaved a big sigh. "It's over. Let's go home."

"Home," Sarn repeated. "Blazing suns, home!" He grabbed Eloise and hugged her. Then, he squeezed Rusty hard enough to surprise a yelp out of him. He danced a little jig while shouting with laughter.

It infected everyone else, and they spent a jubilant five minutes of hugs, kisses, laughter, and even a few tears of relief and joy before Jorl simmered it down and brought them back to the business at hand.

"We five have some homework to do. Mosets, can you familiarize us with the Surnainian controls?"

"I can."

Jorl nodded. "Good. First, Sarn and Khair, take that body out of here."

When the two came back in, every crew member went to their relatively same section of the operations panels. It didn't take long, with the expert help of Mosets, for them to feel confident of their abilities to handle the ship.

Khair then explored the accommodations and reported back to Jorl. "The sleeping arrangements will take a bit of juggling, but since we'll need two shifts to operate this vehicle anyway, they should be adequate. There's also a workable space and facility for the animals' needs. We're also well provisioned."

"Good." Jorl returned his half salute. "Mosets, how about weaponry? Can you handle it?"

"Yes."

"Do we have anything that will destroy without fire or explosion?"

Mosets watched Jorl, attempting to foresee his line of thought. "Yes, there is a laser on board. I take it you want to destroy all . . .?"

Jorl nodded. "I think we should totally demolish all three buildings— the old house and the one on each side of it. All three buildings are part of the landing deck. If we're careful to do just the inside, maybe the natives will not be alerted or alarmed. They'll never know for sure who did what to which, hopefully."

"We can certainly try to achieve the results that you wish, Jorl," Mosets said.

"Start up the pile, Sarn. Mosets, open the sky doors."

By activating a closed circuit on the viewing screen, they watched the hangar doors slide back. Then, they saw the black velvet sky with generous handfuls of stars thrown all over it.

"Bay doors full open," Mosets reported.

"Good. Sarn, bring her up just clear of the doors and hover her."

"Aye, Captain," Sarn replied, also reverting to the role of a trained junior officer.

Jorl went to the bank of screens and watched the scene below the ship. "Mosets, bring the laser to bear. Try for the control room first—fire when ready."

"Aye, Captain." Carefully, with the touch of a maestro, Mosets began using the laser.

Within seconds, a shaft opened up to the underground floor, and Mosets began playing systematic arcs of destruction in the whole area.

"Smoke," Sarn warned. "Probably their power supply is shorting out, so there's bound to be a fire."

"Raise ship twenty feet," Mosets called out. "I need a better view— there is fire now."

"And there goes the fond hope of doing this unnoticed—look." Tarla pointed to a screen, which showed a view of the streets below and the madly racing fire trucks closing in.

"Oh, gee. Oh my goodness," Eloise said. Carol and Eloise were also watching the screen. "Oh, Sarn. Oh, oh, I'm sorry. You're working. But, oh-h my." Eloise was close to tears. Tears of reaction.

Carol, feeling more than a little bit shaken herself from the happenings of the last few hours, took Eloise in her arms, stroked her hair, and whispered soothing sounds of comfort. "The worst is over now, dearest Eloise. All of us are safe and on our way to—to whatever—to the life we chose with the people we chose. Now, let me see a smile, and wipe away your tears and be happy."

"Oh, gee, Carol. You're right." She tried her usual smile, and it worked. Rusty put his big head under her hand, and a big tongue slapped a kiss on her wrist. He sat down and smiled up at her.

"See?" Carol said. "Even Rusty thinks this is for the best." Carol's voice was also a little shaky. She wiped a tear away and smiled at Eloise. She even patted Rusty's head. Even Rusty was surprised.

From nowhere, a crowd gathered and enlarged by the second.

From the height that the ship was, they could look down a good many throats because their owners were looking up with their mouths wide open in stunned wonder.

The ever-enlarging crowd watched the house crumble. They had no idea that a fully cloaked space ship was hovering above them.

"Keep it up, Mosets—damn it. Here come the police. And dozens more cars. Don't touch the wall supports, Mosets. Too many people would get hurt if the building collapsed."

Gradually, the alien structure disintegrated, and even the landing berth beneath them melted away. Consequently, the bay doors were also reduced to safe rubble. The Earthian fire brigade was doing a fine job of controlling the flames and keeping the gathering crowd at a safe distance.

"Take her up. Way up, Captain Mosets," Jorl said.

Tarla smiled and said, "Oh well, the people will have something to talk about for a long, long time." She turned to her controls. "I'll need your help programming our course. I don't understand the Surnainian symbols of destinations.

Mosets got up and went over to Tarla's controls.

Jorl resumed his seat as captain at the helm.

"Khair, before setting course," Jorl said, "try to contact Space Command. We must know if they're on their way here and warn them that the Surnainian Space Fleet could be here also."

Khair hurriedly sat down in front of his communications console and, with the help of Mosets's knowledge of the Surnainian language, began to work on his orders.

"Also," Jorl added, "inform them that we're in a Surnainian ship. After all this uproar, we wouldn't want to be blown out of the heavens by our own people."

"Aye, aye, Captain," Khair answered. "That would indeed be the final straw—to get blown out of the heavens by our own ships. Even after I was dead, I would still be highly annoyed."

"Annoyed? Great blazing runaway suns, I'd come back and haunt them forever."

Chapter 31

Young Lieutenant Kleel made the trip from the bridge of Star Path 1, the flagship of Space Command, to the door of Admiral Emslin's quarters in fifty-nine seconds flat. He paused in front of it to catch his breath and then knocked smartly.

"Enter."

Lieutenant Kleel opened the door, saluted, and advanced to the desk at which the senior, most respected, and regarded with the most trepidation, admiral of the fleet, sat.

He was tall and honed like a functional ship—not an extra molecule of matter in any direction. He returned the slightly nervous lieutenant's salute. "Yes, Lieutenant?"

"We have just made contact with Captain Sandu, sir, and the signal is holding steady. Captain Tron requests your presence on the bridge, sir." Lieutenant Kleel stepped back, saluted, and waited, bright-eyed, for the admiral's reply.

"Thank you, Lieutenant, I will come at once," he answered in a cool, controlled voice. But Lieutenant Kleel did not miss the white knuckles that clenched the edge of the desk. Jorl and Khair were his nephews by his son, Ablendz. The admiral rose slowly and headed for the door ahead of Lieutenant Kleel who followed him at a respectful, but helpful, distance.

When Admiral Emslin entered the bridge, he could almost touch the excited and happy wall of emotions of the crew on duty.

Captain Tron reported and saluted. "Captain Sandu respectfully requests to report, Admiral," he said in the crisp, direct tone of a military man. In a slightly less formal tone, he said, "Thank all the heavens."

"Yes, that is happy news indeed, Captain."

Admiral Emslin walked unhurriedly to the huge communication screen and sat in the elevated command chair behind the communications officer of the watch. "Good evening, Captain Sandu. It is indeed a pleasure to know that our fears for the worst were groundless. I trust the other three members of your crew are safely on board?"

"Good evening, Admiral. Yes, all are aboard and in good health."

"Good. Have you given the coordinates of your position yet?"

"No, not yet, sir."

"Give them. We will come for you at once. Navigator . . ." Admiral Emslin turned and called for Lieutenant Harlz.

Jorl interrupted urgently. "One moment, sir. There are a few things you must know before you lock in."

"Oh? Such as . . .?"

"That the Surnainian Command Fleet could be in this vicinity and that we are aboard a Surnainian scout ship."

"Oh? That is most interesting news. We shall certainly take . . ." The admiral was surprised into silence when he caught sight of the strange animal's head that suddenly appeared over Jorl's shoulder. The surprise tripled when he saw a strange female pull the animal back out of sight. "Captain Sandu, did I see an animal and an alien in the screen just then?"

"Eh, yes, sir. You did, sir. In order to effect our escape from this planet . . ."

"And which planet might that be, Captain Sandu?"

"Planet Earth, Admiral Emslin, sir."

"An observed and protected system, Captain Sandu. And you have an Earthian woman and an Earthian beast of some sort on board. In direct contravention to directives, I might add."

"It's a dog, sir. And there's also a cat. Both of which were directly responsible for our safe escape."

"Indeed? Earthian women are called cats? Either my knowledge, or your translation, is faulty."

"Oh no, sir. A cat is an animal—Eloise is an Earthian woman, sir."

"Well, well. That is three prohibited species. You have been involved, Captain Sandu. Any further bits of, eh, information of which I should be apprised?"

"Yes, sir. We also have another Earthian woman on board."

Admiral Emslin actually blinked in surprise, and his sparse eyebrows rode even higher on his forehead. "Indeed. I shall look forward to your full report, Captain Sandu. It begins to appear that it will be, to say the least, eh, interesting." He steepled his hands in front of his mouth to either hide a smile or a look of displeasure. In the face of any situation, an officer in high command must always look calm, cool, and collected. Unemotional.

"Would there be anything, or anyone, else Captain Sandu?"

Jorl drew a deep breath and continued calmly, he hoped, to finish the list. "Yes, Admiral. We have with us also an Earthian man. And also Mosets, the elder of Mostel is with us, too." Jorl finished in a rush, thankful to have the bare bones of his story laid bare.

"Indeed." Admiral Emslin tightened his steepled fingers. "The Surnainian scout ship—are there more of them in your vicinity?"

"Not to my knowledge, sir. We destroyed the three others of their main task force. However, we have no way of knowing if they had time to contact their fleet."

"Hm-m. Lieutenant Harlz, put up the data and a galactic map of the Earth's solar system."

Lieutenant Harlz punched the appropriate keys, and the computer's large viewing screen displayed the required information.

Admiral Emslin studied the map. Minutes later, he specified the coordinates that Jorl would need to enter subspace from Earth's galaxy. "Is your new, eh, commandeered ship fully operational, Captain Sandu?"

"Yes, sir."

"Good. When you emerge from subspace, you will then proceed with the second group of coordinates that Lieutenant Harlz will give you. You will use signal C of the distress code at 1 point three second intervals and proceed until visual contact is made. You will then proceed immediately to your berthing section and dock. Any Surnainian ship approaching this ship, not using the designated signals, will be blown up forthwith. Understood?"

"Aye, aye, sir."

"Directly upon return to Space Command, I shall expect you to present me with your presence and a full and complete written report from the moment of your departure from this ship. It should prove, eh, most interesting."

"Aye, aye, sir." Jorl was too well disciplined to groan in front of the admiral.

"Oh, a moment more before you return to your duties, Captain Sandu. I wish you to convey my regards to Mosets, an elder of Mostel, and I hope he will be my honored guest for as long as he wishes. Also, everyone here is deeply thankful that you and your crew have escaped unharmed. Well done, Captain Sandu."

"Thank you, sir."

"You will maintain viewing contact from the moment you emerge from subspace. And now, goodnight."

"Aye, aye, sir. And goodnight."

"Sign out, Lieutenant Harlz."

"Aye, sir."

The screen went black.

Chapter 32

✳ ✳
✳

"Captain Tron," Admiral Emslin called.

"Aye, sir?" Captain Tron approached the admiral and saluted.

"Captain Tron, as you know, Captain Sandu's return should be completed in seven hours by ship's time. See that accommodations are prepared for the four alien passengers and the two alien animals. Have the medical staff stand by at the moment of docking and seal off the berth until they give them the medical all clear. The computer should then have enough information regarding their physical health and diet requirements."

"Aye, sir. Eh, sir. Should I . . . must I . . .?"

"Yes, Captain?"

"Sir, do you request a detention squad to stand by?"

The old Admiral's eyes twinkled. "I think not, Captain. After I hear the report, which I have every reason to suppose will be the most interesting of my long career, maybe a mild reprimand will be in order."

Captain Tron's worried expression gave way to a wide grin. "Aye, aye, sir."

The listening silence of the whole bridge crew was broken by a collective sigh of relief.

"If you need me, Captain, or if in the event of a further communication that needs my attention, I shall be in my quarters."

"Aye, aye, sir!" Captain Tron threw a perfect regulation salute.

Chapter 33

*J*orl switched off the screen and swiveled the chair around. "Whew. He's a cool old devil. Well, the worst's over. At least, he knows about our passengers and has some time to think about it."

"I hope that's a good thing," Sarn said, slightly concerned.

"Are you in trouble, Jorl?" Carol asked. "The old boy sounded pretty human to me, but then . . . I don't know much about, eh, alien admirals."

"Oh gee, Jorl, and all on account of us," Eloise said. "I hope you'll be okay. I mean, not . . . not get put out of the army, or the navy, or whatever it is you're in."

"Without the help of all of you Earthlings, we would not be here, safe, on the far side of your moon, now," Mosets said quietly.

"That's right. Anyway, the worst it can be is a demotion and, or, detention. So don't give it another thought, Eloise," Jorl said.

Sarn put his arm around Eloise. "Anyway, we're all in it together. And I wouldn't have missed it for the world."

Jorl got up and then groaned. "The worst part will be making the written report. Where, in black holes, do I start?"

"When we launched from Star Path 1," Tarla said and smiled. "Well, that's what the admiral said."

"We'll all help you, Jorl," Khair said. "We'll just tell it like it was."

"Do you have to report—everything?" Eloise asked and blushed a rosy pink.

Jorl laughed and ruffled her hair. "Yes. All."

"He's teasing you, Eloise," Tarla smiled and said, "Just ignore him."

Khair, who had left the control room a minute ago, came back carrying a tray with glasses and two large bottles of wine.

"Perfect timing," Jorl happily agreed. Khair drew the corks and poured a ruby red stream into each glass.

They raised their glasses and saluted each other. "Here's to interstellar detours." Sarn laughed and hugged Eloise close to him.

"Yes, they can be rather Earth-shaking." Carol, who had Khair's arm around her, hid a grin in her glass.

"Yes, indeed. I still have a . . ." Mosets began just as the ship suddenly filled with the wild clamoring of an alarm system.

"Blazing suns, not again!"

"Maybe it's the wine that sets the alarm off," Khair said with a small smile. "Same thing last time."

The ear-piercing sound of the alarm was filled with clanging crashes and dull thumps. Cat came screaming into the control room, with the deeper howls of Rusty making counterpoint, as he barreled into the control room close behind Cat.

Everyone froze to the spot, totally taken by surprise.

"Now what! Now, what's wrong?" Jorl made it to the command console in two leaps. Tarla and Sarn both lunged for theirs. Khair ran to the area the animals had just left.

Carol and Eloise stayed rooted to the spot and watched Rusty and Cat trying to hide behind anything—or anyone. Bill and Mosets stood alert, prepared to help wherever they might be needed.

In a few seconds, Jorl, Tarla, and Sarn looked questioningly at each other. Nothing appeared to be wrong. But still the terrible noises continued.

With utter relief, the alarm bell stopped screaming. They heard two loud crashes and some splintering ones, then blessed, beautiful silence. Then roaring laughter.

Tension left them with audible sighs when Khair appeared in the doorway, weak with laughter. He pointed to the galley behind him and to the animals in front, laughing so hard he could only point.

The others went to see what was so funny, what the joke was. All over the deck, the bulkheads, and the fittings were broken dishes, bent metal containers, and gobs of food. The place smelled lovely but looked a perfect mess.

Khair managed to stop laughing long enough to tell them what must have happened. "I imagine Cat was curious, climbed up on the auto dispenser, and accidentally activated it. One of them must have blocked it long enough to short-circuit it, and the other one must have jammed the switching mechanism. When I got here, it was spitting out one plate after another like a missile launcher. I managed to disconnect the circuit and shut off the alarm."

"Poor Rusty—and Cat. They must be terrified," Eloise said. "Never mind, Rusty, you're safe now. Come out of there. Good Rusty." She patted his messy head when he warily came out from under a console. "It's okay now—you, too, Cat."

"Yup. And he's smothered in food," Sarn said. "Into a shower first, hug after. Come on." Rusty had tried to cuddle close. Cat began to lick herself. She rather enjoyed the strangely flavored fur.

"You know, this going from the sublime to the utterly bloody ridiculous is almost too much. But . . . but . . ." Carol suddenly dissolved into delicious, unrestrained laughter, probably for the first time in her life.

The rest joined in.

Cheerfully, they proceeded to clean up the uproar. Rusty had had his shower, and Cat was wiped down, somewhat. Cat only half cooperated.

Later, when the place was back to order, they relaxed and drank the rest of the wine.

"Well, here's to love among us, long life, fulfillment, and happiness," Jorl toasted.

Everyone raised their glasses and drank to the toast.

Suddenly, they felt an almost magical bond as they realized the depths of love and affection that connected each one of them to the other, animals included.

"Blazing suns, did this count as our vacation? Or do we still have it coming to us?"

Jorl laughed. "Oh, Sarn, Sarn . . . life would be pretty dull without you," he said and tossed off the rest of his wine.

Tarla checked her console. "We will be exiting subspace in two minutes."

Jorl jumped to his feet, headed decisively to the command console, sat down, and said, "Give me the admiral's heading, Tarla. Let's get home."

"Aye, aye, Captain." Tarla quickly and happily plotted the course.

The End

About the Author

Barbara is widowed and lives in Ontario close to her three married children, Stephen, Roger, and Kathleen.

She loved books and reading from an early age, and she is also a fairly good artist and loves her photography.

Barbara's learned wisdom comes from inquisitiveness, age, and the experiences of life, love, and family, and in the joy of just being alive.